THE BURNING GROUNDS

Also by Abir Mukherjee

A Rising Man
A Necessary Evil
Smoke and Ashes
Death in the East
The Shadows of Men
Hunted

THE BURNING GROUNDS

A NOVEL

ABIR MUKHERJEE

PEGASUS CRIME
NEW YORK LONDON

THE BURNING GROUNDS

Pegasus Crime is an imprint of
Pegasus Books, Ltd.
148 West 37th Street, 13th Floor
New York, NY 10018

Copyright © 2025 by Abir Mukherjee

First Pegasus Books cloth edition November 2025

All rights reserved. No part of this book may be reproduced in whole or in part without written permission from the publisher, except by reviewers who may quote brief excerpts in connection with a review in a newspaper, magazine, or electronic publication; nor may any part of this book be reproduced, stored in a retrieval system, or transmitted in any form or by any means electronic, mechanical, photocopying, recording, or other, or used to train generative artificial intelligence (AI) technologies, without written permission from the publisher.

ISBN: 978-1-63936-985-0

10 9 8 7 6 5 4 3 2 1

Printed in the United States of America
Distributed by Simon & Schuster
www.pegasusbooks.com

*For the booksellers
and the librarians, for all you do for us.*

The only thing that separates women of colour from anyone else is opportunity.
Viola Davis

Day 1

Saturday

ONE

Sam Wyndham

If you're Hindu and you're dead, chances are you'll wind up at the burning ghats.

From twice-born Brahmin to wretched untouchable, this is where you'll find yourself in the end. Countless lives, disparate journeys, yet they all end in the same place, here, upon the funeral pyres at the river's edge. For such an inequitable religion, the burning ghats are a pretty decent leveller.

Some get here early of course, eschewing the recommended three score and ten, often hastened towards reincarnation by less than natural causes, anything from a stranger's knife in your ribs, to a strychnine-laced hilsa fish prepared by a disgruntled wife, and this night, as the rains beat down and the heavens thundered, it was one such early bird that I was staring at.

A bolt of lightning arced through the sky, for a moment illuminating his face. Jogendra Prasad Mullick – JP to his friends – looked up at me from the mud yet seeing nothing on account of him being dead; a nice, three-inch incision across his throat. Neat job, too. His killer knew his business. If he ever fancied a career change, there was probably room for him among the surgeons at the police hospital on Amhurst Street.

J. P. Mullick's career, however, much like his windpipe, had been tragically severed. I didn't know the man other than by what I read in the papers, but on that measure, everyone in the city knew him. You couldn't open the pages of almost any rag without coming across an article extolling his business acumen or his latest act of philanthropy: the establishment of another medical clinic in the name of his dear departed mother, or the bankrolling of yet another tedious, headache-inducing Bengali theatrical production. Yet all that generosity of spirit seemed not to have done his own spirit much good.

Poor Mullick. He was rich, generous, disinclined towards politics and dead. Just the sort of Indian we liked, give or take the last part. Tycoon, patron of the arts and the *burra*-est of *burra babus*. A man among men, right up until the point an hour or so ago when he wasn't. Because from then on he'd been lying here in the mud on the banks of the Hooghly, a shroud covering his modesty and a makeshift cot of wood and string sinking into the slime beneath him.

The stench of the river mingled with the scent of damp wood from the sodden funeral pyres. If it hadn't been for the downpour, Mullick's body might have been cremated and we'd be none the wiser. But for once, the corpse burners weren't doing a roaring trade.

Singh, my subaltern, held the umbrella over my head and muttered a prayer. He was a hulking great chap, like Ayers Rock on legs, an attribute that came in handy these days, what with the natives' growing disregard for the authority of a white uniform, or a white face for that matter.

'Singh,' I said, 'kindly do the needful.'

The young man handed me the brolly, then lumbered forward like a tank division, dropped to his haunches and began going through Mullick's clothing with the dexterity of a pickpocket at Dum-Dum junction. On another day I might have done the job myself, but old JP was fast becoming one with the river and I wasn't overly keen on getting stuck in the mud of the Hooghly, however holy.

Singh looked up. 'Nothing, sir. Body is picked clean.'

His expression was pained, as though he took the dead man's inability to hold on to his possessions as a personal failure. Poor Singh. He was a nice enough lad. Not too much between the ears, which was surprising given the ample volume of his head, but nevertheless keen as mustard.

I turned to the *lal-pagri*, the red-turbaned constable who stood sheepishly at a distance, leaning on his lathi.

'Who found him?'

The man gave a lopsided grin. 'Me only, sahib.'

'And he was just lying there?'

'No, sahib. He was being carried here by some corpse bearers.'

Corpse bearers.

Every district in Calcutta had them. Untouchables of course, but not of the clan that worked within the confines of the burning grounds. They transported the bodies of the deceased from their place of passing to here, their final journey, at least in this life. Ritual dictated they receive a meal from the family of the deceased for their troubles, but these days many preferred their hot rice to be supplemented with cold cash.

'You saw them?'

'Yes, sir.'

'So where are they?'

He rubbed the back of his neck. 'I shout at them to stop, but they drop *chowki* here and run off.'

Of course they had. Nothing in this town was ever simple.

'You get a good look at them?'

'No, sahib. It was very dark already.'

'You didn't question them when they first came through the gates?'

The man grimaced. 'No, sahib. I was doing my round.'

That may have been true, and then again maybe the dear constable had fallen asleep at his post and the men who'd brought Mullick here had simply waltzed past him, dumped the body and run.

I looked him in the eye. 'You're sure?'

'*Hā*, sir.'

'And they were definitely corpse bearers, not *goondahs*?'

His expression curdled. 'They were old men, sir. Too skinny to be *goondahs*. Too poor-looking.' The disgust in his face seemed genuine enough. Untouchables and thugs were different breeds, and it sounded like the constable had seen the former. In the distance, more of their kind were loitering, waiting for the rains to stop so that the funeral pyres could be prepared for the morning.

'You think they killed him?'

'I do not think so, sir.'

No, he was likely correct in his assessment. They would merely have been paid to bring the body here. Pay them enough and they wouldn't ask too many questions, and 'enough' in this case probably wouldn't have been a lot.

Close by, a clutch of white-clad mourners and semi-naked *sanyasis* waited, caught out by the sudden downpour, as four skeletal men struggled to carry the rotund remains of a Brahmin back from his sodden pyre to the shelter of what I took to be a temple. The Brahmin's sacred thread was taut over his ample gut, restraining him from departing this life as though fearful for what the next might hold. When alive, the man would likely have shied away from the men who now carried him, recoiling even from their shadows for fear of ritual pollution. In death though, he seemed less concerned.

I turned to Singh. 'You think they were going to burn Mullick's body?'

The subaltern shook his head. 'Not the ones who brought him, sir. Only the Doms can burn bodies. It is their preserve and their living.'

Of course, I should have recalled. The Doms: that special

sub-caste of untouchables who lived and worked within the confines of the burning ghats. Whoever had transported Mullick here would've known they couldn't have burned his body themselves. The Doms would have beaten them to a pulp if they'd even tried. Cremation was a closed shop after all. If this were England, they'd probably be a guild – the honourable company of corpse burners – with their own livery and a great hall somewhere on the banks of the Thames. But this was India, and while outside the ghats they might be the lowest of the low, inside its grounds the Doms were bestowed a special respect. They were keepers of the sacred fire, the only ones authorised to maintain the funeral pyres, and they made a good living out of that fact. Rumour had it that the head Dom was a very rich man. His house, its lights burning in the distance, was certainly better appointed than my flat.

The question was, why had Mullick's murderers brought his body here? Why risk getting stopped and arrested by the constable who should've been at the gate? A cold wind bristled, the rain-lashed waters of the river shivered, and on the bank, stray marigold petals spiralled heavenward. I pulled my collar up against the chill. I'd been feeling the cold lately, which was ridiculous as this was Calcutta where the temperature never fell below forty even in the dead of winter. Maybe I was getting old, or maybe I was just going native.

An ambulance pulled up, bells clanging like a puja procession.

'Cover the body,' I said to Singh, then turned and headed in the direction of the main gate. 'And make sure it gets to the mortuary. Tell the pathologist that our friend here was a VIP, and tell him I said it might be in his interests to make haste with the post-mortem. Once word gets out, Lal Bazar will be breathing down his neck anyway. We might as well afford him a head start.'

Singh struggled to keep pace.

'*Hā*, sir. You are not staying?'

There wasn't much point. It was late, I was off the clock, and for a good while now, I had fallen out of favour with the high priests of the Imperial Police Force. By the morning, an important case like this would be farmed out to someone else; someone ... amenable; someone with only half a brain probably, but amenable.

'No,' I said. 'I'm off to find a drink.'

TWO

Sam Wyndham

Calcutta.

It was impossible to love it unless you were a sadist of some sort. Impossible, that is, right up until the moment you realised you could no longer live anywhere else, and then you loved and hated it in equal measure. Calcutta was like the splinter that pierced your flesh, an exquisite pain that dulled and ossified till you stopped noticing; a foreign body that became part of you, assimilating you as you assimilated it, yet always there, always ready to hurt you when you pressed too hard. Calcutta was a fever dream, a melange of the infernal and the angelic, its *gullees* and *paras* brimming over with poverty and hunger and fear and brutality. And yet there was that other side too, oft caught only fleetingly, like glimpses from a speeding train, when the city showed you a different face, its humanity and its gentility. And then it was beautiful.

Calcutta was slum and cholera and palaces and culture, it was heat and dirt and white and brown all packed together till you could hardly breathe or tell where one ended and the other began; a hothouse that surrounded and pounded your senses till you accepted this most alien of aggregations as normal and maybe even the correct state of affairs. It was White Town and Black Town and a population segregated by the strokes of a council cartographer's pen. Yet those lines, designed to divide by race, each day would blur and fray and buckle a little more under the simple expedients of commerce and human nature. Because prosperity depended on trade, and trade depended on goodwill and interaction between the races, and because for British and Indian, at least, blood came second to bank balance.

If both races had one redeeming feature, that was it – a tolerance born of the implicit understanding that whatever we might profess to believe, deep down we knew we weren't that different, certainly not different enough to prevent us from making money together, albeit granted that the relationship had been rather lopsided of late. And Calcutta, this bastard city – neither British nor Indian but a deeply flawed union of the two – was the most wondrous flowering of that tolerance.

I still hated it though.

It took a while to find a tonga. On nights like this, when the heavens opened and the roads flooded and even the rats set off in search of less benighted climes, any sort of transport was in high demand and their owners charging wallet-gouging rates. I took the price on the chin and told the driver to make for Park Street.

It was late now, or early depending on your proclivities. Gone 11 p.m., around the time when the city got interesting; when its choice venues opened for business: the clubs and the bars and the places where you only got in if you knew the right name to whisper in the right ear.

It was at times like these when the siren song of the opium sang loudest in my ears. I may have been clean for four years now, but *clean* and *free* are two different things. My former addiction still pulled at my senses, its tendrils reaching into my cerebellum, infiltrating my thoughts, sapping my will.

It didn't get easier; each night, the battle had to be refought, won again, over and over without end; each success feeling less like a victory and more like a stay of execution. The trick, as with so many things in life, was not to put yourself in the way of temptation, so I avoided those parts of town like Tiretti Bazar and Tangra where the opium houses knew me and would welcome me back like the prodigal son or possibly the fatted calf.

Other distractions helped too, and these days, my distraction of choice was a place called the Idle Fox, a gin joint owned by an Armenian called Petros, which, like its owner, had pretensions towards sophistication. When it came to race, though, Petros was a liberal and didn't mind what your skin colour was, so long as your shirt was starched and your wallet was fat.

The Idle Fox was the sort of place where you'd find, if not the city's crème de la crème, then at least the crème that maybe had been left out in the sun a little too long: the businessmen who'd made their money in ways that weren't quite pukka; the bureaucrats who'd gone a little too native to be trusted; the second sons of minor maharajahs; and the educated, high-caste young Indian men who frequented such places for alcohol and an illicit thrill. Around all of them buzzed a bevy of rather attractive women, the kind with looks and brains and who, in a fairer world, wouldn't have to spend their time trying to catch the eye of one of the men in here. But the world was what it was and the Idle Fox was the natural home to these people. It had dark wood, and dim lights, and leather-trimmed booths whose best days were behind them, and it was home to a Chinese singer named Mae with a voice like warm honey and a figure that curved in all the right places. Indeed, it was hard to decide what drew me to the place more: her or the booze. With my limited salary, I was hardly the Fox's ideal patron, but Petros made an exception for men like me – *men with potential*, as he put it, which I took to mean *men with the power to arrest him*.

The doorman greeted me with a nod and opened the door.

Maybe it was the typhoon raging outside but the Fox seemed busier than usual, the air thick with cigar smoke and sandalwood incense and the tang of hard liquor. The usual subdued hum, which I appreciated for it allowed me to concentrate on the sound of Mae's voice and maybe some of her other qualities, had tonight been replaced by a thrum of raucous voices and laughter, mainly from a gaggle of people I didn't recognise and who had pushed Mae from her prime spot on the stage over to a corner by the grand piano, so that they might cut a rug or two. She put up with it but didn't seem best pleased. It wasn't conducive to the sort of evening I wished to enjoy and I might have headed straight for the door were it not for the storm still raging without and the fact that I had nowhere better to go.

To the sound of Mae's tones fighting to be heard over the noise, I made my way over to the long mahogany counter, polished to within an inch of luminescence, behind which stood Axar, the barman, in front of mirrored shelves lined with an impressively diverse array of spirits. I pointed to a bottle and asked Axar for a double. He was as much a fixture of the place as Mae or the leak in the WC, dressed to the nines in white shirt, tie and double-breasted jacket. He poured a miserly measure and I took a seat on a high stool, turned to the stage and contemplated life as Mae leaned on the piano and sang about blue skies.

Recently, I had found myself drifting. I'm not a religious man, which is to say that the Lord and I have not seen eye to eye for some time now, not since the Somme anyway, though to be fair to Him, I have my doubts He was even there. And then, what with the untimely death of my wife in the epidemic at the end of the war, we never really had much of a chance for rapprochement seeing as I wasn't interested in anything He might have to say in mitigation.

The problem with falling out with the Almighty though is that it tends to leave rather a large void in one's existence, and not just at Christmas, and voids by their very nature ought to be filled. In place of religion, I had espoused the philosophy that the universe was cold, capricious and made infinitely worse by the fact that *mankind*, the main actor on its stage, was for the most part, pretty damn awful.

Life, as far as I could tell, served no real purpose, which seemed a tragedy because that made it rather a waste of time and effort on everyone's part. Some Nordic philosophers would tell you that the only sensible thing to do with life therefore was to end it quickly, which sounded perfectly sensible if you had to live in Scandinavia but seemed rather precipitous for the rest of us. Besides, suicide didn't appeal to the contrarian in me. I wasn't about to give either the universe or certain colleagues in the Imperial Police Force the satisfaction of seeing me dead, certainly not before the full-time whistle.

According to Freud, the path to happiness lay in fulfilment at work and in love, which was unfortunate, because I was hardly excelling at either. My relationship with Annie Grant had foundered of late, due apparently to my *inability to move beyond an altar built to a deceased wife*, and my *general tendency to be an arse*.

As for work, I had fallen somewhat out of favour for several years now, for reasons too tedious to mention, suffice it to say that I had followed my conscience and disobeyed the orders of my superiors, not once but twice. I had been sidelined, then frozen out of all but the most mundane of cases; and then, to add insult to a kick in the teeth, was forced to report to a new senior officer called Healey, who was about as competent as the man who'd suggested the Light Brigade take a little canter towards the Russian guns at Balaclava.

The real conundrum was why they hadn't sacked me, or, for the matter, why I hadn't resigned. I sipped my drink and, not for the first time, pondered the question. Maybe it was time to move on, start afresh, maybe somewhere like South Africa for instance, or the Antipodes. Yet my pride would probably keep me here, at least until I had something positive to celebrate. I couldn't bear Annie, or Healey, or anyone else thinking I'd left with my tail between my legs, and anyway, a broken man's home was in a broken city; and they didn't come more broken than Calcutta.

It was then that I saw her: a woman sitting at a table, flanked by half a dozen men in dinner jackets: slim, olive-skinned, and with a figure that could make you forget your troubles if only for a moment. She was the sort of woman you didn't see too often. Not in Calcutta. Not anywhere. The type whose beauty could cause clocks to stop, empires to fall and a thousand ships to launch. The usual laws didn't apply to women like her, maybe not even the laws of physics. I didn't know her, and yet she looked familiar.

She must have felt the weight of my stare, for she turned in my direction and for an instant our eyes met. I found myself holding my breath and sitting up just that little bit straighter. Behind me, Axar called out: 'Another whisky, sir?'

By the time I'd said yes, she'd turned away and was back in conversation with the men around her, smiling politely as some wag made a joke.

'Who's that?' I asked Axar.

He raised an eyebrow as though concerned that I may have been living under a rock, or possibly in Daaca.

'That is Estelle Morgan.'

'Who?'

'The actress? You must have seen her, Captain sahib. They call her the Tasmanian Angel.'

'I don't go to the cinema,' I told him, but the name did ring a bell. Annie Grant had possibly mentioned her on one of the occasions she'd tried to persuade me to accompany her to the Globe or the Picture House.

'You an aficionado of the silver screen, Axar?'

He beamed, exposing faultless white teeth, which soured, I thought, slightly into embarrassment.

'I . . . like the movies, sahib.'

'So what do you think brings this rose to our dungheap?'

He gave a shrug as though the question was better posed to a philosopher, and before I could get more out of him, he moved to serve another patron. I sipped my whisky and turned back to Mae onstage. Normally I'd have been happy to spend a few hours just propping up the bar and listening to her sing, but tonight my attention kept wandering to the woman at the table, the actress called Estelle Morgan.

The men hovered around her like bees around their queen – all except one gentleman, who sat next to her and looked at the others as though he detested them; either that or he was paying for all their drinks. From the vantage of my bar stool, I watched as waiters ferried them champagne that cost more than I earned in a month. It was all rather gauche, I thought, which is not to say that I wouldn't have been right there beside them, doing the same thing, if I were in her company and my finances weren't quite so terminal. Nevertheless I got the impression that she was going through the motions, listening to their stories and laughing at their jokes; but her posture was stiff and her laughter short.

She looked in my direction again, and this time when our eyes met, I was certain. Estelle Morgan was bored. It's a gift I have – a policeman's knack of being able to read a mind from a mere glance – or it might just have been wishful thinking. She threw me a hint of a smile and I raised my glass to her, drank down the last of the contents and then turned to Axar and ordered another. By now I was on to cheaper stuff, the kind that was far easier to appreciate once you'd already had a skinful.

When I turned back, Estelle Morgan was no longer in her seat.

Her erstwhile suitors, meanwhile, made awkward conversation among themselves like guests at a funeral. Maybe it was the alcohol dulling my senses, but I didn't notice her until I caught the scent of her perfume and found her standing next to me, calling out to the barman.

'I'd like to try a local cocktail. What would you recommend?'

Axar seemed as surprised to see her there as I was.

'I could make you a Darjeeling Martini, memsahib,' he stammered, 'or maybe a Bengal Fizz?'

'Tell me about the Martini.'

'It's gin, vermouth, a splash of cold Darjeeling tea, shaken with ice, then poured and served with a twist of lemon.'

'And the Fizz?'

'Rum, fresh lime juice, cucumber slices, mint leaves, watermelon syrup, soda water.'

'Which is better?'

Axar shrugged. 'I could not say, ma'am.'

'I'd go with the Martini,' I said.

She turned to me and looked me over. If it was some sort of appraisal, I must have passed, because she smiled, and in that moment I could have happily spent eternity just looking at her.

'Why thank you, Mr . . . ?'

'Wyndham,' I said, 'Captain Wyndham, but please, call me Sam.'

'Captain Sam,' she said, as though trying out the name, and to my ears at least it sounded rather perfect coming from her lips. 'A nautical man?'

'I would be,' I said, 'but I get seasick in the bath.'

She exhaled a laugh and that made me happier than it should have.

'I was a captain in the army, back in the war.'

That seemed to impress her.

'And now?'

'Now I'm a detective with the Imperial Police.'
That seemed to impress her even more.
'A detective? Now I am intrigued.'

Women have a thing for detectives, assuming, that is, they aren't personally being investigated. I'm not quite sure why. Maybe it's a fascination with death, but then they don't exactly queue up to marry mortuary assistants or funeral directors, so maybe not.

'What sort of things do you investigate?'

'Murder, mostly,' I said, which was rather stretching the truth these days, and gave her a look which suggested that the cares of the world rested on my stoic shoulders. 'And you are?' I asked, doing a decent act of feigning ignorance.

I thought I saw the flicker of something in her eyes.

'Estelle,' she said. 'Estelle Morgan.'

'Well, Estelle, as I said, I'd go with the Martini.'

She pondered for a moment.

'You're sure?'

'Certainly,' I said, and it was true, mainly because I'd never heard of the Bengal Fizz. Indeed, I had a suspicion Axar had just invented it right there on the spot.

'In that case,' she said, 'maybe I'll go with the Fizz,' and gave me a teasing look which seemed to linger. 'Will you join me?'

'I make it a point of never saying no to a lady, or to a drink,' I said.

I turned to Axar.

'Two of your finest Bengal Fizzes, and put them on my slate.'

'No,' Estelle Morgan cut in. 'Put them on the bill of my table over there.'

'That's most generous of your friends,' I said. 'Are you sure they won't mind?'

She arched an eyebrow. 'What makes you think *they're* the ones paying?'

There was something in that comment, that streak of independence, that reminded me of my late wife, and for a moment I felt something akin to guilt.

'Fair point,' I conceded. 'It's just that the modern world has taken its time reaching us here in Calcutta. I'd expect your friends there to insist upon paying.'

She gave me a nod, as though honour had been satisfied. 'They *did* insist as a matter of fact, at least for my previous drink, so it's only right and proper that they pay for these too.'

Behind the bar, Axar filled a cocktail shaker with liquor and ice, closed the lid and set to work.

'So, Estelle,' I said, 'am I to take it you're new to Calcutta?'

'You could say that.'

'And how are you finding our fine city?'

Her eyes widened and she gave me the sort of smile that seemed a tad too bright.

'I haven't had a chance to see much of it yet.'

'I'm surprised,' I said. 'I'd have thought those gentlemen over there would be falling over themselves to show you the town.'

'But a girl should be choosy about which offers she takes up, especially in a strange city. Isn't that so, Mr Detective?'

'Quite,' I said. 'Not every man is as trustworthy as, say, a policeman.'

She laughed at that and touched me gently on the arm.

Axar strained the drinks into two glasses, added a sliver of cucumber to each and placed them on the bar atop two white napkin squares. We reached for our glasses and I raised mine in toast.

'To your time in Calcutta.'

'And to trustworthy men.'

I watched as she lifted the glass to her perfect lips and sipped.

'Now *that*,' she said, 'is a proper drink. What do you think, Captain Sam?'

'Not bad,' I said. 'I could get used to it with a bit of practice. Maybe we should pencil in a few for tomorrow night?'

'I'm afraid that won't be possible,' she said, and I tried not to take it personally.

'So what brings you here, Estelle? Business or pleasure?'

She took a breath and looked as though being here was the most tiresome thing in the world.

'Most definitely business.'

'And what business would that be?'

'Movies,' she said. 'I'm an actress.'

I feigned surprise. 'And you're here to shoot a picture?'

'Alas yes. We've been filming out in the middle of nowhere for the last week. I had to insist we return to civilisation for the weekend. Anyway, it's all so ... boring. I'd much rather you tell me all about being a Calcutta detective.'

'It's a thankless task,' I said. 'Non-violence might be popular across the country, but in this town people still seem hell-bent on murdering each other.'

She looked at me as though this were some sort of revelation.

'Really?'

'I'm afraid so,' I said. 'Calcutta is rather a unique place, unfortunately. The worst of humanity tends to wash up on our shores: Pathan cut-throats, Bihari smugglers, Sikh assassins and more Scots than you can shake a stick at. And then there are the locals. Bengalis are a hot-headed lot. They like to think of themselves as cultured but I've never met a race of people more willing to stick a knife in each other's guts if they feel they've been wronged. They're like Italians but without the virtue of good wine.'

She gave me a teasing glance.

'Well, then they're truly lucky to have such a fine officer such as yourself protecting them.'

'Maybe you should tell them that,' I said.

She took a sip of her drink. 'Oh, I shall, and exactly what should I tell them you've done for them today?'

'Well,' I said, 'I've been investigating a man found with his throat cut.'

'An Englishman?'

'Worse,' I said. 'An Indian, but a rich one. They bring ten times the trouble of a murdered white man. There's always a dozen family members vying to convince you that the murderer was another relative – a son or an uncle or a cousin – and they're generally right.'

'So who do you think did it? Have your powers of detection, the ones upon which the people of Calcutta so undoubtedly depend, led you to a conclusion yet?'

'Steady on, I need time to think. To ruminate. To let theories percolate.'

'Is that why you're in here?'

'Absolutely,' I said, raising my glass to her. 'When it comes to stimulating the brain, I find there's nothing quite like a Bengal Fizz or three.'

She gave my preferred modus operandi an appreciative nod.

'But really, what *are* you going to do?'

The truth was, *nothing*. It probably wouldn't be my case by tomorrow morning, but there was no point in ruining the story for Miss Estelle Morgan.

'Arrest the whole family, I expect. All the way down to second cousins if we have the jail cells. Then wait till someone snitches.'

She looked at me as though unsure whether I was joking, and in all honesty, it was probably as good a strategy as any.

Before I could expound further upon my methods of detection, the sour-looking man from her table got up and made a beeline for us. He was tall, filled his suit well and didn't look like he was coming to wish me a happy birthday.

'Who's that?' I asked. 'Your father?'

Estelle Morgan laughed under her breath. 'My agent.'

'Estelle, darlin',' he said, 'it's time we were moseyin' back to the hotel.'

American, I guessed, judging by the way he mangled the language.

Estelle Morgan turned to me.

'Sam, may I introduce Sal Copeland. Sal, this is Captain Sam Wyndham of the Imperial Police.'

The information seemed to bounce off him. 'We need to go, Estelle.'

'Pleased to meet you, Mr Copeland,' I said, and stuck out a hand which he declined to shake.

'Sure, fella. Good to meet you too.'

Estelle finished her drink. 'Sam's been telling me all about Calcutta and criminals and he's introduced me to this drink which you really must try. It's called a Bengal Fizz.'

To be fair, it was Axar who'd introduced the drink to the both of us, but this was India and it was par for the course that a white man be given the credit for the work of natives. I'm sure Axar didn't mind. Indeed, he wouldn't even have thought to mind. It was just the way of things.

Copeland helped her from her seat.

'Maybe another time.' He turned to me. 'Thank you, Mr Wyndham, for entertainin' Miss Morgan, but she has an early start tomorrow and we really must be goin'.'

'Well, goodbye, Sam,' Estelle said, 'and thank you for the conversation.'

I gave her a nod.

'And thank *you*, Miss Morgan, for the drink. When you're back, if you need someone to show you around Calcutta,' I said, 'you can always find me at Lal Bazar, police headquarters, or failing that, right here on this bar stool.'

And with one last smile she was gone, leaving me to the dregs of my Bengal Fizz and an unexpected sense of loss, and suddenly I didn't feel like hanging around the Idle Fox any more.

The doorman found me a tonga. It didn't take too long, and soon the familiar outline of College Square came into view. Beyond it lay the crumbling buildings of Premchand Boral Street and the flat that I rented on the first floor of a rather shabby edifice, above a brothel and next door to another one.

The street was quiet now, the weather, I imagined, having put rather a dampener on business. Up on the balconies, several girls sat listlessly on the lookout for any passing strays they might persuade to join them upstairs.

One of them called out to me as I descended the carriage.

'Captain sahib, you looking tired. Come here. We look after you.'

The girl was called Mona. At nineteen, she was one of the older ones; old enough certainly to know how to handle men. She smiled coquettishly.

'Don't make me arrest you, Mona,' I said.

She grinned. 'On what charge, Captain sahib?'

'We can start with wasting police time and take it from there.'

I entered my building and climbed the stairs to the first floor. Reaching the landing, I stood for a moment, struggling to fish the key from my pocket. Before I could manage it, the door opened and Sandesh, my manservant, stood there grinning at me like a goat in a rubbish tip. It was a surprise to see him. The man was not exactly the most industrious. Indeed, finding him awake at any time was generally in the gift of the gods, but to see him there, at half past two in the morning, gurning inanely, made me worry he'd been drinking illicit hooch again.

'Master sahib!' he said. 'Look! Look! See who is here!'

He stood to one side and held the door open. There, just beyond the threshold, dressed in a white dhoti and chador and sporting the sort of wispy, travesty of a beard favoured by Bengali pseudo-intellectuals, stood a man I hadn't seen in such a long time.

'Hello, Sam,' said Surendranath Banerjee.

THREE

Surendranath Banerjee

I suppose some explanation is needed.

I had been away from Calcutta, and from India, for several years, far longer than I had originally anticipated. The cause of my flight – charges of attempted murder and sedition – had quickly been dropped, yet it still angered me that they had ever been brought.

If there was a silver lining, it was that their levelling had made one thing abundantly clear to me, namely the nature of British rule in my country. Of course it did not come as a complete surprise. No Indian truly believes that the British administer our country out of sheer benevolence and a sense of Christian charity. Yet the myth that their presence is benign still lingers, and is accepted to some degree by many, most notably themselves. I had once believed I could work with the British to the benefit of my own people. Experience had taught me the naivety of that. A man cannot, after all, serve two masters.

I had spent those years in Europe, remaining because I had nothing pressing in India to come back to. I thought I might be of use among the émigrés drumming up support for the cause of independence overseas. I traversed the capitals of Europe, or at any rate the colder ones: Berlin, Moscow, Vienna, Paris and, for a while, even London. In that time, I learned two things: first, that the only thing worse than an Englishman was a Frenchman, German, Russian or

Austrian; and second, that India's freedom would be won on Indian soil and not in the salons or talking shops of continental Europe.

Maybe I should have come home earlier; the gods know I had seriously considered that. Yet fate contrived to keep me there.

The problem, you see, is that I fell in love.

FOUR

Sam Wyndham

The sight of Suren, after all this time, and dressed like a tea-stall Tagore, made me think I might be dreaming. Maybe I'd succumbed once again? Maybe I was in some opium den and this whole night, from the murder of Mullick to Estelle Morgan and now Suren, was just some sort of fever dream. But no, this was real, and the Suren that stood in front of me was flesh and bone and as tangible as I was.

He'd lost weight, which was a concern, as he'd had precious little to lose in the first place. His face was haggard and his eyes sunken. Perhaps I should have said something; asked about it there and then, but that is not the English way, and anyway, I felt he should be the one to do the talking. He might start by explaining where the hell he'd been for so long. I stood in silence for some moments, long enough for Sandesh to intervene.

'Look, sahib, Suren-*babu* is come!'

'Yes,' I said. 'So he has.' I walked past him into the hall and turned to Suren. 'You're back then?'

He gave a smile, a degree of embarrassment at its corners. 'It would seem so.'

'For good?'

'I don't know.'

'How long has it been?'

'Three years, give or take.'

I nodded.

Three years. Give or take.

Three years since I'd helped him board a ship in Bombay and flee the country. It should only have been for a few months, until the charges against him were dropped. In the end, it had taken even less time than that. He should have returned.

But he hadn't.

'You're two and a half years late,' I said. 'And not a word from you in most of that time.'

He shuffled on the balls of his feet, the look of discomfort on his face only growing.

Good.

'I assumed the censors were monitoring our correspondence,' he said.

I supposed it was possible. Military intelligence had a whole department of eager young ladies, armed, I assumed, with kettles, steaming opening the mail of dissidents and revolutionaries and Ghandi-ites, and preparing reports on whatever they might find inside – mainly talk of illnesses and stomach complaints, one imagined, in the case of the Bengali ones. Still ...

'They dropped the charges,' I said. 'Why would they open your mail? Why would they even need to? Lord Taggart sent you a letter personally requesting you return. I thought it was settled. You were going to come home. You *should* have come home.'

He opened his mouth to speak but then paused and uttered a sigh.

'It was not that simple.'

And there it was, that infuriating way he had of obfuscating. I shouldn't have been surprised. He'd been to Cambridge. He'd learned from the best.

'How long have you been waiting here?' I asked.

'About three hours.'

Three hours. It was nothing in the grand scheme of things, but it was still quite a wait.

'I suppose you'd better come through then.'

He followed me in silence to the sitting room. There he stood, looking around as though this were the Sistine Chapel instead of a flat above a brothel, the place he'd lived in for almost five years. What exactly was he hoping to see? As far as I could tell, the room hadn't changed in the slightest in the time he'd been gone. I headed for the armchair.

'When did you get back?'

'A week or so ago.'

I looked up at him. He was still standing. Awaiting my permission to sit. Well, he could wait a little longer.

'And it's taken you this long to come over?'

He looked to the floor. 'I was not certain you would be pleased to see me.'

'Fair point,' I said. 'You owe me your share of three years' rent.'

I directed him to sit and he took his old spot on the sofa, under the ceiling fan, where, he said, the breeze was muted and less likely to induce a chill, but that was Bengalis for you. No people on God's green earth are more terrified of coughs, colds, bronchial infections and influenza.

'So,' I said. 'The prodigal son hath returned. Should I break out the fatted calf?'

He grimaced. 'You know I don't eat beef.'

'Fine. The fatted goat then, though it's a moot point because I haven't any of either. You'll have to settle for whisky.'

'That would be acceptable,' he said, though the look on his face suggested it was still more hardship than pleasure.

'Dear God, Suren, I'm hardly asking you to drink hemlock.'

I called out to Sandesh, and in that mixture of simple English and pidgin Bengali which served as our mutual medium of communication, ordered him to bring a bottle and fresh glasses, and, given that Suren was now technically my guest, a plate of cashew nuts, assuming we had any.

As Sandesh poured, I cast a glance at my erstwhile friend. Once more I was struck by his sheer wretchedness: he looked almost emaciated, to an extent I was sure must have had his dear mother in tears at the sight of him. Many Indians seemed to suffer a similar fate when living abroad, as though the severance of the umbilical connection to their motherland induced a certain degree of emotional and physical withering. That and the fact that they were just fussy about foreign food.

His skin too was paler, the sheen that came from living in the tropics replaced with a coarseness conditioned by colder climes. It was his eyes, though, which drew my attention. Those eyes, always so full of the spark of life, now seemed hollow; almost haunted.

He picked up his glass in salute.

The drinks in the Idle Fox might have dulled my intellect somewhat, but questions still buzzed in my mind like mosquitoes at dusk. So many things to ask. So much to say, and yet I said nothing, a silence born, I liked to think, of British reserve, but which Annie Grant might tell you was down to my tendency to be a stubborn, pig-headed arse.

In the end it was Suren who broke the ice.

'It *is* good to see you again, Sam.'

'And yet it took you a week to come here.'

'To be honest, I did not expect you still to be living here. I imagined you would have been somewhere nicer, with Miss Grant maybe, in her flat near Park Street. But it seems . . .'

I sipped malt whisky in the hope that it might sweeten my mood and moderate my words.

'Yes, Miss Grant and I are no longer ... that's to say, we don't have ...'

'So I see,' he said. 'I assumed all was well between you.'

I gave him a look which I hoped conveyed my feelings on the stupidity of his assumption.

'Yes, well ...' He coughed. 'Maybe that was naive of me. When did she, I mean when did it ... end?'

I gave a shrug, making it clear that the matter was trivial to me.

'A long time, now. Almost two years, I should think ... And it was a mutual decision.'

'Oh, I'm sure it was,' he said, a tad too vehemently.

'We decided we wanted different things.'

As clarifications went, it was, I realised, rather poor and only opened me up to the fire of further questions.

'But I'm sure,' I continued, 'you didn't come here and hang about waiting for me just to discuss my romantic affairs.'

His face grew grave. 'No. That is quite true.'

He stopped and it seemed the interrogation was over for now. Gratefully, I forced thoughts of Annie from my mind, banishing them back into the shadows, pushing them down to the pit of my stomach and suddenly thoughts of Estelle Morgan filled the void. I did my best to ignore them.

'So what *are* you doing here?' I asked.

He sipped his whisky, then looked me squarely in the eyes.

'Sam,' he said, 'I need your help.'

FIVE

Surendranath Banerjee

What brought me there, to Sam's door in the middle of the night?

The decision was made not by me, nor by my father or mother, but by the arrival at our home of my mother's elder brother, Pranab Chatterjee.

I had practically grown up under the wing of his daughter, Sushmita, though of course that was not the name I knew her by. We Bengalis have two names: a *bhaalo naam*, for forms and offices and the outside world; and a *daak naam*, special, intimate, for family and close friends. I knew her by the latter. I knew her as Dolly.

The first I knew of it was an urgent knocking upon my door. A manservant, one of the new ones employed during my absence, came in.

'*Chor-da, master-da daak-chen.*'

My father was summoning me. A matter of some urgency, apparently. I rose from my bed, made myself presentable and headed downstairs. Even as I descended a commotion of sorts was brewing. From the drawing room came voices. Rapid, agitated words met by my father's calm, deep tones.

I knocked on the door and entered.

There, opposite my father, sat Pranab-*mama*, his eyes dark and sunken, his hair unoiled and the blue-grey of unshaved stubble on his cheeks. He rose to greet me, his face still grave, eliciting little in the way of joy.

I walked over, touched his feet and greeted him, and he took my hands in his.

'Suren. It is good to see you. If only it were under more propitious circumstances. Your father told me you had returned home. I'm afraid I have nowhere else to turn. You are a detective and part my family. I am beseeching you. I need your help and your discretion.'

My father remained impassive, as though this was a matter in which he was merely a spectator.

'Why?' I said. 'What has happened?'

Pranab rubbed at the bristles on his cheek.

'It is Dolly. She has disappeared.'

I took a breath. Dolly had been like a big sister to me, and while we had grown apart over the years, she was still family. Her father's presence here was troubling in the extreme. In genteel *bhadralok* society, young women of caste and breeding did not simply *disappear*, and when they did, terrible things often befell them.

'What do the police say?'

He swallowed hard. 'They told me to go home and not waste their time.' His voice wavered. 'They said she had probably run off with some man.'

The words hung in the air between us. I wanted to ask if that were a possibility. Dolly was five years older than me. To be unmarried at her age was, how should I say, *unusual*. People were beginning to ask questions. But I could not utter the words. In our world, to even ask the question was to imply his negligence as a father. It would only add to his dishonour. Not for the first time, I considered the twisted nature of the society we had contrived to create.

'When did you last see her?'

'This morning,' he said, 'when she left for work. She should have been home hours ago, by five at the latest.'

'Are any of her possessions missing?'

He dropped his gaze to the floor.

'Some clothes, medicine.'

A damning admission. My instinct was to wash my hands of it. Dolly it seemed had left of her own volition. Part of me wished her luck. Yet the grief on her father's face was palpable. He was a good man, one who cared for his family and not just what the world thought of him. My aunt too, I imagined, would be in terrible pain. As for Dolly, I knew she could be headstrong, prone to precipitate action, and in the society in which we lived, women did not receive second chances.

'Pranab-da,' my father interjected, 'Suren is not a detective any more. I do not see how he can help.'

The tears seemed to well in my uncle's eyes. He pressed his palms together in supplication.

'I have nowhere else to turn. This evening I went to her studio. It was locked. The girl who worked for her was nowhere to be seen. I went to the shop next door to enquire if they knew anything. They said there was a commotion earlier in the day. They heard a man shouting. Furniture being smashed. When they went to check, a man burst past them and Dolly's assistant, Mou, was in tears, and there was no sign of Dolly.'

I read the distaste on my father's face. It was his expression, rather than Pranab-*mama*'s grief, that persuaded me. If this truly was a case of Dolly absconding, I would find out why, simply to obtain for her parents a degree of relief. But from Pranab-*mama*'s description of events, it sounded as though it might be more serious. If she was in danger, if she was running from something, or someone, then time was of the essence. I would need to work fast, and now that I was no longer a policeman, there was only one place to start.

SIX

Sam Wyndham

I could have laughed.

'You need *my* help?'

He looked at me with that earnest, hangdog expression that suggested the situation was the gravest imaginable and that, while he regretted his part in it, any comment I might make to try and avoid it becoming my problem was misguided and wholly unreasonable.

'Yes, Sam. I do.'

'What sort of help?'

'A cousin of mine, her name is Sushmita Chatterjee, Dolly to her friends, she is missing. Her father came to see me. He is extremely concerned.'

'And they can think of no reasonable explanation for her absence?'

He shook his head.

'She seems simply to have disappeared. Her father went to her place of work. It was locked shut and there was no sign of her or the girl she employed.'

'Has he been to the police?'

'The police sent him away. They told him she had probably run off with some man.'

'And has she?'

He looked at me with distaste, then scratched awkwardly at his ear.

'I do not know, but my fear is it might be something more serious . . . and so I came to you.'

If he'd hoped that might sway me, he was sorely mistaken.

'You've got a nerve,' I said. 'You bugger off for three years, turn up out of the blue and in the middle of the night and just expect me to dance to whatever tune you play?'

He swallowed back what he really wanted to say.

'I would not ask if it were not important.'

'I'm sure it's very important, to *you*,' I said, 'but why should I bother to make it my concern?'

'Because I think she might be in trouble, and I won't be able to find her without you.'

'Just go back to the police station,' I said. '*You* go with your uncle this time. They'll listen to you.'

He shook his head. 'A missing Indian woman is not a priority for them. And even if they were to investigate, it would set tongues wagging. It needs to be handled discreetly. If she *has* absconded with someone, it could ruin her future.'

'Again, why is that my concern?' I asked.

A small smile creased his lips, as though this were a game of chess and he'd just seen a winning move.

'Because she is the sort of woman you would appreciate: intelligent, headstrong, impulsive. She has a master's degree.'

'Women have been marching out of Calcutta University with master's degrees for almost fifty years now. It's what you need for a good marriage these days, I understand.'

'True,' he admitted. 'As long as they study something inoffensive like art or Sanskrit. But Dolly studied chemistry, and now she runs a business: a photography studio. The first woman-owned and -operated studio in India. She came up with the idea herself, all those women in purdah, all those men who object to the very notion of allowing another man into their houses to photograph their wives. She realised they could have no objection to a woman photographer coming into their homes. Hindus, Muslims, it is a huge market.'

I supposed Miss Chatterjee was on to something there. Still, it couldn't have done her marriage prospects any good.

'If you ask me,' I said, 'it sounds like she probably *has* run off with some unsuitable chap.'

'If she had . . .' I watched him squirm, 'fallen in love with some man, she would not have run off with him. She would have told her parents.'

'Even if he was an unsuitable match?'

He raised an eyebrow. 'Unsuitable?'

'If he was already married,' I said. 'Or a Muslim, or worse . . .'

'Worse?'

'An Englishman.'

'A fair point,' he conceded, 'but I doubt she would do something so foolish.'

I took a sip of whisky. I'd half a mind to send him away with a flea in his ear, but then, if the girl really was in trouble, if something terrible were to happen to her, he would never forgive me, and what's more, I probably wouldn't forgive myself.

'So what do you want *me* to do about it?'

He leaned forward, bringing his face closer to me so that I caught a whiff of his cologne. It smelled expensive. And French.

'What I want, Sam, is for you to investigate.'

'She's only been missing for a day,' I said. 'She'll probably turn up with a perfectly reasonable explanation.'

'You know as well as I do that there are no reasonable explanations for a single woman to stay out all night. She comes from a good family. Her parents do not want their daughter's future blighted by ... a possible indiscretion. And God forbid if something worse has befallen her ... I have to pull every lever at my disposal in finding her.'

I didn't much take to being called a *lever*, and as for helping him, the last time I'd done that it had cost me dearly. But there was no point bleating about that now.

'You could always just rejoin the force,' I said. 'Lord Taggart owes you a favour. I'm sure he'll welcome you back with open arms, water under the bridge and all things forgotten. Probably make you detective inspector.'

He ventured a thought. 'I am not sure he would quite see it that way. And besides ...'

'Besides what?'

He hesitated, lips thinning as though searching for the right words. 'I have re-evaluated my views upon the Imperial Police Force.'

'You do remember that I still work for them?'

'That is different ...'

I didn't labour the point. Instead I summoned Sandesh and the bottle of whisky and ordered him to top up our glasses, or in all honesty, just my glass. If I have learned one thing, it is that one should never underestimate the benefit of pouring single malt on troubled waters.

I took a sip.

'Don't you think you did some good when you were a policeman?'

He considered the question. 'I am not certain that I made much of a positive difference.'

'I recall you saving my life on at least one occasion.'

The hint of a smile came to his lips. 'I suppose then it comes down to one's definition of *positive*.'

I raised my glass in salute.

'So you will help me?' he asked.

I thought for a moment. The Mullick case would no doubt be taken off my plate in the morning. I would be left with nothing but administration and minor offences. I looked at my watch, then downed my whisky and made to stand.

'All right then,' I said, 'let's go.'

He seemed taken aback. 'Now?'

'No time like the present.'

SEVEN

Surendranath Banerjee

'So what were you doing all this time? Living it up in Paris and Rome?' I was seated beside Sam on the poorly sprung seat of an old tonga creaking north towards Cornwallis Street and Dolly's photographic studio.

What was I to tell him? Certainly not of the one person who had made that time meaningful, whose name even now crept into my thoughts. Her name was Elise and I had first met her in a cafe on the Rue de Saint-Sulpice, on a miserable February morning in '25. But that was another story ... another existence. No, I would stick to the mundane.

'I certainly wasn't living it up,' I told him, 'and I never made it to Rome. I was working with the émigrés in France.'

'So not a proper job, then,' he said. 'I suppose your father bank-rolled it all.'

I did my damnedest to ignore the edge in his voice. I needed his assistance. I did not want an argument.

'I paid my own way,' I said. 'I worked.'

'Really,' he said. 'Doing what exactly?'

'Some translation work here and there ... but mainly, if you must know, I worked in the kitchens in a number of hotels: the Adlon in Berlin, the Savoy, and the Meurice in Paris; washing dishes, peeling vegetables, cleaning up after the chefs.'

He seemed momentarily thrown by my response, something I took a degree of satisfaction from, but he soon recovered.

'Isn't all that menial labour rather beneath a vaunted Brahmin?'

I thought back to it all. The terrible heat of the kitchens, the long hours, the cuts on my hands that never healed, the stench on my clothes and my person that never lifted. I recalled the tears I shed, sitting on Berlin park benches, thinking what sort of a life I had left behind in my homeland and what I had been reduced to. I remembered the times I thought about quitting, getting on a steamer and coming home. I thought about how I had stuck it out, how I had learned the ways of the kitchen, how things had gradually become easier. I recalled the references I had received when I left. I recalled learning that I would never starve, because I could always find work somewhere, in some hotel. I recalled learning that true dignity came from one's work and one's efforts, not the family or caste that one was born into.

'On the contrary,' I said. 'Doing those menial tasks, becoming skilled at them, is one of the things of which I'm most proud.'

Thereafter we travelled in silence, each of us, I think, wrapped in our own sullen thoughts, our own righteous grievances. For my part, I remembered my forced return: my guilt and grief at leaving Elise and Paris for Marseilles and a steamer, first to Alexandria and then another through Suez and on to India; my return to Calcutta and the cold, sphinx-like greetings of my father and eldest brother upon the quayside and then the tears of my mother as she rushed to greet me at the steps of our home.

I thought of the following fortnight in which I had stayed in self-imposed purdah, eschewing company and conversation and all but minimal sustenance. If Pranab-*mama* had not arrived at our door, who knows how long I may have carried on in that vein, my days passing in torment, my thoughts an ocean away, my hours spent penning letters which would remain unsent, pondering words that would remain unsaid.

And I thought of the man now sitting beside me. Captain Sam Wyndham. I found it galling that, having swallowed my pride and requested his help, he had made such a song and dance about things, making me practically beg for his assistance. He may have been a friend, but he was still an Englishman, and sometimes his insufferable sense of English superiority still came to the fore. And yet my ire was tempered by a degree of shame on my part. I had ceased communications with him and here I was, brazenly asking for his help. I wouldn't have been surprised if he had simply sent me packing. Certainly I did not expect to be traversing the city with him quite so immediately.

From Premchand Boral Street, it was a distance of a few miles. Sam, I knew, would have preferred to walk, but I prevailed upon him to hail this vehicle in the interests of urgency and shoe leather.

The rain had stopped and the wind had blown itself out and now it was a typical Calcutta night: hot and humid and heavy with the scent of detritus rotting in the gutters.

The silence began to feel awkward, like that between estranged acquaintances thrown together by chance on a train.

'So,' I said, 'how are things at Lal Bazar?'

'Same old, same old.' He waved the question away as though it were some irksome creature: a fly maybe, or a foreigner.

'And . . . are you working on anything interesting?'

'Not really,' he said, 'though I did stumble across a murder earlier today.' He brightened at the thought.

'An interesting one?'

He puffed out his cheeks as though he rather than the deceased were the real victim in all this.

'Might be. It's a body we found at the burning ghats.'

'Is that not rather the point of the burning ghats? Or have things evolved in my absence?'

He seemed unamused. 'Yes, well, this particular corpse turned up with its throat cut, and while that is hardly a novel means of passing in Calcutta, what makes it interesting is the victim.'

'You have identified him?'

'Most likely. I think it was J. P. Mullick.'

I stared at him, dumbstruck, as though I'd been kicked in the head by a mule.

'*The* J. P. Mullick? The one who owns the coal mines and the steelworks and the hospitals?'

'Well, I'm hardly talking about the chap who sells cigarettes at the corner of College Square. Of course the one with the coal mines.'

I felt a hollowness. It was like hearing of the sudden death of the king. Mullick was a hero to many. His businesses competed with the largest British concerns and won. He exported to London and Manchester and Glasgow and turned handsome profits. He was successful and rich and he was one of us. He did, in the world of business, what men like Gandhi did in the political sphere: he gave us Indians back our dignity.

'He is dead?'

'Well, he's in the police morgue right now if you want to ask him.'

'Do the press know?'

'You know how Lal Bazar leaks. If they don't already, you can bet they will by dawn.'

'And his family?'

'They'll be notified in the morning, I expect. Asked to carry out a formal identification. Anyway, it's academic. It probably won't be my case by then.'

'Why?'

'Doesn't matter.'

'Have you upset someone?'

'Why would you say that?'

'No reason. It merely seemed the most likely conclusion.'

His expression soured. 'Well, that's a nice thing to say, seeing how it's the middle of the night and I'm out here helping you.'

That much was true. I should have been more respectful of him, or at least more tactful.

'I apologise,' I said. 'It has been a trying few days.'

'Really? I can't imagine.'

His tone irked me.

'Yes, really. You think you are the only one with problems?'

'Fine,' he said. 'So tell me. Tell me the problems of the vaunted Surendranath, scion of the Banerjees of Bowbazar, recently returned from his grand tour.'

'It doesn't matter,' I said.

'No, tell me.'

'It is complicated.'

He shook his head. 'The only problems that are truly complicated are those involving money or women. If it's the former, simply ask your father, he's hardly short of a few bob. And if it's the latter, well, in that case your position truly is hopeless. So? Does it involve a woman?'

I felt the blood rush to my face.

'No,' I lied.

'Well, then it's solvable.' He sighed. 'If you do fancy telling me what's troubling you, then feel free, though to be clear, I'm just as happy if you don't.'

I sat back and stared at the pools of lamplight stretching northward as College Street yielded to the long, straight stretch of Cornwallis Street and that familiar transition from White Town to an area more variegated, the buildings diminishing both in size and ostentation, becoming more functional, more Indian.

The tonga peeled off into a quiet lane and the horse wheezed to a halt outside a sagging two-storey edifice, its door hidden in the darkness and its windows shuttered. Above the entrance, a weed-sprouting balcony and signage in both English and Bangla proclaiming the Golden Bengal Ladies Photographic Studio. I reached for my wallet and insisted on paying. This was my case after all.

We alighted and took a closer look at the building. The doorway was recessed into the wall so that in the shade of night it resembled nothing so much as a mouth between shuttered-window eyes. The door itself was solid and of the old style – two narrow panels, opening in the middle, their iron ring handles clasped together by a heavy padlock. I pulled at them to no avail.

Sam prised one of the window shutters loose. Behind it, iron bars. He stepped back into the street and took in the surrounding buildings. To one side, a watchmaker's shop, barred and shuttered just as tightly as Dolly's studio. To the other, a *gullee* and a wall, ten or eleven feet high, its top crenelated with the shards of broken bottles.

'Not ideal,' he said. 'I suppose we'll just have to improvise.'

He looked up towards the sign above the door and the first-floor balcony, then pointed to a drainpipe running beside it.

'You're going to have to climb that.'

'Me?' I said. 'But I'm wearing a dhoti. It's hardly practical attire for climbing drainpipes.'

He shook his head. 'Well, maybe you should have thought of that before you came looking for my help, and worn some trousers.'

I could have told him that I had been wearing trousers for the last three years. Was it so terrible that I should seek to wear the clothes of my own people in my own place? But what would be the point? It would not help us find Dolly.

'There is no guarantee the doors and windows up there aren't similarly secure.'

'No,' he said. 'There isn't. But do you want to find this girl or not?'

'Of course I do.'

'Then get up there before we start drawing attention to ourselves.'

I was not entirely convinced that the sight of a man in a dhoti climbing up to a first-floor balcony could do anything but draw attention. Nevertheless I removed my sandals, tucked the ends of the dhoti tightly round my waist and made for the drainpipe, gripping it and hauling myself up, finding footholds between it and the cracked plasterwork as I went. It struck me as I climbed that every previous occasion that I had scaled a drainpipe had been at Sam's behest too, never on my own account or at the request of anyone else. It was worth discussing at a more opportune moment.

As it was, the dhoti presented fewer problems than I had anticipated and I pulled myself over the rusted ironwork of the balcony with bones and modesty intact and with a new-found pride in the versatility of Bengali formal attire. Below, an itinerant cow had come and stood beside Sam, ruminating on a coconut husk.

'I need my sandals,' I called down quietly. 'Throw them up.'

He did so, one at a time, and I, like a fielder at deep square leg, caught them as they came flying up before turning and looking around. There were two sets of doors up here, again of the old style, opening in the middle. Each, I assumed, led to separate rooms. Three windows too, shuttered and no doubt barred. I tried the first door, rattling the ring handles but they remained secure; barred, I imagined, from the inside. The second door too was shut, but here, when I pushed at the doors, a gap appeared. In the darkness I could see nothing, but with my fingers I felt for the ring handles on the inside. I touched rough material – cotton or more likely jute. The rings it seemed were tied together with rope rather than padlocked.

I turned and once more called to Sam. 'Do you have a knife?'

He raised his palms in disbelief. 'Of course not.'

'I need a knife,' I told him. 'I can cut through the ties holding the door shut.'

'Wait there,' he said, then hurried off, disappearing into the night. I saw him once as he passed within the glow of a street lamp and then he was gone, leaving me on the balcony and the cow grazing in the street.

And so I waited, with the sounds and scents of a Calcutta night as my company. The buzz of insects and the smell of woodsmoke. I thought of Elise, and I wished she was there with me instead of half a world away. For an instant, something caught my eye. A figure, was it? In the shadows. I tried to focus, but it was gone and then there was nothing but the cow and the silence of the street.

Sam returned some minutes later and pulled a large knife from beneath his jacket. The sight of it startled the cow. Even in the lamplight, it was an impressive blade

'Where did you get that?'

'Borrowed it.'

'From where?'

'From a coconut-wallah on Cornwallis Street.'

'At this time of night?'

He grew impatient. 'Look, just take the damn knife and get on with it.'

He launched the object towards the balcony and I lost sight of it in the darkness. I threw myself against the wall as the vicious thing arced its path past where I had been standing and crashed to the floor.

'What the devil are you doing? You could have killed me.'

'Don't be ridiculous,' he said. 'Now pick it up and get a move on.'

I did not appreciate the petulance of his actions, yet I said nothing, and it struck me that *there* was the relationship between the British and the Indians in a nutshell. They could do whatever they wanted, but if we complained, we were the ones being unreasonable.

Instead I retrieved the blade and set to work on the rope that tied the ring handles of the door in place.

The jute was thick and the knife less sharp than it had appeared when flying towards my head, and it was the work of some minutes before I managed to cut through. As I did, there came a crash behind me and I turned to see Sam sprawled on the floor of the balcony. Gradually he righted himself.

'I'm getting too old for this type of thing.'

I pushed open the doors and entered the room only to be assailed by the odour of naphthalene and mildew.

I groped in the dark as behind me came a rattle and a flash as Sam lit a match. By the light of the flame, I made out the spartan room. Nothing more than a string charpoy with some bedding rolled up at its foot and two wooden almirahs, their doors hanging open and their contents sprawling onto the floor like disembowelled innards.

The sight of it sent a chill through me.

I made for the far side of the room. There, next to the door, was the black dome of the light switch. I pushed it upwards but the room remained shrouded. Besides, it was the switch for the ceiling fan. I tried that too, and again nothing happened.

'The electricity is off.'

The match-light flickered and died and Sam lit another.

'Let's get a move on then,' he said. 'I don't have too many of these left.'

I passed through the doorway and into a landing, discerning the outlines of another two door frames and a set of stairs leading both down to the ground floor and up to the roof. One of the doors led to a washroom of sorts. In what light fell through the barred window I recognised a stone trough with a bucket of water beside it and a latrine. On the floor beside it, another bucket and, hanging from a hook on the wall, praise be, a hurricane lamp.

I held it to my nose and sniffed. The stench of paraffin. That was good news.

'Suren?'

Sam's voice, its tone grave, echoed from the landing.

'In here,' I called.

'Well, come out. There's something you need to see.'

EIGHT

Sam Wyndham

The match burned down to my fingers, the light flickering then dying. It didn't matter. I'd seen enough.

While Suren had gone off to investigate the interior, I had made for another door, a room also leading out to the balcony but whose exterior door had been barred shut. It must have been used as an office of sorts, though now it resembled more the aftermath of a hurricane, with furniture upturned, cabinets smashed, and everywhere a deluge of papers, negatives and photographic prints.

I reached for my matchbook, ready to rip out another of the flimsy cardboard things, but thought better of it. There were only two left and would need to be utilised sparingly, especially as I was craving a cigarette.

The creak of the door announced Suren's arrival.

'Room's been ransacked,' I told him. 'I'd show you but I'm down to my last two matches.'

He held up what looked like a paraffin lamp.

'This might help.'

'Good work,' I said, taking it from him and setting it down on a corner of the desk, then lit it with the penultimate match. Suren was on his haunches now, picking up random papers and photographs, casting an eye over them, discarding them, picking up more.

I took in the scene. Someone was obviously searching for

something. But this was not a methodical search. It was haphazard; violent. The upturned chair, the filing cabinets smashed open. It was done either in a hurry or with a degree of malice. Not the sort of thing you expected to find in a case of lovers eloping.

The lower floor was little different to the upper, and in a similar state of turmoil, with the exception that here the destruction seemed more flagrant, not confined to single rooms but rather a rolling conflagration of violence that had flowed throughout like a tidal bore. At the foot of the stairs, a hallway, converted into a waiting area, its rattan chairs now thrown about like flotsam, cushions slashed open, bleeding stuffing. Potted plants lay smashed on the ground, dark earth spilling onto stone floor and mingling with shards of terracotta pottery.

I followed Suren into a room which I presumed was the studio. Amid the wreckage of cameras and plates and other photographic equipment lay several large cotton sheets: painted backdrops of palaces and gardens and all the sorts of places people wished to be photographed in preference to the back room of a dingy house off Cornwallis Street. There was even one of the Eiffel Tower, which rather begged the question of how a woman confined to purdah in Calcutta would suddenly find herself transported to Paris, and who exactly would believe she'd been there?

But that was a question for another time and one best answered by Suren's cousin Dolly, who, I now feared, was in a hell of a lot more trouble than I'd first anticipated.

Suren made for a door at the far end of the room, pulling it open and releasing a miasma of chemicals. I followed him in. The room beyond was small and stifling. Suren lifted a handkerchief to his nose against a fog of spilled compounds which clawed at the throat and stung the eyes. I gestured towards the shuttered window.

'See if you can't open that.'

He made for the window, releasing the iron catches from their hooks and pushing open the shutters. As the air and my eyes began to clear, the room took shape, the floor littered with spilled reels of black acetate film coiled like serpents, the smashed glass of photographic plates and bottles which had held the chemical elixirs required for photographic alchemy.

The tables too were strewn with plates and reels and chemicals and photographic papers, their images interrupted in the process of forming, the figures in them ephemeral as ghosts. I held one up to the light. Two figures: a sari-clad woman and a man in the patrician garb of the Bengali upper castes. Both stood with stern expressions, faces fixed upon the lens as they posed in front of a Bengali Arcadia: a backdrop of palm trees and thatched roofed huts.

Suren too was examining the flotsam of film and prints, picking up spools and random plates.

'I do not even know what we should be looking for.'

Anything that might provide a clue as to who's done this, I thought. *And why.*

Before I could say anything, an object hurtled between the bars of the window and smashed onto the cement floor. I didn't need a second glance to know what it was. A bottle, a flaming rag stuffed into its mouth, crashing, shards splintering, fracturing into a hundred pieces, the liquid inside igniting, exploding. A wall of heat and light and fire struck me, blinding, knocking me to the ground. The world contracted and for a split second there was silence; then chaos: the roar of flame; the ignition of photographic film; the stench of chemicals; and the sound of Suren's voice shouting from what felt like miles away. Smoke clouded my vision, and with it the blurred outline of flames, spreading fast, arcing across the room along coiled paths of acetate. Chemical poison filled my lungs, choking, constricting, reopening old wounds. I coughed, deep and hard and bronchial, and suddenly I was back in the trenches, doubled over, reaching for my mask as shouts of 'Gas! Gas! Gas!' reverberated to the screams of men. Around me was mud and blood and the pale, greenish haze of chlorine. The scent of pineapples and pepper. The harbinger of death.

'Sam!'

Suren's voice broke through the maelstrom, but from where exactly wasn't clear. The room hued amber like a circle of hell. I held my sleeve to my mouth and groped frantically for the door but on all sides found only fire and noxious black smoke.

'Sam!'

I turned, disorientated, unsure where the voice was coming from.

'This side!'

Smoke filled my lungs. I fell to my knees, coughing, vision constricting. I had to get to my feet, to move, to fight for life, but it was impossible. All around was flame and charnel and the sound of Suren's voice, ringing out again and again.

'Sam!'

And then I felt his hand on my collar, wrenching me upwards, the support of his shoulder under my arm as we forged a path through the flames to the door and out into the adjoining room. Once more I fell to my knees, gasping for breath, gulping down oxygen. Suren knelt beside me.

'Are you all right?'

Before I could answer there came another crash; once more the smashing of glass, the whoosh of fire. The detonation of another petrol bomb, in the front hallway this time.

'We need to get out of here, Sam!'

He gripped my arm and once more I laboured to my feet.

'We should make for the rear of the building,' he said. 'There must be a door.'

My head pounded. My mind fogged. I fought through it. The rear of the building. That wasn't right.

'No,' I said, pulling him back. 'Upstairs. The roof.'

We changed direction, heading this time for the hallway and the stairs. The flames had spread to the cotton backdrops and textiles, but the path to the stairwell was still unimpeded. We ran, my chest burning with every step, every gasp of breath, reaching the first-floor landing and then continuing, higher, another flight of stairs, into all-consuming darkness, the hurricane lamp just a memory now, discarded in the inferno below. The walls seemed to narrow, closing in on us as we climbed, groping in the pitch-black till suddenly Suren slowed.

'The door to the roof.'

He pulled against it, rattling the thing on its hinges.

'Locked.'

He barged at it with his shoulder but it remained resolute. My head still swam, yet I knew what was needed: a pair of stout, size twelve boots.

'Out of the way,' I said.

We swapped places and I braced myself, mustering my strength and kicked out. A jolt of pain passed through my bones. Another kick and the wood gave way. I stood aside to catch my breath as Suren made his way through the gap. I followed him through, out onto the roof, and fell to my knees, inhaling sweet air, and then looked up to a sky littered with stars.

Suren ran to the parapet at the roof's edge. He crouched down, then slowly raised his head. I fought the pain coursing through my body, rose and made my way over, reaching him and leaning back against the low wall.

'What do you see?'

Suren shrugged. 'Hard to tell. One person most definitely. Could be more.'

One person we could handle, assuming they weren't armed. In the old days I'd have fancied our chances even if they were. But not tonight. Not now.

'What do we do?'

'Keep watching,' I told him. 'We'll think of something.'

The minutes passed. The fire raged on the ground floor, growing, smoke now billowing, escaping through the slits in the shutters and climbing skywards. Across the street, doors opened, spilling yellow light and shouts and bodies into the alley.

'There!'

Suren turned to me.

'Look.'

I got to my feet and looked over the wall. In the street, while others were rushing to the scene, a solitary figure was hurrying away, hugging close to the walls and making for Cornwallis Street. There was something about him – the way he travelled single-mindedly against the crowd, away from the inferno, without even so much as a glance back. It told me what I needed to know.

'Let's go,' I said.

I ran for the side wall, where the roof adjoined that of the neighbouring building, vaulting the parapet and, with Suren a step behind, making for a stairwell at the far end. Once more my lungs rasped. I ignored the pain, reaching the steps and clambering down them.

On the street, a crowd had gathered, their voices raised. A commotion in progress. All eyes focused on the burning building. No one paid us the slightest attention.

Frantically I searched for our assailant among the shadows of the alley.

'Do you see him?'

Suren craned his neck.

'There!'

He pointed to a ripple amid the darkness, a silhouette against the lamplight of Cornwallis Street. He broke into a run, discarding his sandals and sprinting barefoot down the *gullee*, and I did my best to follow.

We reached the corner of Cornwallis Street, I grabbing the nearest telegraph pole for support and Suren desperately scouring the road for our assailant. Somewhere close by an engine growled to life. Suren began running towards it. With a screech of tyres, a car pulled out from the kerb. It roared down the street, headlights blinding white, heading straight for Suren. I raised a hand, shielding my eyes. Suren stood there as though mesmerised. I shouted to him but he seemed not to hear.

With what strength I had left, I ran for him, reaching him seconds before the car, pulling him back towards me, feeling his weight upon me as we both fell to the ground, landing heavily as the wheels of the car missed us by inches.

It roared on into the night, the sound of its engine competing with the thumping in my chest as my breath gradually returned.

I sat up. 'You OK?'

He puffed out his cheeks. 'I think so, though my dhoti is ruined.'

Day 2

Sunday

NINE

Sam Wyndham

Life, all lives, from time to time takes on a monotonous pattern where the daily routine becomes just a series of repetitive actions, carried out through habit and without thought as to alternatives. A malaise, a funk, a morass one is often unaware of, and so makes little attempt to alter. And then something happens, or rather everything happens, all at once, and everything changes.

A murder; a chance encounter with a beautiful, world-famous actress; the return of the prodigal sergeant; and almost being roasted alive. All within the space of a few hours. Such things might make one think the Hindus were on to something with their belief in karma and astrologers and planets aligning in inauspicious patterns. Me though, I put it down to dumb luck and the callousness of the universe.

The next morning was fresh and clear and the walk from Premchand Boral Street to Lal Bazar – that claret-and-white monstrosity that served as police headquarters for the city – was a pleasant one.

I was functioning on little sleep, lots of coffee and several cigarettes, which frankly should be enough for any man still pretending to be in the prime of his life.

Suren would still be in his bed now, and I envied him that. We'd parted ways outside the smoking husk of Dolly's photographic studio, as locals ferried buckets of water from a nearby tube-well and the clang of bells presaged the arrival of the fire brigade.

Neither of us had caught a glimpse of the man who'd tried to murder us, nor did we get a look at the registration plate of the car in which he'd sped off. One thing was certain, though, Dolly was in trouble. Enough trouble for someone to ransack her studio and set fire to it.

Suren was convinced she was still alive, and I thought he was right, though how long she might stay that way was anyone's guess. He was going to keep looking, and I wished him well, offered my assistance, if rather half-heartedly, if there was anything that I might tangibly do, and to which he, perhaps sensing my hesitation, responded in polite, though similarly half-hearted terms.

I pushed thoughts of him from of my head and replaced them with more pleasant memories. Estelle Morgan. Now meeting her had been an unalloyed pleasure. The truth is, the attentions of a beautiful woman, however fleeting, does wonders for a man's self-esteem, and though it might equally have been down to the coffee, I suddenly found myself walking with a spring in my step.

Reaching Lal Bazar, I bypassed the main entrance with its white-uniformed constables standing sentry, and headed for the inner courtyard and the nondescript door which led to the Criminal Investigations Department.

Only as I climbed the stairs did my mood falter. The department was not a cheery place for me these days and hadn't been for some time now. I could trace it back to Suren. His flight from the country had caused a storm, which, when it came to light that I had abetted his escape, broke upon my head. Even though he was soon exonerated, what little chance I may have had to make chief inspector had gone up in smoke.

But the real cause of my professional demise had come about

eighteen months later. There'd been protests in Calcutta; to be fair there are always protests in Calcutta, mainly because Bengalis like to make a nuisance of themselves. Maybe these protests just came at a sensitive time for the authorities, for the man leading them, a man called C. R. Das, had recently been elected the first native mayor of the city.

Of course, many Englishmen took this as a sign that the sky was about to fall on our heads. Attitudes hardened, and when the protests broke out, someone on high decided it might be a jolly good idea to have Das arrested, and I was the one sent to arrest him.

The problem was, I'd met him before and I liked him. Of course, that in itself wouldn't have stopped me doing my job. Over the years, I've arrested quite a few people I've got on well with, but Das was different. Das was a national leader, a man of morals, and a man in ill health. He wouldn't survive another stretch in prison, and I wasn't about to have that on my conscience, so I told him to get out of Calcutta, at least for a while, and he did so; left for Darjeeling, while I told my superiors I couldn't find him. Alas, under questioning, one of his servants claimed to have seen Das talking to me. I denied it of course, and under normal circumstances, that would have been the end of it. My word as an officer and an Englishman would trump that of a native servant, but I was still tarred with the fact of Suren's flight from Bombay. I had, as the bookmakers say, form.

It was not enough to get me sacked, but quite sufficient to have me blackballed, first taken off cases deemed politically sensitive, and then off any that were at all interesting. Not even the advent of a new chief inspector, a man called Healey drafted in from the North West Frontier, had changed matters. As far as the powers that be were concerned, I was *persona non grata*, and the sooner I quit, the better.

I entered the department and passed a chit to a lackadaisical peon sitting on a bench beside the door. There was a time when the fellow would have got to his feet quick-smart as soon as I entered, maybe even following up with a salute. These days I was lucky if he even acknowledged my presence. He took it from me with a nod and then walked the two yards to Healey's office, and knocked on the door.

The note safely delivered, and confident that the late J. P. Mullick would be someone else's problem, I was free to return to the pressing matter of paperwork, the paper in question being the morning's copy of the *Englishman* waiting on my desk, delivered along with a packet of Capstans by an industrious young lad by the name of Sabuj who had a winning smile, an eye for opportunity, and a penchant for exorbitant mark-ups.

'Overheads, Captain sahib,' he would say with a grin, which only became wider when I pointed out that he lived rent-free in some forgotten corner of the building.

The paper was its usual heady mix of fear and outrage, editorials, lamentations and letters from retired colonels in places like Patna opining that the country was going to the dogs and that things would be immeasurably improved if we simply shot Gandhi and a few dozen Congress-wallahs.

Reading the thing was not particularly good for one's health but I read it anyway, out of habit and because it's always good to keep abreast of public opinion, even when public opinion borders on the stark raving mad.

There was no mention of J. P. Mullick thankfully, or even of a body being found at the burning grounds, though there happened to be a small piece about an international actress recently arrived in town. I was about to catch up on news of the Third Test in the Ashes when the sound of Healey's voice rang out across the office like a warning siren before a gas attack: 'Wyndham!' There came the scrape of a chair and the frosted outline of Healey's silhouette making for his door. Yanking it open, he stuck his head out.

'Get your arse in here. *Now!*'

It was about the warmest welcome I'd had all year.

His *office*, if you could call it anything so grand, was a small corner of the department, a salient which had been seized by one of Healey's predecessors and stubbornly defended from the rest of us with thin wooden partitions and a frosted-glass door. It did, though, have its own electric fan hanging from the ceiling and half a window in one wall which offered a slight breeze in the winter months and, if you strained, a partial view of Lal Bazar's inner courtyard. I loitered as close to the door as I thought seemly.

Healey's back addressed me as he made his way towards his desk.

'This J. P. Mullick business. You're sure it's him?'

'Certainly looked like him,' I said.

His chair creaked as he settled into it.

'He been reported missing?'

'Not as far as I'm aware.'

'Where's he live?'

I gave a shrug.

'Well, why don't you go and find out? Get down to his residence, see if it really is Mullick who's turned up dead at the cremation grounds, and if so, figure out what the hell happened to him.'

'Me?'

He stared at me as one would at a German.

'Yes. Is that a problem for you?'

'No,' I said. 'It's just rather unexpected. Is everyone else busy?'

To his credit, he ignored the barb.

'You are still a detective in this department, aren't you?'

'I believe so.'

'Good,' he said, 'because this is your case. I've been told you have a weakness for our native friends, and besides, Lord Taggart believes you're a half-competent, if somewhat unreliable, detective, and competence is something I could use more of.'

He picked up a pen and turned his attention to the papers on his desk.

'You're dismissed. And, Wyndham –' he looked over – 'don't balls this up.'

TEN

Surendranath Banerjee

For the first time since my return to Calcutta, I rose with purpose. Dolly was in danger. Her fate was in my hands, assuming she was still alive, and I was almost certain that she was.

Whoever had broken into that studio was looking for one of two things: either Dolly herself, or something they believed to be in her possession. If they had found her, they would have tortured her, and sooner or later extracted what they wanted. There would be little reason to turn the place upside down. It was possible that they had ransacked the studio *before* finding her, but then why continue to keep an eye on the place, and why attempt to murder Sam and me?

No. It was more likely that Dolly was still alive and in hiding somewhere. That was why they still had the building under surveillance. Maybe they were hoping she might return. Instead they caught us scaling the drainpipe.

Yet the whole incident raised more questions than it answered. Bengali women of Dolly's standing did not, as a rule, involve themselves in matters that could lead to their needing to disappear or the fire-bombing of their place of work. Whatever was going on, it was far more dangerous than Pranab-*mama* had led me to believe. If I was to get to the bottom of it, I would need to speak to him again, this time a little more forcefully.

*

I headed for Shealdah and a train north, out of the city, into a hinterland of high-walled jute mills and circular brick kilns with chimneys that pointed to the heavens like blackened fingers; and then further still, into a countryside of mud-brick and thatch, dust-covered neem trees and palm-fringed ponds that glinted emerald in the morning sun.

I alighted at Ichapore, crossed the tracks and hailed a bicycle rickshaw to take me along rutted roads to Nawabgunge and Dolly's father's house. I wondered what I would tell him. Should I lie about the happenings of the previous night, to at least spare her mother added worry? And yet what good would that do? Would it help bring Dolly back? Or would it only complicate matters?

As I rode, the past came to meet me. I knew this country. Had spent childhood holidays here at my maternal grandfather's house. The place had changed, of course. There were more people now, more buildings, more noise, but they only served to obscure the past, not obliterate it. The landmarks were still there, the shrine to Kali at the base of a banyan tree, the two-roomed school on the corner of a lane. Reminiscences lost to the fog of time now became reanimated, rejuvenated at the sight of them; echoes of my childhood, playing on the *rowak* of this house with Dolly, where the veranda became a carriage, a castle or an entire kingdom from the Mahabharata and we were warriors and kings and queens. How vast that house and its veranda had then seemed. How full of wonder and excitement. And how small it appeared now.

Pranab-*mama* met me at the door, his face haggard, as though he had aged visibly since I had seen him not twenty-four hours earlier. Behind him stood his wife, my *masi*, her eyes puffed and red. I ventured forward and knelt to touch the dust at their feet.

They led me to the sitting room and directed me to the sofa. Pranab-*mama* took a seat opposite and clasped his hands together.

They waited until the maidservant had been sent away and the door closed before continuing. It was my aunt who spoke first.

'We have heard that there was a fire at her photography studio last night ...'

'There was,' I said, 'but Dolly was not inside.'

She looked at me, wide-eyed. 'You are sure?'

'Yes,' I said. 'The studio had been ransacked. As for the fire, it was started deliberately by a miscreant, probably the same person who had looted the place. This matter is more complicated than Dolly simply absconding or eloping, or, God forbid, finding herself in a hospital. Someone extremely dangerous is looking for her. I believe that is why she has fled.'

My aunt burst into tears, my uncle stared stoically ahead. Maybe he was simply stunned, yet I expected more of a reaction.

'What about Dolly's assistant?' I asked. 'What can you tell me about her?'

'Her name is Mou,' he said, 'but as I told you, she was not at the studio when I went there.'

'So where might I find her?'

Pranab-*mama* hesitated. 'Kumartuli. One of the *bustees* around there.'

Kumartuli, the artisans' quarter, where potters and sculptors made the idols of the gods and goddesses which populated our temples. So Dolly employed a crafts girl who lived in a slum. It was an interesting choice, carrying with it the whiff of unorthodoxy. Was that the reason for his reticence?

'Which *bustee*?' I asked.

He shook his head. 'I do not know.'

My aunt was sobbing quietly. Her husband made no effort to comfort her.

'When we spoke yesterday, was there anything you did not

mention to me?' I asked. 'If so, please tell me, however trivial you may think it.'

Pranab-*mama* looked to the floor. It was my aunt who eventually spoke.

'Tell him . . .'

'Tell me what?'

With the *anchal* of her sari, she wiped a tear from her cheek.

'Dolly's friend, Mahalia,' she said. 'Mahalia Ghosh. They had lunch the day before yesterday.'

I knew the name. I had met her. A nice girl. The elder of two sisters. Clever, as I recall. Pretty too. More than one *masi* had opined that she and I might have made a suitable match.

'What about her?'

'She and Dolly are close,' Pranab-*mama* said. 'I went to see her yesterday, in case she knew anything about Dolly's whereabouts. I had even hoped Dolly might be with her.'

'And?'

He gave a sigh. 'She said she didn't know where Dolly was and that they had not spoken for several days. But I felt she was not being honest. I kept pushing her and finally she told me that Dolly had come to her asking for money.'

'Why?' I asked. 'Is she in debt?'

'If so, I was not aware of it.'

Money. Was that at the heart of Dolly's disappearance? A loan from some unsavoury character? The man Sam and I had chased last night? Maybe she now lacked the means to repay. That might explain why her studio had been ransacked. But then, why burn it down? And why try to kill Sam and me?

'Why would she go to Mahalia instead of her own parents?'

My aunt and uncle exchanged a glance.

'I do not know,' Pranab-*mama* said. 'It came as a shock to me.'

'Why did you not mention this to me when we spoke yesterday?'

He bristled. 'Because it is a shameful thing, a *bhadromohila* asking for money like a common beggar. I had hoped you might find her without the need to know such things.'

'If you wish my help, you must tell me everything,' I said, 'no matter if you think it irrelevant or shameful. Now, is there anything else you have kept from me?'

My uncle shook his head.

'I will need to speak to Mahalia urgently,' I said. Where can I find her?'

'At the university,' my aunt said. 'She teaches at Presidency College.'

'Please though, Suren, be discreet,' Pranab-*mama* interjected. 'For both Dolly's sake and Mahalia's.'

I left them shortly thereafter and made my way back to the station and thence to the city, all the time considering my next steps. The path to Dolly, it seemed, might only be navigated with the help of two women, her friend, Mahalia, and her assistant, Mou. I would start with Mou, because the interrogation of a lower-caste artisan could take place in broad daylight, while a meeting with Mahalia, a woman from the same social class as myself, would require greater subtlety. Calcutta can be a small place. *Bhadralok* social circles are surprisingly closed and claustrophobic and governed by archaic rules enforced by stern-faced matriarchs. One step out of line by a young man, one sighting with someone deemed inappropriate, or even too appropriate, is liable to set tongues wagging. And if decent young men were at risk of censure for being seen in the company of unchaperoned young women, then how much worse it was for the women. A meeting with Mahalia would therefore need to be clandestine. The question was, how was I to find a way to do it?

ELEVEN

Sam Wyndham

My first proper case in eighteen months. I took a few moments to smoke a cigarette and let the ramifications sink in.

The first step was to track down Mullick's address, and fortunately it didn't take long. Rich men tend to congregate together. Maybe it's safety in numbers, or maybe they just like to keep an eye on one another. Something else they tend to have is a telephone. One call to the operator and a request for the address for Jogendra Prasad Mullick, and ten minutes later, my subaltern Singh and I had requisitioned a car and were heading to Tollygunge to the south of town, out past Alipore.

Not that long ago, Tollygunge had been little more than a collection of bungalows in the jungle, a weekend retreat among the coconut palms and bougainvillea. But then came the Royal Calcutta Golf Club and everything changed, which was a shame because there is nowhere on earth that isn't made a little worse by the addition of a golf course.

The Mullick residence sat at the end of a quiet lane, a Palladian mansion with Greek pillars and green shutters that seemed a tropical aping of an English stately home; and if that sounded like plagiarism, you should remember that we stole the idea from Italian antiquity in the first place. The grounds were fortified by depressingly high walls and accessed through the sort of wrought-iron gates which might bog down a tank or two.

The driver brought the Morris to a halt and leaned on the horn. There should have been a durwan close by – an ever-faithful servant charged with maintaining the perimeter of the property. Even if he'd been snoozing in the shade of a tree, a few blasts should have brought him to life and running to the gates, but the cacophony did nothing more than force a pair of mynahs from their branches and attract the somewhat lackadaisical interest of a passing cow.

The whole situation was odd. Rich men in Calcutta were never short of staff. Even if Mullick and the whole family had decamped to Darjeeling for the season, he would have kept a retinue here: servants and gardeners and gatekeepers. To do otherwise would be scandalous, because for the rich of Calcutta, leaving your home unstaffed was tantamount to an admission of penury.

The driver gave another blast of the horn for good measure before I told to him to pack it in and switch off the engine. The sudden cessation of noise heightened the silence that followed; the silence of the tropics at least: the call of birds and the buzz of insects.

Singh stepped out, strode up to the gates and rattled them in what I fully expected would be a futile gesture. To both our surprises, the gates creaked open. He turned and shrugged.

He got back in and then ordered the chauffeur to drive on.

With the sun at our backs, we followed a driveway wide enough for several cars, or elephants, all the way up to the front steps. There, I got out and searched for signs of life. The doors were shut tight, which was odd. Indian houses, especially the large ones, hardly ever had their doors bolted during the day. They were kept open to the world and the myriad comings and goings of extended family and staff and all manner of petitioners and flunkeys and hangers-on. To find a mansion such as this,

The Burning Grounds

pristine and yet shuttered, felt unnatural, as though the house too had died along with its owner.

I rapped hard on the door, the sound swallowed by the house and the surroundings. Long seconds passed and the sweat pricked at my collar. Maybe there *was* more to this than just one dead body on the banks of the Hooghly.

We would need to get into the building. Maybe there was a tool shed somewhere? A *mali*'s shack that might contain a hammer or a spade or something else that might help me break in to this upper-class Alcatraz. The gardens were too well maintained for there not to be one somewhere, to the rear, most likely. Hidden away out of sight.

Keeping to the shade, I set off to circumnavigate the exterior. Dragonflies buzzed, their thin bodies shimmering aquamarine as they danced over the emerald waters of a pond. I stopped for a moment, savouring the silence and contemplating, not for the first time, what a wonderful place Calcutta was when you removed all the people.

Beyond lay a flower garden, a riot of red and saffron, row upon row of blossoms, each packed tightly into the black earth of its own individual pot. I wasn't much one for flowers. I could tell you what was a rose and what wasn't, but that was as far as my talents stretched. Bengalis though love them. You can't go five yards in Calcutta without finding a garland hanging from a tree or petals placed at the feet of some little deity at a roadside shrine. It helped that the land was just so damn fertile. Everywhere you looked, the place was in bloom. Indeed, the real mystery was how a place with so many flowers still managed to stink so resolutely.

I knelt beside a pot and pushed two fingers into the soil.

Soft.

Recently watered.

Somewhere beyond the flower garden, a couple of crows gave a squawk of complaint and flapped into flight.

Lazy birds, crows; Bengali ones anyway. Bullocks of the air who generally didn't take flight without a bloody good reason. I stood up and peered through a gap in the blooms. There. In the distance, the top of a head. Black hair moving slowly away.

I set off again, quickening my pace past a thousand blooms.

'Hello?'

The head stopped and turned. A manservant, judging by his attire, pushing a sari-clad woman in a wheelchair. Both seemed surprised to see me. The woman was elegantly dressed. The sari was silk, the necklace at her throat was gold. She gave me the sort of look which the rich had mastered, and which made the rest of us mere mortals question our own right to exist, or at least justify our presence in such proximity to them.

I felt the need to explain.

'My name is Captain Wyndham,' I said. 'I'm a detective from Lal Bazar. Is this the house of Jogendra Prasad Mullick?'

The woman looked up at the servant and then at me. I tried to hazard a guess at her age, but these things were difficult when it came to Bengali women. They often wore their youth well into their fifties. The men too aged slowly, but you could generally hazard a guess at their age by their rotundity, each decade adding a few inches to their bellies like rings on a tree trunk.

'I am rather certain the words *Mullick Bari* are engraved on the pillars beside the gate,' she said. 'In English as well as Bengali. It is the sort of thing I would expect a detective to notice.'

I let the comment pass though it wasn't easy. I do detest the rich, British or Indian, male or female.

'Are you a member of Mr Mullick's family?' I asked.

Once more she looked to the servant before returning her gaze to me.

'I believe so.'

By now the sun was beginning to cook my neck, something

certainly not appreciated by my hangover, and I really didn't have the patience to deal with such riddles.

'Maybe we could talk somewhere out of the sun?'

The woman said something to her attendant, then turned to me. 'Please, this way.'

I followed as the servant wheeled the woman towards the house, through a side door and into a room filled with small palms and banana plants and rows of potted flowers. To one side stood a low table and rattan chairs. The servant wheeled her there, turning the chair so that it faced the windows looking out onto the lawns.

'Take a seat,' the woman said. 'Would you like some refreshment? *Nimbu pani?*'

A glass of the lime juice sounded like it might be good for my head.

'Please,' I said.

With the merest of looks, she instructed the servant, who disappeared into the house.

'Now,' she said, 'tell me how I may help you.'

'I'd be grateful,' I said, 'if you could tell me your name and your relationship to Mr J. P. Mullick.'

She exhaled a laugh. 'My name is Ankalika and I am his wife. Or rather I was. Still, I am the mother of his son.'

Was? Did she know he was already dead?

'I'm sorry?' I said.

'Jogen and I have been divorced for over a year now.'

I rubbed clumsily at the skin at the back of my neck.

'I see,' I said. 'I wasn't aware. It makes things rather awkward.'

The woman arched an eyebrow. 'Why exactly?'

I hadn't considered the possibility of Mullick being divorced. I'd never read anything about it in the papers. The man was a saint and saints weren't supposed to be divorcees.

Still. She had a right to know.

'Mrs Mullick,' I said, 'I'm afraid I must share some rather difficult news with you. We have reason to believe that your husband, your former husband that is, may have been involved in an incident. A body which matches his description was found last night near the Strand Road.'

A flicker of emotion passed across Ankalika Mullick's face and I suddenly wished I'd waited for the servant to return before setting off on this course. If the woman needed comforting, I'd much rather he be the one to provide it.

Mrs Mullick breathed out heavily. 'An incident, you say?'

'I'm afraid I cannot divulge anything more until a formal identification has been made. To that end, would you be able to tell me where I might find your son?'

'My son? Most likely he will be at our other house in Pathuriaghat. Santosh can write the address for you.'

The servant returned with two tall glasses atop a silver tray, each crowned with a mint leaf and a slice of lime. Placing it on the table, he handed a glass to his mistress who took a sip and gave him a nod of approval.

'Mrs Mullick,' I said, 'if I may, I'd like to ask you a few questions about your former husband. Are there any other family members here who might offer you support?'

Her lips thinned. 'There is no one else here, Captain. Just Santosh, the cook and me. Jogen prefers it that way.'

'Can you tell me something of him?' I asked. 'Something other than what I read in the papers?'

There was a glint in her eye.

'Maybe we should wait until you have actually confirmed he is dead. After all, I would not wish to speak ill of the living.'

'You're not on good terms?'

'As good terms as any woman might be with a husband who

discards her, who has doctors prescribe her medicines in order to keep her ... content. But of course, the feted J. P. Mullick cannot be seen to do wrong, and so he keeps me here, in this gilded cage ... what is your English expression? Out of sight, out of mind.'

I didn't know quite what to make of her words. There was the obvious resentment – the understandable bitterness of a woman cast aside – but there was more here. She was accusing Mullick of having her drugged. That was a serious charge to level at anyone, let alone a stalwart of society. But then maybe Mullick wasn't all he'd been cracked up to be. After all, stalwarts of society don't often turn up on the banks of the Hooghly with their throats cut. I took a sip of the *nimbu pani*. It was cool and sharp and I resolved never to drink alcohol again, at least not until the next time.

'You don't consider leaving this place?'

She looked at me as though the question was not worth asking.

'And go where? Jogen pays for this house, for the servants. Here at least, I have a vestige of dignity, and I in turn agree not to spoil his good name.'

'When was the last time you saw him?'

Ankalika Mullick sighed. 'Just before *Poila Baisakh*.'

Bengali New Year. Around the middle of April.

'And how did he seem?'

'Are you asking me about his mental state?'

'If that's how you wish to phrase it.'

'I would have no more insight into that than I would into the workings of an aeroplane. He keeps his inner thoughts under lock and key. All I can tell you is that when he came here he was polite, courteous and in a great hurry to leave as soon as he could.'

It sounded a lot like the way Annie Grant had reacted the last time our paths had crossed. I focused on the matter in hand.

'How was his relationship with your son?'

'With Joyonto?' A shadow passed over her face. 'I shall let

Joyonto speak for himself. Suffice it to say, he is a good son, despite what his father might think. They may have had disagreements on certain matters, but in public Joyonto venerates his father in the way people expect him to.'

'Can you think of anyone who might have a reason to wish harm upon your former husband?' I asked.

Mrs Mullick sipped her *nimbu pani* and placed the glass back on the tray. Slowly she wheeled herself over to a small palm tree which sat in an earthenware pot surrounded by soil and decorative rocks.

'Come,' she said. 'Come, Mr Wyndham, and see.'

I walked over and watched as she lifted one of the rocks. Below it a group of creatures scurried frantically, seeking new shelter.

'There,' she said. 'In answer to your question. I couldn't tell you the names of any of them, but all you need to do is lift some rocks, Captain, and see what lies beneath.'

TWELVE

Surendranath Banerjee

Elise.

I missed her.

Terribly.

What part was love, what part longing, I could not say. All I knew was the ache in my heart and the constant gnawing within my soul. It was a malaise, as debilitating as an illness. It was as though I had become Devdas, the tragic hero of Sarat Chandra Chatterjee's novel, who spends his life pining for the girl he spurned while descending into drink and madness. My thoughts turned to my Elise at dawn, at dusk, in the darkness of the night and at unguarded moments in between. Her face, stealing into my mind like a thief.

I resented her.

Or at least the hold she had on me.

Is this what Sam had spent years dealing with? A torment of love lost? Of decisions made and then regretted and which could not be unmade? I did not want that. I did not want to be Sam, and I did not want to be Devdas.

As I walked, I pushed her from my mind.

If White Town, with its manicured parks, immaculate squares and whitewashed churches, represented the well-ordered, empiric occident, then Kumartuli embodied all that was its antithesis: a warren of winding streets and nameless *gullees*, of craftsmen's huts, of colour and noise and life unbound, replete with the cries of children, the conversation of artisans and the clang of hammer and chisel.

I made my way down an alley near the river, past dilapidated buildings with darkened doorways and crumbling plasterwork that sprouted green weeds and revealed patches of weathered orange brickwork. I knew this place from memory, not from childhood, as I had done Nawabgunge, but from more recent times. From my years as a police sergeant. It was down here, on a particularly rundown stretch of road, that one of my old contacts used to reside, a man by the name of Gopu, a painter of idols. However, the idol business is seasonal, and to supplement his income he also ran an illegal book-making service for the local area.

As criminals went, he was distinctly low-hanging fruit, and despite several stays at His Majesty's pleasure, Gopu never quite managed to reform his ways. Back in '21, with the jails filling with Congress-wallahs and other political types, there had been hardly any room to lock up men like him. Sam mooted that rather than keep arresting him, we should make use of his skills. Offer him a trade, so to speak. As a man who knew the area, if he kept his eyes and ears open and provided us with information now and again, we would stop arresting him and, more importantly, stop the local constables from fleecing him.

I did not know if he and Sam still had the same arrangement, but I hoped he might do me a favour, if not for old times' sake, then at least for a little cash.

I found him, not at the hut where he lived and worked, with its grey, eyeless and many-armed mannequins awaiting the caress of his brushes to breathe life into them, to transform them from straw and clay into facsimiles of the divine, but at a stall close by, on a bench, dressed in a clay-spattered singlet and checked lungi and nursing a glass that held something other than tea. It looked like he had lost weight, which was an achievement. Now he was positively emaciated.

I called out to him.

'Gopu.'

He looked up, his brow furrowed, struggling to make an identification. And then recognition dawned and his face brightened like the skies after a storm.

'Suren-da?' he said, rising to his feet, a smile piercing betel-stained lips. 'Where have you been? Captain Wyndham-sahib said you went to Bilet.'

'Not just Britain,' I told him. 'Other places too.'

'Does your mother know you are back?' he asked. 'You look ill. She needs to feed you ... or find you a wife.'

I took a seat on the bench opposite.

'How are you, Gopu?'

He shrugged off the question. '*Ei-tho.* The days pass.'

I reached into my pocket, pulled out a pack of cigarettes and offered him one. To a man used to smoking bidis, a cigarette was a magical thing and he took it hungrily. I reached for my matchbox, but from somewhere within the folds of his lungi, he extracted his own and struck a match for us both.

'So,' he said, taking a pull, 'you are dressing like a *moshai* now. No more English shirt-pant? I thought you would come back from Bilet a pukka sahib.' He exhaled with satisfaction. 'Good. You are a son of Bengal. You should dress like a Bengali.'

'That much is true,' I said.

'So, what brings you to our humble part of town?'

'I'm looking for a girl,' I said. 'She lives around here somewhere. Her name is Mou.'

He gave a laugh which descended into a hacking cough that bent him over. Eventually the fit passed and he straightened.

'Lots of Mous in Kumartuli. Lots of Mous in Calcutta. Every third girl is a Mohua or a Mousumi.'

'This one works in the Ladies Photographic Studio in Cornwallis Street.'

Gopu nodded as though this was the sort of information that might make a difference.

'Police business?'

'No,' I said. 'And the girl is not in any trouble. I just need to ask her a few questions.'

'I could find out for you. Give me a day or two.'

'I don't have a day or two,' I said. 'I have an hour.'

Gopu sat back and whistled through his teeth. 'That might be harder. I have a lot of work to do. I don't know if I can spare the time.'

'And yet here you are, spending the golden hours sitting outside a shebeen drinking.'

I took out my pack of cigarettes and a five-rupee note and placed them on the table.

'For your trouble.'

In one smooth gesture he palmed the packet and the money, then called out to a boy who sat nearby.

'*Ō-ré*, Sonu.'

The boy jumped up and sauntered over and Gopu barked instructions at him, and the boy nodded then ran off.

'How long?' I asked.

Gopu smiled. 'Long enough for another drink, Suren-da. And it is your round.'

The boy returned some time later, long enough for Gopu to sink not one but two more glasses of the backstreet *cholai*. In his hand, the child held a scrap of paper which he passed to Gopu and which elicited a smile on the man's face and the provision of a couple of cigarettes to the boy as payment.

'You are in luck, Suren-da. The girl in fact lives not far from here. The boy can take you there.'

I knew Gopu well enough not to trust him as far as I could throw him, or, given the enfeebled state he was in, as far as he could throw me. There was a fair chance this child would take me on a tour of the maze of backstreets and leave me lost and confused, and by the time I found my way back here, Gopu would be gone.

'How about we give the boy a rest and you take me there yourself?'

He shot me an ingratiating smile.

'Of course, Suren-da! As you wish.'

He rose from his perch onto stick-thin legs, knees almost wider than his calves, then led the way, navigating the warren of alleys, crossing open drains, negotiating dead ends and stray dogs, into what felt like deepest, darkest Kumartuli; the sort of place where white men might have never set foot, and who, if informed of its existence, would probably launch an expedition to immediately seek it out and name it after themselves.

He stopped outside a small building, little more than a hut, with bare holes for windows and a sagging roof of tiles held up, I felt, by the benevolence of the gods and strategically positioned bamboo poles.

I told him to wait while I knocked on the door. From inside came sounds of movement, yet the door remained firmly shut. The delay seemed to be bothering Gopu. Maybe he thought I might try and claim my five rupees back if I thought he'd been lying to me, which, it is fair to say, I would have. In the end he took matters into his own hands.

He slammed his hand against the wood of the door and shouted.

'*Ey! Dorja khōlō!*'

Surprisingly, his actions seemed to do the trick, and there came the heavy, metallic thud of a bolt being pulled back. The door opened. Behind it stood a grey-haired man in a loose shirt.

'*Kee?*' he said through hollow cheeks that hinted at a mouth shorn of most of its teeth.

I asked to speak to Mou, the girl who worked for Dolly at the Golden Bengal Ladies Photographic Studio.

He eyed me with suspicion, though was careful not to voice it. People like him: poor and uneducated and who made up the vast majority of my kinsmen; the folk we, the supposedly genteel *bhadralok*, referred to condescendingly as *chottolok*, 'small people'; people like him generally showed deference to men like me, at least until they could establish where the real balance of power might lie. I decided to tackle the situation gently.

'I am a relative of Miss Dolly's,' I told him. 'Her studio burned down last night. I am only here to make sure Mou is safe.'

He looked behind him, back inside the dwelling.

'She is fine. Thank you for your concern.'

He made to close the door, but I placed a foot in his way.

'I need to ask her some questions.' I reached into my pocket and pulled out a ten-rupee note. 'The studio will be closed until further notice. This might help temporarily.' It was turning into an expensive afternoon.

The sight of the money helped overcome his inhibitions. He called out: 'Oh, Mou. *Ei-khané aashō.*'

For a moment there was an altercation. The girl may not have wished to come to the door, but the man was now fully decided upon the matter and he duly prevailed. He opened the door wider, and from the shadows, a girl of about sixteen or seventeen appeared. Her face sported a bruise, purple and swollen beneath her left eye, and she looked at me warily.

'Mou?' I asked.

'*Hā.*'

Once more, I spoke in Bangla.

'I need to ask you about Dolly.'

'You mean Sushmita-di?'

Of course. Mou would never presume to call her employer by her pet name. She would only refer to her by her given name.

'That's right, Sushmita. Is there somewhere we can talk?'

The girl looked to the man I assumed was her father.

'We can talk inside.'

I followed them into the darkness of the dwelling. There would be no electricity here. What light there was came in through the small window. At night, there would be candle or hurricane lamp. My eyes adjusted and made out a room of minimal and basic furnishings: a bed, its feet raised off the ground upon a few bricks; a rough wooden chest that would hold their possessions of worth; a single chair of wood and rattan; and a calendar on the wall – Maa Durga on a tiger's back, her spear piercing the flesh of the demon king, Mahishasura. Beyond, an open doorway leading to the only other room, a kitchen of sorts, I presumed.

She gestured me to the chair and took up station, sitting on the bed while her father loitered by the entrance.

'You did not go to work today?' I asked.

'The fire,' she said. 'There was no reason to go.'

'The fire,' I repeated. 'And how did you come to hear about it?'

The girl blinked rapidly. 'I . . . someone must have told me.'

'Who?'

Her eyes flickered like a doe faced with danger. 'I do not remember.'

'We are a long way from Cornwallis Street, and the fire took place in the middle of last night. Surely you would remember who told you such news?'

Her father interjected. 'News travels fast in this part of town. One of our neighbours had to make a delivery this morning, out past Cornwallis Street. He came back and told us.'

I did not believe a word of it, but there was no value in challenging the story. Instead I turned back to his daughter.

'Did you go to work yesterday?'

'Yes.'

'And was Sushmita there?'

'Yes . . . in the morning at least. But she left before midday.'

'Do you know where she went?'

Mou tucked a few strands of hair behind her ear. 'She didn't tell me.'

'But you have an idea?'

'No!'

'You are certain?'

The answer came, but quieter this time. 'Yes.'

I gestured towards her face. 'What happened to your eye?'

She reached a hand up to it, then stopped. 'An accident. I slipped in the dark. Hit my head against the bed frame.'

'What time did you leave the studio?'

A pause. She scratched at the palm of one hand. 'At six o'clock.'

'And when you left, you locked all the doors?'

'Yes.'

I made a show of considering her answers.

'I was at the studio last night, before the fire, and you are right. You did a good job of locking everything. All doors and windows on the ground floor, shuttered, bolted, padlocked.'

'So you can tell her the fire was not my fault.'

'Oh yes,' I said. 'Most definitely. I had to climb a drainpipe and break in from the first-floor balcony. And yet, there is one thing I don't understand. Once I made it inside, I found that the whole place had been ransacked. Papers, chemicals, photographic plates, all strewn everywhere. But how could that be, and who could have got inside and done such a thing, when you had locked all the doors?'

Mou blinked again. 'I don't know what you mean.'

'Did you ransack the place yourself?'

'No!' she said, and this time I believed her.

'So who did?'

'I . . .'

Once more she looked to her father. Now, though, the old man was silent.

'Did someone force their way in?' I asked. 'Did they threaten you? Is that what really happened to your face? Trust me. It is best if you tell me the truth. Otherwise I shall have to summon the police. I used to be a policeman. I still have friends there.'

A tear trickled down the side of her face.

'A man,' she said. 'Dark-skinned. Bearded. At about five o'clock, he knocked at the door. I opened it to ask him what he wanted and he just pushed past me. I tried to stop him but he hit me and I fell. He pulled me to my feet, dragged me inside and shut the door. He asked me where Shushmita-di was. I told him she had left and that I didn't know where she had gone. He asked me where she kept the prints and the plates and the films and I showed him. He asked more questions. He brought out a knife and said he would kill me if I lied to him.'

'What specific questions did he ask?'

The girl shut her eyes tightly. 'I can't remember. He was shouting. I was scared.'

'Please,' I said. 'Think. What exactly was he looking for?'

'I . . . I don't know. I think he asked if he wanted to find a particular picture, how would he locate it. I thought he was a husband, concerned about photographs his wife may have had taken. We have had men like that before.'

'What did you tell him?'

'I told him I just made the bookings. He hit me again. I told him Shushmita-di never shared any of that with me. In the end he bound my wrists and feet and mouth and proceeded to go through the building, pulling out plates, destroying things, making such a mess. I don't know how long he was looking. Finally he came back. He took off my gag and asked once more the whereabouts of Shushmita-di. Again I said that I did not know, and that it was the truth. I told him she would probably come back in the morning.

'Then he brought out the knife and I thought he was going to kill me. I wanted to scream but I knew if I did he would most certainly have done so. I told him my father was ill. That I was the only one who looked after him and brought money. I pleaded with him to let me go. Maybe he took pity on me. In the end he untied me. He told me to go home and to never go back to the studio. He then asked me for the key to the padlock for the door. I gave it to him and then I ran.'

'You did not think to tell the police?'

She looked at me as though the mere notion of such an act was ridiculous. It was her father who spoke.

'People like us, we do not go to the police. Nothing good ever comes of it.'

I took a step back. He was, I suspected, correct in that regard. The police were not the servants of the public, certainly not of the vast majority of poor Indians. They were tools of the British, and, at a push, the well-to-do Indians like myself. But where did all this leave me? The man who had attacked Mou was, in all likelihood, the same man who had tried to kill Sam and me the previous evening. A man looking for certain photographic plates. A husband maybe, or a father, unhappy that his wife or daughter should pose for photographs.

But why had Dolly run? Had she known he was coming? And if so, why not call the police? She was of the class whom the police might actually protect. Why run and where to? Why not back home to her parents where she would be safest?

Maybe her friend Mahalia would have the answers, but I would need to find her first. I looked to the girl now sobbing silently on the bed. The bruise under her eye was, in the gloom, nothing more than shadow upon shadow. She had done nothing wrong and she had been beaten for her trouble. With the studio a pile of smouldering embers, she had no job to go to, no further income with which to support herself or her father. Good jobs were hard to come by, especially for people like her. I wondered how they would cope.

I felt a wave of sadness engulf me. Such was the nature of life in our city for women like her. A constant struggle, of fighting against the odds to build a life and which, in one instant, could be taken away. Suddenly I had no wish to question her further. I doubted there was much if anything more she could tell me.

THIRTEEN

Sam Wyndham

Ankalika Mullick, via her manservant, had furnished me with the address and telephone number of the house in Pathuriaghat where I might find her son. I'd thanked her for her help and returned to Singh and the car for a trip to this second Mullick residence.

It made sense that Mullick should have a place there too. Many of Calcutta's Bengali elite had homes, or more appropriately palaces, there. The Tagore family had even built themselves a baronial castle as though this were the Scottish Highlands rather than the Ganges Delta. More importantly, it wasn't far from the burning grounds at Nimtala where the corpse had been found. Close enough certainly for it to be transported there quickly.

The house resembled the British Museum though maybe larger, complete with colonnaded entrance and an entablature that looked like it had been shipped in from a Greek temple that no longer needed it, possibly because it had collapsed under its weight.

At the gates, a line of people had formed: children and the elderly mainly, all waiting patiently in a distinctly un-Indian fashion. At the head of the queue, two women in white saris were taking small paper packets from large baskets and distributing them to the assembled crowd.

'Alms?' I asked.

'Prasad,' Singh replied. 'After daily prayers at the Mullick house, the devotional offerings are then given to the poor.'

'Very good of them,' I said.

Beyond stood two liveried durwans who drew open the gates as soon as they recognised a police car. Singh and I got out and enquired after both Mullick senior and his son, and the durwans confirmed that, no, Mullick *père* was not at home, but Mullick *fils* certainly was.

A starched servant led us up marble steps, along an incense-infused hallway lined with portraits of patrician-looking Mullicks, each sprouting a moustache fit for a maharajah.

Beyond was a courtyard with a Romanesque fountain at its centre, its waters glinting in the sun. I was rather disappointed not to see exotic wildlife grazing its pastures. There was a tale, back in the day, of one of these Pathuriaghat families having acquired a pair of zebras from the Alipore zoo which they then used in place of horses to pull their carriages around town. Say what you like about the British, we might have made a pretty penny out of this country, but at least we had the good grace not to shove zebras in the faces of the ordinary folk. No, it took an Indian to reach that level of conspicuous crassness.

From a window on the second floor, I spied a man peering down at me. He looked young, maybe no more than twenty. As soon as I caught his eye, though, he was gone, disappearing from sight as though an apparition, almost as if he had never been there at all.

The manservant led us to a high-ceilinged study, its walls lined with leather-backed volumes, all entombed within glass cases, the better to withstand the onslaughts of insects and the elements, and directed us to two chesterfields either side of a tiger-skin rug complete with jaws and teeth.

'Please wait,' he said, 'Mr Joyonto Mullick will be with you shortly,' then retreated whence he'd come.

Within minutes the door opened and in strode a young man dressed in a free-flowing peacock-blue silk robe and red trousers. He wasn't the chap I'd spotted on the first-floor balcony. No, this one bore a decent resemblance to the body at the burning ghat, younger of course, and dressed like the opening act at the Folies Bergère.

I rose to my feet. 'Mr Joyonto Mullick?'

'Yes?'

'My name is Wyndham. I'm a detective with the Imperial Police at Lal Bazar. May I ask you a few questions?'

Mention of the police seemed to trigger something in him. His expression became almost fearful.

'O-of course.'

'Is your father here?'

'I'm afraid not,' he said. 'If you have come to see him, I will probably be of little help.'

'If you'll bear with me, sir,' I said. 'Can you tell me when you last saw him?'

'About a week ago.' His brow furrowed. 'What is this about?'

I asked him to take a seat, then told him what I had told his mother earlier: about the body found last night, not a mile away at the burning grounds.

I watched him closely. His face grew ashen.

'No,' he said. 'That is not possible. My father's not even in Calcutta presently.'

'Can you tell me where he is?'

'Bishnupore.'

That came as a shock. Bishnupore was a sleepy town some hundred miles from Calcutta. Hardly a hotbed of industry or commerce.

'You're sure of that?'

He blinked. 'Well, yes . . . I mean, I never saw him leave, but that was his plan.'

'And have you heard from him since?'

Mullick junior was suddenly tense.

'No, but I did not expect to. I'm not sure there is even a telephone line there. I could send a telegram?'

That sounded sensible and I told him as much. Yet, there was still the question of a body lying in the police mortuary. If it wasn't J. P. Mullick, I wished that confirmation to be made as soon as possible.

'In the meantime,' I said, 'maybe you could accompany me to the Medical College, just in case a formal identification is required.'

Mullick junior looked dazed, which was fair enough. No one particularly wants to see a dead body, and this man looked like a fainter.

'But that is ridiculous,' he said. 'I've told you. My father is nowhere near Calcutta. Just give me a few moments to telephone the office and ask them to cable Bishnupore. We can have this sorted out within the hour.'

I gave him his hour, because the rich expected privileges that the rest of us didn't, and because we in turn were conditioned to provide them. He placed the call and we waited, plied with refreshments of tea and sweetmeats.

The minutes ticked by, and as they did, Joyonto Mullick became more anxious, pacing the floor, placing a second call to the office, berating whoever was on the other end, and then finally, and at my urging, ungraciously conceding that his hour was up.

'You know what the telegraph offices are like in these backward places. The telegram boy has probably stopped to gawp at something and forgotten to deliver the note.'

'Be that as it may,' I said, 'this is a police matter and I'm afraid I must insist on your cooperation. Otherwise I may need to ask another family member.'

That seemed to upset him further.

'There's no need for that. I shall come with you, but rest assured, the moment this nonsense is sorted out, I shall be lodging a formal complaint with your superiors.'

I could have told him it would be a total waste of time, not because he was Indian and I was British, but because I doubted my superiors could think much less of me if they tried.

Mullick left the room, returning minutes later having swapped robe and red pantaloons for a shirt and tie and we set off across the acreage of the house, back to the car for the drive to Calcutta Medical College. I sat with him in the back while Singh took up position beside the driver.

I gave Mullick a few minutes' grace before launching into more questions.

'Does your father have business interests in Bishnupore?'

He gave a grunt. 'There is nothing in Bishnupore save jungle and temples and dirt-poor farmers. No, my father has gone there for *artistic* reasons.'

'He paints?'

Mullick smiled. 'No, he finances. He is bankrolling a motion picture. Some of it is being shot there.'

'Does he always take such a close interest in things he finances?' I asked.

'You must know that he is a keen patron of the arts – I thought everyone in the whole damn country was aware of it. But yes, this film is special. He has obtained the services of a world-renowned actress. This will be the first time such an international star has appeared in an Indian picture.'

I felt my stomach knot. 'You mean Estelle Morgan?'

'The very same. My father convinced her to take the role. He believes this picture will put Indian cinema on the world stage.'

Maybe he was on to something there. I was pretty sure that with Miss Morgan in the frame, even I was now likely to go see it. Yet there was something in Mullick junior's voice, a frustration maybe, or fatigue possibly, that suggested he didn't quite see it that way.

'You're not interested in the film business?'

He gave a grunt. 'Let us say our tastes differ. What's more, my father does not look upon it as a business, rather as an indulgence. The amount of money he has lavished on films . . . we will never see a penny of it back.'

'There is something to be said for art, though,' I offered. 'And isn't it a perquisite of the wealthy to act as patron to such things?'

'Oh, quite,' he said. 'Patronage is all well and good, though not at the cost of beggaring one's own family.'

Was Mullick junior worried about his inheritance? Before I could question him on the matter, the imposing edifice of the Calcutta Medical College came into view.

The mortuary was in the basement and welcomed one with the stench of formaldehyde and flesh. Not exactly the nicest place in the city, but far from the worst either, certainly not when it came to the smell.

Joyonto Mullick and I were led by an orderly into a cramped anteroom with walls the colour of moss and five mismatched chairs which had somehow washed up in there and which now constituted its furniture. I had been in this room more times than I cared to remember, accompanying relatives: the distraught, the subdued, and others, like Mullick here, in complete denial, waiting for a body to be retrieved and brought out for the purposes of identification.

This room was a kind of limbo. A purgatory of sorts. What lay beyond was watershed – a yes or no – a dead loved one or the corpse of a complete stranger. In this room, either outcome was still possible. In this room there was still hope.

All too soon the orderly returned. I rose and led a still indignant Joyonto Mullick out and to the larger post-mortem room where our corpse from the burning ghat lay on one of three metal tables, a sheet covering most of its torso. Joyonto Mullick approached the cadaver as though expecting to be vindicated, probably already planning his letter of complaint to my superiors. He looked at the corpse and then turned to me, his eyes blinking, his lips trembling.

I accompanied him back upstairs and out into the impertinent glare of afternoon. It must have felt wrong to him. Noble men deserved noble deaths. They certainly didn't deserve to be found in the mud of the Hooghly with their throats cut, but then, who did? Maybe he thought great men deserved to be mourned as such, with blackened skies, and sackcloth and ashes, and the wailing and gnashing of teeth. Instead the world carried on unperturbed. The sun shone and the crows screeched.

We stood on the steps of the building and I offered him a cigarette which he accepted gratefully.

A nervous pull. A staccato exhalation.

'Who ... who would do this?'

'That's what I aim to find out,' I said. 'Had your father received any threats at all?'

'Threats?'

'Letters, telephone calls, anonymous or otherwise, threatening him.'

Mullick junior shrugged. 'Not that I know of, but the person to ask would be Ghatak, his secretary.'

'And enemies? He was a popular man, but he was still a businessman. Did he have conflicts? Disagreements with anyone?'

'In business there are always disagreements, but I'm not aware of anyone who had a personal issue with him.'

'I understand this is a difficult time for you, but I'd appreciate a list of your father's close friends and business associates. Anyone you think might be able to shed a light on his life; and I'll need to speak to any other family members, as well as any servants you feel might have an insight into this.'

Mullick sighed. 'If you could give me a day or so, I shall do what I can. In terms of immediate family, there is only me and my mother. As for staff, as I said, the best person to help would be Father's secretary, Ronen Ghatak. He should still be in Bishnupore. My father has been renting a lodge out there for the duration of the filming. Ghatak was with him. I shall cable him to return.'

'No,' I said. 'If your father was staying in Bishnupore, it makes sense that I go there to investigate. I can interview Ghatak there, along with anyone else who has spent time with him these last few days.'

It was proper procedure, I told myself. I could be up there tomorrow morning and return on the evening train, and by then Joyonto Mullick would have had a chance to break the news to his father's nearest and dearest and create the list of people I should speak to. Yes, going to Bishnupore was definitely an appropriate and economical use of my time. And the fact that Estelle Morgan would also be there was just a rather fortunate coincidence.

FOURTEEN

Surendranath Banerjee

What should I tell you of Mahalia Ghosh?

A sweet girl, with heavy kohled eyes and an intriguing smile, she came from a respected North Calcutta family of musicians and poets, several of whom were quite renowned. The younger of two sisters, and proficient in harmonium and tanpura, with a voice that could hold a tune and a mind that loved poetry, she was everything a young Bengali woman of her class and standing was expected to be. Demure, at least upon first encounter, and only later, if you gave her the chance, would you see the mischievousness of spirit, the spark of wit, and the mind worthy of debate.

Over the years, we had met many times, at pujas, functions and receptions, though our conversations had been sadly brief. But that was the way of things in our society: the sexes kept apart until they could be found a suitable match and married off.

That she and Dolly should be friends was, to a degree, surprising. Dolly had a rebellious streak, always ready to charge ahead and break the rules, while Mahalia was more thoughtful, more able to adapt and work out how to bend them.

And those same rules meant approaching her would require tact and delicacy. It would need to be planned and convened at a secluded, ideally secure, location, somewhere we might avoid prying eyes and the poison that spread from people's tongues.

The Burning Grounds

The question was *where*?

According to my aunt, Mahalia taught at Presidency College, not far from Sam's digs at Premchand Boral Street, but that particular location was out of the question. One could not take a respectable girl there. However, there was somewhere else I might use, but I would need permission from the owner.

I made for the post office at Dalhousie Square and availed myself of one of the public telephones, confirming the name and address with the telephonist. I only hoped she would answer.

Half an hour later, I was back at the university, at Presidency College, paying a young lad to deliver a note to Mahalia. He looked at me with a grin, assuming no doubt, some lovers' tryst.

'Don't worry, *dada*, I shall be most discreet.'

I did not bother to correct him. The note contained a request for her to meet me at 3 p.m. at an address in Maddox Street. It mentioned the fire at Dolly's studio and stressed the grave nature of the situation and the urgency of my request.

I loitered at a nearby tea stall until he returned.

'All good, *dada*. Envelope delivered!'

The flat looked different. During my absence from the city, it had been thoroughly redecorated, and in a fashion which could only be done by a person with time, taste, access to international tradespeople and a substantial amount of money. The whole place was now decorated with abstract paintings, murderously angular sculptures and geometrically patterned rugs that might cause headaches if stared at for too long.

A maid led me through to the drawing room where Miss Annie Grant sat waiting.

'Suren!' she said as I entered, rising to meet me. 'When did you get back?'

'A few weeks ago.'

'You've been back several weeks and the first I hear of it is you inviting yourself round to avail yourself of my flat?'

'If it makes you feel better,' I said, 'I only went to see Sam for the first time last night.'

'And already he has you mixed up in his nonsense?'

'Alas,' I said, 'this nonsense is all mine. And I *am* sorry. You are right. It is unconscionable. All I can say in my defence is that things are a tad ... complicated at present, but I am truly grateful for your assistance.'

She nodded, more suspiciously, I felt, than graciously.

'So how is Sam?'

'You haven't seen him?'

'Not for a while,' she said matter-of-factly. 'Not properly at any rate. I suspect he may be avoiding me.'

'I'm sure that is not the case,' I said, more out of duty than honesty. 'I suppose you both move in different circles.'

She gave me a schoolmistress stare. 'Well, he certainly has a tendency to move off at a hundred miles per hour whenever our circles overlap.'

'Yes,' I said. 'He seems to have deteriorated since I last saw him. I don't mean the ...' I left the sentence unfinished, but she knew I was alluding to his former addiction to opium.

'No, he's made strides there, though whisky does a lot of the hard yards.' She looked at me, her expression hardening. 'Why didn't you come back, Suren? Things might have been different if you had.'

I was not sure what she meant, and I told her as much.

'You know,' she said, 'he was hurt when you didn't come back. The police, the military, they threw the book at him. Blamed him for allowing you to leave the country. Even after you were cleared, they didn't trust him. The damage was done. They wouldn't let him near anything important. Even then, he might have been all right, he might have got through. But then you stopped writing. It was as though you'd disappeared. He took it hard.'

I felt as though she had just slapped me.

'I . . . I didn't know,' I said. 'He didn't tell me.'

'Of course not. Did you really think he would? He buries his problems under that foot-thick hide of his, but he has feelings, despite what he'd have you believe. Why *did* you stop writing to him?'

I did not know what to tell her. What exactly was I to say in my defence? That it was necessary for me that I should live without the assistance of Englishmen? That I was an Indian and needed to prove to myself that I could survive in those foreign places? He would only have urged me home, and in my weakness, I might have succumbed.

'My feelings towards Englishmen are rather volatile.'

She weighed my words and found them wanting.

'There are Englishmen and there are Englishmen,' she said. 'He may be an obstinate bloody fool, but believe me, you'll not find a truer friend than Sam. He sacrificed his career for you, and you just cut him off because of what you thought he represented?'

I felt my anger rise. Who was she to lecture me on how to treat Sam? She who had broken his heart and even now was seen about town with another man.

'He had you,' I said. 'He had no need of me. I thought you would be there for him.'

She looked at me as though I had crossed some unwritten line, my words a spark that might cause a conflagration.

'Don't you try and pin this upon me, Suren. I did what I could.'

Manners dictated I not argue further. I reminded myself that this was her house, I was her guest, and she was doing me a favour.

'Maybe we both bear a degree of blame,' I said, 'but he is a grown man. He cannot simply be absolved of responsibility for his own well-being.'

She considered this for a moment.

'No, but we can try to understand what he has to deal with.'

'So tell me,' I said. 'What happened after I left? Between the two of you?'

A wan smile brushed her lips. 'It was the job. It's his burden. I sometimes think it's his penance, as though he has to help find justice for the dead to atone for having been unable to find it for his wife or friends. When, after he helped you escape, and they all but sacked him, he just didn't know what to do with himself. He fell into depression. I had to get out. Simply to save myself.'

The door opened and the maid entered with tea on a silver tray. It was a chance for us both to step back from the edge; back to more trusted ground. I took a seat on the sofa while the maid poured and passed me a cup. Annie changed the subject.

'So who is this girl and why can't you simply question her at a thana or anywhere else?'

'A relative of mine has gone missing. Her parents have asked me to find her, and I wish to question a friend of hers who may know of her whereabouts. You know what people are like. It needs to be kept quiet.'

'Tongues do wag,' she said.

'So you understand my dilemma.'

'Of course I understand.' She sighed. 'I grew up in this city, remember? I know how bad your kind can be. No offence.'

'None taken,' I said.

The conversation was interrupted by a knock at the front door. I rushed to the hallway in time to see the maid open it. There stood Mahalia, her expression hovering between fear and intrigue.

'Mahalia,' I said. 'It is agreeable to see you.'

'Suren-da? *Er māné kee?*' She noticed Annie behind me and switched, as we all do in the presence of the English (and even the half-English), into their language. 'What is the meaning of this?'

'Please,' I said, 'come inside and I will explain everything.'

She crossed over the threshold and I found myself taking an involuntary step backwards.

'Please, Mahalia,' I said. 'Forgive me, I would not have asked you here if the matter were not extremely serious.' I led her to the sitting room and introduced her properly to Miss Grant. Mahalia, never the most forthcoming of girls, now in the presence of the cosmopolitan Miss Grant, seemed to visibly shrink. I did not blame her. Had I not reacted in the same fashion when Sam had first introduced me to this Anglo-Indian woman? The instinct to be awed by the presence of sahibs and mems had been instilled in us over several generations and it was still strong. They were worldly, sophisticated, white. We were parochial and Indian. Mahalia greeted her with palms pressed and averted her gaze.

I would get little out of the girl while Miss Grant remained in the room. I flashed Annie a look and she took the hint.

'Well,' she said, 'I shall leave you to it.'

Once she had gone, Mahalia turned to me. Her kohl-rimmed eyes were tender, her expression one of curiosity.

'Suren-da? Why have you summoned me here?'

I gestured to the sofa.

'It is about Dolly,' I said.

Her surprise seemed to dissipate, too quickly I felt, only to be replaced by a look of suspicion.

'What about her?'

'She did not come home last night.'

'You are certain?'

There was something in the tone of her voice. Not shock or disbelief at the disappearance of her close friend, but the tacit equanimity with which one reacts to news of a train cancellation. She walked over to the sofa, sat down and made a show of thinking.

'Anyway I am sure she is safe.'

'How? Do you know where she is?'

'No. Why would I?'

The protestation seemed rather too quick, too rehearsed.

'When was the last time you saw her?'

'I do not remember exactly.'

'Her parents seem to think you met her for lunch two days ago.'

Mahalia put a hand to her lips.

'Did you?' I asked.

'Now you mention it, I suppose I did.'

'And?'

She looked at me with an expression as sweet as melted jaggery.

'Surely, Suren-da, you are not asking to hear the private conversations of two women? Such a thing would, of course, be shameful.' She smiled. 'Or maybe I have misunderstood?'

Instinctively I felt the hot flush of embarrassment. The woman was clever. She knew of course that my intentions were not to pry, yet she endeavoured to frame my request in such a light. If she hoped to discourage me from my line of questioning, she would be sadly disappointed.

'I am not interested in the details of your conversation,' I said. 'All I want to know is if she told you anything which might shed light on her disappearance. Her mother and father are extremely worried. I know Dolly has a habit of doing whatever she wishes, but this time the matter is serious. If you know something, about where she is, or what she is doing, you need to tell me.'

Mahalia made a show of considering my question, then looked innocently at me.

'I don't think so. No. I am sure. She did not mention anything of the sort.'

'What *did* you talk about?'

'Mainly about a new job I have started in Belgachia.'

'You are no longer teaching at the university?' I asked.

'*Na, na*, Suren-da, it is not like that. This is at weekends only. I have started volunteering at a charity. Teaching the children Bangla, dance, drama, that sort of thing, but it is wonderful. I feel like I am bringing joy to those who have so little. It makes me feel . . .' She beamed, her face radiant like the idols on puja days.

'That is most compassionate of you,' I said. 'What else did you discuss?'

She thought for a moment. 'We spoke about my classes, and a trip my family is planning to take to Digha, a few other things.'

'Such as?'

'They were personal matters. Matters between women. I am sure you do not mean to pry, but I am finding your questioning rather distasteful.'

Mahalia needed to understand the gravity of the situation.

'Let us have no more games,' I said. 'Please answer my questions without obfuscation.'

She affected an air of hurt. 'Am I to be interrogated, Suren-da?'

I added steel to my voice. 'This is a serious matter, Mahalia. Dolly is missing. She may have been accosted or murdered or subjected to unspeakable things. We need to know where she is and what has happened to her, and if I feel you are withholding information, I shall have no compunction in handing you over to my old friends at Lal Bazar. What would your parents say? What impact would that have upon your own sister? It is only out of respect for Dolly's family and your own that I have agreed to question you here, and in private, but if you do not tell me what I want to know, then things will become a lot worse for you. Now you will answer my questions. Where did you meet her two days ago?'

I watched as she reassessed. What was she thinking? Was she realising she had misjudged the situation? Or maybe misjudged me? I saw a subtle shift in her demeanour and then a change in the tone of her voice.

'Very well, we met at a *pice* hotel near Cornwallis Street.'
'At whose behest?'
'Dolly's.'
'And what did she want?'
She looked away from me towards the door.
'She asked me for money.'
'How much money?'
'Whatever I could spare. I gave her what I had. Almost twenty rupees.'
'Why did she need money?'
'She did not say.'
'You did not ask?'
'Of course I asked. She was upset. I could see that. But she would not tell me why. I asked, *Is it the business? Is it your family? Or is it something else?* But she would not say. All she told me was that she needed to go away, but that when she returned, she would pay me back in full.'

It made no sense to me.

'She has her own business,' I said. 'Why did she need money from anyone?'

Mahalia shook her head and gave me a bitter smile.

'You have been away too long, Suren-da. The business has been in trouble for some time. Dolly suspected it was because other photographers, male photographers, were whispering things, bad-mouthing her to customers.'

'What sort of things?'

'That she took photographs of prostitutes and other unrespectable types.'

'Did she?'

Mahalia pursed her lips. 'I told her not to. I told her that such things were dishonourable. That she would acquire a reputation, but she did it anyway. She told me that those girls had every right to be photographed, and who better to document their lives than her?'

I sighed. That was exactly the sort of thing Dolly would do, and hang the consequences to her own reputation.

'What do you think she needed the money for?'

Mahalia shrugged.

'Has she left the city?'

'I don't know.'

The responses had become evasive once more. Maybe the woman needed another shock.

'Did you know that Dolly's studio was set ablaze last night? Before that, it had been ransacked. She seems to have upset someone. Maybe this someone wants to hurt her. Maybe they have found her and are already hurting her. Now I need you to tell me everything you know. If I feel you are lying, I will hand you over to the police and make it known that you have been arrested. Is that clear?'

Mahalia took a breath, prevaricating. When she did answer, her tone was more pliable.

'You are wrong, Suren-da. She did not tell me very much, but I know that it involved some man. Someone unsuitable probably. She could not tell her parents. She said he was in trouble and that she needed to help him. That she would need to hide away for a few days, but after that, everything would be fine.'

'Where is she?'

She shook her head. 'I cannot tell you where she is, because I do not know. But what I can say is that she is safe. Now if that is not enough for you, feel free to have your sahib friends arrest me. What is one more innocent Indian in a British jail?'

'Please, Mahalia,' I said, exasperated at her melodrama, 'you are not Mahatma Gandhi.'

'And you are no Subhash Bose,' she spat back. 'I had heard you were overseas, working for the cause of independence. Now I see it was all lies. You are still a lackey of the British.'

I fought to control my temper. 'Where is Dolly?'

She folded her arms. 'Do what you will. I will not tell you anything more.'

My threat to have her arrested had always been an idle one, and in light of her words, they had, I realised, become even more empty. In the end, Miss Grant escorted Mahalia down to the street as I could not bear further conversation with her. I felt wretched. I had achieved little while upsetting a young woman whom I respected. If there was a silver lining, it was that I could at least tell Dolly's parents that their daughter was alive, even though I did not as yet know her exact whereabouts.

Miss Grant returned to the room and placed a hand on my shoulder.

'Are you all right, Suren?'

'Yes,' I told her. 'I just lost control of the situation.'

'Well,' she said, 'if it's any consolation, I have always known you to be a good and honourable man.'

'Thank you,' I said. 'That means a lot to me.'

Yet the events of the previous night played large. Someone had set fire to Dolly's studio. They were willing to see us burned alive in the process. In those circumstances, how could Dolly be safe? If Mahalia was to be believed, she might still be at liberty, but her life, I was sure, was very much in danger. Nothing had really changed. I needed to find her, and quickly.

FIFTEEN

Sam Wyndham

I decided on an early night, which felt like a novelty. Normally I might have headed to one of the plethora of dive bars and shebeens where a discerning chap like me could while away a few hours. In the old days, of course, I might find myself heading to the *gullees* of Tiretti Bazar or compounds of Tangra in search of opium and oblivion, and even now there was something seductive about the thought. I tried to push it from my head, but that was often difficult. It was probably why I drank so much. One of the reasons anyway. I'd used the O to help me forget about the past and I used drink to help me forget about the O. Now though, for the first time in a long time, I had a murder case on my plate; a good one at that; one that mattered; and an early train the next morning. I told myself I didn't need alcohol tonight, and I certainly didn't need the O.

It was a fine evening. A walking sort of evening, where the scent of jasmine and hibiscus and marigold drifted like ghosts across emptying streets, with the heat of the day ebbing and the perfect balm of night fast approaching.

I ambled back towards College Square, lighting a cigarette and thinking of J. P. Mullick. By tomorrow, word would get out. It would be front-page news in the papers, even the English ones. I wondered how the natives would react. Tears probably, and eulogies verging on the mawkish. Bengalis liked to make a show when they mourned their heroes, especially if they'd never actually met them. As to who had killed him, or why, those were still mysteries, but I had learned a few things about the man and his family and they had surprised me. A divorced wife kept hidden away in Tollygunge, who suspected him of drugging her. A son who might not revere his father in the way others did, worried that his inheritance was being frittered away. Was he eager for power? Eager to step out of his father's shadow and become top dog? There was plenty of precedence for that in Indian history. Just ask the Mughals. Was the son ruthless enough to have had his father dispatched? I wasn't sure. I certainly thought it took a degree of sociopathy for a man to wear a peacock-blue silk dressing gown. And yet the disposal of Mullick senior's body had been almost haphazard. A man with the determination to kill his own father would surely give more thought to such things.

So far so confusing.

Tomorrow though was another day, one in which I intended to make real progress. Ronen Ghatak, Mullick's secretary. He would have answers, such as what Mullick had been doing in Bishnupore all week, and what had made him return to Calcutta without, if his son was to be believed, informing anyone, not even his family.

Somewhere on Wellington Street, my thoughts were interrupted. There, on an advertising hoarding, I saw her: Estelle Morgan; a sketch of her at any rate, in a passionate clinch with Clive Brook in a film called *Fire and Ice*. I must have passed it a dozen times without noticing. Maybe that is why she'd looked so familiar to me when I first set eyes on her in the Idle Fox. Lucky man, that Clive Brook. I turned for home. Tonight, Premchand Boral Street was back to its bustling best, the girls upstairs doing what seemed like brisk trade, so much so that there was no Mona or anyone else with the time or inclination to engage me in witty conversation, which was fine by me.

I noticed the car a moment before the door opened. I should have seen it sooner; indeed I should have noticed it as soon as I turned the corner. Cars didn't often loiter in Premchand Boral Street, mainly because chaps with cars could afford a better class of prostitute. A large man exited the passenger's side. I didn't recognise him, but I knew his type. Six foot and change tall, scuffed brogues and a suit not cut well enough to hide his physique or the gun under his jacket.

He walked over.

'Captain Wyndham? My name's Smith. Would you mind getting in the car?'

I knew where he was from too.

'Let me guess,' I said. 'Your boss is feeling lonely and fancies a chat.'

Smith didn't even crack a smile, possibly because he lacked the facial muscles. If so, they were just about the only ones he was missing.

'I shouldn't like to presume, sir.'

'No,' I said. 'Best not to ask too many questions, not in your line of work. But I'm afraid I can't make it right now. I have an important guest arriving shortly.'

'No, you don't, sir.'

Smith managed to speak the words without a hint of emotion and still convey utter menace. In that sense, he was a chip off the same block as his boss. It had been a while since I'd last spoken to him, which is to say, it had been a while since he'd last summoned me, and I, for my part, would have been happy to live out the rest of my life without ever clapping eyes on him again. And yet it seemed that was not to be.

'Fair enough,' I said and followed Smith to the car.

Our direction of travel came as a surprise: not south to Fort William as I'd expected, but north. Around us passed the shabby streets of Chitpore and the sights of a slumbering Black Town: boarded-up shopfronts and dim embers of light glowing from upper storeys; silhouettes gathered like ghosts around a street vendor's brazier, steam rising, hot oil sizzling; rickshaws lined up and stacked like wheelchairs beside a field hospital, their owners dozing close by; and the ever-present pariah dogs, roaming, scavenging, copulating.

The car turned down a side street, navigating a series of narrow *gullees*, lefts and rights taken at what appeared random but which must have had method for we soon pulled to a stop outside a shabby-looking restaurant. The sign above the entrance probably had a name on it, but at this time of evening it was illegible.

We were, I guessed, somewhere near Allen Market. Not exactly on the beaten track, but then when it came to clandestine meetings, I supposed that was probably the point. Smith exited and opened my door.

'Sir.'

I got out and walked up to the entrance, over the slab across an open drain. It was what Bengalis call a *bondo cabin*: not the most salubrious of venues, tables arranged in small booths, partitioned off from each other by wood panelling, each booth a self-contained world accessed through a curtain. The concept, they said, had originated in Ireland, to allow ladies to take a tipple in seclusion and without judgement, and the idea had been adopted with gusto by Bengalis, especially young couples looking to spend a few illicit moments together. Indeed, most such places were valued more for their privacy than their food. I looked around, trying to spot any security but failed. If they were here, they were damn well disguised as a few down-at-heel native waiters. One of them gave me an oleaginous smile and directed me to a cabin at the far end of the room, directions which really weren't required as all I needed to do was follow the trail of pipe smoke. I made for it, past tired, curtained entrances as overhead an arthritic ceiling fan creaked round as slow as a carousel.

It made quite a change from the Great Eastern, or even the Idle Fox. This was not the sort of place frequented by the great and the good, or even, for that matter, the fairly average. Certainly not the sort of place one expects to find one of the most powerful men in all India. I pulled back the curtain and there he was, sitting at a wooden table, with only his pipe and a plate of fried food for company.

He looked up. 'Ah, Wyndham. Glad you could join me,' he said, as though I'd been given much choice in the matter. I pulled out the chair opposite and sat down. He pointed to his plate.

'Hope you don't mind, but I started without you. To be frank, I wasn't sure when to expect you. I rather thought you might be making a detour via a bar or two, or maybe a trip to your old haunts in Tangra.'

There were many reasons to dislike the man opposite: his lack of scruples; his willingness to use his intelligence assets to bribe, blackmail or cajole to get what he wanted; the casual way in which he destroyed lives if it suited his purpose; or even just the stench of his damn pipe tobacco. For me though, the main reason I disliked the military's head of intelligence for Bengal and much of the rest of Eastern India was because he was a snide, patronising arse.

Before I could ask him why the devil he'd called me to this particular backwater, a thin waiter in a grey shirt that I guessed had started life as white knocked on the wood panelling and lifted the curtain. He passed me a creased menu, then hovered as I scanned it.

'Try the prawn cutlet,' Dawson said.

I ordered as he suggested and, given the military were paying, added a beer too to wash it down.

Dawson motioned to the waiter to disappear.

'So,' he said, swallowing. 'How are you?'

'You know me,' I said. 'I don't like to complain.'

He spoke between mouthfuls of cutlet. 'Word is you've gone off the boil.'

The waiter returned with two beers in a couple of glasses that were all but opaque, placing one in front of each of us. I took a sip of mine. It was warm and sour and rather accurately reflected my mood.

'Well, if that's the price I pay to keep you off my back . . .'

He shot me a frown.

'Now now. No need for that sort of talk. You know I've nothing but the greatest respect for you, and if I've taken an interest in you in the past, it's precisely because you were worth taking an interest in.'

'So what *do* I owe the pleasure then? Or am I just here for the cutlets?'

'Oh, not at all,' he said, cutting himself a piece of battered prawn and dipping it in the small bowl of mustard to its side. 'The devilled eggs are worth a shout too.' He lifted the fork to his mouth. 'I hear you're looking into the death of J. P. Mullick.'

Was Dawson the reason I hadn't had the Mullick case taken from me? Did he want something?

'Is it of interest to the custodians of imperial security?'

'Not particularly,' he said. 'Still, it's a shame when a good man passes on.'

'A good man?'

'Absolutely. He never gave us any problems. Quite a rarity these days when every other Indian is a revolutionary of some sort, even the rich ones. Mullick was a millionaire of the old sort: happy to make money and keep his nose out of politics.'

'My condolences on your loss,' I said.

The waiter returned, placing a metal plate before me, atop which sat two golden cutlets, purple slivers of shredded onion, one dangerous green chilli and a pot of mustard. I cut a piece, dipped it in the mustard and took a bite. Dawson might have been an amoral bastard, but he was right about the prawn cutlets.

'So,' I said, 'if not Mullick, then what do you wish to talk about?'

He leaned back in his chair and stretched. 'I thought we might discuss your old friend, Surendranath Banerjee.'

I looked up from my cutlet. Dawson's face was inscrutable.

'Oh?'

He lifted another morsel to his mouth. 'He's been back a month now.'

'Is that right?' I said. The bugger had told me he'd returned less than two weeks ago. I did my best to hide my surprise.

'And I understand he's recently been spending a bit of time with you.'

I took my knife and chopped the chilli into thin rings, each containing one, maybe two of the seeds that gave them such fire.

'You seem very taken with his activities.'

Dawson took a sip of beer. 'He's a smart chap, that one. I'm glad to see him home, away from all those unhealthy foreign influences.'

'So you can keep an eye on him?'

Dawson picked up his pipe and from his pocket retrieved a pouch of tobacco.

'Yes, well, maybe if you hadn't helped him skip the country, such vigilance wouldn't be required now.'

'He only had to flee the country because he was wanted on spurious charges of terrorism. Charges which *you* could have put an end to.'

Slowly, purposefully, Dawson struck a match and held it to his pipe bowl, moving it so that it kissed the entire surface of the tobacco. Taking a few puffs, he waved out the flame.

'Well,' he said, 'we are where we are. The fact remains he is back now, after spending several years in the company of some rather disreputable characters with a profoundly anti-British bias. It pains me to say it but, like Subhash Bose, I'm afraid your old subaltern has the brains and the standing to become a thorn in our side. I would rather he became an asset. We dropped the ball with Bose. We should never have allowed men like Gandhi to convince him to join the independence movement. He should have been our man. I don't intend to make the same mistake with Banerjee.'

I felt my stomach knot.

'You want him to rejoin the police force? From what he's told me, that's not about to happen any time soon.'

He puffed a rancid cloud of smoke skywards.

'That remains to be seen. But for now, I'd like you to involve him in this Mullick case.'

I nearly choked on my beer. And suddenly it made sense. There had to be a reason for me being allowed a high-profile murder case after all this time.

'Be honest, you could use him,' Dawson continued. 'It's a native case. He's a native.'

'So is my current subaltern.'

He shot me a withering look.

'Please. We both know *he's* hardly the sharpest tool in the box. Why do you think he was assigned to you?'

'What?'

'Well, after your shenanigans with Banerjee in Bombay, what did you expect? That they'd give you another subordinate capable of independent thought?'

'I don't suppose it matters,' I said. 'As for Banerjee, he won't agree to work with me.'

'He will if you tell him you'll help him find this girl he's looking for.'

Should I have been surprised that Dawson already knew about that?

'Do you know where she is?' I asked.

A thin smile crossed his lips. 'Not as such, but I could probably find out if I put my mind to it.'

'I still don't think that would make him rejoin the force,' I said.

'Yes, well,' he said finally. 'There's more than one way to skin a cat.' He reached into his pocket and pulled out an envelope. 'Give him this.'

SIXTEEN

Sam Wyndham

Bengalis, like the Spanish, eat late. It's generally nine or ten before they sit down to a meal, and it can be later sometimes. It's bad for the constitution and may go some way to explaining the preponderance of rotund bellies on so many of them, but it can have its upsides too. It meant that Suren was at the dining table when I telephoned his father's place and invited him to meet me for a post-prandial drink. I'd thought long and hard before making the call. It seemed my involvement on the Mullick case, and thus possibly the future direction of my career, was predicated upon Suren's active involvement too. It wasn't the first time I had been a pawn in someone else's game, but it still rankled. The honourable thing to do would be to refuse point-blank. Inveigling Suren in Dawson's machinations was something that instinctively felt wrong. Like leaving a kid goat tethered in the vicinity of a tiger. What's more, I didn't want or need Suren's help. And yet I yearned to be working the big cases again. Finding the truth; affording justice to those robbed of life and seeking it for those left behind; those were the things which mattered, which got me up in the morning, and I'd been denied them for too long. And as I saw it, I didn't owe Suren anything. Far from a kid goat, he was a big boy now. He could look after himself. If his involvement was the key to restoring my fortunes then I'd swallow my pride and my reservations and bally well do as Dawson commanded.

My venue of choice was the Elephant, a bar off College Square, close to my digs and so affording me plenty of time to settle in.

The Elephant was the answer to the question, *what if you relocate an East End boozer from London to central Calcutta?*, a question, I felt, which would have been better left unasked. The windows were dirty, the floor was timbered, the food an acquired taste, and the latrines best avoided altogether. The interior was a fug of stale beer and cigarette smoke through which one might make out a long bar with photographs of the kings and princes of Europe plastered on the wall behind it. On the plus side, no one of any importance, or indeed with any standards, was likely to stop by, and that suited me just fine.

Heads turned as Suren entered. It wasn't the sort of establishment frequented by Indians, especially not those dressed in a dhoti, and for a moment, a certain section of the clientele, the more well-oiled and loutish variety, seemed to take objection to his presence. One of them stood up as he approached.

'This place ain't for the likes of you, sunshine.'

There was, I thought, an irony in that because I doubted Suren wanted to be there in the first place. Given that the choice of venue was mine, I felt it was down to me to fix things. I too stood up and walked over.

'Some problem here?'

The big chap turned to me. He was not blessed with looks, missing as he was several teeth and half an ear. These deficiencies he made up for by being built like the proverbial brick outhouse. Rolls of fat at his neck obscured a faded tattoo, but the one on his arm was clear and professed love for a woman called Marjorie and I wondered what sin the poor woman had committed to deserve that.

Judging by his sneer, he seemed as impressed by me as I was by him.

'What business is it of yours, mate?'

'Well, firstly,' I said, 'this man is a friend of mine; and secondly, I'm a copper, so why don't you keep your opinions to yourself and sit back down and enjoy your drink before I decide to arrest you?'

I could see him thinking it through. Was it worth a fine and a night in the cells to take a shot at me? Part of me rather hoped he would, because he was three sheets to the wind and I was confident I could put him on his backside without too much difficulty, maybe dislodging another few of his teeth in the process. In the end though, he made the sensible decision. He sat down and took a sip of beer, though the drink seemed to agree with him a little less now.

Suren joined me at my table at the back of the room.

'Nice place,' he said. 'Thank you for inviting me.'

'What can I get you?' I asked.

'A cup of tea.'

'It's a damn pub,' I said. 'They don't do tea.'

'No tea?' he mused. 'No wonder that man was so angry.'

He settled for a brandy, and to my surprise, the barman actually had a bottle.

I returned with his drink and took the seat opposite. 'So how are your investigations going?'

He gave a shrug. 'I am not sure. This is more than a case of Dolly eloping with some man. She is obviously in trouble. I spoke to her parents and her assistant. The assistant claims a man came to the studio the afternoon of Dolly's disappearance. He was the one who ransacked the place. Probably the same man who set fire to it later.'

'Anything else?'

His lips thinned. 'I also questioned a friend of hers, a girl called Mahalia.'

'And?'

'I reduced her to tears.'

'Good work.'

'She is holding something back, but I do not know what or why ...' He took a sip of brandy and looked to me. 'What about you? Was it actually J. P. Mullick you found?'

'It was,' I said. 'The son identified him. And they've kept me on the case.'

His eyes widened. 'Really? I thought you were *persona non grata*?'

'I suppose they had a change of heart.'

'You don't seem particularly overjoyed at the prospect.'

I refrained from telling him that I feared Dawson had pulled strings to keep me on it, and had done so in the hope of luring him back into the fold.

'I'll celebrate when the killer is caught,' I said. 'In fact, the case is why I called you here.' I took a breath. They say the road to hell is paved with good intentions, and while that may be true, in my experience a lot of the route also involves moral compromise, self-interest and self-deception. What I did next might impact the course of Suren's life forever. The honourable thing would be to simply tell him what Dawson had said and let him make up his own mind as to whether to involve himself in the Mullick case. Maybe he would agree to help me. Yet a little voice in the back of my head said otherwise. This wasn't the Suren Banerjee who'd once seen me as some sort of hero. This was a man who now knew just how fallible I could be, and someone I was not even sure I could call a friend any more.

'I wanted to ask you to work on it with me,' I said. 'It's been a while. I'm rusty. I could use your help.'

I saw the distaste register in his face.

'I am not a policeman any more, Sam.'

'I'm not asking you to be. Look, Mullick was a millionaire; a successful businessman; a high-profile Indian. Don't you want to find out what happened to him? You've an analytical mind. More so than I do. And you know how Bengalis think. I could use your insight.'

For a moment he said nothing, merely took a sip of his drink and placed the glass purposefully back on the table.

'I don't know, Sam.'

He wasn't biting. It felt time to bring out the sweetener.

'I'll make you a deal,' I said. 'You help me with this, and I'll see what else I can do re your missing cousin.'

He bit his bottom lip and considered. 'Very well. But this is a one-off arrangement. A quid pro quo. I am not rejoining the police force.'

'That's fine with me,' I said and raised my glass in toast.

'I suppose you had better tell me what you learned today?' he said.

I told him of my conversation with Mullick's ex-wife, whom he'd kept locked away out of sight in Tollygunge, and details of the meeting with his son.

He sipped ponderously at his brandy.

'So what do you plan to do next?'

'Well,' I said, 'I was thinking that tomorrow morning we head to Bishnupore. That's where J. P. Mullick was supposed to be when he turned up dead in Calcutta. That's where his personal secretary is now.'

He raised an eyebrow. 'We? I know I just agreed to help you, but this seems rather precipitous. I don't have the time to traipse into the *moffusil* with you in the cause of a man who is already a corpse. Surely the living trump the dead? I need to find Dolly.'

'I understand that, but what do you propose to do?'

He folded his arms across his chest. 'I thought I might try questioning Dolly's friend Mahalia again. Failing that, I might just follow her. See if she goes to meet Dolly.'

'Seriously? That's your plan? Follow this Mahalia woman around in the hope that she leads you to Dolly? Because believe me, she will not do that, not tomorrow at least, not after your intervention.'

He bristled at my words.

'Maybe she will, maybe she won't.'

I was losing him once more. What had happened to us? Why did this feel like some sort of competition between us to see who was the more competent? I moderated my tone, shifting to one that I hoped was more conciliatory.

'She'll be on her guard tomorrow. Maybe it'd be better to wait a few days, then follow her? Or I could bring her in for questioning at Lal Bazar or another thana. That would really put the frighteners on her. Let her have twenty-four hours. Besides, it's been so long since we worked a case together, it'd be a damn shame if you didn't come to Bishnupore with me.'

Once more he ruminated.

'Very well,' he said finally, and I reached out and patted him on the arm.

'That's the spirit.'

I was about to tell him of my run-in with Dawson and pass him his letter, but he beat me to it.

'Sam, there is something I need to tell you. I saw Miss Grant today.'

For a moment I was too stunned to respond.

'I needed somewhere private to question Mahalia. She was kind enough to let me use her flat.'

I took a sip of beer, hoping to hide my surprise, or rather my chagrin that he would do such a thing. I wasn't sure why – Suren had every right to contact Annie and request her assistance, and yet it still felt disloyal.

'How is she?'

'Well enough,' he said. 'She enquired after you.'

'That was nice of her.'

'She is concerned about you.'

I rubbed at a wet patch upon the table. 'Well, the next time you see her, you can tell her she needn't be. I'm absolutely fine.'

He weighed the comment. 'You could consider telling her yourself?'

'I could,' I said, 'but I have rather more pressing matters to attend do.'

'She feels my ceasing contact with you placed a strain upon your relationship.'

I looked up at him. He seemed to be struggling with something. Was it the first stirrings of guilt? Well, I could tell him that while there certainly were things I blamed him for, the ending of my relationship with Annie was not one of them.

'Well, that's ridiculous,' I told him. 'Annie and I had a difference of opinion, that's all.'

And that much was true. She was of the opinion that I was selfish and let my job consume far too much of me, and given that I was effectively frozen out, maybe I should consider, if not an alternative profession, then at least a sabbatical. I on the other hand was of the opinion that she was talking nonsense.

Things had degenerated somewhat from there, with accusations levelled in both directions, none of which required detailed exposition to Suren, suffice it to say that in the end we both decided that I should refrain from visiting her quite so often. That had been the best part of two years ago, and yet the pain remained.

'I understand she has been seen around town with a foreigner.'

The words felt like a punch to the gut. In fairness I had heard as much myself, but hearing it from Suren still stung. A Russian, by all accounts. A man by the name of Ostrakhov, Count Nikolai Ostrakhov, to give him his full title. Some chinless blueblood probably, with lands and estates and serfs somewhere on the great Russian steppe. At least until the Bolsheviks arrived and relieved him of the lot. The thought made me smile. I wasn't sure where I stood on the matter of communism, but any ideology which advocated shooting the aristocracy couldn't be all bad. And now, here he was, washed up in Calcutta with all the rest of the flotsam.

'So I believe,' I said. 'Did she tell you about him?'

He had the decency to look embarrassed.

'No. I must have picked it up somewhere else. He is probably a dilettante. A passing fancy.'

I lifted my glass to that, saluted him and downed the remnants of the beer. I didn't know if he was right, but it was good of him to voice the sentiment. But Annie could do what she liked. It was none of my business. Odd that Suren should have heard about it though. I thought back to what Dawson had told me, about Suren's actual date of return to India.

'When did you really get back to Calcutta?' I asked.

'Excuse me?'

'For someone who claims to have been back less than a fortnight, you seem to have picked up a fair amount of intel.'

He stared hard at his glass. 'Almost a month.'

'A month? And in all that time you've been holed up at your father's?'

His expression darkened. 'Something like that.'

'Do you want to tell me why?'

He closed his eyes momentarily and sighed. 'It is not easy to explain.'

'So who is she?'

He looked up at me.

'What?'

'You've been back a month and you've spent nearly all that time holed up in your room. That means it's either illness or love, though the latter is really just a subset of the former. And given your symptoms, I am guessing your affliction is of the amorous variety, so I ask again, who is she?'

He lowered his gaze and stared at the table. 'It doesn't matter. Nothing can come of it.'

So it *was* a woman. Suddenly I found my petty resentments evaporating. Suddenly everything made a lot more sense. The poor, deluded chap was in love. That was why he was being such a petulant arse.

'It bloody does matter,' I told him. 'Come on. Where does she live? We'll go round to her house right now and I'll tell her some lies, like what a good chap you are.'

An embarrassed smile crossed his lips. 'That will not be possible. She lives at a distance from here.'

'Howrah?'

'Paris.'

I looked at him with a new-found appreciation.

'How the devil did you manage to find an Indian girl in Paris?'

'She's not Indian,' he said. 'She's French ... well, half French. Her father is English. Her name is Elise.'

'Right,' I said, trying to come to terms with it all. 'Well, this really is a turn-up for the old whatsits, isn't it? A French girl ... And how exactly did you meet this mademoiselle?'

'At a conference for democracy.'

'Of course you did,' I said. 'How very romantic.'

'Politics can be romantic,' he said.

'Only to Bengalis. How long ago was this?'

'Almost a year, though it took a while for me to get to know her.'

'So what happened?' And then the penny dropped. 'You told your father, didn't you?'

'It was the correct course of action. I wrote him a letter.'

'And he told you to leave her and come home, didn't he?'

'I had no choice. It was a question of family honour.'

I shook my head. 'Honour is overrated, Suren. What did honour ever do for Gordon at Khartoum or the band on the *Titanic*? So how did you leave things with this mademoiselle?'

'I asked her to meet me. We took a walk through the Tuileries Gardens and I explained the circumstances: my father's demand that I return; his insistence that no relationship was possible between us; the problems of religion and culture and so on.'

'How did she take it?'

He didn't answer.

'I'm sorry,' I said.

'It was the hardest thing I have ever had to do.'

'If it's any consolation, I know what loss feels like: the emptiness; the gnawing; the constant thoughts, day and night, about what you've lost, what might have been.'

'Does it get easier?'

I took a sip of beer and considered what to tell him. In the end, I decided on the truth.

'A little,' I said. 'And then only slowly. In the meantime it'll hurt like hell … every day, every hour. Are you sure that's what you want?'

He drained the last of his brandy.

'I'm sure that I have no other choice.'

Day 3

Monday

SEVENTEEN

Sam Wyndham

I should have given him Dawson's letter the previous night. I should have handed it over and warned him that whatever Dawson offered, he should decline. I should have told him that the reason I still had the Mullick case was because Dawson wanted to pull Suren back to our side. I should have told him all of those things but I didn't. Instead we talked of Elise and my wife, Sarah, and of Annie, of love and of the fleeting nature of happiness. And then it was too late.

Now, as the car swept along the Strand Road towards the pontoon bridge, and the morning mist clung to the river like a lover, he sat beside me, meditating upon his own thoughts as the smoke from the cigarette between his fingers snaked skywards. Up front, Constable Singh remained silent, no doubt brooding over who the chap sitting next to me was and why he was accompanying me to Bishnupore.

Despite the hour, the city was already coming to life. To one side, a banner proclaimed one of Mullick's free schools, this one for the sons and daughters of rickshaw pullers. Scrawny children, maybe aged eight or nine, sat barefoot and cross-legged in the courtyard, chalk in hand and hunched over small slates, busily writing as a teacher pointed to letters on a blackboard. The classes started at dawn and finished by nine, in order that the children might get to their workplaces on time.

Soon the bridge arrived. Suren wore that hangdog expression that I knew from old. It was concerning to see how tired he looked. At least now I understood the cause. Unfortunately for him though, there was no cure. That burden, the one he had borne since that day in the Tuileries Gardens, was unlikely to be lifted any time soon. Before I could offer any encouragement, however, the great station of Howrah was upon us.

The station was its usual mix of the manic and the infernal, the air a noxious combination of locomotive smoke and the stench of humanity. It was thousands of *babus*, and box-wallahs, and *bibis* with baskets of vegetables upon their heads, spilling from the bellies of trains and onto platforms and concourses, while the calls of chai-wallahs and paan sellers and fruit vendors and bootblacks rose high into the soot-stained ironwork above.

I made for a newspaper stall, a small booth festooned with prints and publications, some clipped to its sides, others hanging on arcs of string across the ceiling like oversized Christmas cards. A thin note of grey-blue incense wisped uncertainly from the glowing tip of a reed-thin joss-stick which sat atop a shrine at the rear of the booth. At the heart of it sat the goddess Saraswati upon her lotus leaf, sitar held gently between two of her arms. The goddess of learning. Good choice, I thought, for a seller of newspapers.

I bought a copy of the morning's *Statesman*, scanned the headlines and sighed.

'News of Mullick's death is out,' I said.

'Does it say he was murdered?'

'Thankfully, not. And there's no mention of where or how he was found. But there are already calls for a city-wide day of mourning.'

'People loved him,' Suren said. 'He provided them with schools and hospitals ... and dignity.'

'Tell that to his ex-wife,' I said.

I stowed the paper and we commenced the struggle through the tide of bodies, first to the ticket booths and then to the platform where stood the morning train to Bishnupore, steam sprouting from its funnel. We climbed the steps of a first-class carriage, I having quickly and forcibly dissuaded Suren of his ridiculous Gandhian wish to travel third class, telling him in no uncertain terms that the end of British rule in India would not be hastened one jot by our travelling cattle class, and that while his desire to commune with his fellow Indians was admirable, the last thing that the farmers, peasants and other assorted hoi polloi of third class needed was to spend their journey in the company of an English policeman and an Oxbridge-educated Brahmin recently returned from the Côte d'Azur.

The compartments of the carriage were already filling up, a mix of military officers and civil servants by the look of them, and now and then the odd memsahib, all heading upcountry, no doubt to some second-rate outpost of empire such as Patna or Faizabad and which in embittered, gin-soaked moments they might wish were swallowed into the ground. The penultimate compartment had been colonised by several gentlemen in shirts, ties and woollen suits totally unsuited to the tropics. Each wore an expression of discomfort that suggested either a bad meal had the night before or a career forged in accountancy, neither possible explanation filling me with an urge to explore further.

That left the final compartment, one which through the glass appeared occupied solely by a pale, thin gentleman in a dark suit, with his nose in a book and the air of someone not partial to too much conversation. I gave thanks to the Almighty for small mercies and slid open the door, realising only as he looked up at me that he sported the dog collar that marked him out as a man of the cloth, and suddenly I regretted not taking my chances with the accountants. With Suren already barrelling into the back of me, a retreat was impossible, and before I knew it, I was two feet inside the compartment.

The clergyman offered us both a nod but reserved a smile for Suren. You can tell a lot from a clergyman's smile. The mere act of it denoted that the man was not a Scot. Scottish clergy do not smile, certainly not while there is still sin in the world. No, the smile suggested he was English, a suggestion reinforced by his inoffensive suit, Oxford brogues and the faint hint of lemons emanating from his aftershave, from which I took him to be C of E, as a priest of the Catholic persuasion wouldn't care for a fragrance quite so insipid.

Yet that smile had been proffered solely to Suren, and that muddied the waters. It suggested a streak of the evangelical, the need to proselytise and to save brown souls from damnation. There weren't too many C of E vicars that went in for that sort of thing these days, and those that did weren't the type to wear polished brogues.

There was another possibility of course, and one probably worse than the man being either evangelical or Scotch. There was the chance that he was a progressive: one of those high-minded young clergymen who believed we had no business ruling India, and that the sooner we left the better for everyone; which rather begged the question why they hadn't already left themselves. Instead, most of them were falling over themselves to make friends with Indians, especially the nice, educated, neatly coiffured types like Suren; and while my own views on our continued presence in this country were of a similar vein, I at least had the decency to arrive at them out of spite, self-loathing and a realisation that whatever else they might be, Indians could be no more callous and incompetent at running the place than we were, so why not let them have a go?

In the end, I suppose the impetus for the smile did not really matter. What mattered was the sheer fact of it. For the smile signified a willingness for conversation with perfect strangers and that was never a good thing. At least he had the good grace to wait for us to be seated before engaging us.

'A fine day for it,' he ventured.

For what? I wondered. *For investigating a murder, or just for being on a train?*

'Oh, most certainly,' Suren replied.

The clergyman proffered a name.

'Kemp. Reverend Archie Kemp.'

Suren returned the kindness, giving him two for one.

'Surendranath Banerjee, and this is Captain Wyndham.'

The reverend nodded sagely. 'Going far?'

'Bishnupore.'

The Englishman's face lit up. 'It falls within my parish. My new parish, I should say.'

'You are recently arrived in India?'

'Almost two weeks now. First posting from the bishop of Calcutta. Can't wait to get stuck in. I daresay it'll be a challenge getting to know the parish and its flock, but I'm looking forward to it. I've heard it's a lovely place.'

'Yes,' Suren agreed. 'Many beautiful temples dating from the sixteenth century.'

Kemp's face suggested this was wondrous news. 'You know it well?'

Suren shook his head. 'No, but I have seen pictures in books.'

The reverend seemed disappointed, but rallied quickly. 'So a first time for us both. What about you, Captain ... Wyndham was it?'

'Same,' I said, and in truth I had less of an idea of the place than either of them. All I knew was that Bishnupore sat about a hundred miles north-west of Calcutta as the crow flew and substantially further as the train trundled.

'And will you be visiting the temples?'

Sightseeing was not high on my agenda. All I wanted to do was to head from the station to the film set, interrogate whoever we needed to, find out what we could that might provide an insight into J. P. Mullick and his murder, maybe spend a little time in the company of the beguiling Miss Morgan, then catch the evening train back to Calcutta. But you couldn't exactly tell a reverend that.

'Alas, I don't expect we'll have time.'

A guard's whistle and a gentle jolt of the carriage announced our departure and precipitated a lull in the conversation as the reverend turned his attention to matters possibly spiritual and certainly beyond the window. The train fell quickly into its rhythm, clicking over tracks and fenders as the factories and mills of Howrah provided a brief, brick-built intermezzo before the emerald-green embrace of rural Bengal: a tapestry of paddy and pond and palm awakening under a rising sun.

This was the Bengal of the artist's brush and the poet's pen. This was the land that all those Calcutta-centric Bengali intellectuals like Suren pined for: villages of mud-brick and thatch; velvet fields and ink-green pools; serpentine rivers that bordered and bound and bisected the land and sustained its people. And this was the best way to see it – at a distance and from the comfort of a first-class compartment.

The look on Suren's face suggested he felt something similar, though possibly without the postscript, and I suppose it was a mercy he didn't suddenly break into song about the whole thing.

As the train moved on, though, he and Kemp were soon engaged in a conversation as wide-ranging as it was banal, bonding over a shared membership of the Liberal Club in London. I knew of the place, of course. It stood like an Italianate castle on the north bank of the Thames not far from Parliament. It cost a pretty penny to join and was a gentlemen's club for those men who disliked other gentlemen, or at least those with the zealously imperialist sentiments that were traditionally found in other clubs. I closed my eyes and left them to it.

When I awoke it was to a dry mouth and the screech of brakes. The train slowed, juddering fitfully to a halt beside a station platform. The Reverend Kemp was staring out of the window like a child at the zoo. On the platform, hawkers went from window to window, crying out their wares of oranges and cucumbers and cheap tin toys for the children. I rubbed the ache from my neck.

'Where are we?'

He turned and smiled. 'A place called Midnapore. I might step out and stretch my legs.'

'Don't wander too far,' Suren told him. 'The trains here have a tendency to set off on a whim.'

Kemp slid open the door and I watched him head down the corridor like Columbus off to discover the new world. His absence left our little six-seat compartment dangerously empty. With only Suren and me seemingly in residence, it might appear a tempting berth for any newly boarding passengers. I got up and laid my jacket on Kemp's seat.

'To keep it safe for him,' I said to Suren.

He ruminated before speaking. 'I have never understood your antipathy towards your own kind. It is most confusing.'

'That's rather unfair,' I said. 'My antipathy extends far beyond my *own* kind. It is catholic in scope and liberal in application and encompasses almost everyone everywhere.'

'What about Miss Grant?' he asked. 'Does it extend to her these days?'

The question caught me like a right hook.

'Why would you even ask that?'

He smiled. 'You remember in the old days, how you would wage that campaign against Miss Grant's suitors?'

I told him I didn't have the foggiest idea what he was on about.

He arched an eyebrow. 'You don't recall the time you convinced that French doctor chap who was courting her that she had been married twice before and had six children in a boarding school near Yeovil?'

'Crossed wires.'

'You claimed to be one of her ex-husbands.'

'Nonsense,' I said. 'I merely told him that I'd attended a wedding *with* her. It's not my fault the man's grasp of English was shaky.'

'That is not quite my recollection.'

'It doesn't matter,' I said. 'He wasn't right for her.'

'How can you be sure?'

'Because for a start, he was French,' I said. 'Frenchmen are famous for their dalliances of the heart. You must know that having lived there. Indeed, your Elise probably found you a breath of fresh air compared to dalliance-loving Frenchmen. What Annie needs is someone solid and dependable.'

'Like a German?'

'No,' I said. 'Not that dependable.'

'A solicitor, then?'

'That would be more appropriate.'

'There was a solicitor, as I recall,' he said. 'You told him she was the prime suspect in a murder investigation.'

'Well, she *had* been a suspect.'

'Almost two years prior. And it was *you* who'd made her a suspect and then proceeded to find her to be completely innocent.'

From the platform came the shrill tone of a whistle. The train would be moving soon, and suddenly I had the fervent desire that the good Reverend Kemp should return forthwith. The platform beyond the window began to slip gently by. I reached into my pocket for a pack of Capstans.

'Is there a point to all this?'

In the corridor outside, the figure of Kemp appeared like the archangel Gabriel himself. The compartment door slid open and he entered, a grin on his sunburned face and a slice of watermelon between handkerchiefed fingers.

'I was just wondering,' Suren said, 'if you were planning a similar campaign vis à vis this Russian gentleman.'

The thought had, I admit, crossed my mind, but only fleetingly. There comes a point in any doomed relationship when one has to face up to the hard truth that it is better to bury the past and look to the future, however uncertain that might appear. And when it came to my relationship with Annie, it seemed that point was drawing inexorably closer.

I gave him a shake of the head. 'Sometimes you just have to let people make their own mistakes.' And even as I said the words I wasn't sure whether I meant her or me.

EIGHTEEN

Surendranath Banerjee

Bishnupore arrived with a hiss of steam and the scream of brakes. We said our adieus to the Reverend Kemp, I having exchanged addresses for correspondence. He was of that new breed of Englishman, earnestly interested in the ways of Indians, almost as keen on understanding us as in telling us what to do. I hoped his fervour might continue. Too often, though, the eagerness to understand us was blunted by the hard business of actually spending time with us.

Sam and I descended from our carriage. Further down the platform a wave of bodies spilled from third class, washing onto the concourse, colliding with others trying to board. There was the usual jostling, the single-minded pushing and shoving, the raising of voices. A typical Indian scene: grinding progress achieved through utter chaos. One saw it not only at stations but at post offices, cinemas and any place else in the country where demand exceeded supply. It was frustrating. We had spent the last 150 years aping the British and in all that time we had singularly failed to adopt their one truly virtuous quality: the ability to form an orderly queue. Why this should be was unclear to me, though I suspect it may have had something to do with our respective religions. Christianity, with its belief in only one route to God, seemed the natural environment for the development of a queuing mentality, whereas Hinduism, which taught that God (and by extension, trains, cinemas and temples) could and should be reached by many routes, was a philosophy which all but guaranteed the evolution of an anarchic free for all.

We steered a course away from the crowd, past an uninterested ticket inspector and through the station, emerging into the heat of late morning and the bustle of provincial life and commerce. Beyond the railings sat a small market: maybe two dozen hawkers, men and women, sitting cross-legged on the ground, surrounded by their wares and calling out to a gaggle of officious housewives and servants, cloth bags in hand, eager to secure a bargain on everything from cauliflower and brinjal to mangoes and jackfruit.

I stopped beside a vendor selling bunches of small green bananas and pointed at one.

'*Kotho?*' I asked.

He picked up the bunch, placed it on an old metal scale, adjusted the weights, adding a pound and subtracting ounces till the pans balanced and he named his price.

'What are you doing?' Sam called out.

I paid, picked up my bananas and showed him my prize.

'Cheaper than in Calcutta.' I pulled off a pair of the fat, stubby fruits and offered one to him which he accepted without ceremony.

'Probably fresher too. Ask your new friend if he knows anything about the film being shot here.'

I had my doubts as to whether a hawker of bananas would have much knowledge about such things, but then again, street vendors sat at the nexus of gossip and hearsay in many locales in Calcutta, seeing and hearing everything that went on within a two- or three-mile radius. Why should Bishnupore be any different? So I asked him and his face lit up like the sun. He embarked upon a detailed history: the arrival of a train of sahibs, memsahibs and shirt-pant-wearing Indians; a carriage-load of crates which had required all the porters in Bishnupore station as well as additional strong-backed men from the local populace to transport, first to a hunting lodge where the arrivals had established camp and then, for the last week, to and from one of the nearby temple sites.

I thanked him and explained his words to Sam as we headed for the shade of a nearby tree to eat our bananas and consider our options.

'At this time of day,' he said, 'chances are, they'll all be out filming. Did he tell you which temple they've gone to?'

I looked out at the road in front of us, choked with carts and cows and bicycles.

'No, but I would imagine every tonga-wallah in town knows where they are.'

A smile creased his lips. 'Good point. You sure you don't miss being a detective?'

He walked towards the road, searched until he saw a tonga and, banana skin in hand, hailed it down. After a brief discussion with the tonga-wallah, he beckoned me to join him and gestured to the driver, a moustachioed fellow in a shirt and checked lungi and head shielded from the sun by a loose turban.

'This chap says he knows where to go, but he's asking a fare for which I'd expect him to take us all the way back to Calcutta.'

I shook my head. 'Either he thinks you are with the film people and will pay whatever is asked, or that you are just an idiot sahib with deep pockets. I suggest you pay him half of what he asks.'

He did as I advised, telling the tonga-wallah exactly what we were willing to pay, and I added my two annas' worth on the subject. The man gave a snort then yanked the reins of his vehicle and headed off without us.

Sam looked to me.

'Yes, not quite the result I was hoping for, Suren.'

I shrugged. 'I don't think this is entirely my fault. You have lived in India for almost seven years now, while I have been absent from it for three years. Anyway, tongas are as common as crows. There will no doubt be another along in a minute.'

Alas, the tonga supply proved less like crows and more like hens' teeth, and ten minutes elapsed before another appeared, a dilapidated-looking thing with a grey-haired driver who quoted a fare higher than the previous chap, and which we now accepted without complaint.

The vehicle made surprisingly swift progress given the age of both driver and beast. In time the roads narrowed and the buildings thinned, yielding slowly to trees and fields and open ground. And then, in the distance, the gentle, sloping *chala* roofs of Bishnupore's temples, like the thatched canopies of our traditional huts but reincarnated in stone and terracotta.

I admit I felt my stomach knot at the sight of these divine structures created centuries ago by *my* forefathers, long before the British or the French or the Portuguese or any of the rest of those Europeans arrived on our shores, cap in hand and seeking trade. Certainly long before they presumed to tell us that our land was theirs and their ways superior to ours. I wished that Elise might be here to see them with me, to show her that we too were a civilised people. That we were capable of great feats of architecture. But that would never happen. It was maybe just as well, for I also felt a certain melancholy to see them in such condition, their perfect, rust-red skins cracked and hacked open by the elements, the bricks beneath shattered, crumbling, assailed by the spirits of the jungle who saw fit to strangle them in the roots and shoots of trees and bush. Anger, too, that we should allow the treasures of our past, the bequest of our ancestors to fall into such a state of disrepair. And yet it was not unexpected. We were a subjugated people whose shackles extended from the physical to the mental. We discarded the wisdom of our heritage in order to ape the ways of others and we called that progress. We threw out kurta and dhoti so that we may sweat in trouser and starched collar. It was madness and yet we did it, believing it would improve us. We were a people who despised ourselves in the present. Why then should we care about our past?

That melancholy, that bitter taste in my mouth and in my heart, transformed seamlessly into another pain. Elise invaded my thoughts yet again. There, in that moment, I realised that the manner of my parting from her had similarly been driven by certain feelings of inferiority. I was not good enough for her. How could I be? She was European. Her people had conquered the world. And we? We were the subjugated. How absurd, then, that my father should object to such a match on the grounds of culture and religion, as though her presence would somehow sully our bloodline. How terrible. How pathetic. But what else could one expect from an upper-caste Bengali? We were taught from birth to believe in our superiority, strutting around as though we were lords sent from heaven, while in reality we were just as subjugated as our lower-caste kinsmen; viewed as just as inferior by our occidental overlords.

Sam broke my introspection.

'Suren,' he said, 'would you look at that!'

NINETEEN

Sam Wyndham

The place was in disarray. Less a film shoot and more like the retreat from Mons. A chaos of men running in all directions, storing equipment, carrying boxes, loading carts. *Some* men, anyway. To one side, a few elegant souls stood leaning against crates, smoking and shooting the breeze. Actors, probably. You could always tell artistic types by their reticence to do any of the hard work.

I paid the tonga-wallah, got down and collared a couple of chaps carrying a crate the size of a tea chest.

'Who's in charge here?'

Both looked at me blankly, so I tried again, this time in Bengali.

'*Borro sahib kothai?*'

A smile broke out on Suren's lips.

'Very good,' he said. 'Let us see if you can understand their response.'

In truth I couldn't follow much of it. Bengali, when spoken at speed by a native, is like trying to understand English spoken by a Glaswegian: a noble endeavour, but one doomed, pretty quickly, to utter failure. Fortunately, one of the pair answered with a gesture of the head towards a gaggle of men, one of whom, wrapped in a chador, cotton satchel hanging from one shoulder, and with a cigarette burning between his fingers, appeared to be the centre of attention.

I gave them my thanks and headed for the gentleman in question. He looked every inch the artistic Bengali: thick black glasses, cheap cigarette, and an air of grave superiority that illuminated his bearded face. I took an instant dislike to the fellow yet consoled myself with the thought that if men like him had one redeeming feature, it was that they loved the sound of their own voices and generally had decent English. Better than a Glaswegian's, certainly.

He noticed our approach and took a pull on his cigarette.

'I'm looking for the director,' I said.

He smiled graciously and afforded us an exhalation of cigarette smoke. 'Then you have found him. And you are?'

'Captain Wyndham of the Imperial Police. And this is my... This is Mr Suren Banerjee.'

The man granted us a nod of acknowledgement.

'Mitra. Dipankar Mitra.'

'We'd like to ask you about Mr J. P. Mullick. I take it you've heard the news?'

Mitra grunted a laugh. 'Look around, Captain. This all is a result of *the news*. Without him, without his money, we are ... *khatom*.' He pulled a hand across his throat; an unconscious echo of the state of Mullick's body in the mud.

'I'm sure his death is difficult for his loved ones too.'

His expression softened. 'Yes of course. His passing is tragedy for so many. Do you have any idea what happened?'

Sometimes, the best way to get someone talking is to make them believe it's an exchange of information rather than an interrogation. People are often happy to divulge confidences if they think they'll get something in return. I took a breath, then said surreptitiously: 'I wonder if we may go somewhere to talk?'

He thought for a moment, then flicked the ash from the end of his cigarette. 'Come,' he said. 'Follow me.'

I turned to Suren. 'Stay here and have a look around. Find out what you can.'

He stared at me, unamused.

'About what?'

'You know the drill. Just look out for anything odd. Keep your ear to the ground and your nose in other people's business.'

'I'm not a policeman any more.'

'Yes, but you were always good at this sort of thing. Admit it, you'll find it a thrill.'

'Eavesdropping?'

'Talking to people. Look, artistic types are always gossiping. Go ingratiate yourself with some actors.'

He gave a sigh. 'Very well.'

Suren wandered off across the grass and I followed Mitra away from the chaos, round the side of one of the temples, its walls and brickwork inveigled by vines and creepers. The noise of men fell away as Mitra continued to puff on his cigarette like a one-man locomotive.

Up ahead stood a marquee of sorts, greyish canvas walls flecked with the mildew of a dozen monsoon seasons.

'My tent,' he said. 'We can talk there.'

As tents went, this one wasn't half bad. There were houses in Calcutta that were smaller. Beyond the threshold, things became, if anything, even more impressive. It was like something out of the *Arabian Nights*. Carpets covered the bare ground, and upon them stood several wood-and-canvas folding chairs, a daybed with an intricately carved back, drowning under a surfeit of silk cushions, and a lacquered chest pressed into service as a table. Maybe if I looked hard enough I'd find electricity and running water, and then the place would well and truly be better than my flat.

'Please.' He gestured to a chair. 'Some tea?' He did not wait for a reply before calling out: 'Bipin-da! *Cha niyē-ai!*'

Lowering himself onto the daybed, he crushed the stump of his cigarette into a glass ashtray which sat on the chest.

'So, Captain, what would you like to know?'

'Maybe you could start by telling me a little about the film you're shooting?'

Mitra's face brightened. 'It is an epic. The greatest Indian film ever to be shot. The story of a princess in the court of Tipu Sultan, of her love for the man and the terrible fate that awaits them both. It will be love story and tragedy.'

'Quite the magnum opus,' I said.

'It will be. Most certainly. Assuming it is ever finished. Without Mullick-da, who knows what will happen?'

'When was the last time you saw Mr Mullick?'

Mitra stroked his beard. 'Two maybe three days ago.'

'Which was it?' I asked. 'Two or three?'

'Three,' he said, a nod confirming his recollection. 'Friday. Early morning. Most sudden. Some business in Calcutta he had to go for. All very unexpected. He said he would be returning very soon.' He threw up his arms. 'But he is not coming back, and this morning we are receiving the terrible, most worst, news.'

The man seemed distracted. He flicked a stray flake of cigarette ash from his shirt. Maybe it was the thought of his film going down the swanee or the imminent loss of his Arabian tent, but he didn't seem like a man in hoc to grief at the death of one of Bengal's greatest sons, not to mention his own patron.

'And who gave you that news?'

'*Oi tho*, Mr Mullick's secretary, Ghatak.'

'And Ghatak is here, I believe?'

Mitra nodded. 'Very much he is here.'

'Did he tell you why he didn't return to Calcutta with his employer?'

He took a long puff. 'No. I assume Mullick-da must have told him to remain. He was going for short time only.'

'Do you know what matter took Mr Mullick back to Calcutta at such short notice?'

'I was not asking. He has many business matters. You should speak to Ghatak. He will know.'

In normal circumstances I'd have had Constable Singh beside me with his notebook and pencil to inscribe such information, but in his absence I had to do it myself.

'Was this the first of your films he was financing?'

Mitra leaned back. 'No. He has long time been involved in such things. Not just my films. Other films too,' he added, almost defensively. 'I mean, he is . . . he *was* great supporter of such things.'

'Was he in the habit of spending time on set?'

Mitra cleared his throat and looked around. 'Where is that damn fellow with the tea? Oh, Bipin-da! *Cha koi?*'

He bent down, reached into the folds of his satchel and rummaged till he found what he was looking for.

'Cigarette?'

He proffered a battered pack, then took one himself, before conjuring up a cheap matchbox, shaking it before pulling out a thin sliver of a match. The withered strip of emery on the side of the box was almost worn smooth and it took three strikes before the matchhead erupted. With his hands, he cupped the flame, sheltering it against a non-existent breeze and brought it over to me, lighting my cigarette before seeing to his own.

He sat back, took a pull and exhaled.

'The brand is to your tastes, I hope?'

'It's fine,' I said.

'Gauhar Be Baha. Most oldest cigarette in whole of India.'

The fabric of the tent rustled and in stepped a rather diminutive fellow balancing teacups and biscuits on a battered tray. He set the whole lot down on the chest and took a step back.

Mitra gestured to the cups. 'Please, have.'

I reached for a cup and sipped. 'You didn't answer my question,' I said. 'Did Mr Mullick always spend time on set?'

Mitra ordered his manservant from the tent, took another pull on his cigarette and waited while the little man departed.

'In some films more than others.'

'Any idea why?'

Cigarette between his fingers, he lifted the cup to his lips and took a sip without spilling a mote of ash. His face remained inscrutable.

'I don't wish to speculate.'

'I'd rather you did,' I said. 'Less than forty-eight hours ago, your patron was murdered. I have been tasked with finding his killers and I would very much like to accomplish that as quickly as possible, certainly without needless hindrance. So unless you'd prefer to continue this conversation at Bishnupore thana, I suggest you tell me everything I wish to know.'

Mitra placed his cup back on its saucer. '*Murdered?* So then the talk is true. I was told only that he had passed.'

It felt like the first unambiguous reaction that the man had given me.

'Who's been saying that?'

Mitra shrugged. 'Who knows where these rumours come from? In any case, this is not a matter for me. To Mullick's secretary, Mr Ghatak, you must pose these questions.'

'And I shall. But first I'm posing them to you, and I expect your full and frank response.'

The director rubbed at the bristles on his chin. 'How should I put this? His interest in any particular film was often dictated by matters other than the script.'

'Meaning?'

'Meaning that often it was dictated by his view of the actresses involved.'

Well, that was interesting. It sounded like our saint had an eye for the ladies. He certainly wouldn't be the first. Was it possible he'd gone back to Calcutta to see a woman? But there was a rather attractive lady already on set. One whom he'd personally convinced to come.

'And had he taken an interest in your actresses on this shoot?'

Mitra gave a laugh. 'One particular actress, and more than an interest. You have heard of Estelle Morgan?'

'I've seen her on advertising hoardings.'

'Of course,' said Mitra. 'She is big actress in England . . . and she is starring in this film.'

'Quite a coup,' I said. 'How did you manage to persuade her?'

'You can thank Mullick-da for that. I don't know how much he paid her. However much, still it is not enough bring a smile to her face.'

That was a surprise. She'd been nothing but smiles when I'd met her in Calcutta.

'She finds it difficult,' Mitra continued, 'to be filming out here in Bishnupore. She even rowed with Mullick-da about it. Finally he agreed to let her go back to Calcutta for the weekend. It was complete disruption to our shooting schedule.'

'Did he usually involve himself in the casting process?'

'Most of time he was happy to let me be handling such matters, but he always insisted on meeting the cast I had selected. Sometimes, though, he would bring some girl and say to me, "Include her, Mitra-da. She has talent." I would put them in background, in one, two scenes, maybe. Most did not have what it takes.'

'And what does it take?'

'Presence.' He intoned the word as though it had tangible weight. 'Simple good looks are not enough.'

'And Estelle Morgan?'

'Estelle Morgan,' Mitra nodded appreciatively, 'she has *real* presence. It is obvious why she is sought in England and America. You know she goes to Hollywood as soon as she is finished here? The sooner the better, in my opinion. She and her agent have been nothing but trouble.'

I thought back to the Idle Fox and the man who'd insisted Estelle call it a night.

'Tell me about her agent?'

Mitra exhaled blue smoke. 'American gentleman by the name of Copeland.'

'Is it common for an agent to turn up on set?'

Mitra snorted. 'In this country, actors do not even have agents, not professional ones at least. And yet this chap comes halfway across the world to be on set with his client. But then Americans, I have heard, are odd fellows. Smart, too. Copeland insisted that Mullick pay Miss Morgan's fee to him in advance. As for the rest of us...'

'You and your crew haven't been paid?'

Mitra puffed out his cheeks. 'Not yet. I have been paying some wages and bills from my own pocket. The gods alone know what will happen now.'

'Is that why you're packing up?'

'No,' he said. 'We are packing because those are the orders of Mullick-da's son, Joyonto. He wants to discuss the future of the film with me.' He sighed. 'Unlike his father, Joyonto Mullick has not much passion for film. He may cancel the whole thing. I just hope Mr Ghatak manages to smooth the path.'

'I shall need to talk to Mr Ghatak,' I said, 'and Miss Morgan too, preferably without her agent in tow.'

Mitra smiled. 'That will not be a problem. Copeland is not here. He did not return with her from Calcutta. In fact, the last time I saw him was before he caught the train back to Calcutta with Mullick-da.'

'Wait,' I said. 'Copeland was on the same train back to Calcutta as J. P. Mullick?'

'I believe so. Estelle Morgan too.'

TWENTY

Surendranath Banerjee

It was all well and good Sam saying '*find out what you can*', but what was I supposed to do? I was not a policeman now and so the usual threats of violence or jail which were the basic tenets of police interrogation work, at least in India, were unavailable. Nevertheless I set off, reluctantly, towards a group of individuals gathered around a table upon which sat plates of *shingara* and fish and mutton chops and a large urn of tea.

The *shingara* were still warm and, taking a napkin, I helped myself to one, lifting it to my mouth and taking a bite. Potatoes and peas, simple ingredients, brought to life by the zest of cumin, ginger and green chilli. The taste of my youth. It may have been a month since my return, but the renewed pleasures of Bengali cuisine were still a joy. Indeed, the hardest part of my European sojourn had been the food; worse than the climate, the foreign languages and other Indians. In fact, it may be said that I was driven from Germany by the state of the culinary fare. To this day I do not understand how a nation so powerful could be built upon a diet comprised exclusively of sausage, cabbage and beer. As for France, while their cuisine is no doubt of a higher standard, too much of it is based upon doing unspeakable things to sheep, ducks, geese, frogs, pigs, snails and most upsettingly cows. And then, of course, there was Britain. I fear there is little one can say in defence of a nation who had expended so much blood and treasure conquering the parts of the world where the spices grew, yet had never let this bounty come anywhere near its own dining tables. I had said as much to Elise one time when I had cooked for her: a dish of curried brinjal. It had not turned out quite as I had hoped and I was embarrassed to serve it to her, but she had smiled, professed to enjoy it and had eaten every last morsel. Maybe that should be the definition of love.

I spotted a gentleman standing by himself to one side, a cigarette in his hand and that smouldering, faraway look that marked him out as an actor. I recognised him at once, from the film *Bilet Pherat*. If I was to question anyone, it may as well be a film star. Taking another bite of the *shingara*, I walked over, and before I had the chance to introduce myself, he gave me a smile and began addressing me in Bengali.

'You're the chap who turned up with that detective sahib.'

'That's correct,' I said, pressing my palms together. 'Surendranath Banerjee. And you of course are Dhirendranath Deb.'

He looked at me as though surprised that I should recognise him.

'Please, call me Dhiren.' He held the cigarette to his lips. The tip glowed red between his fingers. 'They're saying Mullick-da was murdered. Is it true?'

'Who's been saying that?' I asked.

He took another nonchalant pull on his cigarette. 'Who knows? On a film set, gossip carries on the wind. We practically breathe it. There is little else to do when the cameras aren't rolling. So is it true?'

'Unfortunately.'

He sniffed, then exhaled a whisper of blue.

'You do not seem particularly shocked,' I said. 'One of Bengal's greatest men, murdered.'

He gave a wry smile. 'One of Bengal's *richest* men, certainly. I would hesitate to place him among its greatest.'

I struggled to hide my surprise. 'What about the hospitals and the schools?'

Deb gave a snort. 'A man can be many things: philanthropist, benefactor, scoundrel. Sometimes he can be all of them all at once.'

Suddenly my eye was caught by a woman walking across the grass. She was tall, fair-skinned and the sight of her seemed to take the very breath from my lungs. Deb noticed my reaction and laughed.

'Yes, she is quite something, isn't she? Her name is Miss Estelle Morgan, and she has come from England to grace us with her presence.'

'It must be a great honour acting opposite such an actress,' I said.

'Opposite a memsahib, you mean?'

'I only meant I have never seen a film before where the hero is Indian and the leading lady is, as you say, a memsahib.'

'Well, unfortunately you may not get to see this one either. Without Mullick to bankroll it, I doubt this film will ever be finished. In fact I'd be surprised if any of us see a paisa from it. Any of us except for Miss Morgan, of course.'

'How much was Mullick-da paying her to star?'

'More than he was paying me, for sure. Probably more than he was paying for everyone and everything else combined.'

'He must have admired her tremendously.'

Deb shot me a glance.

'Yes, that is certainly one way of putting it.'

It took a moment for the penny to drop.

'But Mullick was a respectable man,' I said. 'A fine man.'

He shook his head and smiled. 'Fine men can also do un-fine things. Sometimes they do it simply because they can.'

'I cannot believe that a man like Mullick would force himself upon a woman.'

He took a final pull on his cigarette, then discarded it to the wind. 'A man like Mullick would not need to use force. He would see it as sport. A chase; a game to be played. A right afforded by his wealth and to be exercised at his choice. I would not be at all surprised if you discovered that he was killed by an irate husband or father. There must have been at least half a dozen who would happily have stuck a knife in him.'

I could not help but feel depressed at his words.

'You knew him well?' I asked.

'Not particularly,' he said, 'but it is common knowledge in our circles. Believe me, your Mullick-da was not all he was made out to be. You will be surprised how little a man's reputation rests upon good deeds and how much upon good solicitors.'

I thanked Dhiren Deb for his time and walked in a daze, back across the grass in the direction that Sam and the director, Mitra, had headed. A bitterness began rising in the pit of my stomach, sour and black, growing and spreading and threatening to colour my thoughts. During my sojourn overseas I had sustained myself in the belief that morality dictated that India deserved independence. Our leaders therefore had to be moral men and women. And not just our leaders but all of us, especially those we looked up to. And Mullick was a leader in the field of commerce and business. He was a titan. But if Deb was to be believed, the man was the worst type of scoundrel; and if a man like Mullick could be a snake, then what hope was there? What hope for our country when even our heroes were tainted? As Gandhi said, if we were to be worthy of our freedom, we needed to be better than our oppressors, certainly morally. Because, otherwise, the freedom we earned would be hollow, tainted and hijacked by unscrupulous men.

TWENTY-ONE

Sam Wyndham

So Estelle Morgan had been on the same train back to Calcutta as J. P. Mullick. That had certainly come as a shock. It seemed I had more to question Miss Morgan about than I'd originally anticipated.

Mitra was good enough to lend me the use of his tent to carry out my other interviews, and also of his servant, Bipin, to bring me both my required individuals and a steady supply of tea.

First came Mullick's secretary, Ronen Ghatak, a subdued young man in a white shirt, thin tie and black suit that was well on its way to a shiny dark grey. Watchful eyes stared back from behind cheap, wire-framed spectacles. He looked about twenty-five and like he hadn't slept in most of that time. I offered him a seat on the daybed recently vacated by Mitra.

'My name is Captain Wyndham,' I said. 'Of the Imperial Police.'

'Ghatak,' he said, proffering a nervous hand. 'Ronen Ghatak.'

Unbidden, Bipin entered with fresh cups of tea and set them on the chest between us and loitered in a corner until I told him, quite unceremoniously, to sling his hook. Then he bolted like the proverbial scalded cat and I got on with my questioning of the secretary.

'My condolences on the death of your employer.'

Ghatak nodded and mouthed words that never came.

'It must have been a terrible shock.'

'It was.' He shifted, attempting to attain some degree of comfort upon the daybed. 'I still cannot quite accept it.'

'When did you find out about his death?'

'Yesterday. I received a telegram from the office, two in fact. The first asking as to Mullick-da's whereabouts. I responded saying I had no idea and that he had not returned from Calcutta. Then, a few hours later, I received the second, informing me of his demise.'

'Did you tell anyone about this?'

He shook his head. 'Not last night. The second telegram requested I mention nothing. Then this morning, I received a third telegram ordering that all filming cease and that we return to Calcutta as soon as possible.'

'Do you still have the telegrams?'

'The one that came this morning, yes. The others I must have thrown away.'

'May I see the one you have?'

'Certainly.'

He fished around in his pocket, drawing out a thin rectangle of paper, unfolded it and passed it to me. At the top, the crest of the Indian Posts and Telegraphs Department; the message itself, sent at 8 a.m. that morning from the telegraph office on Dalhousie Square, was short and to the point:

> *Further to prior*
> *Immediate cessn to filming*
> *All to return Cal earliest.*
> *K Sarkar*
> *Dir.*

'Do you mind if I keep this?' I asked.

Sweat glinted on his forehead.

'Please,' he said. 'It is a most terrible occurrence.'

'It certainly is,' I said. 'You see, Mr Mullick was murdered.'

Ghatak raised a hand to his forehead and chest, twice in quick succession, the Hindu equivalent of a Catholic crossing himself in the face of the malevolent.

'So the rumours are true. I was hoping they would not be. Have you ... have you any idea who is responsible?'

'That remains to be seen,' I said. 'How long have you been working for Mr Mullick?'

He seemed not to hear the question.

'Mr Ghatak?'

'Oh, three years, nearly. Originally as assistant secretary, and the last two as principal secretary.'

'And how did you come to be in his employ?'

'I applied for the post of an administrative clerk at his office. I was not successful but then Mullick sahib interviewed me himself. He asked about my family, my background. When I told him I had only recently arrived in Calcutta and had no family here, he provided me with accommodation and hired me as assistant secretary instead.'

'What were your duties as principal secretary?'

From his pocket he took a handkerchief and mopped at his brow.

'I assisted him with many things: appointments, meetings, travel arrangements, notes and dictations, typing his correspondence, keeping supplicants at bay.'

'What triggered his return to Calcutta?'

Ghatak reached for his handkerchief, this time taking it to the back of his neck.

'I can only tell you that he was scheduled to remain here for another week. Then, on Friday morning, he informed me he would return to Calcutta by train with Miss Morgan and her agent. He said some last-minute business had come up in the city, but that he would return by this morning.'

'He didn't tell you what exactly?'

'No.'

'I thought you said you were responsible for managing most aspects of his life.'

Ghatak scratched at his neck. 'Most, but not all. There were certain things which Mullick sahib did not share with me.'

'Such as?'

'I have no idea.'

'You organise a man's life for three years and you were never curious about what he might be doing in those moments he kept secret from you?'

His shoulders stiffened. 'He had his right to privacy, and it was not my place to enquire.'

'Not even a quiet chat with his chauffeur, to see where he might be going? Or a word with his valet?'

Ghatak blustered. 'I would not indulge in such petty gossip, especially with the likes of a chauffeur or valet.'

Suddenly I regretted asking the question.

'Did Mullick receive any communication which might have caused his sudden return to the city?'

'Not that I am aware.'

'No cables or telephone calls?'

'Nothing.'

'Then how did he come to know of this "last-minute business" matter which had suddenly cropped up?'

Ghatak blinked. 'I . . . I could not say.'

'He just woke up and decided to go back to Calcutta?'

'He did not tell me everything,' he protested. 'He was . . . he was a man of ideas. At any time some thought might strike him and then it would preoccupy him and he would suddenly change his plans completely.'

'Is that what you think happened? He had a *thought*?'

'Businessmen can be mercurial.'

'But if it was a business matter, wouldn't he have shared that thought with you? Wouldn't he have asked you to make plans for his return to Calcutta?'

Ghatak shrugged. 'I cannot speculate further on his motivation for going. All I can say is that he did not share those motives with me.'

'Do you think he simply wanted to accompany Miss Morgan on the train?'

The secretary blinked again. 'I do not see why. Anything he might wish to discuss with her or her agent, he could have done here.'

The secretary was being willingly obtuse, though whether it was out of loyalty or for more nefarious reasons, I wasn't sure. If Mitra was to be believed, Mullick had a bit of a roving eye. No doubt, Estelle Morgan would have caught it.

'Come now, Mr Ghatak,' I said. 'Miss Morgan is a good-looking woman, and it's clear that your employer had, let us say, an appreciation of beauty. He was the one who secured her services in the film here, isn't that so? I'm asking you if there is a possibility he returned to Calcutta because Miss Morgan was going there.'

His concession was grudging at best.

'It is possible, I suppose.'

'And his emotional state? When he left on Friday morning, was he anxious, or different in any way?'

'He seemed perfectly content.'

'Not someone who was worried over some last-minute business matter?'

'I cannot speak to his state of mind.'

'What about his relationship with his son? Can you speak to that?'

There was a flicker of something, as though he'd just been jabbed by a red-hot pin.

'They had their disagreements.'

'You mean they didn't get along?'

Ghatak chose his words with care. 'I would imagine it is difficult to live under the shadow of a great man, especially when they have high hopes of you. Joyonto-da did not live up to what his father expected of him. But he would never do anything to harm his father. It would never occur to him to do such a thing.'

The secretary was hardly proving to be the oracle I'd hoped. At best, the good and faithful servant, remaining loyal to his fallen master. At worst, he was hiding something.

'Did you make any arrangements for his arrival in Calcutta? His car to take him home, maybe?'

Ghatak shook his head. 'He said he would make his own arrangements.'

'And what of Miss Morgan and Mr Copeland?'

'What about them?'

'Did they accompany him to the station?'

'No. The cast and crew are mainly staying in an old hunting lodge nearby but Mullick sahib values his privacy and instead ordered me to rent a separate house. He asked that I send them a car to take them to the station, however.'

'And this house which Mullick was renting, you stayed there too?'

'Naturally. He required me to be close at hand.'

'Was anyone else invited to stay there?'

The secretary seemed to twitch. 'Such as?'

'Miss Morgan?'

Ghatak cleared his throat. 'She and Mr Copeland were billeted in a hotel in town. At Mr Mullick's request, I made an invitation to them to take rooms in the house Mullick-da had rented. He did not want such a famous actress as Miss Morgan to be put out, staying in some third-rate place in the middle of nowhere. He thought she might appreciate a modicum of privacy. Mr Copeland, however, insisted they remain at the hotel.'

I bet he did.

'What sort of a man was Mullick, in your opinion?'

'In what sense?'

'Did he have any enemies? Anyone who might hold a grudge?'

He shook his head as though the question was absurd.

'You only need to read the papers to know the esteem in which he was held. Everyone loved him.'

'And someone loved him so much, they were willing to slit his throat.'

The blood seemed to drain from Ghatak's face.

'Is . . . is that what happened?'

'It is. And that's why I need you to answer my questions truthfully. There is at least one person out there who didn't much care for your boss, and I intend to find out who. So I ask you again, are you aware of anyone who might have held a grudge against your employer?'

This time Ghatak was less flippant.

'There were certain people who had disagreements with him.'

'Anyone in particular?'

The answers came faster now.

'Angus Carlyle.'

'The jute baron?'

'The same. Ever since Mullick sahib was elected chairman of All Bengal Commerce Association ahead of him.'

I made a note of the name.

'What about here? Were there any disagreements on set?'

Ghatak's brow furrowed. 'In what sense?'

'Any problems between Mullick and the director or the cast around money, maybe, or creative direction?'

'Not significantly,' he said. 'Always there will be complaints about money. That is just the nature of the business. Actors, directors. They are happy to spend it like water. None of them know what it is to do a real day's work. As for creative matters, Mullick-da generally kept out of those things.'

'And yet he was the one who obtained Miss Morgan's services,' I said.

Ghatak conceded the point only partially, as if Mullick's involvement was trivial. 'He might, on occasion, intercede on behalf of an actress or actor pushing for a larger role, but he was never insistent. If he could help those artistes, then he would, but not at the expense of his relationship with the director.'

'What about his relationship with Miss Morgan's agent, Mr Copeland?'

This time Ghatak stared at me, hard.

'They did not get along, that much is true, but Mr Copeland is American. They are unused to our ways. They do not understand that a man like Mullick-da deserved deference and respect. Their relationship was certainly abrasive.'

'Abrasive enough for violence?'

A momentary shiver seemed to pass through Ghatak. 'I would not think so, but who knows with Americans?'

'Did Mullick ever receive any threats?'

Ghatak's expression hardened. 'Nothing that passed my desk.'

'You're sure?'

'There was the odd crank. Madmen, lunatics, poor people who would send letters or turn up at the house or the office, alleging this or that. All nonsense of course. With some, I would threaten to call the police. With others, if they appeared destitute, I would send them away with a donation, we would say for their temple or mosque or whatever. Of course, whether the money always reached its intended destination is debatable.'

'A donation?'

'Mullick-da authorised it. He was a very generous man.'

'These *cranks*. What sort of accusations would they make?'

Ghatak looked away. 'I don't recall. There were not many.'

Not for the first time, I felt Ghatak was holding back.

'Come now,' I said, 'surely you can remember one case.'

He raised his palms. 'I'm afraid not. It was all minor issues. Trivial matters. One hardly paid them any attention even at the time.'

I doubted that. Ghatak struck me as the type who paid attention to everything. Yet if he wasn't going to open up, and in the absence of a prison cell or thumbscrews, it was better to try a different tack.

'Was Mullick a good employer?'

'I cannot complain,' he said matter-of-factly. 'A stable job is hard to come by these days, even for a man with a college degree. He gave me a job when I had none.'

I took a long look at Ghatak, this thin man in a tired suit, his shirt frayed at the cuffs and the cracked leather of his shoes. It didn't seem like such loyalty cost much.

'And the pay?'

He smiled in that self-deprecating manner Indians have when you ask them such things.

'It was enough to cover the rent and fill my plate, though it would have been nice to have had a little more.' He gave a bitter laugh. 'How can I complain about the past, when it is the future that is black? Who knows what I shall do now? Mr Mullick junior, that is Joyonto-da, may keep me on for a period, at least until his father's affairs have been settled, but then?'

'I'm sure you'll find an opening somewhere,' I said.

'In Calcutta, employers like Mullick sahib do not exactly grow like flowers. And what should I put on my CV? That I was personal secretary to a murdered man? We Indians are a superstitious people. A *boro babu* will think twice before employing someone who might bring such misfortune into their lives.'

'A British employer, then,' I said. 'Someone less prone to such things.'

He shrugged. 'It is difficult without connections.'

'Miss Morgan seems to have made some acquaintances in Calcutta,' I said. 'Maybe she can provide you with an introduction.'

He did not reply, but the idea hardly seemed to bowl him over.

'On the subject of Miss Morgan,' I continued, 'why did Mullick cast her as the heroine?'

'Mullick-da was a great fan of her work. Her role as Anne Boleyn in *Henry the Eighth* was a favourite.'

'It's rather unusual for a British actress to play a role in an Indian film, isn't it? However did he convince her to take it?'

The secretary gave a wan smile. 'Perhaps you have heard the tale of the Maharajah of Alwar? The maharajah, while on a trip to London, had cause to visit a showroom for Rolls-Royce cars. The salesman, seeing only a brown face, gave him short shrift. The maharajah could have made a scene. He could have dragged that salesman over the coals, asked to see the manager, ensured the man's sacking from his post, but he did none of those things. Instead he returned the next day in full ceremonial regalia, bought all the cars in the showroom and had the attendant accompany them to Delhi where he promptly decreed that the municipal authorities use them for refuse collection.'

'Your point?' I said.

'My point is that sometimes Indian money trumps even British snobbery.'

TWENTY-TWO

Sam Wyndham

The secretary departed, the cares of the world upon his narrow shoulders. I summoned the servant, Bipin, availed myself of another cup of tea and asked him to call Estelle Morgan to the tent.

As he left, Suren stepped in.

'Making progress?' he asked.

'Not enough. The director, Mitra, hinted at a few things regarding the sort of man our friend Mullick might have been, but the secretary, Ghatak, wouldn't corroborate any of it. He's a strange fish. Called Mullick a generous man.'

'And?'

'Well, to look at the man, you can tell he's hard up. His clothes look a hundred years old and he's not exactly red of cheek and plump of bicep. Whatever salary Mullick was paying him, I doubt it would be termed generous.'

Suren shook his head at me.

'Seven years in this country and you still do not know us. Labour is cheap. Abundant. Men like Ghatak are ten a penny. Just having a job, even if the pay is pathetic, puts him in a better position than myriad others. It means he has the potential to move forward in life. Without this job, he could not marry. In that sense, Mullick was indeed generous to him.'

'Fair enough,' I said, mulling his response. 'You see. That's why I asked you to come along. You have an insight into these things that I don't. Anyway, how have you been getting on? Find out anything useful?'

He pondered the question.

'I had an interesting conversation with an actor. There is something troubling I need to tell you about J. P. Mullick.'

'Let me guess,' I said. 'He wasn't quite as pure as the driven snow as you'd expected?'

He didn't respond.

'I've heard similar,' I said. 'And that secretary of his is holding something back.'

Maybe it was talk of holding things back, but I suddenly remembered Dawson's letter to Suren in my pocket. I reached into my jacket and retrieved it. I realised I had been putting off handing it to him. My procrastination, I feared, was precipitated by the fact that I was concerned for him; worried about what Dawson might want with him.

But this Suren was a different creature from the boy I'd first met seven years earlier. This Suren was more confident. He didn't need me to act as mother hen.

'Here,' I said, holding it out. 'I meant to tell you. I was summoned by your old friend Colonel Dawson last night. He asked me to give you this.'

Suren was taken aback. 'You went to see him?'

'Not out of choice,' I said, then told him of my late-night journey across town to the eatery in Allen Square and the request from Dawson at the other end. I kept the details vague. Giving him chapter and verse would only complicate matters.

'You think he wants to arrest me? To question me about what happened back in '23?'

I laughed under my breath. 'The man controls the largest security network in the country. If he wanted to arrest you, he could've done it at any time since you got back, or probably even in France, for that matter.'

He took the envelope, slit it and extracted its contents. He read it over quickly.

'Well?'

Suren looked up. 'He wants me to meet him. There is a number I should call to arrange time and place.'

'That's it?'

'More or less.'

I wasn't sure I believed him, but before I could question him further, the tent curtains parted, in glided Estelle Morgan in a sleeveless silk dress, and the world stopped. Even the breath in my throat seemed to forget what it was doing.

'Captain Wyndham! This is a surprise!' A perfect smile lit up her face. Beatific, the sort that suggested you were in the presence of the divine.

For a moment I was lost for words.

'When Bipin told me there was a policeman wanting to see me, I hardly thought it might be you!'

I stammered some monosyllabic reply.

She turned to Suren.

'And who is this?'

'May I introduce Mr Suren Banerjee,' I said. 'A former colleague of mine, recently returned from Europe.'

'Lovely to meet you, Mr Banerjee,' she said.

Suren looked like a rabbit hypnotised by a snake.

'P-pleasure is mine,' he said, and looked over at me. 'You did not tell me, Sam, that you were acquainted with such a famous actress.'

'Yes, well,' I said. 'It's amazing what you miss when you go away for three years.'

He gave me a glance which I chose to interpret as new-found respect, though it might just as easily have been disbelief.

'Anyway,' said Miss Morgan, 'I'm just glad you're here.' And in that moment, I was keen to believe her. 'This news about JP, it's terrible.' She raised a hand to her mouth. 'Wait. Is this the case you mentioned to me the other night?'

'It is,' I said. 'And I'm afraid I need to ask you a few questions.'

She looked surprised. 'Very well, but I'm not sure how I can help.'

'It's nothing to worry about,' I said, directing her to the daybed. 'Sometimes even the most innocuous detail can turn out to be useful.'

'Crucial, even,' Suren chimed in.

At that moment, the servant, Bipin, stuck his head round the door.

'*Cha*, sahib?'

The question was directed at me but his eyes were on Estelle. He didn't wait for a response, instead conjuring up a tray with a pot and even china cups this time. He placed it on the chest and poured, handing a cup to Miss Morgan.

'Chugar?' he asked.

I told him in no uncertain terms to get out, and as he left, I caught a glimpse of a grey-haired woman in a sari standing by the entrance.

Estelle Morgan took a sip of tea.

'Did you know J. P. Mullick well?' I asked.

She placed the cup on the lacquered chest.

'Not really. I mean, not before coming to India. But in the few weeks I've been here, he has been a most gracious host. May I ask how he died?'

Explaining the truth to her, that he'd had his throat slit and been left in the mud of the riverbank seemed somehow inappropriate, like dropping a pile of manure at the feet of the Madonna. So I kept it brief and sanitised.

'He was murdered, by person or persons unknown.'

She raised a hand to her mouth. It took a moment for her to regain composure.

'When did it happen?'

'We believe sometime on Saturday evening.'

'But I saw him on Saturday.'

'So I understand. You and your agent, Mr Copeland, were on the same train back to Calcutta, is that right?'

'Yes.'

'And how did he seem to you on the train?'

She thought for a moment. 'No different from normal, I suppose. A tad subdued maybe, but I put that down to the early hour. To be honest, Sal and I were in a separate compartment, so I didn't much speak to him; just a few words when we boarded and then at the station in Calcutta, before he rushed off to find a taxi.'

'And was that the last time you saw him?'

'Alas yes. I spent the rest of the day in town with Sal and then caught up with some people I'd met the previous week. I was with them when I met you in that club later.'

'Maybe you could give me an insight into Mullick's state of mind while he was out here then. I understand he rather threw himself into the role of playing the good host to you.'

There was a momentary glint in Miss Morgan's eye; the slightest curl of the lips.

'It's true, he did afford me a certain degree of attention. But in terms of his state of mind, I don't know what to tell you.'

'Did he seem preoccupied at all? Did his behaviour change? Especially in the last few days here.'

Estelle Morgan bit her bottom lip. 'Well, now you come to mention it, he did seem rather ... distracted. I rather had the feeling it was a business matter. I assumed that's what took him back to the city.'

'He didn't tell you as much?'

A shrug of tanned shoulders. 'He just said it was an urgent matter and that he'd return in a few days. And now he's ...'

In her eyes, the first tears glistened. She tried to wipe them away with her fingers. Suren and I reached for our handkerchiefs in tandem, holding them out for her. She refused both, retrieved her own and dabbed at her eyes.

'I'm sorry, Captain. I don't mean to get emotional.'

'Not at all,' I said, perhaps a tad too vociferously, and stowed my handkerchief. 'You returned to Bishnupore yesterday, is that correct?'

'That's right. You'll remember Sal made me leave that charming club where I met you because he'd booked me on the early train.'

'But he didn't come back with you?'

'No,' she said. 'I came back with my maid. Sal had some contract business to take care of, something important sent over from Hollywood. The telephone lines out here are not the most reliable. From here, he said he'd be lucky to get through to Calcutta let alone California. He doesn't much care for India, or Indians for that matter.' She turned to Suren. 'No offence.'

'What did he think of Mullick?' I said.

The hint of a smile crossed her face and she did her best to hide it.

'Sal and JP didn't exactly get on. Sal didn't want me coming to India. He certainly didn't want me taking this part. He said it was a distraction; that my future lay in America.'

To be fair to Sal Copeland, I felt he might have a point.

'So what did persuade you to take the part?'

She gave a sigh. 'Maybe I'm just a romantic. I've always wanted to see India. My father was stationed here, and my mother, well, she had ties to the place too. And this country is so different.' She shot me a look that landed like a slap. 'You meet such interesting people out here. So when JP got in touch, I just didn't want to turn down the chance.'

'Have you seen much of the country?'

'Not really,' she said. 'Only Calcutta... and Bishnupore of course, but that doesn't really count. I was hoping to have time at the end to visit the Taj Mahal. I would like to see it in the moonlight. Tell me, Captain Wyndham, is it truly as romantic as everyone says?'

'I'm afraid I've never been,' I said, and wondered why that should be so. Almost seven years in India, and apart from Delhi, Bombay and a few out-of-the-way places, I'd singularly failed to see much of the country outside of Bengal.

'Well, maybe if you had the time, you might consider accompanying me?'

For a moment I was stunned into silence, my train of thought completely derailed. In my defence, I think most men in my position would have been similarly thrown off course. Beside me, Suren coughed.

Estelle Morgan's cheeks flushed. 'As long as you don't think I'm being too forward. I'd hate for you to feel uncomfortable. It's just that in my world a girl learns to be direct.'

'Not at all,' I said, pulling myself together. 'It would be my pleasure. But alas, with the investigation into Mr Mullick's death, I doubt I shall have the time.'

My response seemed to wrong-foot her as surely as her question had me, which in its way was gratifying. She recovered though, with aplomb.

'Well, in that case,' she smiled, 'you'll just have to solve the whole thing very quickly.' She checked the silver watch wrapped round her wrist. 'Now, is there anything else I can help you with? I'm afraid I'm rather tight for time. I need to go and pack. Mr Ghatak is organising transport for me to return to Calcutta. At least I hope he is.'

There was one question, but it was too direct and I doubted whether the answer to it would mean anything in terms of my inquiry.

Miss Morgan, I wanted to ask, *did J. P. Mullick ever proposition you?*

I decided against. Instead I accompanied her to the mouth of the tent. At the threshold, she turned.

'There's a party being held at some mansion in Calcutta tomorrow night. It'll be absolutely tedious and I'll know hardly anyone there, but now that we're no longer shooting out here, I suppose my agent will insist I attend. Would you consider accompanying me?'

I felt my stomach knot. 'I'm honoured,' I said. 'I'll try of course, but I can't make any promises.'

Estelle Morgan flashed another of her million-watt smiles. 'I'm taking that as a yes,' she said, and then she was gone.

I watched her as she went gliding across the grass like a silk scarf on a banister, the sari-clad maid a pace behind her.

'Sam?'

Suren's voice broke through the fog in my mind.

'Sam!'

'Yes?' I said, turning to him.

'I think she is trying to cloud your judgement.'

'Nonsense,' I said.

'How well do you really know Miss Morgan?'

I told him the truth. That I'd met her about forty hours earlier in the Idle Fox.

'So hardly at all, then?'

He looked at me witheringly, like a father disappointed at his child's stupidity.

'She knew the victim; she was with him a few hours before he was murdered; and now she is inviting you, the investigating officer, to take her to the Taj Mahal or at least a party?'

'You think she's hiding something?'

'Don't you?' he said. 'She was certainly rather forward with you.'

'She's an actress,' I said. 'As a species they're generally quite forward.'

'You have met many?'

'No,' I said, 'but that's not the point. And it takes more than a bat of the eyelids from a pretty girl to throw me off the scent.'

He didn't seem convinced.

'Really?'

'Of course! You know me. The job always comes first.'

'So you will not go to this party with her?'

'Certainly not,' I said. 'Well, not unless it's in the line of duty.'

TWENTY-THREE

Surendranath Banerjee

The next train back to Calcutta was scheduled for a quarter past six, and while I suggested a punctual return to the station, Sam insisted upon a detour via the local post office, a small, whitewashed building on the town's main thoroughfare.

Inside, a punkah swung gently upon the ceiling. Sam walked up and accosted the bespectacled clerk, pulling out his police identification card and placing it on the counter between them.

'I need some information about certain telegrams that were sent and received from here in the last few days.'

The man looked from Sam to the ID card and then back again.

'We are not at liberty to divulge the contents of telegrams, sir,' he said in a manner which may have been noble, although he may have simply been laying out his stall for the receipt of a bribe.

Sam short-circuited the process and placed two rupees on the counter, then, when the man seemed unmoved, added two more, at which point all four were quickly transferred to the gentleman's pocket.

'Right,' Sam said. 'I understand several telegrams arrived yesterday, addressed to a Mr Ronen Ghatak, and that he, in turn, would have sent at least one back.'

'That is correct,' the man said.

'You're certain?'

'Yesterday was Sunday. It is a quiet day. Not many telegrams sent or received. I remember Mr Ghatak.'

'How many telegrams did he send?'

The clerk thought for a moment. 'Just one. But he made several telephone calls.'

'Can you tell me the numbers he requested?'

The man shrugged. 'I did not keep a note. But they were placed to Calcutta. Same thing on the previous day and the one before.'

Sam looked to me, then back to the clerk.

'So Mr Ghatak came in here on Friday, Saturday and Sunday?'

'Yes. On Friday evening and on Saturday he seemed most anxious.'

'You didn't happen to overhear anything he might have been saying?'

The clerk hesitated and Sam reached once more for his wallet, but the man raised a hand to stop him. He pointed to a wooden cabin at the far end of the room. 'Telephone calls are made from inside. Impossible from here to make out what was said.'

Thanking him for his time, we turned and made for the exit.

The clerk called out from behind us. 'There is one more thing. He placed a telephone call this morning. I might recall a detail or two.'

Sam and I looked at each other, and Sam reached for his wallet.

'Would five rupees help jog your memory?'

He walked back and placed the note on the counter from where it instantly disappeared into the clerk's hand.

'He asked to be put through to the Great Eastern Hotel in Calcutta.'

'What do you make of that?' I asked as we exited.

Sam shoved his hands in his pockets.

'Hard to say. The call to the Great Eastern. Estelle Morgan's agent is staying there. It might have been to him. But then, it might have been to any number of others. As for the rest of the calls, Ghatak said he hadn't heard from Mullick since his departure on Friday, so unless he's lying, those calls were to someone else. The fact that they were made over the weekend suggests they weren't run-of-the-mill work matters. Anyway, there's no point speculating. The best thing to do is ask him.'

'You want to go back to the film set?' I asked. 'We shall miss the train and there are no more tonight. You can stay if you want to, but I cannot afford to lose another day. I must get back to finding Dolly.'

'We won't need to go back,' he said, gesturing at a passing car. I looked over. There, beside the driver, sat Ronen Ghatak, with the director Mitra and Dhiren Deb, the actor, in the rear.

'Where are they going?' I asked.

'Judging by *that*,' he said, as a second, luggage-laden car passed, 'I'd say the same place as us. It stands to reason, I suppose. There's no point in them staying any longer. Mullick junior has probably summoned the director back to Calcutta to find out just what the devil all the money his father's lavished on the project has bought him. Ghatak needs to get back to the office, and as for the actor, well he's a VIP.'

It was a fair assumption, though I had expected Mitra to remain with his troops for the retreat to Calcutta. *That*, it appeared, was not the director's style.

We walked the short distance to the station. There, Mitra, Deb and Ghatak had spilled from their car and were busy instructing a retinue of porters, each now laden with suitcases or with a trunk atop his turbaned head. The luggage, it became apparent, belonged to Mitra and Deb, for Ghatak fielded his own battered cases with two hands.

'Should we question him about the telephone calls?' I asked.

'Not here,' he said. 'We'll do it on the train, out of earshot of his friends.'

Night was falling, the heat of day replaced by the caress of an evening breeze. Crickets chirped and moths danced in the glow of station lamps. The platform was congested, and Ronen Ghatak and his compatriots, together with their retinue of porters, pushed their way down the platform. In the crush of people, the trunk atop one of the porter's heads slipped and crashed heavily to the ground, earning the poor man a vociferous and expletive-laden rebuke from Mitra. As we passed them, the actor Dhiren Deb saw me and nodded, but made no attempt to come over and talk. Indeed, thereafter the trio kept their distance from us, that awkward space that parties acquainted, but not *well* acquainted, tend to maintain when faced with such situations.

Any further thoughts I might have had on the matter were curtailed by the arrival of another group walking down the platform. This time there were three porters, two in red shirts with trunks held aloft and the third, probably a local man roped in to help for a few rupees, doing his best to juggle several smaller cases, one in each hand and another tucked awkwardly under an arm. Before them swept Estelle Morgan as though she were the Rani of Jhansi on the Promenade des Anglais, dressed in silk blouse and flowing trousers and a wide-brimmed hat that did as much to attract attention as it did to offer shade. A half-step behind came her maid, the grey-haired Indian woman I had seen earlier outside Mitra's tent. Now she carried a tapestried travelling bag which I assumed held those essentials either which Miss Morgan could not do without, or which would not fit within the portmanteaux that comprised her baggage train.

She aimed a polite word or two at Mitra and Deb, then continued along the platform to where Sam and I stood. 'Captain Wyndham. Mr Banerjee,' she beamed. 'We must stop meeting like this.'

Sam responded with a garbled sentence.

'I thought you were taking alternative transport back to Calcutta... I don't mean... Not that it isn't a pleasure to see you again.'

Poor chap. For an intelligent man, his faculties are too easily scrambled by the attentions of a beautiful woman. It is a failing common in men, but dangerous in a detective.

Miss Morgan placed a hand on his arm. 'That is kind of you to say, and yes, well, a car had been procured, but it seems the gods had other ideas. It broke down about a mile into the journey. Something about a sheared axle.'

I wondered if it had possibly collapsed under the weight of her luggage, but it is not the done thing to point such matters out to an English lady.

'The chauffeur-wallah said a replacement vehicle wouldn't be ready until this evening, by which time it would be too late to make the journey tonight. And so here we are,' she said with a glint in her eye, '*forced* into taking the train with you instead.'

'You have my sincere condolences,' Sam said. 'Rest assured, however – Suren here is a noted raconteur. He will no doubt keep you entertained with his many stories. He has recently returned from France and has tales of the goings-on in Paris and St Tropez.'

Estelle Morgan's face brightened. 'Is that true, Mr Banerjee? I do hope you'll share some of your stories.'

I coughed. 'I really don't –'

'You just try and stop him,' Sam interjected.

I tried to protest but my words were drowned out by the whistle of the approaching locomotive, shunting into the platform a leisurely seven minutes late, which, I supposed by the standards of the railway, was practically early.

The first-class carriages stopped conveniently close by and Sam and I made way for Estelle Morgan and her maid to board. I looked back and saw Mullick's erstwhile secretary Ghatak bid his adieus to Mitra and Deb and head down the platform towards second class. Beyond him, the usual scrum around the third-class carriages took hold as passengers battled for ingress. Estelle Morgan's maid, I imagined, after settling her employer into her first-class seat, would similarly make the journey down the train to find a place among the lower orders.

It did not take long to find an empty compartment. At the far end of the carriage, Mitra and Deb slid open the door to another one.

'So will you join us?' Sam asked Miss Morgan.

She looked along the corridor to the compartment into which the director and the actor were disappearing, appraising the situation before turning back to him.

'Yes, why not?'

To my surprise, the maid piped up, a look of consternation writ large on her wrinkled face.

'Memsahib? Maybe a separate compartment?'

Estelle Morgan smiled and patted her on the back. 'I think we can trust the Captain and Mr Banerjee, Madhu,' then turned to Sam. 'You must forgive her, Captain. She's been my maid simply forever and she's very protective. She thinks all men are out to take liberties.'

I marvelled at how an Indian woman had become maid to a girl from Tasmania. No doubt it had something to do with her father's time in India. Sam on the other hand seemed to find the situation rather amusing.

'She is quite right,' he said. 'A woman travelling alone can't be too careful.'

'Absolutely,' Miss Morgan replied. 'But what better protection could I ask for than from a detective of the Imperial Police?'

With a blast from a stationmaster's whistle, the train shunted to life. We settled in to our compartment, I closest to the window, with

Sam beside me and Estelle Morgan opposite. To my surprise, the maid too, after ensuring her employer's copious luggage was safely stowed in the baggage compartment, rejoined us and took a seat.

'I like to have Madhu close at hand,' Estelle Morgan explained. 'In case I should need anything.'

The train gathered momentum, shrugging off the cocoon of luminescence of the station and slipping into the darkness. In the distance, lights flickered like stars. I made myself comfortable and turned to see the maid staring at Sam with a look I struggled to divine but which, if I had to guess, I'd say was probably somewhere between hostility and disappointment.

I had seen other maids look at him in similar fashion. Annie Grant's maid, Anju, used to specialise in such looks too, reserving I thought, her most bilious glances for him. Ladies' maids as a species seemed to be rather protective of their charges in a way that gentlemen's butlers never were. Anju had often looked at Sam as though he was not good enough for her employer, and if there was an irony in an Indian maid feeling that an Englishman was not an appropriately refined suitor for her Anglo-Indian mistress, it was certainly lost on her. Or maybe that was simply the standard reaction of ladies' maids the world over. Had not Elise's maid acted the same way with me? But then in our case, there was the matter of skin colour to be considered. But why in the world should it be so? When one's skin is dark, one is almost conditioned to expect prejudice from the lighter races, and then we, many of us at any rate, begin to accept this blind prejudice as scientific fact, and when someone comes along, someone like Elise, who sees beyond mere colour, it comes as a shock. One sees these prejudices for what they are – the fears generated by a closed or uneducated mind. My own people suffered from the same evils. Why was it that so many refused to see beyond skin or caste when for others, like Elise, it came so naturally? What was it that drove the difference between the closed mind and the open one? Was it fear, or conditioning, or something else? Maybe fear and prejudice were the natural state of the world and that those with open minds were the exceptions, the anomalies? After all it was easy to submit to fear and prejudice. Had I not submitted to it myself? I had accepted it the minute I acceded to my father's order to end my relationship with Elise and to return home forthwith.

Estelle Morgan leaned forward. 'Were your investigations today productive, gentlemen?'

Sam rubbed at the back of his neck. 'They've been useful,' he said.

The actress arched a perfect eyebrow. 'So you've figured out who killed him?'

'No,' Sam said, 'but we may have a better idea of why he was killed.'

I supposed that much was true, even if I wouldn't have volunteered that information quite so readily. We knew more about the sort of man Mullick had been, one surprisingly different from how the world saw him. Not for the first time was I struck by the ease with which wealth allowed reality to be refashioned into whatever form a rich man might seek; how easy it was to whitewash a reputation through hard cash and shows of public piety.

The maid, Madhu, rose to her feet.

'Memsahib, I should see to your luggage. Make sure everything is in order. You will excuse me please?'

Her English was impressive. But then, she had been in the employ of an English family for many years. Her mistress gave a nod and she slid open the compartment door and stepped out into the corridor. Miss Morgan waited until the door had closed again before turning back to Sam.

'You don't think it has anything to do with the film, do you?'

Sam hesitated and Miss Morgan sensed his unease.

'I mean, there's no risk to us, is there? Madhu is very fragile.'

Sam shook his head. 'You don't need to worry, Miss Morgan. Rest assured, you and Madhu are perfectly safe.'

She smiled. 'Well, I'm going to hold you to that, Captain.' She turned to me. 'Mr Banerjee, what say you? Do you think I can entrust my safety to Captain Wyndham?'

'Oh, I'm sure,' I said. 'Though the captain is a very busy man, I am sure he will give you his full attention.'

I saw the irritation on Sam's face and it made me smile. It appeared to amuse Miss Morgan too.

'It seems Madhu and I are indeed fortunate to have you watching over us, Captain. I must say though, Mr Banerjee, you two make a rather odd couple: an Englishman and an Indian. How ever did you become friends?'

Something about the comment made me bristle. I looked to Sam. Maybe we were both asking ourselves the same question: *were we friends now, or merely fellow travellers, thrown together out of common purpose?* The thought induced melancholy. At one time we had indeed been close. I had saved his life and he had saved mine. When considered in that context, were not our present differences petty? Did they not stem from our own inflated sense of pride? I tried to put the matter from my mind.

'Such are the fates,' I said. 'Our acquaintance goes back to 1919, when the captain first arrived in Calcutta and I was a police sergeant. Captain Wyndham was charged with solving the murder of a British administrator, a Scotsman as I recall, and I assisted him with the investigation.'

Estelle Morgan's eyes sparkled. 'And did you solve the case?'

'Most surely,' I said, 'though it was not without its trials.'

'The biggest one being there was no shortage of people ready to murder a Scotsman,' Sam added.

'But you're not a policeman any more, Mr Banerjee?'

'That is correct.'

'So why are you involved with this case?'

I sought direction from Sam. He smiled and urged me to continue. Maybe he too was weighing up our squabbles against our historic friendship. I turned back to Miss Morgan.

'I suppose I was simply keen to see the temples at Bishnupore.'

We fell into silence and after a while I thought back to the note from Colonel Dawson. His name was enough to conjure fear into the hearts of those familiar with it; and for those millions who weren't, I did not know whether they were to be envied or pitied. For the man was a linchpin in their continued subjugation in their own land, and while ignorance may be bliss, it is only through knowledge that we change things.

There had been more to the note than I had imparted to Sam. In it Dawson intimated that he was privy to knowledge that might prove useful to me. Information regarding a relation of mine. It could only be Dolly.

Why had I not told Sam this? I am not certain. Maybe it was fear or maybe foresight, but I had held back. Dawson was not a man who dispensed favours freely. If he was offering me something, he would want his pound of flesh in return, and my fear was that his price would be exorbitant, something that I should refuse to pay, and who knows what compromises I would have to make with my conscience.

There was a knock and the door of our compartment slid open. An Anglo-Indian in the uniform of the railway company entered, asking to see our tickets. His check was perfunctory, and once happy there were no second- or third-class stowaways in with us, bade us good evening and stepped back into the corridor.

Sam rose from his seat.

'Excuse me, Miss Morgan,' he said and followed the man out before sliding the door closed.

The actress looked from the door to me.

'How very strange,' she said. 'Is the captain in the habit of running off like that?'

'Oh, most definitely,' I said. 'He probably has some questions for the man,' and, I thought, after that he will have some for Mr Ronen Ghatak.

TWENTY-FOUR

Sam Wyndham

It is a universal truth that all train conductors have a well-developed sense of their own importance. Maybe it is the uniform, or the cap, or the heavy, metal ticket clipper which they wield like a transportational sword of Damocles over the heads and fate of poor passengers. Whatever it is, I've never found it easy dealing with them. Still, once you got over the prickly starts, dealing with them often proved fruitful. After all, on a train, they're basically God. They see all and hear all that happens within their domain.

I closed the compartment door behind me and called out to the man, and he turned as I pulled my warrant card from my jacket pocket. 'Imperial Police,' I said. 'I'd like to ask you a few questions.'

The man raised an eyebrow.

'Were you the conductor on this train three days ago?'

He thought for a moment. 'The Friday? Possibly.'

'Is that a yes?'

'I suppose it is.'

'Good,' I said, walking him to the end of the carriage. 'There were two men who boarded the train at Bishnupore that night, first-class passengers both of them. One was a Bengali, well dressed no doubt.' I went on to describe Mullick, not the way he'd looked on the riverbank or the mortuary, but in better days, from photographs of him I'd seen at his abode. 'Do you remember seeing him?'

The man shrugged. 'Again, it's possible.'

It wasn't the most helpful of responses, but then I doubt ticket conductors are paid to be helpful.

'The other was a sahib, an American gentleman.' I described Sal Copeland as best as I could remember him from the other night in the Idle Fox: dark hair, about six foot tall and a face as sour as milk left out in the Calcutta sun for a day. 'He would have been travelling with the young lady in my compartment back there. Do you remember him?'

The man grinned. 'I remember the lady. And yes, there was a man travelling with her.'

'Were all three travelling together? In the same compartment?'

He shook his head. 'I don't think so. The woman and the American were alone.'

'Did you see the American talk to anyone else? Someone matching the description of the Bengali?'

He thought for a moment. 'Now that you come to mention it, I did see him with someone. On one occasion when I was passing through the carriage, I saw him in a different compartment with an Indian. They didn't seem to be getting on. Having a rather heated discussion they were. You could hear it from the corridor. To be fair though, it was the American gentleman who was doing most of the shouting. Very shocking manners for a sahib.'

'Did they get off the train together?'

He shrugged. 'I don't know. I'm certain that at Howrah the American and the young lady left together.'

I thanked him, and as he walked off, I lit a cigarette. I still had my questions for Ghatak about his telephone calls to Calcutta, but I needed to order my thoughts first. Sal Copeland had been arguing with an Indian gentleman. It stood to reason that the Indian would have been J. P. Mullick. The question was what had they been arguing about? Money? Or something more sinister?

Maybe Estelle Morgan knew? And if she did, would she tell me? Either way, I'd make sure to get the answer from her agent back in Calcutta.

I finished the cigarette, flicked the butt out of the open window. Behind me the compartment door slid open and I turned to see Estelle Morgan standing there, a quizzical look on her beautiful face.

'Everything is all right I hope?'

'Fine,' I told her. 'I just needed to check a few things with the conductor.' I considered holding back what I'd learned, but my need for answers outweighed thoughts of caution. 'He mentioned that on the train a few days ago, he saw your agent having a heated conversation with a man who looked like J. P. Mullick. Do you know what that was about?'

Tentatively, she raised a hand to her mouth.

'Sal has a tendency to pick fights wherever he goes. It's simply his nature. And are you certain it was Mullick that Sal was speaking to?'

'Quite certain.'

'Well, whatever it was, he didn't mention it to me.'

She came and joined me by the window, her shoulder brushing against mine. We fell into silence and she looked out into the night, at a world contracted to mere flickers of light in the darkness. The train rocked and clacked its way east.

'I could do with a drink,' she said. 'Do you think there's a bar on this train?'

I could have done with a drink myself, a single malt would have been perfect, but the chances of finding such a thing on an Eastern Railways train were about the same as finding an Irishman sober on his birthday.

'I might be able to track down some tea,' I said. 'Would you care for a cup?'

'Isn't there a little chap who comes round and takes your order?'

'It's certainly possible,' I said, 'but I wouldn't bank on it. We might die of thirst in the meantime.'

'In that case,' she said, taking my arm, 'I should very much like to come and help you track it down.'

With the train rocking gently, we made our way along the corridor. There would probably not be a buffet car, not on a service such as this. More likely there would be a galley kitchen where tea and rudimentary meals would be prepared; and while those dishes might lack finesse and, in many cases, flavour, they did have one redeeming quality: the power to unite. Indeed the Indian Railways omelette sandwich, prepared with onions and green chillies, in primitive conditions and at fifty miles an hour, was probably as close to a national institution as we'd managed to forge in this country, bridging the divide between races, regions, religions and culinary prejudices. There was a universality to that omelette, an ability to cross boundaries. It was like tea, or cricket, only better, because it filled a hole in your stomach.

I considered sharing the thought with Miss Morgan, but I doubted she'd appreciate the insight, especially as she'd probably never been subjected to an omelette sandwich before.

The galley was two carriages further along and acted as a border between first and second class. The aroma of hot oil and spices filled the air. Behind the counter stood an Anglo-Indian, boiling in a regulation railway shirt, tie and jacket. Ignoring me, he directed his attention and a smile towards Estelle, and to be fair, I didn't blame him.

'What may I prepare for you, madam?'

'Tea?' Estelle turned to me for confirmation. 'For two.'

'And anything to eat?'

Estelle Morgan stared at the board propped up on the counter, a meagre list of dishes marked upon it in chalk.

'I must warn you,' I said, 'the food's edible but not exactly cordon bleu. And I can't vouch for the hygiene.'

'The railway cutlet,' she said, with a certainty that surprised me.

'You know what it is?' I asked.

'Vegetables mainly. Is that right?'

'Absolutely,' I said. 'Carrots, beans, peas, and a few other odds and sods probably, all covered in crumb and fried.'

'Beetroot too,' she said. 'In the odds and sods.'

I looked at her. 'You've tried one?'

'Madhu likes them,' she said. 'She's made some for me. I might as well try the real thing.'

'Fine,' I said. 'Let's take our lives in our hands.'

I turned back to the attendant.

'Two cutlets.'

He gave a nod and disappeared behind the hatch. I felt Estelle Morgan's eyes upon me.

'What?' I asked.

'I'm wondering how a man like you ends up in India.'

'A man like me?'

'You don't seem to be particularly enamoured of the place.'

'I've no issue with the place,' I said. 'It's the people I object to. And before you say anything, I mean the British as well as Indians. My problem is I dislike the British back home even more.'

'Is that why you left?'

The directness of the question took me by surprise. One does not expect such philosophical queries while awaiting the delivery of railway cutlets. Nevertheless, I found myself answering her with candour.

'The England I returned to after the war wasn't the one I'd left three years before. Actually, that's not the whole of it. I wasn't the same man as the one who'd gone off to war, and then …' I was about to tell her of my wife, Sarah. Of her passing, but stopped. Some things were sacred.

'And then?'

'And then, I got the chance to come here.'

A scream pierced the air. Another followed. Coming from the far end of the carriage.

Estelle looked to me. 'Is that –' She didn't finish. I was already running. The train juddered then screeched to a halt. Momentum threw me forward and I hit the floor hard, the metal plating jarring my wrists. Estelle Morgan was more fortunate, grabbing the handrail just in time. I got to my feet and headed once more down the carriage. Ahead, the connecting door opened and in staggered Madhu. She saw me and stopped dead, then noticed her mistress and rushed forward. I held out my arms and caught her.

There was blood on her sari.

'What's happened?'

'It is Mr ...'

'Who?'

She pointed behind her, towards the connecting door. 'He's through there,' and then she burst into tears.

I moved past her into the next carriage. A crowd had gathered, the conductor among them, his face ashen, remonstrating with a couple of passengers.

The conductor looked over, his expression grave.

'What's happened?' I asked.

'See for yourself.'

He moved aside and gestured towards the carriage's WC. I pulled open the door. Ronen Ghatak, J. P. Mullick's secretary, sat slumped on the floor, mouth open, eyes staring glassily ahead, a bloody wound at his neck, the life drained from him. A look of surprise was frozen on his face as though he couldn't believe someone had had the audacity to kill him.

I turned to the conductor. 'Get these people out of here.'

Estelle Morgan pushed her way through.

'Please tell Suren to get over here,' I said.

I checked his wrist. No pulse. Body still warm. I searched his pockets and retrieved his wallet. Twenty rupees nestled within its folds. Whoever had robbed Ghatak of his life had left his money.

Not robbery. A targeted attack, then. And afterwards, someone had pulled the emergency cord and stopped the train.

How long ago had that been? No more than three or four minutes now. Enough time to get off the train and make a run for it, but not enough to get very far. I needed to move, fast.

'Do you know who pulled the communication cord?' I asked the conductor.

He gave a shrug. 'No. But I can tell you it was pulled in this compartment.' He pointed down the corridor to a cord that hung limply from the ceiling.

'How many men do you have on this train?'

'Eight – me, the driver, the engine crew and the galley boys.'

'I'm putting you in charge,' I said. 'Get word to all of them. Seal the train. Make sure no one gets off.'

I made for the nearest exit and found Suren coming the other way.

'Sam? What's happened?'

'Ghatak,' I said. 'He's dead. Stabbed in the neck.'

He blinked. 'What?'

'Come on,' I said. 'I need your help.'

At the far end of the carriage, I opened the door and peered out into the night. 'Check the other side,' I told Suren, then jumped down onto the tracks.

In the darkness, I walked towards the rear, past the length of the train, listening for any sound amid the undergrowth, searching for any sign of movement.

The track sat atop a ridge, the seething, living jungle about ten feet distant. I scrambled down the bank and made for it, stopping only at the tree line. From it came the crick of cicadas and the croak of bullfrogs and the howls of bigger animals. And then, I thought, came something else. The distant snap of a twig underfoot. Maybe it was real, or maybe I had imagined it. Maybe it had been nothing at all, just a whisper beyond the tree line. Then came a rustling, and the pad of something in the undergrowth. Beast or man? I couldn't say. I was unarmed, my Webley warming its holster back in Premchand Boral. I made my choice, and stepped into the void, the jungle reacting around me with whoops and warning cries. I kept on, further into the black, straining to see and hear, trying to block out the sounds of the jungle, searching out a telltale sound that might be man-made.

To my right, a click. I swivelled. A noise above my head, then a screech, blood-curdling, inhuman, and the rustle of leaves. I stepped back.

Something flew over my head. A knife? An owl?

Behind me another noise. Ragged breathing. I turned, fast.

Again came that inhuman howl. I stepped towards it and saw movement. Fleeting. Grey against black, and then nothing. I gave chase, made ten steps and caught my foot on the root of something. The world turned upside down and then I was on the jungle floor, creatures crawling on my skin. I brushed them off, righted myself, got to my feet. From somewhere came a laugh. It might have been human or monkey or jackal. I spun round and lost all track of my bearings, stumbling a few steps first one way and then another, searching, straining for any sign of the train lights but finding nothing in any direction save the black of night and the hiss of the jungle.

I called out into the void. 'Hello!'

'Sam!'

Suren's voice. Distant. A world away. Thank God. I uttered a silent prayer. I called out again.

'Suren!'

'Sam. Where are you?'

'Here!'

I followed the sound of his voice, slowly backtracking till I reached the tree line. Suren stood there impassively.

'What are you doing in the jungle? It is dangerous to go wandering off.'

'I thought I heard something,' I said. 'Someone was out here.'

He looked at me. 'You saw them?'

'I heard them. I heard something at any rate.'

'You are certain? No one in their right mind would try to escape into the jungle at night,' he said. 'These places are haunted. All manner of creatures which feed on human flesh.'

'Nonsense,' I said, as a shiver passed through me. 'Someone was out here. I know it.'

Suren mulled this over. 'Even if you are correct, there is little chance of us finding him now. Come, we best head back to the train.'

Ahead the lights of the carriages illuminated the darkness, the locomotive hissing smoke.

'We should continue to Calcutta,' he said. 'There is a chance our killer is still on the train. We can check for suspects on the way.'

I supposed he was right. It was dark and we were in the middle of nowhere. The thought of running blindly through the jungle with its bandits and snakes and man-eating tigers might not be the best of ideas.

Maybe, as Suren said, the killer had pulled the cord as a diversion. Maybe he was still on board.

'Fine,' I said. 'I'll inform the conductor. You make sure the scene of the crime is secured and that no one tampers with Ghatak's body.

After that, we check the train for suspects, anyone looking suspicious; anyone with blood on their clothes.'

He gave a mirthless laugh.

'What?'

'Am I being paid for this?'

'You rejoin the force,' I said, 'and I'll backdate the cheque myself.'

TWENTY-FIVE

Sam Wyndham

The train shuddered, coming to life, building up steam, picking up speed. I left Suren to go through the third-class carriages with the train conductor.

Madhu was in shock, by Estelle Morgan's estimation at least, and not in any state to answer questions. I gave her half an hour's grace and commenced the search of the first- and second-class carriages, checking faces, looking for traces of blood, all of which proved fruitless.

I turned to questioning those who'd known Ghatak, notably the director, Mitra, and the actor, Deb, but neither had left their first-class compartment since boarding the train, a fact vouchsafed by an elderly couple with whom they shared it. Both men seemed genuinely shocked at the news of Ghatak's fate, with Mitra in particular looking like he might vomit.

'What if all of this is linked to the film? What if someone is coming after us next?'

Deb, though, was more sanguine. He lit a cigarette.

'No one is coming for us. If this was about the film, they'd hardly have gone after a mere secretary who had nothing to do with it. No one kills for art, only for money or love. A terrible state of affairs, but there you have it. And with Ghatak's murder, coming so soon after Mullick-da's, it would suggest that the motive is most likely not love but money.'

I couldn't fault the actor's logic. He might even have made a half-decent detective if he'd had the inclination. I told him as much, and he took that as licence to continue his theorising.

'This must be related to some business dealing of Mullick's. A disagreement over contracts, possibly. Maybe someone has signed a contract with him, had second thoughts and then tried to back out. Maybe they met Mullick and asked him to rip up the contract and when he refused they killed him? Yet the contract would still exist. Maybe they went after Ghatak in the hope of finding the papers and destroying them.'

As theories went, it was possible. Yet Deb was possibly overestimating one thing: Ghatak's loyalty to his fallen boss. In my experience, a hard-up secretary like Ghatak was unlikely to give up his life for a boss who was now dead and whose very employment was now under question. More likely he'd have struck a deal; handed over any such contract for a sum of money. Still, it was worth following up. I made a note to check Ghatak's luggage, just in case it had been stolen or tampered with.

I left them to their theories and returned to my own compartment where Estelle Morgan was seated, her maid's hand held between her own and with a cup of tea resting beside her.

I sat down opposite them.

'Tell me what happened, Madhu.'

The maid sniffed, her expression unreadable.

'I do not know... that is to say... I am not certain... exactly.'

'Just tell me what you remember,' I said.

She took a breath and nodded. 'I was returning from the baggage car where I had checked upon memsahib's luggage. I was passing through a second-class carriage. The door to the latrine was open. I made to close it, if only to ward off the smell, and then I saw him.

Only his leg at first, but then ...' She stifled a sob. 'In the darkness, I saw a body, lying there on the floor of the latrine. I thought maybe someone had fainted. I went to check, to see if they were all right.' Estelle Morgan passed her a handkerchief. 'As I knelt down, I saw it was Mr Ghatak. I went to revive him and then I noticed the blood ... on my hands ... on my sari ...'

She broke into tears. Estelle Morgan placed a hand on her arm and made the sort of soothing noises that women do. She looked to me, her expression disapproving; harsher than I'd seen before.

'I think that's enough, Captain. Don't you?'

'I'm afraid not,' I said. 'A man is dead after all and your maid is the one who found the body.'

She accepted the fact, though with the resentful air of someone who doubts its veracity and who reserves the right to challenge it later. I turned back to the maid.

'Please, continue.'

'There is little more that I can remember. I saw the blood and panicked. Then I ran for help.'

'What about beforehand? Did you see anything untoward prior to coming across Ghatak's body?'

The question seemed to throw her.

'Untoward?'

'Anything, or anyone, unusual,' I said.

'There was one thing. As I was walking through the carriages, a man came running in the other direction, and pushed me out of the way with his shoulder. By the time I made to remonstrate, he was already approaching the far end of the carriage. I shouted after him, asked him didn't he have any respect for old women, but he just carried on.'

'And this man was Indian?'

'Of course. A sahib would never have done such a thing.'

Well, that was nonsense. Quite a few sahibs I knew would

have no hesitation in knocking a native maid to the ground if circumstances dictated, or if they simply felt like it. And if the man had been white, I doubted Madhu would have plucked up the nerve to shout after him. Such was the way of things in this fine country.

'Can you describe him?'

She let out a sigh. 'It is hard to recall. It happened very fast. He was tall. Not as tall as you, but tall for an Indian.'

She said the last word with such disdain that I wondered for a moment that in spending so much time with her British mistress, if she had forgotten that she herself was actually Indian.

'As for what he was wearing ... shirt, pant. I can't recall much else.'

'Would you recognise him if you saw him again?'

She shrugged. 'I do not know.'

'Right,' I said. 'I'm going to need you to accompany me on a tour of the train.'

Estelle Morgan got to her feet. 'Captain Wyndham, I really must protest. Madhu has just been through a terrible ordeal. She needs to rest, and your man has no doubt left the train already when it was standing idle.'

'That may be so,' I said, 'but there's a chance he's still on board and I cannot discount that possibility. Now please, Miss Morgan, let me do my job.'

Once more, she relented, and once more, it was resentfully. I derived no pleasure from the situation, indeed, quite the opposite. I told myself that I should not judge her harshly for her intervention. That she was willing to consider the feelings and the well-being of a native maidservant was admirable. How many Calcutta memsahibs would have done so?

With Madhu a step behind, I walked out of the compartment.

*

To add insult to injury, the effort proved fruitless. Whoever Madhu may have seen, it did not appear that they were on the train any longer, at least not as far as she could tell.

She stopped a few times as we progressed from carriage to carriage and stared hard at a few individuals. Men, all of them, wearing white suits and dark trousers, and all superficially similar – dark hair, medium height, but nothing that singled them out as our killer, certainly there was no blood on any of them.

I returned her to our compartment, then stood in the corridor outside with Suren and a cigarette.

'You went through Ghatak's luggage?'

He gave a nod. 'As far as I can tell, it has not been tampered with. Certainly the passengers that were seated with him attested that no one had approached his bags. But it is hard to be certain without knowing what to look for. In any case, I have secured them in our compartment.'

The train shuddered as it passed over a set of points.

'Did they say anything about Ghatak's demeanour, or what took him from the compartment?'

'Only that he did not utter a word. One of the passengers said he looked nervous, that he kept kneading his hands together, nothing else. And then he simply got up, asked the fellow in the seat beside him to watch his bags and left. The chap assumed he was going to the latrine.'

'Did he open his luggage at all?'

'Not according to the others there.'

'None of it makes any sense,' I said. 'Why kill the secretary of a dead man? And why here? Why on this train?'

Suren exhaled cigarette smoke. 'I suppose it is possible the killer was hoping to get to Ghatak's bags but, with Madhu finding the body so quickly, never got the chance. Maybe the answer still lies in there somewhere?'

'Maybe,' I said. 'How much longer till we reach Calcutta?'

'Still an hour at least, according to the guard,' he said. 'And no sign of our murderer. I trust the authorities will be waiting for us at Howrah station.'

I gave him a nod. I'd ordered the driver to stop at the next station along the line. From there I'd sent a message via the telegraph to both police headquarters at Lal Bazar and the stationmaster's office at Howrah informing them of the situation and requesting a welcoming party of officers.

'And when we get there, what are you going to tell them?'

'I'll give them the facts. What else can I do? Someone attacked and murdered J. P. Mullick's secretary, then most likely escaped into the jungle while the train was stopped.'

Suren dropped the butt of his cigarette on the floor and ground it under the sole of his shoe. He shuffled uneasily beside me.

'What?' I asked.

'The killer running off into the jungle. It would be a desperate act. Probably foolhardy.'

'You're not going to start on about ghosts again, are you? For an educated man, you really can be ridiculously superstitious.'

'I heard one,' he said. 'Out there, when I was looking for you. There are many kinds of spirits which inhabit the jungles and the forests. Most of them are evil.'

'You heard an animal, not a ghost.'

'It did not sound like an animal. Besides, certain ghosts take the form of animals. Penchapechi take the form of owls. They follow travellers in the forests until they are alone and then strike, killing their victims and drinking their blood. And Begho Bhoot, the ghosts of men killed by tigers. They are said to roar like the tigers that killed them. Or Kanabhulo, like your sirens in Greek mythology. They target lone travellers in remote places, hypnotising and then devouring them.'

'For the last time, it wasn't a ghost.'

'Either way, it is a foolish man who ventures into unknown jungle in the dark.'

'What are you saying?'

'I am saying, if the murderer was, as Madhu said, an Indian, I doubt he would have run off into the jungle. I'm saying maybe the cord was pulled as a diversion. I'm saying maybe the killer *is* still on the train and Madhu in there simply failed to recognise him, or . . .'

'Or?'

'No one else saw this man running through the train. Not the guard, not any other passengers. We only have her word for it.'

'So Madhu killed Ghatak?'

He shook his head.

'I'm simply stating that it is a possibility.'

'What reason could she possibly have?'

'I don't know. What reason could anyone have for killing him?'

The lights of civilisation pierced the dark, solitary orbs at first, flickering in the wilderness, then more: twos and threes and then tens. In our compartment, Ghatak's bags now sat on the shelf above my head. I kept one eye on Madhu who'd remained mute from the moment we'd entered while Estelle Morgan continued her ministrations. I admit I was surprised and impressed by Miss Morgan. I had not expected the milk of human kindness to flow through her so readily. Here she was, an international film star, tending to an old Indian maid from some village somewhere, and while it hardly restored my faith in mankind, it did at least rekindle hope in it.

'Miss Morgan,' I said, 'we may need to question Madhu again. You, of course, are free to leave town, should you wish to. However, I'm afraid Madhu will have to remain in Calcutta at least for a few more days.'

The maid looked to her mistress. There was fear in her eyes.

Estelle Morgan took her hand in her own, gave a squeeze and offered the woman a few words of comfort. Then she turned to me.

'In that case, Captain, I shall just have to remain in Calcutta until you are done with Madhu. We'll be at the Great Eastern Hotel, just so you know where to find us.'

TWENTY-SIX

Surendranath Banerjee

The police were waiting at Howrah. A line of constables and an English officer, sealing the platform like overzealous ticket inspectors.

'What are they going to do?' I asked Sam. 'Arrest every Indian male on the train and question them till one confesses?'

It sounded ludicrous, but in British India, it was always an option.

'No,' he said, 'but their presence might help unnerve someone. We'll get Madhu to have another look over the men as they disembark. Maybe it'll jog her memory.'

'Maybe,' I said, 'that's if she was telling the truth in the first place.'

Sam sighed. 'I don't think she killed him. You saw her, she was in shock. And what motive could she have? Or do you think she killed Mullick too? Because they have to be linked.'

I considered telling him that Madhu would have been in Calcutta too when Mullick had been murdered, assuming she'd come back with Miss Morgan and her agent, but the whole thing felt like an uphill struggle. Sam was right. Why would the maid kill either of them, and did she even have the strength to do so?

I hoped the police would handle the situation delicately. Tempers were already frayed. The last thing we needed was heavy-handed police inflaming an already tense situation.

'What now, then?' I asked.

'I'll wait here and see how Madhu gets on. If she fingers anyone, I'll deal with them. Otherwise I'll accompany her and Miss Morgan to the Great Eastern. There's no need for you to hang around.'

That was fortunate, for I had no intention of waiting in the first place.

'What about Ghatak's luggage?' I said. 'Do you want me to take a look at the papers?'

I am not certain why I offered. Maybe Ghatak's murder had affected me on some personal level. After all, while Mullick had been Sam's case, Ghatak's murder had been proximate. It seemed like a personal slight. I felt compelled to help find his killer.

He gave me a smile.

'That would be most kind. And tomorrow, let's meet early. Come to the flat for nine? We need to give some thought to Dolly.'

And so I left him there, chaperoning Miss Estelle Morgan and her maid while the constables double-checked the passengers for anyone the latter might find suspicious. The station concourse was still busy, despite the hour, and I eased my way past travellers, railway workers and hawkers, out into the night air. The lights of the city on the far bank reflected off the waters of the river; myriad vessels sat moored like sleeping dragons. I walked down stone steps worn smooth by generations of feet, past dark corners where itinerant men and even families slept, bedded down for the night under the flimsiest of cover. The tonga rank was a few minutes' walk away, at the distant end of the courtyard. I walked towards it, lighting a cigarette as I went. Calcutta is a city that lives in the open, not behind doors like London or Berlin. Its streets and squares and public spaces are thronged with life while other places slumber. Here, outside the station, the area hummed with tea-stall *adda* and cottage industry. Bodies brushed past, faces coming into focus in the lamplight, then receding just as fast, to be replaced by yet others. It was then, out of the corner of my eye, that I saw her. Through gaps in the crowd, a young woman, standing near the rank, a silhouette in a sari. As I drew closer, she took form. She looked, I thought, familiar. Maybe I imagined it. Maybe I was simply exhausted, seeing what I wanted to see; for the woman bore a stark resemblance to Dolly.

I told myself it could not be her. Not here. Not in Howrah in the dead of night. It made no sense.

Ghatak's cases in hand, I picked up my pace. For a split second she turned in my direction, and then the crowds closed between us.

Was it her?

'Dolly!' I shouted.

I pushed my way through the crowd, but she was gone. Frantically I scanned the scene: towards the station and then the full 360 degrees.

There! A woman heading down the steps, towards the warehouses and the ghats, and then once more she was gone, disappearing into the darkness. I gave chase, down the steps, past the *gullees* and the dogs and the detritus of the day's commerce. I fought past bodies, frantically searching doorways and alleyways, then stopped. There was no point continuing. Whoever the woman had been, she was gone, disappeared into the night.

I cut my losses and made once more for the tonga rank.

The gates to my father's house were barred and locked to the world, and I had to shout several times before Bhulo-da, our old durwan, came running, toothless grin upon his face, to open them.

'*Shob thīk aché, chhor-da?*'

'All is fine,' I told him, and headed inside, through the courtyard, and up to my room.

I turned on the lamp and closed the door behind me and placed

Ghatak's cases on my desk. I pictured him, lying dead in the WC cubicle on the train. Murdered under our very noses.

And I thought of Dolly. Why had someone ransacked her studio? Had it really been her I'd seen in Howrah tonight? What did it all mean? From my pocket I took Dawson's note. It was too late to telephone the number now. I would, I resolved, call it first thing in the morning.

I removed my jacket, then lay down on the bed and tried to put her out of my head.

In time, my thoughts turned to my own future.

I had spent the last few years wandering Europe, meeting émigré Indians and sympathetic foreigners, and discovering the truth: that while there were many warm words expended by our hosts, when it came to practical support for the cause, there would be precious little. The more I learned, the clearer it became. If our freedom was to be won, it would be purchased here, on our soil; not through force of arms or foreign influence but through our own sweat and blood and suffering. It would, as Mr Gandhi had stated, be achieved by convincing our oppressors of the morality of our case and the immorality of their own, so that in the end they would leave of their own accord. There were many who considered such an outcome mere fantasy. Never in human history had a people's freedom been secured in such a way. After all, one did not make friends with one's oppressor. One fought him, and slayed him, and inflicted defeats upon him until he no longer had stomach for the fight. *Liberty or death*. Was that not the truth? Freedom had always required violence.

Yet what if Mr Gandhi were right? What if it *was* possible to achieve it through peaceful means? What if we could lift a people, hundreds of millions of men and women and children, from subjugation without the need for violence? Would that not be something? Would it not be a beacon, not just for Indians and Britishers, but for all mankind? That is what Mr Gandhi preached and that was also the conclusion to which my recent sojourn had led me.

And why did I believe it was possible? Partly because of the very nature of our oppressors themselves. It is a funny thing, but three years in Europe had, surprisingly, led me to a relative appreciation of the British. For all their faults, they are a people governed by rules, their own rules of course, but rules nonetheless. And while there are other nations who espouse rules – the Germans definitely; the Japanese also, at least so I have heard – what separates the British from these other peoples, I think, is the willingness to reassess. Where a rule is wrong, a German may continue to follow it because rules and laws are there to be obeyed. The British though are different. If a law is absurd or immoral, the British will decide it is stupid and most likely break it. It is what they call *common sense*. From what I have seen, it is probably easier to convince an Englishman that he is wrong than it is to convince a Frenchman or a German of the same thing. That does not mean it is easy. Most of the time it takes a herculean effort to show them the error of their ways, but they do, generally, get there in the end.

Why are they different from the continental Europeans? Maybe it is their splendid isolation, or maybe it is because of their time with us? Maybe these last few centuries that they have been exposed to Indians has tempered them in a way that the other Europeans have not. Maybe of all the subjugated peoples and all the colonisers, the only two who *can* participate in a non-violent struggle for freedom at this time are we Indians and our friends the British.

Whatever the reason, I was certain that our freedom lay down the path of non-violence, and that my life, henceforth, should be dedicated to the struggle.

Day 4

Tuesday

TWENTY-SEVEN

Surendranath Banerjee

I slept fitfully, my dreams plagued by visions of Ghatak's lifeless body, the howls of ghosts in the jungle and of a woman running through the backstreets of Howrah. By five in the morning, I had given up. Instead I rose to the chorus of birds and the Mohammedan call to prayer.

Beneath the window, on my desk, sat Ghatak's luggage – his suitcase and briefcase. If I was to be cursed by lack of sleep, I might as well do something useful. Slowly I rose from the bed, walked over to the desk and sat down.

I reached for the briefcase. Black leather, frayed and scuffed in places, held shut by a two-paisa lock that was more for show than security. I pressed down on the clasp and the lock clicked open.

Inside were several bundles, each held together with rubber bands or string tags. In addition there were two fat folders of manilla-coloured card. I lifted the whole lot out and placed it on the desk and took a cursory look at the folders. The first contained several documents: title deeds by the look of them, embossed and with the stamp of the king emperor. The other contained a variety of things: scraps of paper with scribbled notes; a ledger with its pages divided into seven columns; chequebooks issued by the Imperial Bank of India, some hollowed out to their stubs, others still fat with blank foils.

I put them to one side and turned to the bundles of papers, removing the band that held together the papers of the first pack. It was a legal contract of sorts, an agreement for the establishment of a school for the arts somewhere near Darjeeling. The Tagore family had founded something similar, a university in Bholpore. Did Mullick wish to rival the Tagores? If so, it was a lofty ambition that now would probably never see fruition.

I studied the contract, reading it through, carefully at first, then more casually as it delved into issues of land and construction which proved too dry to follow closely. Twenty minutes later, I turned the final page and sat back. I was no more the wiser as to why Mullick or Ghatak might have been murdered. There were still several bundles to go. I longed for a cup of coffee to sustain me, but the maidservants and the cook would not prepare breakfast for at least another hour and I had no idea how to go about finding its constituents (coffee, milk, sugar) and the utensils, let alone brewing a pot in this house. Strange that in Paris and Berlin, in the smallest of garrets and bedsits, I could make a cup of coffee, but doing so in my own father's house was beyond me. Yet such is the way of things in this country. I recalled making coffee for Elise in my frozen room on the Rue Saint-Sulpice, she, all but hidden, tucked under the blankets up to her nose, surfacing only when I handed her a cup.

A hollowness engulfed me. An emptiness in my soul, to be filled with a lifetime of guilt and regret. I could not go on like this. How long would it take for the pain to ebb? How long till I could forget? I thought of Sam, seemingly destined to spend his days in self-sabotage, as though it might constitute penance for his dead wife. Was my fate to be similar? Was I destined to spend my life grieving for a love cut short, unable or unwilling to find happiness elsewhere? But now was not the time for such self-pity. Two men were dead and I had Ghatak's papers to examine.

I ploughed on, picking up the second bundle of papers. This

batch appeared to relate to the film being shot in Bishnupore. The document was a costing for the film: spending plans covering everything from set design and transport, to the costs of film crew and, interestingly, the amounts being paid to the actors and actresses. Dhiren Deb, as he had already intimated to me, was not being paid a particularly handsome amount. The real surprise though was Estelle Morgan. While Deb had been correct, and her remuneration was higher than his own, it was by no means as high as I had anticipated, certainly not what I imagined an actress on her way to Hollywood might expect to earn. It was not clear why her agent had been against her taking the part, and while she had explained to Sam that she had done so out of a desire to see India, it appeared that desire flew in the face of financial acuity.

I read the document closely, but other than Estelle Morgan's fee, I could find nothing else of interest, though in fairness I had no idea what I should be looking for.

The other bundles were just more of the same. Contracts and legal documents, costings and plans, some annotated in red ink, in an expansive hand which I took to be Mullick's, and others in blue ink or pencil, in a smaller, more spidery style, which I imagined had been the secretary's.

That left only the two manilla folders. I reopened the one with the land deeds. They related to property somewhere in the east of the province, a sizeable plot of two thousand *katthas*: about sixty acres. It was possible that it might be relevant to the murders, but then again, so, potentially, could any of Mullick's business dealings. I made a note of the names mentioned, a Mr Hemchandra Bose and a Mr Aziz Ul-Haq, both had signed the document with their thumbprints, and moved on to the final folder.

I opened it and tipped the contents onto the desk – the scraps of paper, the seven-columned ledger and the chequebooks. The scraps I found to be receipts, everything from taxi fares to Mullick's tailor's

The Burning Grounds

bills. I moved on to the ledger, running my finger down columns of expenses, checking the details of suppliers and goods purchased.

It was halfway down the second page that I saw it.

My blood froze.

One thousand rupees. Made out to the Golden Bengal Ladies Photographic Studio. My heart pounded in my chest. Dolly's studio. But why would Mullick be paying Dolly? It had to be a mistake. I needed to be sure. The payment was dated three weeks earlier. With sweat prickling at my collar, I picked up the chequebooks, running through the stubs until I found the one I was looking for. There, in Ghatak's spidery handwriting, were the same words: *Rs 1,000 – Golden Bengal Ladies Photographic Studio.*

There was no doubt now. Mullick, or at least his secretary Ghatak, had known Dolly. They had paid her a thousand rupees – a princely sum – for what exactly? Both men were now dead and Dolly was missing. I needed to tell Sam.

It was Sandesh who opened the door, his eyes drowsy and bloodshot.

'Wake Sam sahib right now,' I said.

Sandesh padded dazedly back down the corridor and knocked on the door to Sam's bedroom.

'Sam sahib?'

He turned to me and shrugged.

I left my sandals at the door and rushed down the corridor, knocked loudly, then let myself in.

'Sam, get up.'

His sleep-tinged voice answered from behind the mosquito net. 'Suren? What time is it?'

'Almost half six.'

'I thought we said nine?'

I held out Ghatak's briefcase. 'This can't wait. There's something you need to see.'

A minute later, with Sam beside me in his dressing gown, I spread the papers on the dining table.

'This is Ghatak's ledger of expenses,' I said, flipping through the pages until I found it.

'There.' I pointed to the entry in Ghatak's scrawl. 'Look.'

Sam looked.

I watched as the penny dropped.

'Is this what I think it is?'

I nodded. 'Ghatak paid a thousand rupees to Dolly three weeks ago. I believe the payment was made on behalf of Mullick.'

He whistled through his teeth. 'One thousand rupees. That's a hell of a lot for a set of photographs.'

'It's not clear what the payment was for,' I said. 'Maybe she had taken photographs for Mullick? His ex-wife maybe, or his extended family.'

'But a thousand rupees? These were photographs, not oil paintings.'

'The answer might lie at Mullick's office,' I said. 'Ghatak seems to have been a stickler for filing. I'd wager the invoice is in a cabinet there.'

He smiled and placed a hand on my shoulder.

'You should have been an accountant.'

While Sam got dressed, I headed down to the street. In the light of dawn, and shorn of its patrons, the place looked almost respectable: the brothels closed, the girls resting, the balconies festooned with the first of the day's laundry. This street held so many memories. A *daab*-wallah, his cart loaded with thick green coconuts, wheeled the contraption slowly down the lane. It was the same man from years ago when I'd lived here. We smiled at each other like old acquaintances suddenly brought to mind, and he reached for a coconut and held it out to me.

'*Dada*, how long since you bought a *daab* from me? Come. Have.'
'Make it a good one,' I said.
'All good ones, *dada*. Only the best.'
He took the coconut, hacked off the top with his machete and poured the juice into a glass.'
I sipped and stared and thought of the past, of my life here in this street. So much had transpired in the time since I had left it. I was a different man now. Older, and if not wiser, then at least more sceptical. I sported life's bruises now upon my soul.
The coconut water went down too easily. I returned the glass, paid the man and lit a cigarette, drowning my thoughts in tobacco smoke until Sam came down the stairs.

We took a tonga to Mullick's office. It was still early, but some of his people would be at work. En route I told Sam about the woman I'd seen at Howrah, the one who'd resembled Dolly and who had disappeared into the backstreets.
'You certain you didn't just see what you wanted to?'
I shrugged. 'I do not know.'
'Why would she be at Howrah at that time of night?'
'I thought maybe she was preparing to leave town.'
'It's possible,' he said, 'assuming it really was her, and not a figment of your imagination.'

Mullick's office was on Hare Street, occupying several floors of an imposing pillared building which looked as though it might eat lesser buildings for breakfast.
'A chance to kill two birds with one stone,' Sam said as we walked up stone steps, through the revolving doors into a marbled atrium two storeys high. Beside the stairwell stood a statue of what I took to be Atlas holding up, if not the world, then at least the second floor. Around us, and despite the early hour, a blizzard of

souls weaved to and fro: file-laden box-wallahs, suited Englishmen and even the odd Anglo-Indian secretary in skirt and blouse, all rushing as though the world was ending and there was still paperwork to be completed.

'Do you think it is always like this?' I asked.

Sam shrugged. 'For their sake, I should hope not. We should split up,' he said. 'You go through the files while I go and see Mullick junior.'

'Divide and conquer,' I said. 'The British way.'

After taking directions from the front-desk reception-wallah, we parted company at the top of the stairs, Sam heading for the office of Joyonto Mullick and I for that of Ronen Ghatak.

I stopped a young man and asked for directions to Ghatak's cabin, and was informed to keep going, past several departments, to the end of the building where finally I reached a large room animated by the buzz of conversation and the clack of typewriters. There, a score or so of men were hard at work under a bank of whirring fans. In the corner was a door to a smaller office, and behind a desk beside it sat a young woman in a blue sari.

'I'm looking for Mr Ghatak's cabin,' I said.

'I'm afraid Ghatak-*babu* has not come to office today.' She offered me a smile of apology. 'I am not sure as to his current whereabouts.'

I could have told her that Mr Ghatak's current whereabouts were most likely a drawer in the mortuary at Medical College Hospital, but some knowledge is best left unshared.

The question remained, therefore, as to how I was to obtain access to his cabin and, more particularly, to his filing system and hopefully an invoice from the Golden Bengal Ladies Photographic Studio.

'My name is Banerjee,' I told her. 'Accountant working for Joyonto-*babu*.' I raised a digit and pointed upwards. 'All this business with the death of JP-*babu* has put a strain on everything. I need access to certain records. Can you help me?'

She seemed unsure, so I persisted, appealing to her charity, and when that failed, to her sense of self-preservation, insisting that Joyonto-*babu* himself had personally requested the records as a matter of urgency.

Once more I pointed to the ceiling, and once more she followed with a gaze.

'Very well,' she said. 'This way.'

TWENTY-EIGHT

Sam Wyndham

I parted ways with Suren and found myself in a world of wood panelling and portraits that might have graced a Mayfair gentlemen's club. Here, though, there was also the whiff of incense, suggesting a mix of East and West that I found slightly jarring.

Half a dozen men in shirts and ties huddled beside the stairwell, busily conferring about something in hushed tones. Beyond them, a secretary was seated behind a desk, affecting nonchalance but with one eye and possibly both ears trained upon their conversation. Perhaps aware of being caught in the act, he looked over in alarm as he suddenly noticed me.

'Yes, sir?'

I introduced myself and told him I needed to speak to Mullick *fils*.

He made a show of checking a diary half the size of the desk.

'Mr Mullick is in meeting. You have appointment?'

'I'm the police,' I told him. 'I don't need an appointment.'

He gave me a nod and directed me to an armchair beside a low table, then got up and walked hastily down a corridor. By now the huddle of suits had paused their deliberations and eyed me as though I might be Typhoid Mary. From the table I picked up a copy of the morning's *Englishman*. No mention of Mullick on the front page and certainly no mention of his now dearly departed secretary either. For want of anything better to do, I turned its pages, stopping at the editorial. Recently the paper seemed to have been expending a tremendous amount of vitriol, as well as newsprint, on the current mayor of Calcutta, a man by the name of Jatin Sengupta. The editor, it seemed, along with a fair few other British gentlemen in Calcutta, had never quite got used to the idea of a mayor elected by the popular vote, basically because, by dint of sheer numbers, that elected mayor was likely to be Indian. And while the position held little real power, the very notion of a brown man being the first citizen of our city seemed to stick in not a few craws. Democracy they felt, like certain fragile plants, was something best unplanted in Indian soil. The *Englishman* and for that matter many an Englishman, not to mention Scots, Welsh and Irish, had spluttered in outrage when C. R. Das had been elected the city's first mayor a few years earlier, and with his passing the previous year, the mantle had been passed to Sengupta who, like pretty much every Indian thorn in our flesh, was an Oxbridge-educated lawyer. Indeed, if the *Englishman* really wanted to preserve British control over India, they might be better served advocating the banning of all Indians from studying law.

My deliberations were interrupted by the return of the secretary, scurrying back along the corridor like a schoolboy.

'Captain Wyndham, please come with me.'

I followed him along the corridor as the scent of incense grew stronger. Its source soon apparent: a small shrine erected under a portrait of J. P. Mullick, his image garlanded with strings of marigolds, *ārtis* and joss-sticks burning at its foot. The secretary knocked on a door, then opened it wide.

Joyonto Mullick stood to greet me. Like his father's portrait in the corridor, he was dressed in white kurta and dhoti, though with a red carnation in his buttonhole. If he was in mourning, it seemed he was doing his grieving outside of business hours. The room around him was furnished in the style I imagined would grace that of a City of London banker – thick carpet, thicker curtains, a leather-topped desk of dark wood, the kind that looked like it would sink, and a couple of wing-backed chairs. Joyonto Mullick directed me to one.

'Captain Wyndham. You have news?'

I got to the point. 'Yes, but it's not good. Ronen Ghatak was murdered last night.'

I read incomprehension in his face.

'Ronen? But . . . how?'

'Stabbed. On the train returning from Bishnupore. I shall need details of his next of kin and his place of residence in Calcutta.'

For a moment Joyonto Mullick stood there as though in a trance. I coughed and he snapped back to the present.

'I'm sorry, Captain Wyndham, you were saying?'

'Ronen Ghatak. His next of kin?'

'I can't say. I think he came from somewhere near Murshidabad. I don't think he has family here. I shall have the details sent to you.'

'Have you any idea why someone might want to kill him?'

'No more than I have about why anyone might want to murder my own father.'

'We believe the two murders are linked. With regard to your father's death, we have been pursuing several disparate lines of inquiry, but with Ghatak's murder, the scales tip firmly on the side of this being related to some business dealing. So I must ask you, are you aware of any such matter, some transaction or other which your father was involved in, which may have precipitated his murder?'

Mullick junior shook his head.

'Prior to his murder, I questioned Ghatak. He gave me a name: Angus Carlyle, a man who might hold a grudge against your father. Can you shed any light on that?'

Mullick junior dismissed the name with a wave of his hand. 'Carlyle had his nose put out when my father was elected chairman of the commerce association. Some Britishers have an issue with

Indians in positions of authority. My father found it amusing. But that is hardly grounds for murder. And why would he kill Ronen? However, my father did not involve me in all aspects of the business, which is why –' he raised his arms in frustration – 'I am now trying to fathom all of the things which were kept from me.'

I blinked. 'Kept from you?'

'Financial outgoings, donations, charitable commitments. There are so many costs that were not discussed with me.'

'I'm afraid I need to ask you for an account of your movements three nights ago, the evening your father was murdered.'

He looked up. 'Me?'

'At this point we're investigating all avenues. You, like anyone else, must be ruled out as a suspect, more so as you are his next of kin and presumed primary inheritor of his estate.'

'Well,' he said, indignation rising in his tone, 'I certainly did not kill him.'

'So you can tell me where you were three nights ago?'

Joyonto Mullick paused. 'I'm afraid I cannot tell you that.'

'Why?'

'Because according to the laws of this country, I was in attendance at an illegal event, and I would not wish to endanger others.'

I sighed. An illegal act could be one of so many things from the sexual, through the narcotic to the political.

'I'm not interested in any crimes other than your father's and Ronen Ghatak's murders. I don't care if you were at a brothel, smoking *gājja* and plotting the abduction of the viceroy, so believe me when I say, it's in your best interests to tell me where you were the other night.'

A smile graced the corners of his mouth.

'If you must know, I was at the theatre with a friend, a new production of *Nildarpan*. You have heard of it?'

Of course I'd heard of it. Every policeman in the city had.

Nildarpan – The Indigo Planting Mirror – some play written fifty or sixty years earlier about the indigo rebellion and the suffering of Bengali peasants at the hands of unscrupulous British overlords. The powers that be had done a decent job of hushing the whole rebellion up, of course; the good people of Eastbourne or Edinburgh or even Delhi wouldn't have seen much mention of it in their morning papers; but then the damn play came along and threatened to open up the whole can of worms again. It made the Indians angry and worse, got the blood up of certain people of conscience within the British community – the clergy mainly, and no doubt some women too. And so, rather than address the issues, we had of course done the sensible thing and banned the play. We even introduced a censorship law – the Dramatic Performances Act – to stop any similar native plays *likely to excite feelings of disaffection to the government established by law in British India.*

The Indians had been bleating on about it ever since, rather gracelessly pointing out that such a law didn't sit particularly well with our ideals of freedom of speech, but then British ideals were for British people and not Indians, and their insistence on trying to make us spell it out was just plain rude.

'So you were at the staging of a seditious play?'

'Yes.'

'And there are others who can corroborate that?'

He scratched at his earlobe. 'If you remain true to your word that no charges will be brought.'

Bloody Bengalis and their bloody plays. I sometimes wondered if there was a more infuriating people on the face of the planet. It was as though they considered themselves a nation of Napoleons, their every intellectual act a blow against the mighty British Empire, when in all truth they were more like fifteen-year-olds drinking alcohol, thinking they were doing something terribly rebellious when actually no one really cared.

'You have my word,' I said solemnly. Indians appreciate solemnity when it comes out of a British mouth.

'In that case, I think I can provide corroboration.'

'At what time did the play end?'

'Around half past nine.'

'And after that? Where did you go?'

'I . . . I came home.'

'Directly?'

'Yes.'

There was something in his tone. Something forced.

'You are certain?'

'Of course. My driver can confirm.'

I was sure his driver would confirm anything Mullick told him to.

'Was anyone else with you?'

Once more, he hesitated.

'It's in your interest to tell me everything,' I said. 'If we later find out you've omitted anything, or God forbid lied, then things might get rather more complicated for you.'

He took his time answering and I watched a range of emotions fly across his face.

'I returned with a friend.'

'I'll need a name,' I said, 'and where I might find them.'

Mullick junior took a breath.

'Is there any way we can keep these details between us, Captain? It is a delicate matter.'

I looked at him. 'As I told you, I'm not interested in your personal life.'

'I have your word that it will remain between us?'

'You do,' I said, and I almost meant it.

'His name is Hirok Bhattacharya. He is currently a guest at my house.'

Well, that certainly put the cat among the pigeons. It took a lot to make that sort of admission, especially to a policeman. Word or no word, I wondered why he had told me. Maybe the threat of what would happen if he lied to me had hit home. Or maybe part of him wanted to tell me, to unburden himself of his secret. It wasn't the first time a suspect had yielded such information, even at the risk of being hanged, as though, when it came to the need for a confessor, a policeman was the next best thing to a priest.

I wondered too if Mr Bhattacharya was the young man I'd seen fleetingly on the balcony the other morning when I'd visited Mullick's house in Pathuriaghat. It didn't matter. What was important was whether or not he could provide an alibi for Mullick junior, and I rather suspected that he could.

It wouldn't rule Mullick junior out completely of course. A clever chap like him could have, probably would have, organised others to carry out such a deed while making sure he himself had an alibi, but in that case why not arrange a better alibi? Why not be seen in the centre of town by a thousand sets of eyes? Why go to a performance of a banned play and then bring home a young man, a lover even, if you knew the police would be checking into your whereabouts?

I was overthinking this. So far, nothing ruled young Mullick in or out.

'Did your father know?'

'About Hirok? No.'

'More generally?'

'You mean, did he know that I am a *confirmed bachelor*? Yes, he knew. He blamed my mother. He said she had been too soft in raising me.' Joyonto Mullick looked to the window. 'I was disgusting to him, abnormal, a curse from God. He tried many times to *fix* me. On more than one occasion he tried to wed me off, but with my mother's support, I refused. I told him if he forced my hand, I would create a scandal the likes of which would ruin him. After that, we hardly spoke. The lauded J. P. Mullick, father to a ...' He turned back to me. 'Every man has two faces, Captain. The one shown to the world and the one kept hidden. The hidden face is generally the truer one, and sometimes, it is the face of a monster.'

There was no anger in his voice, no resentment, merely resignation, and in that moment I did not know whether he had meant himself or his father.

'I ask you again, Mr Mullick,' I said, 'is there anything about your father's return to Calcutta or his subsequent murder that you haven't told me?'

He shook his head. 'You are asking if I had him killed. The answer is no, Captain, and I mourn as a son should. But part of me is relieved he is gone. Now if there's nothing else, I must get on. What with the funeral prayers, I have a tight schedule.'

'There is one other thing,' I said. 'Did your father ever mention a woman called Sushmita Chatterjee, or the Golden Bengal Ladies Photographic Studio?'

Mullick junior paused. 'The name is not familiar. Why do you ask?'

'Ghatak recorded a payment of a thousand rupees made to Miss Chatterjee three weeks ago. She seems to have disappeared around the same time as your father was murdered and her studio was ransacked.'

He stared at me without blinking. 'I assume he had some photographs taken.'

'A thousand rupees seems rather a lot for a few photographs.'

'Then maybe some photographic equipment?'

'Your father was interested in photography?'

'Not to my knowledge. Maybe it was for some film project?'

'It's possible,' I said, 'but it doesn't explain why Miss Chatterjee should vanish around the time of your father's murder or why someone would seek to ransack her premises.'

Joyonto Mullick shrugged. 'I do not know this woman, Captain, and I rather doubt my father did either. Our companies make thousands of payments every week. My father certainly wouldn't have direct knowledge of most of them or the parties to which they were made. He controlled an empire. He wanted something done, he snapped his fingers and a dozen men like Ronen Ghatak made it happen. If you ask my opinion, I think you are wasting time with this photography business.' He made a show of checking his pocket watch and began to rise from his chair. 'Now if you don't mind, I must get on.'

'Of course,' I said, 'but I shall have to speak to your friend Mr Bhattacharya, and I'll need the names and addresses of those who were at the play with you three nights ago, and the name of the director.'

His expression darkened. 'Is that really necessary, Captain? I fear it would impact my reputation with my friends if they think I am divulging information to the police.'

'I'm afraid it is,' I told him. 'But I shall be discreet.'

I stood on the steps of the building, sucking on a cigarette and inhaling petrol fumes and diesel smoke in the morning light. I tried to make sense of Mullick junior. He was a man conflicted. Duty and honour and respect for one's father were principles ingrained into these people from birth as though etched onto their foreheads. And yet, when that respect was shattered, what replaced it? Hatred? Anger? I hadn't seen those from Joyonto Mullick, but that did not mean he was innocent.

TWENTY-NINE

Sam Wyndham

Suren came down the steps to join me, and we took refuge from the sun under the shade of a banyan tree that was busy destroying the pavement.

'Did Mullick junior tell you anything?'

'Not too much. I'll need to question this chap Angus Carlyle though. He doesn't seem to have been too keen on Mullick. What about you?' I asked.

He shook his head. 'Nothing. No invoice, no order of purchase, no record at all.'

'Where does that leave us?'

He shrugged.

'You're sure you checked thoroughly?'

He gave me a withering look.

'So a clandestine payment, then,' I said. 'For a large amount. To a woman who goes missing the day Mullick is murdered.'

'And her studio is ransacked,' he added. 'But what could be so valuable as to warrant murder?'

I stared at him and sighed. For someone so smart, he really could be naive in the ways of the world.

'Photographs,' I said. 'Compromising material that could be used for blackmail. Maybe it's some business competitor. Maybe some politician.' *Maybe his own son?* 'Whatever the truth, I think

Miss Chatterjee may have got herself embroiled in something she did not anticipate.'

The question was, where did we go from here? Whatever the connection between J. P. Mullick and Dolly Chatterjee, without finding her, we were no further ahead.

'We should search his digs. There might be something there. Did you find an address?'

'Yes,' he said. 'I found a letter addressed to him in his office cabin. The address is a *mess bari* in Howrah – 22 Round Tank Lane. Before that, however, we need to find Dolly.'

'Yes,' I said, 'she just became our top priority.'

'It was always my priority,' he said.

'Well, she's mine too now,' I said. 'She may be the key to the whole thing.'

'How do we do that?' Suren asked.

'We find that friend of hers, Mahalia. She might not have told you where Dolly is, but she'll sure as hell tell the Imperial Police. First, though, we head to the Great Eastern.'

When they came to town, anyone who was anyone stayed at the Great Eastern. It had always been so. Rumour had it the place had once been a bakery. The bread must have been good, because before long it had become a meeting place for new arrivals missing the comforts of home. Soon a hotel was tacked onto it, not just any hotel but, they said, the finest hundred rooms in Asia. It was said a man could walk in at one end of the hotel, buy a suit, a wedding present, seeds for the garden, have a decent meal and a *burra* peg at the bar, and if the barmaid was agreeable, walk out the other end, engaged to be married. They didn't sell the seeds any more, but the rest was all still perfectly feasible.

The lobby was gilded, and bedecked in enough marble to give the Victoria Memorial a run for its money, and looked like the sort of place that gave your wallet palpitations before you even made it five steps inside.

Behind the front desk stood a morning-suited native who studiously did his best to avoid my eye. I brought my hand down on a brass bell the size of a large rat that sat atop the counter, which seemed to get his attention.

'May I help you, sir?' he said, though his tone suggested that any help that might be forthcoming would be purely coincidental.

'I need to speak to one of your guests. A Mr Copeland.'

His expression curdled as though I'd suggested something vaguely clandestine.

'And is Mr Copeland expecting you?'

I pulled out my warrant card and placed it on the counter in front of him.

'Why don't we surprise him?'

Five minutes later, Suren and I were seated at a booth in Wilson's, the hotel bar, while a bellboy had been ordered to Copeland's room, armed with a summons to meet us here. It was early, too early for a drink at any rate, and Wilson's was next to deserted.

A white-jacketed waiter came over and Suren ordered tea, which I assumed would cost more than any beverage had a right to, and for which I would have to foot the bill.

'And for you, sir?'

'Nothing,' I said. 'Maybe just a glass of water.'

The waiter nodded and turned on his heel, leaving Suren and me to contemplate the decor, which had probably left several acres of Burma treeless.

I was not particularly looking forward to speaking to Mr Copeland. For starters, he was American. I had never met an American who wasn't at least a couple of inches too tall, who didn't speak too loudly, or who didn't seem to believe himself and his nation to be God's gift to the rest of mankind. And those were just the good ones.

The waiter returned, holding aloft a silver tray with a glass of water and more bone china than was strictly necessary for the brewing and consumption of a cup of tea. He placed the glass of water in front of me, then turned to Suren, laying down cup, saucer, milk jug, sugar bowl, tea strainer and teapot, and then a second pot of hot water.

At that point, Sal Copeland walked in. He was dressed in a dark blue suit and patent leather shoes that wouldn't last a week in some of the more picturesque parts of town. Tall, tanned and with the air of a man who had better places to be, he strode over. Suren and I rose to meet him.

'Mr Wyndham.'

'Captain Wyndham,' I corrected him, 'and this is Surendranath Banerjee.'

'Copeland,' he said to Suren, 'Sal Copeland.'

'Just to confirm,' I said, 'you are Miss Morgan's agent, is that correct?'

He gave a cursory nod. 'You here about Mullick?'

'That's right.' I gestured to the banquette. 'Please, take a seat. We'd like to ask you a few questions.'

Copeland composed himself as the waiter reappeared.

'Something to drink?' I asked.

He shook his head and waved away the waiter. 'I'm in a hurry, so let's make this quick. How can I help you gentlemen?'

'A hurry?' I asked. 'I was under the impression that the film was on hiatus, at least until the recipients of Mullick's estate decide whether to continue providing the financing.'

Copeland spat a laugh. 'It's dead, Captain. Believe me. As dead as a raccoon in a room full of alligators. The director might think it's on hold, but believe me, it ain't, and I'm getting Estelle on the next boat out of here.'

'I meant to ask you about that,' I said. 'Rather odd, isn't it, that an actress of her standing should take a part in some Indian film?'

'You're telling me. I told her not to take it. How many people are gonna see some two-bit flick set in India? I told her the risks, coming out here, catching malaria or typhoid or whatever. Soon as she finished shooting that last film in London, I told her we should head straight to California, but Estelle was set on it. Said she wanted to come to India. Said she might never get another chance.'

'I expect the money was good too.'

Copeland shot me a look of disdain.

'Believe me. I could've gotten her a helluva lot more in Hollywood.'

'Did you tell Mullick that?'

'What?'

'I assume you negotiated the deal. Didn't you ask Mullick for more?'

'Course I did.'

'And?'

He scratched at the side of his head. 'Like I said, Estelle wanted to come. Can't exactly play hardball when your own client's cooing about how much she wants to come do the picture.'

'Hardball?' Suren asked.

'Baseball term,' Copeland said. 'Like your cricket, but actually interesting. Means to be tough in one's negotiations. Anyway, it's done now. Over. Time to get out of this dump.'

'You don't like it here?' I asked.

He snorted a laugh. 'You ever been to Alabama, Captain?'

I told him I hadn't had that particular pleasure.

'Alabama is too hot, too dull and too stuck in the past. This place is like Alabama, but without the charm.'

'What did you make of Mullick?'

His face was blank. 'Didn't really know him.'

'Come now,' I said. 'You negotiated Estelle's deal with him. You must have got a sense of the man.'

'Didn't much care for him, if you must know. Kinda uppity, if you know what I mean.'

'You mean he was a brown man with opinions?' Suren said.

Copeland shot him a look. 'I mean he was a difficult son of a bitch. I know y'all worship him here like he was one of your gods, but the man was a bastard, or as your friend Captain Wyndham might say, not my cup of tea.'

He was wrong there. If I thought it merited, I'd have been happy enough using the word *bastard*.

'I believe you and Estelle came back from Bishnupore on the same train as Mullick,' I said.

'S'right.'

'What brought you back that evening?'

Copeland huffed. 'Honestly? Estelle just wanted to get the hell out of Bishnupore. She was going crazy sitting out there in the middle of nowhere. She wanted a night off among the lights of Calcutta. As for me, I had some business things to deal with. It's why I stayed on while she went back on the Sunday. I needed to send some cables to the States. Urgent matter regarding one of my other clients. I won't name him, but let's just say there are certain rumours floating about which I needed to squash. Had to threaten a rag of a magazine with a lawsuit.'

'On the train,' I said, 'how did Mullick seem to you?'

Copeland shrugged. 'Seemed fine. We didn't really speak much.'

I leaned forward. 'Really? Because the ticket inspector on the train that night recalls Mullick and a foreign gentleman in the same compartment engaged in a rather heated conversation. I'd rather assumed that gentleman was you. Are you saying I'm mistaken? Because we can always ask the ticket inspector.'

Once more Copeland scratched his head. 'Yeah, well, we had a little disagreement about Estelle's contract.'

'About what exactly?'

'The shoot was running late. I've got pictures lined up for her in Hollywood. Pictures she's contracted for, with studios that'll sue if she's not there on time, not to mention kill her career stone dead. I told Mullick as much. Said we needed to be out of Calcutta by Friday at the latest, and that if he was as big a fan of Estelle as he claimed to be, he wouldn't make a fuss about that.'

'And what did he say?'

'He said she had a contract and that he would hold her to it. When I say we didn't speak much, it's because there wasn't much to say after that.'

'Did he happen to tell you why he was returning to Calcutta that night?'

'He didn't say and I didn't ask.'

'Did he seem at all anxious?'

'I don't know. He wasn't in the best of moods, if that's what you mean.'

'And when you got to Calcutta, what happened?'

'We went our separate ways.'

'Did you by chance see if Mullick was met at the station by anyone?'

'Can't say I did. Estelle and I got off and headed straight for the taxi stand.'

'And you came straight here to the Great Eastern?'

'Absolutely. Why's it even an issue?'

'Because, Mr Copeland,' I said, 'as of now, you're the last person we know to have spent time with J. P. Mullick before he was killed.'

Copeland swallowed, his Adam's apple bobbing in his throat. 'Well, he was alive when I left him, and there's a whole station full of folks who would've seen that. I suggest you go find some of 'em.'

'When did you hear about Mullick's death?'

He made a show of looking up at the ceiling. 'Yesterday morning. Got a cable from his man Ghatak.'

'Do you still have it?'

'What, the cable? Can't rightly say. Might be in my room, or I might have thrown it in the trash, in which case the maid will have taken it away when she cleaned. They're pretty efficient here.' He checked his watch.

'Have you spoken to Miss Morgan this morning?' I asked.

He looked at me suspiciously.

'No. Why?'

'Because Mr Ghatak was murdered last night, on the train back from Bishnupore. Miss Morgan's maid discovered the body.'

Copeland was suddenly subdued. 'Hell. I didn't really speak to the feller, but that's tragic.'

'How long were you up in Bishnupore?' I asked.

'Bout a week.'

'One week there and you didn't speak to Ghatak? Didn't you liaise with him when you needed something, or wished to talk to Mullick?'

'Once or twice, maybe,' he conceded, 'but only briefly.'

'Tell me, Mr Copeland,' I said, 'did you ever happen to meet a woman called Sushmita Chatterjee?'

He looked at me blankly.

'No. Any reason why I should have? Now listen, gentlemen, as enjoyable as this is, I really need to get going. There's a liner leaving for Shanghai in a couple of days and I need to arrange passage.'

I looked to Suren.

'That seems rather hasty,' he said to Copeland.

'I don't care how it seems.'

'My colleague is right,' I said. 'We're in the middle of a double murder investigation. Your desire to flee our fair city in such a hurry might be construed negatively. At the very least, it's unhelpful to the inquiry.'

Copeland shook his head. 'I don't really give a damn. Now unless you plan on arresting me, I believe I've every right to leave when I choose to.' He rose from the table.

'The maid,' I said.

He stopped and looked down at me.

'What?'

'Miss Morgan's maid. She's a witness to a murder. Whatever else happens, she's not leaving the city until I say so.'

Copeland stared for a moment. 'That's no concern of mine,' he said. 'Good day, gentlemen.'

And with that he was gone, striding out the room like he was off to kill some Red Indians or at least offer them bit parts in a film.

Suren sipped his tea.

'What do you make of that?'

'He was one of the last people to see Mullick alive,' I said. 'He had an argument with him on the train. He stood to lose a lot of money if Estelle didn't make it to America in time for her next film.'

'Is that enough of a motive for murder?'

'Money is always a motive for murder, especially for Americans.'

'But even if he had reason to kill Mullick, the man was alive when he and Copeland parted ways.'

'Copeland would have hired someone to do his dirty work,' I said.

'But he had no motive to kill the secretary. Indeed, he wasn't even on the train last night when Ghatak was murdered. And he has no connection to Dolly.'

'You're right,' I said. 'I can't see a connection, but that doesn't mean there isn't one, we need to consider all possibilities. And there's something else I don't understand. Copeland could have broken the contract. Mullick was hardly paying Estelle a fortune. Copeland could have got her out of here, paid Mullick whatever damages he wanted and still made more money for Estelle on another picture in Hollywood, so why didn't he?'

'Maybe he has nothing to do with this at all,' Suren said.

'Possibly, but there is *something* fishy about him. His answers were evasive.' I looked at him. 'You noticed it too, didn't you?'

He nodded. 'Don't you know? I used to be a detective.'

THIRTY

Sam Wyndham

I returned to the lobby to find my friend the concierge still manning his post behind the reception desk.

I told him I needed to speak to another of his guests, Miss Estelle Morgan's maid, and told him to once more dispatch the bellboy with a message.

He looked at me as though, in the whole history of the Great Eastern, no one had ever requested to speak to a lady's maid before.

'Police business,' I said.

As the bellboy made for the stairs, I joined Suren in the arcade of boutiques that seemed to run the length of the ground floor and halfway to Howrah. He was standing outside a milliner's, staring at a green bonnet with feathers protruding from the top.

'Why would anyone wear such a thing?' he said.

'It is a bit much for Calcutta,' I agreed.

'A bit much for anywhere,' he said. 'I shall never understand European women's fashion.'

'Bit rich,' I said, 'given you come from a land where maharajahs wear turbans ten times more flamboyant than that. I don't remember you complaining.'

He smiled. 'Maybe my time in Europe has made me more of an egalitarian and republican?'

'Quite,' I said. 'Off with their hats.'

'Sam?'

The voice came from behind us. My stomach knotted.

'Annie?'

She smiled, one of those smiles that used to lift my spirits while taking my breath away. Now, though, it felt like a knife twisting in my chest.

'And Suren in tow,' she said. 'Thick as thieves. Have you found your cousin?'

Suren looked bashful. 'Not yet.'

She turned to me. 'What brings you to the Great Eastern, Sam?'

'A case,' I said. 'Murder.'

Annie looked as though I'd just poked her with a stick.

'Of course. You and your cases. Well, I'm glad they've got you working on them again. It seems you're happiest when avenging the dead.'

I let the comment pass. This was hardly the place for an argument, and anyway, she was probably right, and the dead had their virtues. They didn't make snide remarks for one thing.

'And you?' I asked. 'Doing a spot of shopping?'

'I'm here with a friend, if you must know.' She turned distractedly in the direction of one of the boutiques. 'He's in there picking up a suit.'

He.

I felt that familiar punch to the gut whenever Annie mentioned a male friend. I assumed that the man in question would be that Russian fellow she was spending so much time with these days. Well, if Annie wanted to run about town with some rich idiot who had nothing better to do of a Tuesday morning than buy a suit, that was her business.

A tall, emaciated-looking figure emerged from the tailor's shop diagonally opposite. He looked like those pictures of the poet Shelley I remembered from school textbooks: pale and willowy and with the sort of boyish, other-worldly looks that appealed to a certain type of woman who frankly should have known better. It was a shame really. Until now, I'd rather admired Shelley – for his political stuff if not for all his later nonsense about love.

The man carried an oversized bag containing, no doubt, a new suit, and suddenly I had the feeling that it had been paid for not by himself but by Annie.

Annie breathed in. 'Well, it was nice to see you both,' she said and turned to leave.

'Wait,' I said. 'Aren't you going to introduce us to your friend?'

The thin chap stood hovering at the tailor's door, unsure of whether to advance or retreat. Finally, Annie beckoned him over.

'Sam, Suren. This is Nikolai.'

'Nikolai, these are friends of mine, Sam Wyndham and Surendranath Banerjee.'

The waif gave a curt bow. 'A pleasure,' he said. 'Count Nikolai Ostrakhov.'

Suren eyed him suspiciously. Quite rightly, I thought. There were too many damn foreigners running around India, lately.

'A count,' I said to Annie. 'You're going up in the world.' I turned to Ostrakhov. 'Russian?'

'That is correct,' he said, in heavily accented English.

'And what brings you to Calcutta, Mr Ostrakhov?' I asked.

'*Bis-niz*,' he said. 'I am hoping to start trading of tea.'

'Nikolai's an émigré,' Annie said, putting a hand on his arm. 'The Reds have taken absolutely everything from him except the shirt on his back.'

It was a shame they hadn't spared him a suit.

'I imagine,' I said to Ostrakhov, 'that it's hard to start a business with only your shirt as capital.'

'It is,' Annie answered. 'That's why I'm providing the finance. We're to be partners.'

It seemed she was paying for a lot more than a suit.

'Tea for two then,' I said. 'Lovely.'

Annie seemed suddenly in a hurry to change the subject. 'This case of yours,' she said. 'I thought you were *persona non grata* these days, having offended, well, pretty much everyone in the city.'

'Desperate times,' I said.

'I must say, I'm surprised you've returned to the fold,' she said to Suren. 'Three years abroad and you come back only to resume working for this genius.'

Suren shook his head. 'I'm not working for him. I'm merely helping him. Sometimes his genius needs a push.'

'Well, that much is certainly true,' she said. 'Preferably off a cliff.'

I tried to think of a witty retort but nothing came to mind. Instead I addressed Ostrakhov.

'So what do you make of the tailor, here?'

'Very good,' he said, beaming.

'I should hope so,' I said. 'I generally go to an Armenian chap in Park Street. He's excellent and probably less than half the price of these hotel johnnies. Let's have a look then.'

Before Annie could stop him, the chap had opened up his bag and lifted out a dinner jacket.

'Very nice,' I said. 'You'll be ready for all those parties with other tea traders.'

'Tea parties,' Suren said.

Ostrakhov looked confused. Annie looked like she might wish to shoot one of us.

'If you must know it's for a party tonight. A rather famous actress will be in attendance.'

'I see,' I said. 'Well, we mustn't keep you. I'm sure the count here will need time to get ready.'

Ostrakhov seemed to be struggling to follow the conversation. I smiled at him and he brightened at the sight.

'Good day,' he said, with a nod of his head.

'And to you too,' I said.

I looked on as Annie, Ostrakhov and his new suit walked off towards the exit, and felt less than happy with myself. I should have been gracious to both of them. Instead, I had been petty and childish. But then Annie had started it, parading Ostrakhov around like a new pet. Someone to lavish time and money and suits upon.

Suren just stood there, staring at them.

'What?'

'Nothing,' he said. 'I just have this feeling that you might be regretting your decision to turn down Miss Morgan's invitation tonight.'

'Now hold on a minute. I didn't turn it down, exactly,' I said. 'And now I come to think of it, it might be a good opportunity to question that chap Copeland some more.'

'Naturally,' he said. 'And Ostrakhov too.'

'What?'

'Oh, nothing. What did you make of him, by the way?'

'Not much.'

'He seems to have become quite friendly with Miss Grant, to the extent that she is going to be backing him financially.'

'You think he plans on stealing her money?'

He looked pensive. 'He is not right for Miss Grant.'

'True enough,' I said.

'So how do you intend to remedy the situation?'

For a moment, I wasn't sure I'd heard him correctly.

'Are you asking me how I intend to split them up?'

He smiled. 'Far be it from me to suggest such a thing.'

'Those days are over, Suren,' I said. 'I fear Annie and I are never going to see eye to eye on things. I've a mind to let her make her mistakes. Let her find out the hard way.'

'She is still your friend,' he said. 'You should not want to see her hurt.'

'Have you seen the state of him? I think the only thing our friend Count Ostrakhov is likely to hurt is Annie's bank balance.'

He pondered my words. 'I'm not so sure.'

THIRTY-ONE

Surendranath Banerjee

I was unnerved by this Count Nikolai Ostrakhov. There was something unwholesome about him. Sam, it was clear, had not taken kindly to him either, yet my hostility was not rooted in the same soil as his. Indeed, Sam, through romantic malice, took a dislike to any man upon whom the attentions and affections of Miss Grant may be dispensed. No, my antipathy lay elsewhere and was harder to pin down. I had never met Count Ostrakhov before, yet he looked familiar. That pale skin, that tall, spare frame and sharp, angular nose that put me in mind of nothing so much as a common crane.

Had I seen that face before? It was unlikely. Even in Europe, I had not rubbed shoulders with such nobility. And yet I could not shake the feeling that I *had* seen him. Maybe then in a past life? A past incarnation? I could not tell this to Sam, of course. He would simply have laughed. But in our traditions, such things were eminently possible. In fact they occurred more regularly than one would think. What the French called *déjà vu*, that feeling of having already experienced a certain situation, what was it but the echo of a past life? This, however, felt different. This familiarity with Ostrakhov was tinged with something darker. Something malevolent.

'Come on,' he said. 'No time to daydream.'

A bellboy had just handed him a note.

'Miss Morgan wishes that we call upon her in her suite, and that we speak to her maid in her presence.'

I pushed thoughts of Ostrakhov from my mind and followed him towards the stairs.

Miss Morgan's suite was on the second floor, reached by a staircase that was ornate to the first floor, where, out of sight from the lobby, it became a much simpler affair. Madhu opened the door and, with her gaze directed at the floor, led us into a corner sitting room with French windows open to the view: the gardens and dome of Government House visible in the distance. Miss Morgan, draped in a dressing gown of green-and-gold silk in the Chinese style, wafted in from the balcony, a cigarette between two elegant fingers.

She greeted Sam like a long-lost friend, calling his name and with arms out seeking to embrace him. She turned to me and smiled. 'And Mr Banerjee. Please, won't you both have a seat? Shall I have some tea sent up?'

She reached for the brass button on the wall but Sam stopped her.

'It's all right, Miss Morgan. We won't keep you long. We've just a few more questions for Madhu here.'

The maid looked to her mistress. Sam directed her to the sofa while he pulled up a chair opposite. Miss Morgan sat next to her maid, while I took up station near the French windows to the balcony and reached for my notebook and pencil.

'Now, Madhu,' Sam said, 'I want you to tell me again exactly what happened in the minutes leading to you finding Ronen Ghatak on the train last night.'

The woman clasped her hands together then commenced her account, retelling how, upon returning from checking on Miss Morgan's luggage, she chanced upon Ghatak's body in the WC; and how she had knelt down to check upon him only to come away with blood upon her hands and sari; how, in her panic, she had screamed and run from the scene, colliding with Captain Wyndham near the carriage housing the galley kitchen. Once more she mentioned the Indian man who had pushed past her, heading away from the WC, a man she had later failed to identify when Sam had taken her through the train.

Sam asked his questions, the same as the previous evening, and received the same answers. There was little the woman could tell us that was helpful.

'And when you found the body, did you pull the communication cord to stop the train?'

She shook her head. 'I don't recall doing so.'

'Why were you checking Miss Morgan's luggage?' Sam asked.

The woman brushed at her eye, then glanced at her mistress. 'It is a rather delicate matter.'

'A man is dead, Madhu. I don't care how delicate you think it is, you need to tell me.'

The maid looked to the floor, then to her mistress and received a nod, before turning once more to Sam.

'It is a ladies' matter. There were certain things which I should have packed in Miss Morgan's day bag which unfortunately ended up in the suitcases in the guard's van. I needed to fetch them.'

I watched as Sam's face turned the jewelled pink of pomegranate segments. Miss Morgan looked away.

'Yes, well, I think that's all fine,' Sam said, struggling to extricate himself from the situation. 'We won't take up any more of your time, Madhu.'

His questioning had been perfunctory at best. The Sam I knew would never have been put off by a little embarrassment. He would have continued, like a dog fighting for a bone until he had wrung every last morsel of information from the woman. Maybe he was getting old. Or maybe he just didn't want to offend Miss Morgan.

I, though, was not satisfied. The idea that Madhu might fail to pack according to her mistress's requirements struck me as odd. She seemed so dedicated, so concerned for Miss Morgan's well-being, that such an oversight seemed out of character. I suppose it may have been just that – an honest mistake – but Sam should have pressed harder.

'If I may,' I said. 'I have a few questions.'

All eyes turned to me: the maid, wary; Miss Morgan with a look that suggested she'd forgotten I was even in the room. Sam seemed almost relieved.

'May I ask how long you have been in Miss Morgan's employ?'

Her brow furrowed. 'You mean, how long I have worked for memsahib?'

'That's correct.'

'Since she was a child.'

Miss Morgan stirred beside her. 'My father was in the army. He and Mamma were posted to Lucknow for eighteen months. It's where I was born. Madhu was hired as my ayah and when we left for Australia she came too. She's been with me ever since.'

'You were *born* here, in India?' I asked.

'Yes,' she said. 'That is part of the reason I was so keen to see the country. And it meant Madhu might see her homeland again.'

'It must have been difficult for you, Madhu,' I said. 'Leaving your people and moving thousands of miles.'

The woman shrugged. 'Our fate is our fate.'

'Your family, your parents, they did not object?'

'I have no family,' she said.

'Very well,' I said. 'Just so I am clear, the baggage car where you had stowed Miss Morgan's luggage. How many carriages distant was it from the one in which you found Ghatak's body?'

'Four, maybe five cars back, I think.'

'So, having retrieved the items your mistress requested, you travelled back through the packed second-class carriages. A stranger pushed past you, heading in the opposite direction. You then reached the carriage before the buffet car where you chanced upon the open WC with Ghatak inside. After realising what you had chanced upon, you screamed, and on regaining your wits, ran in the direction of the front of the train, towards the buffet car and the first-class carriage, at which point, someone pulled the communication cord.'

'That is correct.'

'Why that direction?'

'Excuse me?'

'Why run for the buffet car? You had passed so many second-class carriages full of people. Why not run to alert them?'

She looked at me blankly.

'I do not know. I suppose I thought maybe the conductor would be there, or maybe Captain Wyndham.'

'Yet I understand that, moments later, when you were leading Captain Wyndham to the scene of the crime, the conductor was already on the scene, which implies he must have been in one of the carriages further back. Furthermore, the fact that he reached the scene before you had returned with Captain Wyndham suggests he could not have been more than one carriage further back. You would have passed him on your way. Did you not think to run back and tell him?'

The maid shook her head. 'I don't know. Maybe I saw him. I-I do not recall exactly.'

Miss Morgan interjected. 'Come now, Mr Banerjee. Poor Madhu had just stumbled upon a murder. She was in shock. Given the state she must have been in, you don't honestly expect her to recall every detail such as where the conductor might be.'

'Very well,' I conceded. 'Let us move on. The man you saw, the one who pushed past you. This event transpired in the same carriage as where you then came upon Ghatak's body. Is that correct?'

The maid nodded. 'Yes. At the opposite end of the same carriage.'

I made a show of checking my notes. 'And then when you turned to confront him, he ignored you and continued into the next carriage.'

'That's right.'

'Very well,' I said. 'That is most helpful.' I turned to Sam. 'I've nothing further at this moment.'

Once more the maid dabbed at her eyes then looked to Miss Morgan. 'If I may be excused, memsahib?'

Miss Morgan shot a glance at Sam. 'I take it you have no objections, Captain?'

Sam indeed had none and Madhu rose and silently left the room. Miss Morgan took this as her cue to rise too.

'Well, if there's nothing else ...'

Sam got to his feet. 'There is one more thing,' he said. 'This party being held in your honour tonight. My diary seems to have opened up. If you haven't changed your mind, I'd be happy to accompany you.'

Miss Morgan beamed. 'That's wonderful! I'd be delighted!'

I followed Sam out of the door and lingered at a distance as Miss Morgan bade him her goodbyes. The whole process seemed to take longer than it should have. The British tend to be efficient in their adieus. A curt goodbye and a handshake usually sufficing. Not Miss Morgan and the captain though.

It was only when we were back downstairs and safely outside, that we spoke.

'Did you know that Estelle Morgan was born here?'

He shook his head. 'I suppose it explains why she was so keen to come here.' He fished in his pockets for a cigarette and came up empty-handed. 'So what did you make of the maid?'

I was not sure what to say. I'd been disappointed at how quickly he had given up his line of questioning, but it was not in his nature to react positively to any sort of criticism, be it constructive or otherwise; and yet I owed him the truth.

'I do not think she was being entirely forthcoming.'

He smiled. 'Good! And did you spot it?'

'What?'

'The anomaly in her story.'

'What anomaly?'

'The communication cord.'

'What of it?'

'According to the conductor, the cord was pulled in the carriage where Ghatak's body was found. He hadn't pulled it himself and Madhu said she didn't do it. So the assumption has to be that it was pulled by Ghatak's murderer in order to stop the train so that he could get off and escape. Now, if he's the man who pushed past Madhu and who then moves into the next carriage and vanishes, when does he pull the communication chord? And if he didn't pull it, then who did? It's possible he doubled back, but why? There was a perfectly good communication cord in the next carriage. I checked.'

'So, either he needlessly doubled back or someone else pulled the cord. Or Madhu is lying and there was no man and she pulled it herself. Would she even be capable of such a thing?'

'A stab to the neck? Why not? It's certainly possible if he wasn't expecting it. They were known to each other. She could easily have caught him off guard. And she had his blood on her sari.'

'But what reason would a common lady's maid have to murder Ghatak? There is one other possibility. Maybe the killer, whoever it might be, was someone whom she recognised? Maybe she is being cajoled into silence?'

Sam nodded. 'You haven't lost your touch, Suren.'

My ears burned. 'I'm embarrassed to say that I thought you might have lost yours.'

He laughed. 'In that case, I'm hurt.'

'Well,' I said, 'what with your fawning over Miss Morgan, it was hard to perceive your methods of detection.'

He looked at me and shook his head. 'Police work is more than just the application of intelligence. It can entail subterfuge, too. I can't help feeling that whatever the maid is hiding, Miss Morgan is aware of it.'

I admit I was rather taken aback. Sam had a certain, let us call it *a blind spot* when it came to women. More than once it had led to complications. Now, though, it seemed that he had matured somewhat. It was good to see.

'So all that business of inviting yourself to this party, it is all a ruse to find out what Madhu might be keeping back?'

'Partly,' he said. 'And partly because it'll be a damn good way of annoying Annie Grant.'

THIRTY-TWO

Sam Wyndham

We left the Great Eastern and walked along the shaded side of the street in the direction of the university, where Suren left a note in Mahalia Ghosh's pigeonhole, asking her to meet him at 4 p.m., inside the English cemetery on Park Street, near the grave of the famous Rose Aylmer, whose untimely death from eating too many pineapples had been recorded in verse and made her famous. Thereafter we headed to Bowbazar and the sort of cheap eateries that my wallet, if not my palate, preferred. Past crawling traffic and the usual midday hustle of hawkers and traders, resting rickshaw-wallahs and tiffin-time box-wallahs.

We settled on a Chinese place on Temple Lane set on the ground floor of a melancholy-looking building that seemed as though it might collapse if one stared at it too hard. But in Calcutta, the more dilapidated the building, the better the quality of the food. In seven years of eating in such places, I was yet to be proved wrong.

The interior was no better. The walls, a faded, grime-encrusted brown, enclosed an area just about large enough to swing the proverbial cat, assuming you didn't mind hitting a patron or two in the process. Between them sat a cluster of rough wooden tables and chairs that might have dated back a century or so. The menu consisted of half a dozen dishes written up in English and Chinese on a chalkboard nailed to one of the walls.

A young Chinese waitress in a red-and-gold silk dress added some colour to the place and quickly brought over a pot of tea and two small cups, then stood by as we pondered the fare on the chalkboard.

I looked to Suren. 'Chimney soup followed by the gobi Manchurian?'

'Perfect,' he said. I ordered. The girl left and I took a sip of tea. 'So what have we learned?'

Suren sighed. 'Where to begin?'

'With the facts,' I said. 'J. P. Mullick was found murdered three nights ago after making a hurried and unscheduled return to Calcutta. His secretary tells us it was for a business matter, but no one in Calcutta was expecting him back; not his family nor his chauffeur or the staff at his office. On the train, he argues with Sal Copeland about releasing Estelle Morgan so that she may fulfil film obligations in America. He takes a taxi, we don't know exactly where to, but not back to his home in Pathuriaghat. He's killed, then transported to the burning grounds, presumably in the hope that his body will be disposed of without anyone being any the wiser.

'The same day Sushmita Chatterjee disappears from the Golden Bengal Ladies Photographic Studio, which is later ransacked, and when we turn up at the scene, someone tries to burn the place down. Two nights later, Mullick's secretary, Ronen Ghatak, is murdered on the train back from Bishnupore. He is found by Madhu, Estelle Morgan's maid, who claims to have seen a suspicious man who pushed past her, but who then disappears when someone pulls the communication cord, thus stopping the train. Among Ghatak's possessions is a record of a payment of a thousand rupees to the Golden Bengal Ladies Photographic Studio – a rather princely sum for photographs. Our search for any receipt or invoice as to what payment might be for has proved fruitless, suggesting that whatever it was for might not have been exactly above board. Have I missed anything?'

'Only that last night I saw a woman at Howrah who might have been Dolly, and her friend Mahalia is probably our best bet for finding her. But what does it all mean? What could be worth killing Mullick and his secretary for?'

The waitress returned with the soup and ladled it into bowls from the black stove pot with red coals burning under it which gave the dish its name.

'I can't help thinking the key to this whole thing is the link between Mullick and your cousin, Dolly. What exactly was he paying her for? We have to assume it was something illicit.'

Suren shook his head. 'I find that hard to accept. I have known her my whole life. Yes, she can be headstrong, even arrogant at times, but I doubt she would be involved in anything untoward.'

'With respect,' I said, 'your problem is that you're a bloody romantic. You want to believe the best about people, which, by the way, is a terrible mindset for a policeman. And you haven't even been in the country for three years. People change.'

He lay down his spoon and sat back. 'Still, I cannot believe she would do such things.'

'Then give me a legitimate reason why Mullick would pay her a thousand rupees.'

The question was met with silence.

'Face it, Suren, whatever she's done, it's serious enough for someone to ransack her studio, and instead of going to the police, your cousin goes into hiding.'

He picked up his spoon once more. 'Very well, let us assume you are right, and that Dolly and Mullick were involved in something unsavoury. What could be so bad as to get Mullick and now Ronen Ghatak killed?'

'Blackmail, maybe?' I said. 'Let's say Mullick paid Miss Chatterjee to take photographs which are compromising in some way.'

'But why would he choose a woman?'

I looked at him. 'What?'

'There are hundreds of male photographers in Calcutta. Surely one of them would be a more suitable character to take such photographs? Why go to the only woman photographer in the city? A respectable *bhadromohila* at that.'

'I don't know,' I said. 'But the fact remains, Mullick paid her the thousand rupees for something, and now she's in hiding.'

Suren shrugged.

'Look,' I said, 'Mullick's personal dealings were less wholesome than people thought. The man had his peccadilloes. Maybe that film director Mitra was on to something when he suggested Mullick's murder was the revenge of a wronged father or husband?'

Suren rubbed at his cheek. 'But that would not explain the murder of Ghatak.'

'It might do, if Ghatak was the one procuring these women for Mullick? It stands to reason. A man like Mullick would not get his hands dirty. If he wanted something – or someone – he would get somebody else to arrange it. His own son told me that. Ghatak would have been the perfect candidate. I know you don't want to hear this, but Dolly might also fall into that category. Her whole business is photographing women. What if she were sharing those photos with Ghatak? A menu of options for Mullick?'

I saw the distaste in his face.

'I am telling you, she would not do such a thing. There must be another explanation. Maybe this is some family feud? Maybe Mullick's son is responsible. You said yourself that his relationship with his father was strained. Or maybe his ex-wife. Maybe it is her revenge for Mullick's treatment of her.'

'But why would either kill Ghatak?'

'Maybe he knew some business secret. Where the corporate bodies are buried, so to speak. Maybe they felt it better to be rid of him than risk him turning against the family.'

'And the link to your cousin, Dolly?'

'What about *your* Miss Morgan?' he responded.

'What about her?'

'She might be involved. You said her agent is holding something back, and her maid is hardly telling us the whole story.'

'Where's the motive?' I asked. 'She's an international actress. First time in India –'

'*Second* time,' he corrected. 'Remember, she was born here.'

'You're splitting hairs,' I said, 'but fine, first time since childhood. She hardly knows Mullick or Ghatak. I grant you, that agent of hers, Copeland, is a shifty fellow, but even if he did stand to lose money if Morgan didn't get to the USA in time for her next picture, is that enough of a reason to kill Mullick? It would have been far easier just to break the contract. And again, why kill Ghatak too? Not to mention *how*? Copeland was back in Calcutta. How would he have even known Ghatak was on that particular train last night, let alone have him murdered? No, the only plausible theory linking Mullick, Ghatak and Dolly is the one I laid out. Ghatak was finding women and girls for Mullick, and Dolly, maybe by providing photographs, was helping him for a fee.'

Suren folded his arms across his chest. 'What about the possibility of a business deal gone wrong – are we not being hasty in dismissing that? Either a bona fide venture, or possibly something illegal.'

'I would imagine it's more likely to be something illegal,' I said. 'Calcutta businessmen are not in the habit of slitting each other's throats, at least not physically.'

'True enough.'

'So let's assume Mullick is murdered because he's crossed someone in the criminal fraternity. Maybe he's reneged on a deal; maybe he owes someone money. Fine. So what about Ghatak? Do they kill him because he knows too much? And Dolly Chatterjee? If she's as pure as you say, why is she running for her life?'

'Maybe she has witnessed something she shouldn't have? Maybe she witnessed Mullick's murder? That might explain a lot.'

'It still wouldn't explain why Mullick paid her a thousand rupees. Unless . . .'

'What?'

'You're not going to like it.'

He pursed his lips.

'What if Mullick and Dolly were having an affair?'

THIRTY-THREE

Sam Wyndham

A telephone call to Angus Carlyle's office informed us that he was probably at his club. Most of the city's captains of industry, the white ones at any rate, were members of the Calcutta Club or the Bengal Club, but a few, the ridiculously wealthy and the ridiculously titled, favoured the rarified atmosphere of the Imperial Club, whose membership criteria were as strict as its fees were high.

I thought it best to take Sergeant Singh along. He'd seemed stone-faced since I'd ditched him for the trip to Bishnupore in favour of Suren, and I hoped this would make up for things. The last thing I wanted or needed on my hands was a sullen Sikh, and besides, the thought of this strapping great fellow throwing his weight around within the hallowed walls of the Imperial Club gave me a frisson of delight.

The club itself was an imposing whitewashed mansion situated on a large plot on Chowringhee overlooking the Maidan.

'Feel free to chip in with your own questions, Sergeant,' I said as we drove through its gates and along the driveway to the portico entrance and eliciting the first smile I'd seen from him in several days.

A liveried footman pulled open my door and, leaving the driver, Singh and I made our way up the steps and into the blessed cool of a mahogany-panelled hallway, its walls decorated with plaques and portraits of the great and the good, and the stuffed and mounted heads of several large herbivores unfortunate enough to be minding their own business while in the vicinity of some wag who considered it heroic and daring sport to shoot an unarmed creature from 250 yards with a .375 Holland & Holland Magnum.

Under the whirl of ceiling fans, we made our way to the front desk where Singh brought out his warrant card, laid it on the counter and enquired of the reception desk-wallah as to the exact whereabouts of Angus Carlyle. The man looked at him with disdain, then looked to me for reassurance.

'It's a fairly simple question,' I said. 'Maybe you should answer it.'

The man composed himself and straightened his tie with a gloved hand. 'Mr Carlyle is likely to be in the reading room on the first floor.'

Singh thanked him and we made our way past white-jacketed waiters and what I presumed from the hum of voices and smell of cigar smoke was the door to the bar, to a rather grand staircase with banisters of polished rosewood.

We climbed to the first floor, past more portraits of men in uniform all sporting the sort of sideburns favoured by our ancestors and which were generally thicker than a sheep's coat.

'Reading room?' Singh enquired of another waiter at the top of the stairs, and we followed his directions to a door at the far end.

The reading room was the sort of place I wouldn't mind retiring to: two of its walls lined with bookshelves and another marked by several large windows through which shafts of the Calcutta sun fell, illuminating the pirouetting patterns of smoke from half a dozen cigars and cigarettes. The silence was broken only by the rustle of newsprint and the odd cough from some superannuated resident slumped deep in a wingback leather chair.

On a table next to the door sat the day's editions of the *Englishman* and the *Statesman*, as well as slightly older versions of *The Times*, *Punch* and several other publications from the motherland.

To one corner, beside a rather too large wooden globe of the world, the British possessions painted a reassuring pink, stood another white-coated steward who seemed surprised to see us, or possibly just Singh's turban, and hurried over.

'Can I help you?'

'Angus Carlyle,' Singh said. 'Which of these gentlemen is he?'

The man gestured to a gentleman sitting close to the window, the salmon-pink pages of a newspaper open in front of him like a sail.

'Mr Carlyle?' I said as we walked over.

The newspaper lowered, revealing a blond-headed, bespectacled face which was even pinker than the newsprint.

'Yes?'

'My name's Wyndham,' I said, 'and this is Sergeant Singh. We're from Lal Bazar. Would you mind if we asked you a few questions?'

He took a moment to appraise us, then closed the newspaper. 'Not at all,' he said, folding it and placing it on the table beside him. 'Take a seat. Rather a relief actually.'

'Excuse me?' I said, as Singh pulled over a couple of empty chairs.

'Cotton futures,' he replied. 'You know much about them?'

'Fraid not,' I said, taking a seat.

'Yes, well, they're going down the pan,' he said grimly. 'Because of the Americans. It's always the Americans.'

'I thought you were a jute man.'

He looked at me and with one finger pushed his spectacles up the bridge of his nose.

'I am, but it's a fool who keeps all his eggs in one basket. Didn't your mother ever tell you that the key to happiness is a diversified portfolio?'

'My mother wasn't much one for financial advice,' I said,

momentarily wondering if my life had been mortally hamstrung by that fact.

'So what can I do for you, Mr Wyndham?'

'J. P. Mullick,' I said.

He nodded. 'Yes, terrible business. A great loss to Bengal and all that. What happened to him?'

'He was murdered, Mr Carlyle.'

That seemed to grab his attention. 'Really? They didn't mention that in the paper.'

'No, sir,' I said. 'I understand you were well acquainted with him, from a business perspective at least. I wonder, could you tell me what you made of him?'

A sniff of derision. 'What can I tell you? The man was an arrogant, preening popinjay. Whip-smart though, and cunning. The natives aren't like us, Wyndham. They play by a different set of rules. In the early days, when he was first establishing himself, I tried to work with him. We were looking at buying coal mines in Bihar together. I thought we'd agreed a deal, and put a joint bid on the table, only to find that he'd then gone behind my back and put in a higher bid himself. We never really saw eye to eye after that.'

'Did you ever meet any of his family? His wife or his son?'

He gave a sly laugh. 'I've met the son a few times. He's soft, like all the young men who've grown up in luxury. Hardly a chip off the old block. As for the wife, I met her once about fifteen years ago; around the time I thought we were going to be partners on that coal mines deal. He invited me to his house. She was quite a beauty, I remember that. Can't say I've seen her since.'

I was about to probe him further on the question of Mullick and beautiful women when Singh piped up.

'We need to ask you, sir, your location on Saturday evening last, between 6 and 10 p.m.'

It was hardly the smartest query. A man like Carlyle would

never need to get his hands dirty committing such an act himself; and indeed the question, or perhaps the questioner seemed to rile the businessman.

'Me?' he said incredulously, his voice raised to a degree sufficient to turn heads in our direction. 'What the hell have my whereabouts got to do with anything? For goodness' sakes, man, you don't think *I* had anything to do with it, do you?'

I felt the need to interject. 'We are merely following all lines of inquiry. As you've said, you were hardly on good terms, and we've been informed you and he were at loggerheads regarding the chairmanship of the commerce association.'

'Yes but that hardly constitutes grounds to murder the man!'

The steward walked over, a nervous expression on his face.

'Sorry, sirs, but I must ask you to refrain from raising your voices.' He pointed to a sign above the door forbidding loud conversation in the reading room.

Carlyle waved him away but lowered his tone all the same.

'Look, I wasn't the only one who had an issue with Mullick. He seemed to take relish in putting one over on us British. But that's the problem with natives like him. They're ungentlemanly.'

'Of course,' I said. 'That must be why they're barred from gentlemen's clubs such as this. Now if you would please answer the question.'

'I believe I dined at the Polo Club that night if you must know, with two friends: James McMillan, a tea planter down from Assam, and an officer from the garrison at Fort William, a Major Fitzroy. McMillan and Fitzroy were my guests.'

'And where we might find these gentlemen?' asked Singh.

The question, or maybe the questioner, seemed to irritate Carlyle. He gave a theatrical sigh.

'McMillan is on his way back upcountry. As for the major, he was due off on a tour of East Bengal. I'd imagine you could find him somewhere between here and Chittagong. Or you could simply ask the maître d' at the club. He'd tell you I was there all evening.'

I didn't doubt it. I didn't doubt that the maître d' would say anything that Carlyle wanted him to say, true or otherwise. Yet the fact remained, Carlyle's alibi or lack of it meant little. I'd not come here intent on accusing him of anything, merely to understand the gentleman, his relationship with Mullick, and just as importantly to discover more about exactly what sort of a man Mullick was. Singh's intervention had rather set the cat among the pigeons and now Carlyle was on the defensive and I rather feared he wouldn't tell us anything of note.

I thanked him for his time, and with Singh in tow, made a tactical withdrawal out of the room and back down the stairs.

'Head back to Lal Bazar,' I said. 'Check out his alibi with the Polo Club and see if you can track down those two men. Start with the major at Fort William, then move on to the tea planter. Let me know what you find out.'

'You are not coming?' he asked.

I checked my watch.

'Alas no,' I said, 'I've got a prior engagement.'

I didn't have much call to wear black tie these days, but this party I felt deserved the effort, so I got Sandesh to dredge my dinner suit out of the back of the wardrobe and give it a brush down.

He held it up on its hanger for me to see.

It was getting on for a decade old and carried the distinct air of mothballs, but the trousers still fitted and that felt like a victory. I donned a dress shirt starched to within an inch of rigid, and in front of the bathroom mirror, fumbled with the bow tie till my patience wore thin.

I returned to the sitting room to find Sandesh out on the balcony, loafing and ogling the girls across the road. I coughed and he spun round, wet rag in his hand as though he were in the process of cleaning the air out there. He smiled at the sight of me.

Before he could say anything, the telephone rang and he rushed to answer it.

'Captain Wyndham residence,' he said. 'Who is may I ask calling? ... Oh, Suren-*babu*! One-minute-one-minute, I call sahib.' The contraption in hand, he turned to me. 'Suren-*babu*, sir.'

I walked over and took the telephone from him. 'Suren?'

'It is Mahalia, Sam.' He sounded out of breath. 'She did not come to the cemetery. I waited almost an hour. I went back to the university, hoping I might find her, but there was no sign. I think we may need to go to her home, arrest her and force her to talk.'

I told him to calm down. 'Maybe she didn't get your note, or maybe she just couldn't get there in time? Didn't you say she was teaching kids somewhere up town?'

'It is possible,' he said.

'So let's not get ahead of ourselves. You can try again tomorrow. If she doesn't cooperate, we'll bring in the heavy artillery.'

That seemed to mollify him. I ended the call and turned to Sandesh. 'So? How do I look?'

'Very nice, Captain. You are pukka sahib!'

With his endorsement ringing in my ears, I made my way down to the street, receiving several comments from the girls up on their balconies, which I chose to take as complimentary, and hailed a tonga at the corner of College Square.

The driver was a Bihari by the look of him, puffing away on a small brown bidi that, I knew from experience, could burn a hole in the side of a dreadnought. The smell of it is different from that of a cigarette, more earthy. I ordered him to make for the Great Eastern. With one last puff, he threw the burning embers into the gutter, then yanked the reins and the nag set off at an amble. That was fine with me as I was beginning to have second thoughts about the whole endeavour. I wasn't one for parties, and my earlier desire to cock a snook at Annie Grant now seemed to have dissipated almost completely.

We came to a stop outside the hotel at a few minutes before eight. I handed the man a few coins which he touched to his forehead and then stowed in a tin box at his feet. A uniformed doorman in a fanned turban offered me a parade-ground salute the sheer majesty of which almost made me salute back in return. In the lobby, my friend the concierge was still at his post. Maybe it was my formal attire or maybe he was just warming to me, but this time he was most gracious in his greeting.

'Captain Wyndham. Miss Morgan is expecting you. May I send a boy up to her room to inform her of your arrival?'

'No need,' I said. 'I'll go up myself.'

I took the stairs to the second floor and knocked, muffled voices and hurried footsteps sounding behind the door. Madhu opened it, looked me up and down with an expression that suggested I'd overdone the cologne. Nevertheless she bade me enter and led me once more to the suite's sitting room.

'Won't be a moment, Sam.' Estelle's voice carried from the bedroom. 'Help yourself to a drink.'

I spied a well-stocked sideboard and headed over to it. 'Take your time,' I said, reaching for a tumbler.

I had poured myself a whisky and taken a first sip by the time I heard her footsteps. I turned to see her enter, dressed in a green-and-gold silk sari, and it was all I could do to keep from choking on my drink.

She tried to hide a smile. 'Did I startle you?'

'Not at all,' I said, coughing. 'I just didn't expect to see you in a sari.'

'Is it all right?'

'It's beautiful,' I said. 'It's just not the done thing among Calcutta's crème de la crème.'

Her face fell. 'You think I should change?'

'On the contrary, I think it might do them good to see a woman dressed the way one should in such a climate,' I said, receiving in response the sort of smile people paid good money to see on the silver screen. The room suddenly felt too warm.

'A drink?' I asked.

'If you think we have time?'

'This is Calcutta,' I said. 'There's always time for a drink.'

'A gin sling, then.'

I looked at her. 'Alas I might need some help with the constituent parts.'

She walked over. 'Really, Captain. And I was beginning to think you knew everything.'

'Almost everything.'

'It's gin, lemon juice, sugar syrup and a couple of dashes of bitter.'

She passed me the cocktail shaker and I proceeded to implement her instructions.

'And then some ice. A *lot* of ice.'

I reached for the ice bucket.

'And now you shake it till the ice inside freezes your fingers.'

I did as ordered, and as my hands went numb, poured the drink into a tall glass.

'Now tonic and soda water,' she said. 'Equal measures.'

The final touches added, I passed her the glass.

'Well? How is it?'

Another smile. 'Perfect.'

It is curious how the accomplishment of even the most basic of tasks can bring joy to a man's heart when it's done on behalf of an attractive woman. I caught sight of Madhu loitering near the door, watching me like a shopkeeper spying on a schoolboy for signs of larceny. Estelle, I felt, must have noticed it too, for a moment later she took me by the arm.

'It's stiflingly warm in here, Sam. Why don't we go out to the balcony?'

It seemed a jolly good idea to me and so I accompanied her outside and into the evening breeze and looked out onto the lights of Government House. Letting go of my arm, she took a sip of her cocktail.

'This city is rather beautiful in its own way.'

'It certainly looks better in the dark,' I said.

'I think I shall miss it,' she said. 'I'll be on a boat heading for Shanghai soon.'

My stomach seemed to fall. 'That is a tragedy.'

She turned and looked at me curiously. 'For whom?'

'For the city.'

Her smile wavered. 'And for you?'

I took a sip of whisky and pondered the question. Meeting her was definitely the most interesting thing that had happened to me in a long while, the double murder of Mullick and his secretary notwithstanding. She'd certainly brightened things up a bit, like a beam of sunlight entering a long-shuttered room. I found myself wishing she were staying longer.

'It'll be tough,' I said. 'I doubt I'll get invited to any more glamorous parties.'

She looked at me with what I thought was real tenderness. 'Well, I shall certainly miss you.'

And suddenly I found myself wishing that might be true.

'You'd tire of my company soon enough.'

'I don't believe that,' she said.

'Trust me,' I said. 'I'm hard to put up with on a regular basis. I'm whatever is the diametric opposite of an acquired taste.'

'You know what I think, Sam?' she said. 'I think you're scared to be happy.'

Maybe there was truth in that. Or maybe I was just scared to let anyone get close to me in case they realised how hollow, how broken I was.

I drained my glass and turned to her.

'We're late,' I said. 'We should get going.'

The venue was Firpo's on Chowringhee, a Calcutta institution that claimed, alongside many other Calcutta institutions, to be the finest establishment east of London. It was where visiting royalty came to dine, dance and be entertained, and might have been made for a woman like Estelle Morgan.

The noise was audible before the place came into sight, the hubbub of voices competing with the strains of a string quartet. The building was hard to miss, lit up as it was like the seafront at Blackpool in season, its whitewashed walls gleaming as though the paint might still be wet. Carriages, their distinguished guests delivered, now idled along the length of the street, coachmen clustered in small groups smoking or playing cards.

A liveried attendant helped Estelle from the tonga and she took my arm amid the scent of jasmine and frangipani for the short walk to the entrance.

Inside was everything I had come to expect from the upper classes in this city: opulence and extravagance and people having too good a time of it all. Calcutta's elite, the white parts of it at any rate, were out in force, well oiled with drink and having a whale of a time. Women were draped in satin and summer patterns, some sporting enough diamonds to furnish a chandelier; and the men were in uniform or sported black tie, which in its way was just another uniform, and while my dinner jacket was maybe not the smartest or the newest, I was the only man there with an internationally renowned actress on my arm.

Upon our entrance, the hum of conversation seemed to diminish.

Heads swivelled to appraise us. Estelle seemed to notice it too and I felt her stiffen somewhat. Yet I couldn't help but feel a stab of something, not pride exactly, but a sense of satisfaction, that the great and the good of this damn city were all staring at the woman who'd walked in with *me*, a bloody policeman who had no real business being in their midst. Yes it was infantile, but it was also rather marvellous, and I wished it would happen more often.

A turbaned waiter approached, a silver tray of champagne flutes held aloft like an offering to the gods. I took two and passed one to Estelle.

'Here, this might help.'

'Help?'

'You seem rather tense all of a sudden.'

She breathed a laugh. 'You are a most observant man, Sam.'

'I'm a policeman. It's my job,' I said. 'Though I'd have thought you'd be used to this sort of thing.'

She took a sip of champagne. 'I *am* used to it. But that doesn't mean I like it.' She raised her glass. 'Still, a drink or two should see us through.'

'If you don't enjoy it, why bother to come tonight?' I asked.

'Publicity,' she sighed.

'Do you really need it? Here, I mean? It's not as though India is the centre of the cinematic world.'

She smiled ruefully. 'But India is impossibly exotic, at least to the great American public. The press will be here tonight and it will make good copy. And anyway, if you're not seen, you're forgotten. At least that's what Sal says.'

'Ah yes,' I said. 'And where is the illustrious Mr Copeland this evening?'

She took another sip of champagne. 'He should be around here somewhere.'

Sure enough, it didn't take long to spot the American as he was already making a beeline for Estelle, forging a path through the crowd like a steamroller.

'Estelle, darling,' he said, taking her hand. 'I do hope you're having a good time.'

She looked up at him. 'We've just arrived. Captain Wyndham here is looking after me. He's being the most perfect gentleman.'

Copeland gave me a nod and, surprisingly, the hint of a smile. 'Captain Wyndham. Thanks for looking after our girl here. I won't lie to you, it's been a rough week and I'm glad you've been here to keep things on the straight and narrow, so to speak. I know your presence has been a great source of reassurance for Estelle.'

'Really?' I said. 'That didn't seem to be your view earlier today.'

He had the decency to look abashed. 'Ha! Yes, well, you didn't exactly catch me at a good time. I was waiting on news from the States. A potential role for Estelle in a new picture.'

'And you've received that news now?'

'Oh yes. And good news it is too. In fact, if you don't mind, might I prise Estelle away from you for a few minutes? There's a few things about it I need to discuss with her.'

It didn't seem like a request I could refuse. I turned to Estelle. 'If you'll excuse me.'

'Of course,' she said. 'I'll come and find you when we're done.'

I left her, feeling rather more melancholy than I had expected, and, to the strains of 'The Blue Danube', wandered through the throng in search of a proper drink. Conversations swirled, light and frothy and tinged with laughter. I had hoped to find a waiter. What I actually found was a mirrored bar, complete with waistcoated barman, a modern, art-deco thing – the bar, not the barman – all curves and black-lacquered surfaces, with three rows of bottles on its mirrored shelves. I headed for it like a docker does a pub on payday.

'Whisky,' I said to the barman. 'Neat. Single malt if you've got it.'

He turned and reached for a bottle behind him, brought it round and showed it to me, seeking my approval as though it were a bottle of wine and I a Frenchman. It was an Islay, one with an unpronounceable name, and that was fine with me because I had found that any good whisky, whatever its name, generally becomes unpronounceable by the third measure.

I told him to make it a double.

The chap, bless him, dispensed the liquor with a liberal largesse before handing me a hefty crystal tumbler. I toasted his good health and I meant it, then took a sip, waylaid a passing waiter and relieved him of a morsel of sheekh kebab skewered on a toothpick and followed the music through the hallway and into a gilded ballroom. Here the glittering notables of Calcutta society mingled while a troop of uniformed natives flitted between them with trays of drinks and canapés. Some of the faces were known to me: gentlemen I'd crossed paths with, civil servants who directed the fates of millions, tycoons who'd made fortunes in tea, teak, jute or pretty much anything that could be extracted from this country at a profit. Of those who plied their trade in the opposite direction – the pale men from Manchester or Wigan, here to hawk the wares of their British-based concerns, be it shirts from Leeds or soap from Bristol; or the red-faced Scots from the Clyde who sold girders and factory machinery by day and drank the town dry by night – well, there were fewer of them in attendance, though one or two, the more successful or the better connected, could be spotted here and there, looking as out of place as politicians at the gates of heaven.

I had a passing familiarity with some of the women too, mainly from my early days in the city when I was considered an acceptable if not particularly prized catch for quite a few ladies. Most of them, I suspected, had spent the intervening years avoiding me, not that I bore them any ill will for that, as, given the option, I'd probably have done much the same myself.

And then I spotted her, the one woman who had always stood out from the rest. Annie Grant, on the arm of that foreign fop, Ostrakhov. I felt that familiar sensation, the one I always felt when seeing her on the arm of another man: like being hit by a runaway bull. A silent, invisible blow that still had the power to wind, completely; and suddenly I felt I should have followed my instincts and stayed in the other room with the barman. Annie looked as Annie always did, radiant, tonight in a blue-green dress that shimmered in the brilliance of the chandeliers. Around her neck, a piece of diamonds and sapphire that probably cost more than an honest man made in a lifetime.

She caught my gaze, eyes widening as she began to walk over, Ostrakhov on her arm as if glued there. I took a generous gulp of whisky and steeled myself.

'Sam?'

Her expression suggested she found my very presence here somehow astonishing and annoying, which was nice.

'Annie,' I said, and gave a nod to Ostrakhov who greeted me with a grin that I was sorely tempted to wipe off his face with my fist.

'I'm surprised to see you here, Sam. You didn't mention you were coming.'

'Well, you know me,' I said. 'I live for these social occasions.'

She looked less than convinced. 'I *do* know you, Sam, which is why I'm even more surprised by your presence. And how are you finding it?' She looked around. 'I see you've made the usual number of friends. Shouldn't you be introducing yourself to people?'

I held up my tumbler. 'I thought I might introduce myself to a drink first. Dutch courage and all that.'

Ostrakhov's eyes lit up. 'What is this you drink?'

'Whisky,' I said. 'Single malt. But I'll be buggered if I can tell you what it's called. It begins with a "B" but the name is practically unpronounceable.'

'Bunnahabhain?'

'That sounds about right,' I said, impressed as much by his knowledge of Scotch whisky as his ability to pronounce the damn thing. Then again it was probably easier to say in Russian than it is in English.

'Are you a connoisseur of whisky, Count Ostrakhov?'

'I liked very much. Back in Russia. But that was long time ago.'

Maybe I'd misjudged the man. It seemed he might have a few redeeming qualities after all. I held out the glass.

'Have a sip, tell me what you think.'

He reached out a hand. 'Very kind.'

'Well, what do you think?' I said, noticing the look of distaste on Annie's face as he took a sip.

A grin creased his face. '*Is* good!'

'Yes, I thought so too. There's a lovely chap behind the bar in the other room who will pour you a large one if you want. I'd be happy to introduce you to him.'

Ostrakhov looked to Annie as though seeking permission. She, however, was looking at me.

'You don't need to do that, Sam. I'm sure Nikolai and I can find the bar on our own. Speaking of which, you aren't here alone, are you? I didn't see your name on the guest list. Or are you working? Are you here because of your murder case? Frankly, that would make a lot more sense than you simply turning up to a party you weren't invited to.'

At that moment I spotted Estelle Morgan entering the room, Sal Copeland a step behind. She saw me, beamed and began to walk over.

'Come now, Miss Grant,' I said. 'I do have a life outside of work, but you're quite right, I wasn't invited. I'm here as a plus one.'

Annie did her best to hide her surprise, but it's hard to hide such things from a seasoned detective.

'Really?' she said. 'And who, pray tell, is the lucky lady?'

'Here she comes now,' I said. 'Let me introduce you.' I moved past her and took Estelle's hand. 'Estelle,' I said, 'I'd like you to meet Miss Annie Grant and Count Nikolai Ostrakhov.'

This time there was no hiding the shock on Annie's face, and though her natural composure quickly reasserted itself, in that brief moment I experienced a degree of blissful satisfaction that even Hindu holy men only occasionally achieve.

'A pleasure,' Estelle said, reaching out a hand which Ostrakhov was more than happy to kiss.

'Sam,' Annie said, 'you didn't tell me you knew Estelle Morgan?'

Estelle stepped in before I could reply. 'Oh yes,' she smiled. 'Sam and I have become quite good friends.'

'How wonderful,' Annie said, the words seeming to struggle from her lips. 'And has he shown you much of our fair city?'

'Oh indeed,' Estelle said. 'He's been an absolute darling.'

I struggled to recall showing Estelle anything at all of Calcutta, and I wasn't sure why she was saying these things but I was glad she was.

Annie nodded as if this was the most interesting thing she had heard all day. 'And will you be staying long in town?'

Estelle sighed. 'Alas no. Unfortunately I need to leave shortly.'

'Oh, that is a shame,' Annie said. She turned to me. 'Couldn't you convince Miss Morgan to stay a little longer, Sam?'

'I'm certainly trying,' I said.

'Yes, he is,' Estelle cut in, 'but I have no choice. My agent tells me there's a role in King Vidor's new movie for which he wants me to audition. But I *am* trying to persuade Sam to join me out in Hollywood.'

Annie blinked, her smile wavering. 'I didn't know you were thinking of leaving, Sam?'

I could have told her that it was news to me too, but I admit

I was interested in where this was going. I shrugged. 'It's just a thought. A change is as good as a rest, isn't that what they say? New worlds to conquer and all that.'

'Oh, Miss Grant,' Estelle interjected, 'please try and convince him.'

I wondered what she was playing at. Still, I had to hand it to her. She certainly was a good actress. She'd almost convinced *me* that I should go to America with her.

Annie mumbled something which was lost amid the sound of the orchestra striking up a new tune. The strains seemed to revive her.

'Miss Morgan,' she said, 'please do excuse us. I absolutely adore this waltz. Come, Nikolai, let's dance.'

Old Nikolai looked like he'd much rather spend some more time with us, or possibly he just wanted to follow up on my offer of showing him to the bar before the whisky ran out. Either way, he didn't look exactly thrilled as Annie dragged him off to dance. A part of me actually felt sorry for him. A small part though, and only a little bit sorry.

Estelle too watched them go. 'Miss Grant seems to like you, Sam.'

'You can tell that from a two-minute conversation?'

She gave a laugh. 'It didn't take two minutes. It was obvious enough from the way she looked at you. And the way she looked at me when I took your hand.'

'Maybe you should give Hollywood a miss and become a detective here?'

'Maybe I will.'

'On second thoughts,' I said, 'you are clearly too talented an actress to even consider doing anything else.'

'You think I was acting? Oh but I *would* like you to come to America with me. I may have hammed it up a little for your friend there, but only because I thought you might appreciate it. There's obviously some history between the two of you – women can sense these things – and I get the feeling this Nikolai isn't the first chap she's brandished in your face. I just thought she might like to see what it was like when the shoe is on the other foot. She's not English, is she? I mean, not wholly.'

'No,' I said. 'She's Anglo-Indian.'

'Really?' she said, her eyes widening. 'I've not seen many of them here.'

'No,' I said, 'you won't. Most of them don't move in the circles Miss Grant does.'

Estelle seemed to ponder this. 'It can't have been easy for her. I imagine it's difficult for people like her to fit in, neither fish nor fowl.'

'You really are quite perceptive,' I said.

'It's good to see someone like her thrive though. However did she manage it?'

'Brains,' I said, 'and a bit of good fortune. She came into some money and invested it extremely profitably. And she is fortunate to be here in Calcutta. On the whole, it is a more liberal place than most of the country.'

'Most of the world too, I'd imagine,' she said. 'Sal says that in America, any hint of miscegenation is looked upon as a terrible sin. He says it can destroy careers *and* lives. It's even illegal in some parts of the country. People are lynched. Imagine that. To be condemned for loving the wrong person.'

'Well, I don't think Miss Grant will be venturing to America any time soon.'

'Well, that's not my concern,' she said, taking my hand. 'I'm much more interested in whether *you'd* consider coming.' She gave me a smile. 'Now. How about we have a dance?'

Sometimes the demands of being a policeman run contradictory to those of being a man. My training, my experience, my whole damn life told me that it wasn't normal for a woman like Estelle to lavish such attention on a man like me. Suren, no doubt, would have told me that if something felt too good to be true, then it almost certainly was. But Suren wasn't here, and while caution and scepticism might, in the cold light of day, be the obvious and correct course of action, there and then, in the heat of a Bengal evening, a double whisky or two to the good and in the glow of this beautiful woman, I wanted to believe every word from her lips and every touch of her fingers. I told myself there was no harm in it, that for one night I could pretend that this woman by my side might mean the sweet words she whispered to me. Tomorrow was a different day. Tomorrow, I could return to cold, hard reality.

It was some time after midnight that Sal Copeland sauntered over to us and took Estelle by the elbow. His speech was slurred, his accent honeyed by alcohol.

'Estelle, darlin', time to go. It's late an' there's a lot we need to sort tomorrow.'

Estelle protested, but Copeland was having none of it. Eventually she relented, but not without a final gambit.

'You don't mind, Sal, if Captain Wyndham takes me back?'

Copeland gave me a hard stare. 'As long as he promises to be a good boy.'

'I'm sure the captain will be a perfect gentleman,' she told him, with a degree of conviction I wasn't sure was quite merited.

The night hours are the best hours in Calcutta. The roads are still, the air is cool and, if the breeze is blowing in the correct direction, suffused with the scent of hibiscus and marigold. Tonight, the wind was gentle and perfect and the short journey back to the Great Eastern was like riding through a dream. As the tonga drove,

Estelle rested her head against my shoulder and I looked up at a sky full of stars and sighed.

Estelle lifted her head. 'What's wrong, Sam?'

'Nothing,' I said.

'Are you sure?'

'I'm just conscious that you'll be leaving soon.'

She took my hand. 'You know I have to go.'

'I suppose I could have you arrested,' I said. 'That would keep you here.'

'True,' she said, 'though it might kill the romance. It would be far better for you to come with me.'

In that moment I couldn't tell if she was joking.

The whole conversation felt surreal. Maybe the whisky had loosened my tongue because for once I spoke frankly.

'You don't want that, Estelle. You hardly know me, you have the world at your feet, and I'm a copper whose only talent is tracking down murderers and even that's debatable these days.'

She breathed in. 'I've seen enough of men to know the difference between a good one and a bad one. And you, Captain Sam, are one of the good ones.'

I listened to her words but feared to believe them. She must have sensed my hesitation.

'Seriously, Sam. Think of it. America. The land of opportunity. You said yourself you could do with a fresh start.'

I couldn't recall uttering the words, but then it had been one of those evenings, and the sentiment was certainly true. But I couldn't just up sticks and leave.

'There is the small matter of a double murder that needs solving.'

'Mullick and his dogsbody? Surely there are others who could deal with that?'

I sensed a hardening of her tone.

'When I asked you about Mullick the other day, you said he'd been nothing but a gentleman towards you. Now that was before ... well, before you came to know that I was, as you say, one of the good ones. From what I've found, it seems there was another side to the man, a less savoury one. I need to ask, were you being entirely honest?'

She turned towards me. 'I'm asking you to come with me to America and all you want to talk about is Mullick?'

'I need to know if he ... if he *hurt* you.'

'No,' she said definitively, 'he didn't. He surely *hurt* others though, and you're correct in so much as he wanted to hurt me too. But I've met so many men like him before, men who think with their wallets, who think wealth entitles them to anything and anyone they want. I've learned how to handle them. As for whoever killed him, have you considered that they probably saved other girls from the same treatment at Mullick's hands?'

It is hard to describe how I felt in that moment. I felt the pain in her voice, and the suffering, and a manner that suggested she had locked it away, much as I had my own pain, behind a door in her soul. In that brief instant, following her to America did not sound quite so preposterous or fanciful but something that was both possible and necessary. In that moment, I wanted to protect her, to stay by her side, to help her heal. But as the night air refreshed my senses and the whisky released its grip, I recognised the sentiment for what it was – a fantasy.

'Why *did* you come here, Estelle? Why did you take a role in some tinpot little Indian movie?'

She looked at me, and for a moment I felt she was about to tell me something. Something she'd kept hidden, not just from me but from the world; something buried and camouflaged with a skill only an actress could manage. And then it was gone. That beautiful mask descended once more and she smiled.

'Maybe it was, what do the Indians call it ... kismet? Maybe it was so that I might meet you?'

The tonga turned the corner and pulled up outside the hotel.

I got out and helped her down.

'Well,' she said, 'I suppose this is it.'

'Yes, I suppose it is,' I said. 'Thank you for a rather wonderful evening. I really didn't expect it to be quite so ... enjoyable. I ... It's just a pity that we had to meet under these circumstances.'

'But without these circumstances, we wouldn't really have met at all.' She leaned in and kissed me and if that moment had lasted an eternity, I wouldn't have minded one jot. But then it was over.

'I will miss you, Estelle,' I said.

She smiled. 'How about you walk me up to my suite?'

'I would like that,' I said.

'And I suppose I could always make one last attempt to change your mind about America.'

I walked her through a sleeping lobby, lights dimmed, deserted of life save for a bellboy dozing in one dim corner and the night manager enthroned behind his desk looking like Canute holding back a tide of marble flooring. He looked up and afforded us a nod as we passed.

We took the stairs in silence, her arm in mine, each of us, I suspected, lost in our thoughts of what might have been had circumstances been different. Indians are a fatalistic people. The Hindus started it, of course, with their notion that one's destiny was written in stone, etched unchangeable by the gods and the stars, but over time those of other faiths seemed to have also adopted it. I too, in my turn, had succumbed to the notion, at least in part. My fate, predestined or otherwise, could not lie with Estelle Morgan.

Yet each step seemed to loosen the bonds that tethered me to this land, to this city: to Annie Grant; to friends; to the job; to Premchand Boral Street; to Sandesh and the girls on their balconies; to

Suren Banerjee; to the threadbare, empty coat that was British rule of this place. With each step the chains slackened as I dared to dream.

And then the face of Sarah drifted into my conscience. Eight years. Eight *long* years since she had passed. Some days it felt like only yesterday that I had felt her touch, heard her voice. On others, it felt like decades. And yet, she was always there. The voice of my conscience, the exasperated angel at my shoulder.

If my coming to Calcutta had been an attempt to flee the memory of her death, then what now were thoughts of this new emigration? How would she view it, especially if it was in the wake of the woman now on my arm? A woman I hardly knew? And in search of what exactly? Sarah would, I was sure, want me to be happy; she would want me to move on with life, but would she judge this potential step progression or foolishness?

The landing to the second floor came upon us with a haste that felt unseemly, and there, up ahead, was the door to Estelle's suite. It was as we reached it that she turned to me.

'Well, Sam, I shan't ask you again. If you said no to me now, there would be a finality to it. I'd rather you tell me you'll think it over. That way I can pretend that maybe you will come.'

'You know I need to get to the bottom of Mullick's murder,' I told her. 'But after that ...'

A half-smile played on her lips. Not like the smile she had given me the first time I had met her, full and radiant and confident, but something more natural, more fragile, and so, in a way, more precious, more beautiful.

'If you do find those responsible, remember what I said. Try not to judge them too harshly. They might have been acting from noble intentions.'

'Estelle,' I said, 'is there something you're not telling me?'

She shook her head. 'You already know everything there is to know about Mullick.'

As I struggled to make sense of her words, she spoke once more.

'You will write to me, won't you, Sam?'

'I shall,' I said. 'If you tell me where to send the letters.'

'I'll send you a telegram, care of the police, as soon as we reach Los Angeles.'

'Then it's settled,' I said.

'Save one thing,' she said. 'You haven't kissed me.'

Before I could reply, the door to her suite opened. There stood Madhu, looking for all the world like an irritated mother hen.

'Miss Estelle, come inside. Is very late now.'

Estelle looked as though she had no choice but to obey the command of her own maid.

'You owe me that kiss, Sam. I'll collect it in America.'

I left Estelle to the admonishments of her maid and, my head spinning, walked slowly back down the stairs of the Great Eastern and out into a night subtly changed from when I had walked in.

I stood on the pavement, lit a cigarette and inhaled. None of this could be real. I knew that much. And if it wasn't, what did that mean? Why was this woman weaving this spell? What could she hope to gain? In that moment I could think of nothing. Nothing that I might have to offer her.

And then my thoughts turned to America. With or without Estelle, why should I not go? Truthfully, there was little to keep me in Calcutta. My relationship with Annie Grant was dead, in spite of, or maybe because of, our best efforts, our unending struggle to build something from nothing. She was with Ostrakhov now, and that sat less uneasily with me than I had anticipated. Maybe it was the influence of Estelle upon me, or maybe it was because Ostrakhov, penniless weed that he was, seemed less of an arse than I'd expected. Whatever the reason, Annie and I were happier, it seemed, when we were apart than when actually together. Things with Estelle Morgan might end up no differently, but surely it was better to take a chance on something new than to continue along a path that would lead nowhere. And if things didn't work out, there was always Canada. I thought I might like Canada. I had a feeling people were less optimistic there.

A tonga-wallah on the far side of the street eyed me hungrily. At this time of night, transport was in short supply and I, in black tie and dinner jacket, looked like just the sort of gullible fool who'd be easily parted from his money. He was probably right in that.

'*Kothai jeté chān, sahib?*'

'Premchand Boral Street.'

He nodded sagely. '*Teen takā.*'

And for once the price didn't sound that steep.

'*Chalo*,' I said, and ascended the buggy.

With a gentle pull of the reins, he set off, then turned left into Bentinck Street and continued in the direction of College Square. The road was peaceful, a canyon between slumbering buildings. It struck me, that if I *were* soon to depart India, it was only a precursor to a wider exodus. The rest of my countrymen would eventually follow, and then these buildings would be our legacy. They would stand long after we packed our bags and finally acknowledged the truth, that we were masters in another's house and that they wanted it back. But there would come a time when they too would crumble, and then the dead and their tombstones in the cemeteries of Park Street would be all that was left of us here. In which case, it was important to do what good we could while time remained. The moon disappeared behind a cloud and reality dawned once more, hitting me like a slap in the face. There would be no America, no Canada. There would be the search for Mullick's killer and Ghatak's killer, and for Dolly Chatterjee, and after that, who knew? But whatever lay in store, one thing was certain. It would find me here, in India, in this cursed city of Calcutta. The only place fit for a man like me.

The flat was in darkness, Sandesh asleep under the dining table. I left him to it. If anyone needed their beauty sleep, it was him. I thought about hitting the hay myself, but after the evening with Estelle, sleep would not come. Instead I wandered through to the living room in search of a nightcap.

I poured myself a whisky – a restrained measure, at least by my usual standards, and was about to head to the balcony when Ghatak's briefcase caught my eye. Suren must have left it here prior to our dash to Mullick's office that morning. I picked it up, extracted the ledger in which Ghatak had so assiduously recorded every expense incurred on behalf of his master, and leafed through the pages. It had already yielded one nugget of information: the payment to Dolly's studio of a thousand rupees; maybe there were more secrets waiting to be found. Whisky in hand, I made my way to the armchair for some bedtime reading.

In neat, regimented rows, Ghatak had laid out the costs of everything, down to the last rupee and paisa. I wasn't sure what I was looking for. Anything that seemed out of the ordinary. The first few pages didn't yield much – indeed, the sheer banality of it threatened to do what the whisky was supposed to, and help me fall asleep. But then suddenly I saw something that made me sit up.

An amount with no explanation beside it. Twenty-five rupees. I flipped the pages. There, seven days later, was an identical amount, again with no details of what it was for or to whom it was paid. I kept going. Throughout the ledger, every seven days without fail, a payment of twenty-five rupees.

I went back to the first entry and scanned the payments around it. Nothing untoward seemed to jump out. I kept going, moving seven days on and to the second payment; then again, moving forward another seven days to the third payment. It was then that I saw it. Each week, on the line following the mystery expense, Ghatak had recorded payments made to something or someone with the initials B.C. He'd then thoughtfully added 'dinner' against each entry. The same initials, and each week roughly the same amount.

It might have been nothing and I'd have dismissed it if it had been a one-off, but the same initials, time and again, and always on the line after the mystery payment of twenty-five rupees. Maybe it meant something. The trifling amounts – a few rupees each time – suggested it wasn't Mullick having dinner, but Ghatak himself. The secretary had struck me as a creature of habit.

I let my mind wander. Was Ghatak going somewhere each week and then stopping to have dinner? Was the twenty-five rupees payment for illicit services? It seemed an awful lot for a prostitute, at least from what the girls in Premchand Boral Street told me. Maybe rent for a property then? That would explain why Ghatak found himself in the same location having dinner each week. But again, it sounded like a lot of money for a week's rent. What then? I took a sip of whisky and looked to Sandesh snoring under the dining table. Maybe it was a payment to someone? Did Mullick keep a woman in a house somewhere? Was Ghatak paying her a weekly amount? That would make sense. It would also explain the lack of any description beside the payments. After all, it wouldn't do to label them *'payments for boss's woman on the side'*. Maybe Ghatak went for his dinner, at this place labelled B.C., while his boss was down the road ... otherwise engaged?

I drained the glass of its whisky. The more I thought of it, the more convinced I became. The two payments – the mysterious one for twenty-five rupees, and the ones for Ghatak's dinner marked B.C. – were intrinsically linked. The key was to finding out what B.C. was, and where, and I knew one person who might be able to help.

Five minutes later I was back outside, hailing a tonga from the rank on College Square. The first in line was a young chap I'd not seen before.

'Where to, sahib?'

'Cossipore,' I said, 'and make it fast.'

THIRTY-FOUR

Surendranath Banerjee

Colonel Dawson.

I had telephoned the number he had provided and an anonymous voice had given me an address in Dum Dum and a time: 11 p.m.

I headed for Dum Dum cantonment, to a house not far from the station, on a street called Subhash Nagar Road. An odd choice of venue. Dum Dum was a suburb to the north of the city, crowded and unremarkable, which, come to think of it, may be why the colonel had chosen it.

The address was on the edge of a bustee, across the tracks from the station, and best reached, according to the instructions given me, via the number 3 rail gate. The house itself was a two-storey structure, door closed and windows shuttered, at least on the ground floor, circled by a veranda and situated at the end of a courtyard.

I climbed the few steps to the veranda, the door opening before I reached it. Beyond stood a figure shrouded in darkness, yet his build and his garments marked him out as Bengali rather than British. He closed the door behind me, and in the light of a candle, I caught sight of his face. Forty-ish, balding, thick eyeglasses. Nothing to distinguish him from a million other gentleman of his age. And yet this unassuming man *was* different.

'Follow me,' he said, before turning and making for a door at the far end of the room. He was, I assumed, an agent of the British. How many others, I wondered, ordinary-looking men like him, walked among us? And who was I to judge? Had I not spent years in the service of the same authority? My role may not have been clandestine, but did that exculpate me of guilt? No doubt many of my kinsmen had viewed me with the same distaste with which I did this man. The question was whether they would always see me as tainted, or whether redemption was possible.

I followed him upstairs to a door on the upper floor and waited as he knocked before entering. Dawson was staring out of a window into the night. He turned, cane in hand, pipe clamped between his jaws, shirtsleeves rolled up, and affected a lopsided smile.

'Young Mr Banerjee. It is a pleasure to see you.' He gestured to some chairs around a rough wooden table. 'Won't you have a seat?'

He hobbled over and joined me.

'Some refreshment?'

'No,' I said. 'Thank you.'

'Cigarette maybe?'

He pulled a pack from his pocket, a Turkish brand, unsealed it and held it towards me. I took one and he held out a silver lighter, clicking it aflame. I put the cigarette to my lips and inhaled. 'There,' he said, patting me on the shoulder, then taking a seat on the other side of the table. 'I must say, you're looking in fine fettle. Have you put on a little weight since returning? I find one's own cuisine has that effect, especially after all that foreign muck they'll have subjected you to in France and Germany. Spent a bit of time in the old Deutschland myself back in the day. Lost almost a stone in weight. Would've lost more if it wasn't for the beer, and a certain young woman.'

He gave a chuckle.

'I'm told you became rather friendly with a young European woman yourself. French, in your case, or so I understand. I hope you've left those things behind you, young man. I'm sure your father wouldn't approve of that sort of dalliance.'

I tried to hide my shock, though in retrospect it should have come as no surprise that the colonel knew of Elise. It was common knowledge that they opened the mail of what they termed *subversives*. But I never thought that I might be included on that list. The real question was why.

'May I ask why I am here?'

'Absolutely you may, and I shall get to that presently. First, though, I had hoped you might tell me what your plans are now that you have returned. I know your former colleagues at Lal Bazar would be delighted to have you back. I understand Lord Taggart would wish to give you a significant promotion, with salary to match.'

It was my turn to smile. 'That is most gracious,' I said, 'but I think my policing days are behind me.'

Dawson nodded as though he had already reached that conclusion.

'Maybe a position in the administration, then? I am sure we could find a suitable place for you within the ICS. Not some minor position, but something with some real substance. Times are changing. It won't be long before Indians fill the topmost roles with the Indian Civil Service and you could be one of them. Imagine it, you'd be one of the elite, the heaven-born.'

I sat back and took another pull on my cigarette. The heaven-born. The name given to the *burra*-sahibs of the ICS, the thousand or so Englishmen who ruled over our several hundred million. And Dawson, if he was to be believed, was offering the keys to me.

'And what would you seek in return for such a generous gift?' I asked.

He held his hands up. 'Nothing. Nothing at all. And it wouldn't be a gift. Let me be frank. You're a Cambridge man, aren't you? It is in India's interests to have a man like you in government. I imagine you may one day even have the viceroy's ear. That can only benefit us all.'

Dawson, one of the most powerful and feared men in the country, was asking me to believe in his altruism.

'That is most gracious,' I said, 'though at present I am not certain what I intend to do. Nevertheless, whatever I choose to do, I doubt it will be in the service of the present rulers of this country.'

Dawson lifted his pipe, tapped it once on the palm of his hand, then placed it in his mouth and with a long match proceeded to light it. When he looked at me again, his face seemed different.

'I see. Well, then we shall speak no more about it. Let me tell you why I have asked you here tonight. I've been informed that a relative of yours, a Miss Chatterjee, a photographer I believe, has disappeared.'

I sat up straighter. 'Did Captain Wyndham tell you that?'

He seemed to find that amusing. 'The day I need to rely on a man like Wyndham to tell me things is the day I retire. I've also been told that you may be looking for Miss Chatterjee.'

'Yes,' I said hastily. 'Is she alive?'

He puffed on his pipe, then exhaled, taking it in his hand. 'She is. At least for now.'

A wave of relief flooded through me. 'And you know where she is?'

'I hear things. I believe she has become embroiled in some dangerous business. Whatever it is, I doubt she will remain at large for long.'

'So you will tell me where I can find her?'

He paused before answering. 'Well, that's a difficult matter. Anything I tell you might compromise people who work, as you so eloquently put it, for the present rulers of this country; people, Indians I should say, for whom I feel not just a professional loyalty, but a personal one too. I couldn't jeopardise them simply to assist someone to whom I owed nothing.'

And slowly the penny dropped. If the carrot would not work, then Dawson would use the stick. If I did not do his bidding, Dolly might die. Indeed Dawson, out of spite, might even hasten her death. Was I prepared to gamble with her life?

'What would it take for you to tell me?' I said, my voice cracking.

And then the smile returned to his face. 'How well do you know the mayor of Calcutta?'

THIRTY-FIVE

Sam Wyndham

The tonga-wallah took me only so far.

It is a fact not often stated, that while India may or may not be on the road to liberation from the firm yet benevolent fist of British rule, there are parts, in Calcutta at least, where a degree of de facto independence has already been achieved, where British writ does not hold, and where a white man, or even an Indian unfamiliar with the local topography, would be well advised to steer clear of if he valued his life or the contents of his wallet.

Somewhere north of Cossipore sat a half-square-mile warren of blind lanes and dead-end *gullees* that constituted one such kingdom. During daylight hours it was like a hornet's nest, peaceful enough, as long as you didn't poke it, that is to say, do anything that might grab the attention of its denizens. And anything resembling a uniform might, if it tarried too long, be taken as provocation and be encouraged on its way with a barrage of bottles, half-bricks and choice epithets in English, Bengali and Hindi. After dark, though, was different. After dark, the place obeyed the law of the jungle, and now I was off to try and track down the king lion.

Uddam Singh was a survivor, a piss-poor immigrant from piss-poor Bihar who had come to Calcutta as a teenager with little more than his smarts and a fondness for cut-throat razors. Rumour had it that his talents were spotted by a gangland boss who had taken him under his wing and taught him the secrets of the city, only for Uddam to repay him by slitting his throat and, for good measure, those of his family too. The story might have been apocryphal, invented by Uddam himself for all I knew, but once you'd met the man, it didn't seem at all far-fetched. What wasn't in doubt though was that through a combination of entrepreneurial flair and extreme violence, Uddam had managed to install himself as kingpin of an organisation that controlled much of the trade in narcotics, prostitution and other such wholesome economic activities in North Calcutta.

He held court in the back of a shebeen in a wretched, though aptly named lane called Golla-Katta Gullee. Cut-Throat Alley. One wondered if the name had been the reason why Singh had chosen it for his base of operations, or whether he'd been the one who'd christened it. Whatever the truth, it wasn't the most salubrious of addresses, even for this part of town. The shebeen didn't have a name, at least not one that anyone had cared to tell me, and was a squat construction of mud-brick and board, topped off by a roof of terracotta tiles that pitched at a precarious angle and which, if it didn't outrightly defy the laws of physics, then was certainly contemptuous of them. It sat sinking into the mud, hemmed in between two boarded-up buildings whose erstwhile owners had, I imagined, decided to up sticks and leave rather than lodge a complaint with the proprietors.

The last half-mile I covered on foot. It had been a while since I'd last ventured here, and this presented a slight dilemma. While I was known to Uddam and a few of his lieutenants, there was no guarantee that an excitable young hoodlum, wet behind the ears and eager to prove himself, might not react to my presence with rather too much enthusiasm, and before I had a chance to explain, pursue a course of action we might both regret. It was, I decided, best to carry my Webley, the sight of which I have found often settles disagreements in my favour.

Avoiding the minefield of cow dung and dog muck that lay strewn at intervals along the lane and ever-ready to claim a shoe, I crossed over the open sewer and introduced myself to a rather diminutive thug, a gentleman possibly wider than he was tall. He seemed rather nonplussed at my presence, which was fine with me, given the most likely alternative was outright hostility.

'I need to see Uddam Singh,' I said. 'Is he in tonight?'

The man looked up at me, smirking as though the question had been imbecilic.

'No speak English.'

'Of course you do,' I said, moving my jacket an inch to reveal the outline of my revolver. 'Smart man like you. I'm sure you understand more than one language.'

He shook his head, laughing. 'Uddam-da does not come here any more.'

'So where can I find him?'

The man shrugged.

'Well,' I said, 'why don't you go inside and send out someone who does know where he might be? I'll wait here.'

The man nodded and turned for the door. For an instant, I thought he might just do as I asked. Instead there came the telltale sign, almost hidden in the dark, the hand going to the waistband, the quick swivel, the lunge forward with the blade in hand. Fortunately I'd seen it all before, a hundred times, in Calcutta and London and a half-dozen places in between, and when he turned, it was to the sight of me, a few steps back now, with my Webley pointed at his head.

The door behind him opened and out stepped a man I did recognise. A bald-headed ox of a chap who went by the name of Gupta. He looked at me and smiled, then grunted something in what I presumed was Hindi, but could just as easily have been some version of English. The diminutive thug whose head I had my revolver trained on slowly lowered his blade but continued to glare at me as though confident that his scowl might stop a bullet, and for a moment, I admit, I was tempted to find out.

'Mr Wyndham,' Gupta said, 'it has been a long time, no? Please lower your weapon. There is no need for such things, and I would hate for you to be injured.'

I did as he asked. He grunted again to the thug, who took a step back.

'Now tell me, Mr Wyndham. To what do we owe the pleasure of your company this evening?'

'I was hoping for a word with your boss,' I said, 'but it seems to be harder than obtaining a meeting with the viceroy.'

Gupta smiled graciously. 'I cannot speak for the viceroy, but Uddam-da is a very busy man.'

'Come now,' I said, 'surely he has a few minutes for an old friend.'

He stepped out into the lane. 'I cannot guarantee it, but we can try. Come with me.'

I bid adieu to my diminutive new friend and fell into step with Gupta.

We walked, by my reckoning, a mile or so. I couldn't say in which direction as the route was a meandering, indeterminate sojourn along Dickensian backstreets of tumbledown buildings with shuttered windows, past rancid *gullees* and open sewers. The sort of streets where the dogs might be rabid but still had the sense to be scared of the rats. Every now and again, voices carried on the wind, snatches of conversation from darkened doorways which guillotined as we passed.

Gupta kept the talk to a minimum. I had the impression that while this was his master's turf, he was still on edge, alive to the slightest sound or movement out of the ordinary.

'How much further?' I asked.

'Not far,' he said. 'I hope, Mr Wyndham, that you have something to share with Uddam-da. Something I can tell him to make it worth his while.'

'Oh, you needn't worry,' I said. 'Just tell him Wyndham is here and that it'll definitely be worth his time.'

Finally we turned into a narrow lane, double-storey buildings crowding it on both sides. A whistle from one of the rooftops. Then another. Our progress noted and reported.

Eventually we reached a house that sat a little back from the path. In front, several men sat lounging on stone benches built into a veranda. They stiffened as they caught sight of me, a pack of wolves sensing danger. A few words from Gupta put them at their ease.

The building itself was nothing unusual. A cracked cement facade, crumbling in places to reveal the brick beneath. A few windows, shuttered on the ground floor and barred on the upper level.

'This way,' Gupta said and I followed, up the stone steps, into the building, then along a darkened corridor to a room at the back of the house.

'Wait here.'

Gupta exited and another man entered, dressed in a loose turban and kurta. Fair-skinned and built like the Red Fort. A Pashtun, I guessed, or something similar, from the North West Frontier or some such bedevilled place. A hard face whose acreage was dominated by a rather large, rather broken nose and an almost ginger beard that put me in mind of an Irishman in fancy dress. He stared at me and I gave him a nod, which seemed to bounce off him.

'Have we met before?' I asked.

The man grunted. 'You arrested my brother.'

Now I looked closer, he did seem familiar. It was perfectly possible, I supposed.

'Really?' I said. 'One arrests so many people these days, it's hard to keep track. And how is your brother?'

'Dead,' he said. 'TB in Alipore Jail.'

'I'm sorry,' I said, and I was. Genuinely.

The ensuing silence was broken by the sound of heavy footsteps on the wooden stairs in the hallway, the awkwardness thankfully banished by the reappearance of Gupta.

'Uddam-da will see you.'

I followed him from the room and up the stairs to a door. Gupta knocked, opened it wide and bade me enter.

Uddam Singh was seated behind a large, leather-topped desk that had no business being in this part of town. The walls were covered in paintings that, like the desk, had probably been liberated from residences across Calcutta or possibly an art gallery. On a sideboard sat a decanter of amber liquid and some glasses. A far cry from the back of the shebeen where he used to do business and where the most one could hope from the hooch was that it wouldn't send you blind. Business, I assumed, was good.

Singh grimaced through fractured teeth. He'd lost a son a few years earlier and I had tracked down the man who'd been responsible. That didn't make us friends, but it did mean we had an understanding.

'Captain Wyndham *sahib*,' he said, emphasising the final word, and thereby somehow contriving to cheapen it. 'They told me you had been sacked. This is fortuitous timing indeed! I was going to reach out to you and offer you a job.'

I couldn't tell if he was joking.

'That's very kind of you,' I said, 'but you were misinformed. I don't know how many constables you have in your pocket at Lal Bazar, Uddam, but in terms of intelligence, it doesn't look like you're getting your money's worth.'

'So to what *do* I owe this pleasure?'

I dispensed with the niceties. 'I need the name and address of an establishment. A restaurant or hotel or shebeen with the initials B.C.'

Singh made a show of mulling over the letters, as though he'd never heard them before in his life.

'I am afraid, as you English say, nothing springs to mind. Maybe if you told me why you want to know?'

'J. P. Mullick,' I said.

Singh stared back blankly. 'What of him?'

'You're aware he was found dead three nights ago?'

'Naturally. A great loss to the city and to the country.'

'He was murdered.'

Singh feigned surprise. 'You are sure? Well, that is certainly tragic news. The streets of this city become more dangerous by the day, Captain. If only the police would do more.'

'Well, maybe you could tell me what you know about it.'

He looked affronted. 'Captain Wyndham sahib. I must protest! You cannot think that I had any hand in this business.'

'If I did,' I said, 'we'd hardly be having this pleasant chat in your office. We'd be at Lal Bazar in an interrogation cell and I'd be the one sitting down.'

He smiled graciously. 'Of course. Where are my manners? Please –' he gestured to a chair – 'sit. Would you care for a rum?'

I took a seat and declined the drink.

'So what do you know of Mullick's death?'

'I heard you found him at the burning ghats.'

'Yes. He was brought there by four men. I want to know who killed him and why.'

Singh puffed out his cheeks. 'That is a lot to ask, Captain.'

'Well, let's start with those initials then,' I said. 'Do you know what B.C. stands for?'

Singh pondered for a moment. 'Let us say that I did. What could you offer me in return?'

'Nothing,' I said. 'It would be an altruistic gesture on your part that would be seen favourably by me.'

Singh laughed, a deep growl that went on for some time, then stopped. He looked at me and his expression hardened.

'I admire your nerve, Captain.'

He stood up and leaned over the desk, his face close enough to mine that I could smell the alcohol on his breath.

'You come here to waste my time, is that it? From what I understand, your star is not on the rise at Lal Bazar. I could kill you right here and now and I doubt anyone will miss you. They might not even bother to mount a search.'

'You could try,' I said, 'but you're not that foolish. I'm a sahib and a policeman. You kill me and, popular or not, you'll have the full might of the Imperial Police descend upon you like the heavenly host to smite the living daylights out of you. Even if you did survive, it would only be to spend the rest of your life in a three-by-four cell in the Andamans. Now wouldn't you rather have me as a friend instead?'

Singh glowered, weighing up his options, possibly considering whether it might be worth killing me anyway and hang the consequences. He stood tall and straightened his shirt.

'Very well,' he said. 'I will tell you what I know, not because of some petty threats but because I understand that you are under a cloud and I wish to see you do well and because you are an honourable man. Think of this as a favour, one which I shall seek to call on in the future.'

I kept mum. Better to let him think we might have a deal than to open my mouth and force the issue.

'Before that, though,' he said, 'how much do you really know about Mr Mullick?'

'Enough to understand that he wasn't quite the saint he was made out to be.'

'Very good, Captain! Maybe you are smarter than you look. Mullick, for all his hospitals and charities, had another side to him. One that led our paths to cross more than once.'

I raised an eyebrow. Mullick's world was a gilded one. Singh's was back alleys and knives to the ribs. Their paths should never have crossed. Unless . . .

'Was he involved in any, how should we put it, economic activities which might be frowned upon?'

Singh grinned. 'You have a way with words, Wyndham. But if you are asking if he made money from illegal activities, I do not believe so. There were rumours that he funded certain opium and hasheesh suppliers, but I never saw any proof. Believe me, if I had, I would have paid him a visit long ago. But there was no reason for him to do so. He made enough money from iron and coal and jute. Why worry about drugs? No, his interests lay in another direction.'

'Prostitution?'

'Very much so! He had an eye for a pretty girl, especially the kind less common in Calcutta: Nepalese, Naga, girls from Goa with green eyes. The more exotic the better. He would pay a handsome amount for the right girl.'

'Who procured these girls for him?'

'The usual flesh traders with their sources across the country. Some bring in girls from as far away as China and Tibet.'

'You say your paths crossed?'

'A few times. He used to rent a place not far away. Which is to say, his flunkey did. Mullick never handed over a paisa himself. All transactions carried out by his subordinates, but I knew it was Mullick. He would come there once, sometimes twice a week, to be *entertained*. Nice building. Very clean.'

'Tell me where.'

Singh shook his head. 'No point. The arrangement stopped a few years ago. They say he bought a building in Burra Bazar and used that for his assignations. Now I think of it, it's not too far from the burning ghats. And this B.C. – there's a place in Burra Bazar with those initials. It's called the Butterfly Canteen.'

'And the address?'

He gave me a look which signalled exasperation.

'You're the detective, Captain. Why don't you find it?'

I gave him a nod and got up to leave.

'And remember, Captain. You are in my debt now, and as you know, I am a man who collects upon them.'

Day 5

Wednesday

THIRTY-SIX

Surendranath Banerjee

Sometimes one makes a pact with the Devil because the alternative feels worse. In reality, it is because the benefit is immediate and the consequences, however dire, remain in the realm of the future.

The mayor of Calcutta was a man named Jatin Sengupta. An Indian, democratically elected, and no fan of the British. Dawson wished me to get to know him. He simply wanted, he said, an insight into Sengupta's thoughts, and was at pains to stress that this was merely for the better functioning of the government ... so that there might be fewer misunderstandings between British and Indian. I did not of course believe him, and he was quite aware of that fact, but sometimes a fig leaf is required to save us all embarrassment.

I had left Colonel Dawson and that house in Dum Dum and travelled back to my father's house in Shyambazar, and while I had agreed to nothing, I knew that I would do as he had asked. A night of fitful sleep changed nothing. Dolly was in danger. Dawson knew where she was and would only tell me if I did his bidding. If she were to die, I, knowing that I had the chance to save her, would never forgive myself.

In the morning, I bathed, shaved and dressed, requested breakfast from the maid, then went in search of my father who at that hour was generally to be found on the east veranda, shawl around his shoulders and a cigarette between his fingers, taking in the sun and the morning's newspaper headlines.

He looked up.

'Suren?'

'*Baba*,' I said, 'I have been thinking about our conversation regarding my proposed choice of career.'

He folded the newspaper and placed it on the rattan table beside him. The cigarette he kept in his hand.

'*Ha, bollō*. What conclusion have you reached?'

I paused for the moment, my throat suddenly dry.

'The British have intimated that, should I wish, I could rejoin the police at a senior position. Alternatively they have proposed that an application to join the ICS would be looked upon favourably. Both would be important positions,' I said, 'and offer significant influence.'

My father's face was a mask offering no indication of what he might be thinking.

'And?'

'I wanted your advice before I took a decision.'

He was silent for a moment. 'I take it that these offers were conveyed to you through your friend Captain Wyndham?'

I nodded. The gesture was easier than an outright lie, and the truth, that they had been put to me by the head of Section H, was not one I wished to disclose.

'What does he say?'

'He wishes me to rejoin the Imperial Police.'

That at least was true, even if the context had been omitted.

'Of course he does. They see you for what you are, and what you can be: a potential asset to them ... or a formidable thorn in their side. And what do you propose to do?'

'I am minded to turn them down. I have no wish to work once more for the British, but as you said, other than police work I have no skills, no experience of anything practical. Nothing that I can use for the betterment of the country. I wish to rectify that, and I think a good place to start would be right here in Calcutta. I was considering applying for a post with the Calcutta Corporation. Something that would provide political experience while also benefitting the people.'

He seemed pleasantly surprised with me, which felt unusual.

'It is not a bad idea,' he said. 'What exactly did you have in mind?'

'I am not sure,' I said. 'Something where my experience of the police might be useful. Maybe advising the mayor on police matters? He may be elected, but the police are still wholly under the control of the British. Perhaps I could provide him with some independent insight into such things.'

My father scratched at the skin beneath the strap of his wristwatch, then reached out a hand and placed it upon mine.

'I would expect Jatin-da could use that sort of assistance.'

'So you will effect an introduction to him?'

He smiled.

'I will do more than that. I shall tell him, one old barrister to another, that you will be indispensable to him, and that if he has any sense, he should employ you on the spot.'

And so I left the house that morning, armed with a letter from my father addressed to Jatin Sengupta, Mayor of Calcutta. I hailed a tonga, headed, not for the Corporation's offices, but Sengupta's home near Free School Street. I pondered whether to call in on Sam en route but decided against. He would want to know all the details of my meeting with Dawson and I was not yet sure what I was prepared to tell him. Anyway, I would see him soon enough.

Sengupta's house turned out to be a simple bungalow, dwarfed by the buildings on either side. I went through the gate and up the short path to the front door, which opened as I reached it. Beyond stood a maidservant who enquired as to my business.

'Is Jatin-*babu* at home?' I said, proffering the letter from my father and my card as my bona fides. The maid bade me wait in the hallway while she disappeared. The room was shadowed in darkness. I waited, serenaded by the sounds from the street: the calls of hawkers, the blare of bicycle rickshaw horns and the growl of motorised vehicles. She returned soon enough, this time accompanied by a woman in a sari.

'Mr Banerjee,' she said, 'I am afraid Jatin is indisposed at the moment, but he asks that you wait and he will see you shortly.'

Her English was perfect; her accent flawless. She came forward out of the gloom and for a moment I stood there, speechless. The woman smiled.

'Please come with me.'

I obeyed dumbfounded. She was tall and striking, but I had seen such women before. What I had not seen before though was an Englishwoman in a sari.

It took a few moments to get over the shock. Jatin Sengupta, the elected mayor of Calcutta, the successor to the beloved C. R. Das, was employing an Englishwoman as his secretary? And one that wore a sari, no less. If Dawson needed a spy in the mayor's office, then why me? Why not this woman? And what was this woman doing working for the mayor anyway, and in his home, too? Was it not scandalous? What did his wife make of it?

I followed her into the sitting room and sat down, stupefied.

'Won't you have some tea, Mr Banerjee?'

I stammered some response which she took to be in the affirmative. The Englishwoman whispered some instruction in Bangla and the maid quickly and silently disappeared once more. The woman returned her attention to me and perused my letter of introduction.

'I see you have recently been in Europe,' she said. 'Did you spend much time in England?'

'Alas, no,' I told her. 'I am afraid I spent most of it in France and

Germany, though I am familiar with England, or at least parts of it. Cambridge and London, mostly.'

She smiled. 'You're a Cambridge man. I could tell. Jatin too. Downing College. It's where we met. I'm Nellie, by the way. Nellie Sengupta.'

THIRTY-SEVEN

Surendranath Banerjee

'You . . . you are married to Jatin-*babu*?'

If my surprise at seeing an Englishwoman in a sari was palpable, the shock at hearing that she was the wife of the mayor was nothing short of seismic. Nellie Sengupta seemed to take pleasure from my stupefaction.

'Oh dear, Mr Banerjee, is it really that appalling to you? I'd have thought a Cambridge man would be rather more broad-minded.'

'I . . . on the contrary,' I said, 'I am merely surprised, most pleasantly, I should add. And please, you must call me Suren.'

Her demeanour brightened. 'Very well, Suren it is. *Pleasantly surprised*, you say. In what respect? That an Indian man should take an English wife?'

'No,' I said, 'more that the families, on both sides, should allow it.'

'Yes, well,' she said, 'sometimes you just have to force the issue.'

There came a soft knock at the door and the maid returned with a pot of tea and china cups, placing the tray on a small table in front of me. Mrs Sengupta, Nellie that is, poured out two cups while the maid retreated once more.

'Milk?'

'Please,' I said. 'And I am curious to know more of how you met your husband.'

She smiled wistfully and passed me a cup upon its saucer.

'Well now, that really is a tale. I don't know how familiar you are with my husband, but his family comes from Chittagong in East Bengal. His father sent him off to Cambridge to study law.' She brandished my letter of introduction. 'Well, *you* must know what that's like. It can be a wonderful place, but also quite lonely for an Indian boy.'

I did indeed know how that felt. To spend years as a second-class citizen, from a subjugated people, in the land of the master race. Even those who did not look down on the likes of me outright, displayed a parochialism, a patronising attitude, as though we Indians should gawp at their splendour and their civilisation and be thankful for their beneficence.

'My parents,' she continued, 'would provide lodgings to some of them, and our house became a sort of meeting place for a group of them, where they could be themselves and not parodies of little Englishmen, and where, most importantly, they might have a meal more suited to their own culinary tastes than the fare served to them in college.

'That's how I met Jatin. He came to our house one day, dressed up to the nines and thin as a rake. Shy too. At least at first. Little by little, though, I got to know him and at some point we fell in love. Of course, we kept it secret. Even among university types, such relationships aren't always looked upon benignly. Only our closest friends knew. Of course, the time came when we decided we had to tell our parents. Ma and Pa had, I think, worked it out already, or had at least suspected. They had their reservations, naturally, but they were willing to let me choose my own path. Jatin's parents on the other hand . . .'

She took a sip of tea.

'Well, you can imagine their reaction. Jatin's father sent a letter to my parents outlining his objections – the difference in religion, the chasm in culture, the notion that I would not be able to adapt to living within an extended family in India; and at the same time, he wrote to Jatin ordering him back to India.'

Suddenly the room felt too hot. I felt the sweat break out on the back of my neck. Jatin-da's father seemed cut from the same cloth as my own. Jatin-da, however, appeared to be fashioned from finer metal that me. He had done the right thing by the woman he loved.

'I see he did not follow his father's command.'

'He *did*, actually.'

She caught my surprise and smiled.

'Up to a point, at least. He followed his father's instructions, got on the boat at Southampton and duly sailed off.'

'But then ... how do you come to be *here*?'

'He had a change of heart at Suez. He decided he couldn't live without me and sailed all the way back, cabled me from the ship and I was waiting for him. We set off together soon after and were married at sea. And when we finally came ashore in Chittagong, I met my in-laws dressed in a sari. I wouldn't say it's been plain sailing ever since, but it's not been quite the calamity they were expecting. The sky hasn't fallen on anyone's head and I think we've surprised a few people.'

She could include me in that assessment. I thought of Elise. Like Jatin-*babu*, had I also not received a summons from my father, recalling me to India? Had I too not boarded that ship for home, sacrificing happiness, and yes, let us call it what it is, *love*, for familial ties and responsibility? The only difference was that Jatin had turned around at Suez, while I, shamefully, had continued, all the way back to Calcutta.

Nellie Sengupta must have mistaken my silence for disapproval, for the smile on her face faded. I quickly set her straight.

'I think the actions of Jatin-*babu* were most honourable. Yours too. The world would be a better place if only more people had your courage.'

The door creaked. Nellie Sengupta and I both turned as in strode a patrician-looking, bespectacled gentleman in dhoti and chador. I rose and pressed my palms together in *pranam*.

He smiled affably. 'Jatin Sengupta, at your service. And you must be the famous Surendranath Banerjee.'

I blushed. 'I am surprised you have heard of me, sir.'

'I have my contacts in Europe,' he said, reaching out and taking my hands in his own, 'and they speak most highly of you.' He turned to his wife. 'I hope Nellie has been looking after you?'

'Very much so,' I said.

He nodded. 'Good, good. So, Suren-*babu*, what brings you here?'

I took a breath. It was true that I had little choice but to be here. Dolly's life might depend on it. And yet, these were good people, fighting the good fight, at the forefront of the struggle for independence. Jatin Sengupta should have been an example to me. Instead I was here to inveigle myself into his confidence and then what? Betray him to Dawson? Was I to sell out the cause of my country's freedom or retreat with my soul intact?

But there was Dolly to think of.

'Mr Sengupta,' I said, 'I'm sorry. I think I have wasted your time.'

THIRTY-EIGHT

Sam Wyndham

The Butterfly Canteen was on Armenian Street. A call to Lal Bazar had confirmed the address. It was within walking distance of my digs but the morning was already uncomfortably hot and would only get hotter. Instead I accosted a loitering rickshaw-wallah, one I had passing acquaintance with, and who generally gouged me less than some of the others.

'Armenian Street,' I told him, as I climbed aboard.

The lane passed around me, punctuated by the creak of the wheels and the tinkling of the bell on the end of the rickshaw's stalk, till we reached the junction with College Square and then such sounds were drowned out by the noise of everyday life.

The Butterfly Canteen was open and doing a brisk trade in breakfasts. About half of its dozen tables were occupied by a clientele that was exclusively native. A few heads turned as I entered, but not that of the old gent behind the counter. He looked about sixty, was dressed in a shirt that didn't look much younger, had a head of silver hair and a face which hadn't seen a razor in several days. A rag to dry crockery, or possibly to blow his nose into, lay draped across one shoulder. I walked over and finally he looked up.

'Please, sahib. Take seat, I will come for your order.'

I took out my police identity card and passed it across the counter. 'What I need is some information. You live around here?'

He scratched nonchalantly at his neck. '*Hā*, sahib. Upstairs. Lived here fifty years.'

'J. P. Mullick. You know the man?'

'The *borro babu*?'

'That one.'

'Sahib, everyone knows Mullick-da.'

'Did you ever see him around here?'

'Only after dark.'

'I'm looking for a building. One that Mullick might have owned. You know it?'

The man smiled. A graveyard grin inhabited by a few tombstone teeth. 'I might do.'

'Well, you should tell me. I'm the police.'

'And I'm the proprietor of this restaurant. You should order something. Toast and omelette?'

I slipped two rupees across the counter. 'Keep the change,' I said. 'And the food.'

He took the time-worn rag from his shoulder, placed it on the counter, then made for the door. I followed him out into the street and he pointed across the road, a few doors down, to an anonymous, three-storey building with weeds growing out of its guttering.

'That building.'

'You're sure?' I asked.

'I live in this *para* long time, sahib. I see everything.'

I thanked him and made to cross the street.

'You come back when you finished,' he said. 'Toast and omelette waiting.'

I threaded my way through the traffic of carts and lorries, arriving unscathed on the opposite pavement. Even standing in front of the building, there was little to distinguish it from its neighbours. The ground floor boasted a stationer's, its frontage open to the street. The name on the board above it read *Himalaya Pen and Pepar*. Behind the counter stood a woman, a girl actually, who looked like she should have been at school, maybe working on her spelling. It was the kind of place that sold pens and notepads and inks in various colours and of questionable quality to a cost-conscious clientele. Beside the shopfront sat an anonymous wooden door, solid and padlocked, a thick chain running between the ring handles. Above it, two sets of shuttered windows.

I caught the girl behind the counter watching me and decided she was as good a place to start as any.

'Do you know who lives upstairs?'

She shied away, looked round into the back of the premises for assistance, and when she failed to find any, turned back, warily.

'I not knowing, sahib.'

'You ever see anyone going in or out?'

A shake of the head. 'I not seeing no one. Door is locked always.'

I took out my identity card and laid it on the counter.

'Is there another way in?'

'There is stair. In back.'

'May I use them?'

Again she looked round, this time calling out. '*Oh, Dulal-da! Shooncho!*'

Whoever Dulal was, he didn't seem inclined to answer. The girl appeared at a loss.

'I tell you what,' I said. 'How about I buy one of your best pens and you let me through to the courtyard?' I pointed to a maroon-and-gold fountain pen in the glass cabinet beneath the countertop. It was a gaudy thing, and the thought of Suren's face when I gifted it to him lifted my spirits.

My purchase safely wrapped and stowed in my pocket, the girl showed me through the back room of the shop, past battered crates of stock and stacks of cheap writing pads, to a small courtyard at the rear strewn with the detritus of general Calcutta life: discarded newspapers, empty cigarette packets and a thousand terracotta shards of broken clay *bhars*.

To one side stood the stairwell, zigzagging up the rear of the building, past a door on each landing, till it reached the roof. I nodded my thanks to the girl, climbed to the first floor and tried the door. It was shut tight, probably barred on the inside. The one on the next floor was much the same. I continued on to the roof, clambering over the low rampart. In the middle stood the entrance to the building's inner stairwell. Even from this distance it was clear the thing had been forced. Slivers of wood lay strewn on the cement like shrapnel and the rest of the door hung lopsided from one of its hinges.

I covered the ground quickly, reaching what was left of the door and pausing, listening for any sound inside and hearing nothing. I looked around at the sea of other rooftops festooned with lines of multicoloured washing and potted plants. I imagined whoever had taken an axe to the door would have entered under cover of darkness. To do so during the day would have been to risk attracting attention from the nearby houses. Chances were that the perpetrator was long gone. Nevertheless, I reached for my Webley before kicking open the door and pushing on into the darkness of the stairwell. In terms of instilling confidence, the Webley was a useful thing. Though I'd still have preferred a torch.

Silently, I navigated the steps, my free hand out against the wall for support, attuned to any sound from below. I caught the scent of something, one I had encountered before. I gripped the butt of the Webley tighter and headed on, down to the second-floor landing. A shaft of light speared through a crack between a door and its frame. I pushed it open. The scent was stronger here. In the half-light I saw a bed, a mosquito net spread high over its four posts. Around it, the first flies buzzed impotently, unable to penetrate its mesh. Beneath it, half obscured by pillows, lay a body. I walked over and lifted the net. The body of a woman. Native. Semi-clothed. The sheets stained crimson with her blood. Her face disfigured, purpled, swollen. One eye bruised shut. Her throat cut.

I touched her skin.

Still warm.

A rush of air rustled the netting. From behind me a noise, a figure, a native man rushed towards me, one arm rising, a knife in his hand. In an instant he was across the room, lunging. I parried, pushing the dagger away, knocking his arm against a bedpost, throwing myself off balance. I fell. Ended up on my knees. He came again, this time wrapping his arm around my neck. I saw the blade approach. I reached out, grabbed his wrist, slowed its progress towards my throat. My vision began to blur. With all my strength I pushed up onto my feet. The blade drew closer. I stepped back, one foot then another, then slammed my attacker into the wall behind me. His grip loosened. I dug an elbow into his gut and he cried out. The knife fell to the floor. In an instant he was down, scrabbling for it. I backed away, searching for my gun. *Where was it?*

He found the knife first. Got back to his feet, stepping forward once more.

There! On the bed, beside the dead girl.

I dived for the bed, reaching for the Webley, but it was caught up in the mesh of the net. There was no time to free it. The man lunged. I twisted out of the way of the blade and kicked out, sweeping his legs from under him, then pushed the knife into the netting. He uttered a curse, cut short when my fist hit his jaw. He reeled backwards and I reached once more for the Webley. It took time to free it. The man rose, struggled with his knife and threw it. I ducked and fell to the ground as it whistled past my ear. Finally the gun came free, landing on the floor beside me. I picked it up, pointed it at him and then he ran.

I fired, but he was already out of the door, stumbling into the darkness of the hallway and out of sight. I got up, ran after him, through the doorway and into the blackness. I heard his footsteps, his ragged breathing. From somewhere below, a crash, the iron clang of a metal door. The courtyard. There had been a door leading to it from the ground floor. I ran, downwards, reaching the door, seeing the sliver of light seeping in through the crack between it and the world outside.

Hauling it open, I stepped through, the glare of daylight blinding me. Shielding my eyes, I scanned the courtyard. *There!* Making for the narrowest of *gullees*, a man in a dark blue shirt disappearing between two buildings. I set off after him, sprinting, lungs burning, reaching the corner just as he exited into the bustle of the street beyond. There was no time to think. If he made it to the main road, any chance of stopping him would be gone. I called out, ordering him to stop, then raised my revolver and fired. This time the bullet flew true, hitting home, finding its mark. The man clutched at his shoulder, a crimson blossom on his blue shirt. He kept moving though, turning the corner into the street.

I sprinted on, sure now that I had him. At the corner I scanned the maelstrom. It took a moment, but then I saw him, on the opposite side, diving into an alley. His wound it seemed wasn't severe. Maybe the bullet had simply grazed him. Yet with so many bodies in the way, there was no way of letting off another shot.

I forged a path across the road, pushing past pedestrians, slipping between vehicles, halting traffic, almost knocking over a hawker's stall of tat and trinkets, reaching the mouth of the lane, but there was no sign of my assailant. The *gullee* was a short one, leading to another road, just as busy as the one behind me. I raced on, reaching the end and scanning left and right and finding nothing.

For several minutes I kept up my search, wandering down the street, peering into shops and doorways, then retracing my steps and checking the other direction, but gradually the truth dawned that I'd lost him.

I let out a curse.

I'd had him and let him escape. And who knew what the consequences might be.

Slowly, I made my way back towards the house. The building would need to be secured and the body taken away. And I had to find Suren. He needed to know. Because the woman in that building. I had a feeling she might be his cousin, Sushmita Chatterjee.

THIRTY-NINE

Sam Wyndham

The closest police station was a block away on Harrison Road. I ran, dodging traffic, making for the pavement and fighting my way past more hawkers and pedestrians, the ten minutes in the noonday heat feeling like an hour, sweat dripping, the shirt sticking to my back.

I needed to find Suren, to explain to him the fear that was rising within my breast. I staggered up the steps of the police station, past a shocked constable who, had I been Indian, would probably never even have let me inside the building. In the shade of the interior, I sought out the desk sergeant and showed him my identity card.

'Wyndham,' I said. 'CID. There's been a murder in a house in Burra Bazar. I need as many men as you can spare. We have to seal off the premises.'

The sergeant, a tall fellow with an imposing moustache, went off, roaring his subordinates into action. For my part, I reached across his desk, picked up his telephone and dialled the operator and asked her to put me through to Lal Bazar and my boss, Healey.

He didn't sound pleased.

'Where in God's name are you, Wyndham?'

I kept it brief. Told him I'd found a woman's body inside a building in Armenian Street.

'I'm going to need a police van down here, along with a fingerprint man.'

'What the hell's going on? You were supposed to get to the bottom of Mullick's murder and instead you bring me two more murders. First his secretary and now some woman.'

'It's complicated,' I told him. 'The woman was found in a building I think was owned by Mullick. I'll make a full report shortly.'

'Just find me Mullick's killer,' he said. 'Lord Taggart is breathing down my neck, and if you don't give me something positive soon, we'll both be in the shit.'

I cut the connection then dialled again. This time, I gave the operator Suren's father's address and asked to be put through. The maid answered and I told her I needed to speak to Suren.

'He is not here, sahib,' she said. 'He returned a little time earlier and I give him your previous message. He has gone to your house only.'

Once more I cut the line, then asked the operator to be put through to my own number. Sandesh answered on the fourth ring.

'Please tell me Suren's there,' I said.

'*Hā*, sahib,' he said. 'He is here. He was waiting for you, but he is leaving now.'

'Don't let him go!' I said. 'Call him to the telephone. I need to speak to him.'

Seconds later, Suren was on the line.

'We've found a body,' I said. 'A young woman. You need to come down to Armenian Street. Get over here as fast as you can.'

There was silence for a moment before he spoke.

'Is it Dolly?'

I couldn't think who else it could be.

Back in the main room, the sergeant had corralled a motley contingent of constables.

'Get a set of bolt cutters,' I said. 'We're going to need them.'

We hurried back to the house and I stationed a couple of them at a distance to keep away the usual gawkers who, like flies around shit, would no doubt gather at the first hint of the extraordinary, then ordered the sergeant to take the bolt cutters to the chain that held the front door padlocked.

The remaining constables poured in, checking each room for signs of life, and death, but under strict instructions not to touch anything, not until the fingerprint johnny arrived from Lal Bazar.

There was thankfully little else to find. The building was spartan, its few rooms sparsely furnished: in the one where I'd found the woman, there was, other than the bed on which she lay lifeless, an almirah and not much else; in another, a sofa and a few cheap paintings on the wall – saccharine sunsets and thatched huts and *naukas* sailing down rivers, the imagined Eden which Bengalis harked back to, before we British arrived like the snake in their garden.

The rooms on the ground floor were more functional: a kitchen of sorts, the metal cylinder of an Icmic steam cooker sitting on a sideboard beside a meat safe, its mesh cage empty, the water in the bowls under its four legs long since evaporated. And then, at the back of the house, a room set up with photographic backdrops similar to the ones that had existed at Dolly Chatterjee's studio before the fire had put paid to them. I was examining them when Suren arrived, wheezing, his face dark like the grave.

'Where is she?'

'Upstairs.'

'How did you find her?'

'This building,' I said. 'It belongs to Mullick. I broke in.'

I led him up the stairs, past a police constable and to the threshold of the bedroom. A team of orderlies stood waiting, ready to take the body to the mortuary. I had ordered them to wait until Suren arrived. I showed him into the room and waited at a respectful distance. The net was still in place over the bed: a muslin veil over the scene. He walked over, lifted it, and let out a cry.

'*Hai Ram.*'

'Is it Dolly?'

He turned towards me. There were tears in his eyes. 'It is Mahalia Ghosh.'

We made our way back downstairs and I forced a cigarette into his hand. He was in a state of shock. I felt the need to confess.

'If I'd been an hour earlier,' I said, 'she might still be alive.'

He took a pull of the cigarette and stared at me blankly.

'What?'

'The man who killed her was in the building. He almost killed me too. I managed to fight him off, then gave chase but I lost him in the *gullees*. Got a few shots off though. I might have managed to wing him.'

He slumped against a wall. 'What was she doing here?'

'I think her killer brought her here. I also think Mullick might have been here the night he was murdered. It's not far to the burning ghats. There's a good chance this is where he was killed.'

Suren shook his head in confusion. 'I do not understand any of this. What would Mullick's killer want with Mahalia?'

'The same thing we did,' I said. 'He wanted to know where Dolly is hiding. There's no doubt now. Whoever killed Mullick is after her.'

'You think she told him?'

'She's been tortured. I wouldn't expect her to have held out.'

He turned to me. 'Are we responsible?'

'What?'

'Mahalia. Is she dead because of us?'

I put a hand on his shoulder.

'I don't see how.'

'Do you think someone saw me question her at Miss Grant's? It was the morning after the attack on Dolly's studio,' he said. 'What if someone had been following me?'

'Whoever attacked us that night drove off at speed. I doubt he'd have been able to tell you from Adam. There's no way he could have identified you, known where you lived and then followed you. No, whoever killed her tracked her down without our help.'

'You are certain?'

'Completely,' I said, with as much conviction as I could muster. It didn't matter if I was right. What mattered was that Suren not burden himself with guilt.

'We need to find Dolly,' he said. '*Now*. I won't have another death on my conscience.'

'How?' I said. 'She might be anywhere in the city.'

'There is one person who knows,' he said. 'Colonel Dawson.'

'Dawson?' I said. 'Is that why he wanted to see you?'

'In a way. He proposed a trade. He would supply me with the address if I did something for him.'

I sighed. 'Please tell me you didn't agree.'

'I said I would consider it. And now I don't see that I have any option but to accept his terms.'

'So you're going to make a pact with the Devil? That always ends well. You know he'll destroy you.'

'I have no choice,' he said. 'Now are you going to help me?'

FORTY

Surendranath Banerjee

It did not matter what Sam said. Mahalia was dead because of me. I should have found Dolly by now. I should have taken up Dawson's offer last night, there and then. I had put my conscience first and as a result an innocent girl was dead. I thought of her parents and her sister. How could I ever again look them in the eye? I thought of the children at the charity in Belgachia whom she seemed to derive so much joy from teaching. I thought of a meaningful life cut short. I would not let Dolly suffer the same fate, and if the only way to avoid that was to mortgage my soul to the British, then that is what I would do.

'I need to see him,' I said. 'I shall call the telephone number he set out in the letter.'

Sam seemed incredulous. 'For Christ's sake, man. That would be a mistake. Besides, I know how these intelligence johnnies operate. The number in that letter will have been disconnected five minutes after you called it.'

'I won't let anyone else die,' I said. 'Can you get me into his office in Fort William?'

Sam looked to the heavens. 'What am I, the bloody viceroy? You can't just go barging into the most heavily guarded place in the city without an invitation. They wouldn't let us in the front gate.'

'There *has* to be a way, though.'

His expression changed.

'There is,' he sighed, 'but you need to be certain, and I mean as sure as you've ever been about anything, that you want to go through with this.'

I felt as though the ground was opening up before me. A chasm ready to swallow my future. And yet I had to do it. I had to jump in.

'Tell me,' I said.

He exhaled, long and hard. 'Very well. As long as you're aware of the consequences. I have a telephone number, a different one, to be called if I need to contact him, but only *in extremis*.'

'I think this qualifies.'

Sam led me outside and to the local thana. The station was all but deserted with only a young constable behind the desk. He hardly looked old enough to shave. Sam ordered him from the room then picked up the telephone and spoke to the operator. He gave her a number and a moment later he was through.

'It's Wyndham,' he said. 'I need a meeting with the colonel. It's urgent.'

He looked over at me, his face ashen, the telephone receiver still at his ear. There was silence, and then Sam was talking again.

'No. It has to be private. I shall be bringing someone. Someone he's spoken to quite recently.'

Then a nod.

'Twenty minutes. Fine.'

He replaced the receiver and turned to me.

'Come on.'

We headed back out into the heat of the day.

'Where are we going?' I asked.

'To church.'

In the street he flagged down a passing car, then proceeded to ignore the chauffeur and talk directly to the passenger in the rear.

The occupant, a rather red-faced sahib in a tweed suit that had no business being this close to the equator, seemed somewhat taken aback. Any thought he might have of remonstrating soon disappeared, however, as Sam pulled out his warrant card.

Negotiations completed, Sam looked up at me.

'Get in.'

We headed straight down Strand Road, the city passing in a frenzy. To the right, the Hooghly, flowing southward, matching our pace. I sat in the rear, beside the rather worried-looking Britisher whose vehicle this was, while Sam sat up front, encouraging the driver to ever greater turns of speed. I apologised to our host and assured him that we would not waylay him for long, though in truth, I had no idea where we were going.

In the end, the journey took no more than fifteen minutes. The Church of St John was one of the oldest in Calcutta and modelled on St Martin-in-the-Fields in Trafalgar Square. It even had a stone spire, which was impressive given that when it was built there was very little stone to be found anywhere within a hundred miles of the city.

I descended the vehicle and followed Sam under the pillared portico and through the doors of the church. While I have been inside churches many times, they had all been in Europe. I had never before set foot in one in India. There had never been any need.

On another day I might have taken time to look at the pipe organ or the plaques or the paintings. There was, they said, a copy of Da Vinci's *The Last Supper* in here, painted by a local artist who used the faces of Calcutta grandees for Jesus and his disciples, but today none of it mattered. Today, all that mattered was Dolly.

The place was empty save for a few silent souls sitting scattered among the wooden pews, heads bowed or fixed stoically at the cross on the bare altar. In the air, the sound of voices in song. A choir, I assumed, rehearsing in another room close by, singing those hymns of theirs that sounded so strange to our ears. Remarkably grave, I always felt them to be, exhorting the faithful to rejoice while somehow sucking all joy from the experience.

'You don't need to do this,' Sam said. 'We'll come up with another way to find Dolly.'

I shook my head. 'There is no time to find another way. If you're right, if Mahalia *has* revealed Dolly's location to her killer, then there's no time to lose.'

'He's wounded,' Sam said. 'I shot him in the arm. At the very least, he'll need to get that seen to before he can find her.'

'Unless he has accomplices,' I said, 'in which case ...'

'Just bear in mind there's no coming back from this. You take a favour from Dawson and he will own you.'

I felt nauseous. 'I understand,' I said. 'And I am reconciled to it.'

He patted me on the shoulder. 'Very well. In that case, let us pray.'

We sat down on one of the rearmost pews. The sound of the choir grew louder, reaching a crescendo before fading.

'Are we awaiting divine intervention?' I asked.

'No, we're awaiting the verger. He should be along shortly,' he said. 'The gospel according to Dawson. As for divine intervention, I wouldn't bank on it. The Almighty has never shown Himself to be overly concerned about assisting the Imperial Police Force before, at least not to my knowledge.'

'But I'm not police any more,' I said. 'Maybe He might look upon me more favourably.'

'Yes that would be just my luck,' he said. 'Toiling thanklessly all my life in the service of the one true God, only to have Him turn round and reward a bloody heathen instead.'

We did not have to wait long. The choir next door had hardly started upon another hymn when a chap who, from his features, the colour of his skin and the fact that he wore clerical vestments and had a cross hanging around his neck, I assumed was South Indian came walking towards us. While Bengal had proved relatively stony ground for our religious friends from Europe, the Christian missionaries had certainly found our South Indian brethren more amenable to their proselytism. I cannot say why exactly. Maybe it was a matter of temperament. I have often thought of our southern cousins as being calmer and quite possibly smarter than us hot-headed Bengalis.

He stopped in front of us and nodded. 'Gentlemen, this way please.'

Sam rose and I followed.

Footsteps echoing upon the stone floor, the chap led the way to a side door and out once more into the courtyard. A large black car stood idling. As we approached, the chauffeur, a Britisher built like a gorilla, stepped out and opened the rear door, revealing a pair of polished brogues and a walking cane.

Sam stood back. 'Maybe you should do this alone.'

In truth I wanted him by my side, but he was right. If I was going to compromise myself, it was better to do it without witnesses. I stepped in, pulled the door shut, and took the seat beside Dawson. The colonel took his pipe from his mouth and rested it beside a leather briefcase.

'I must say, Mr Banerjee, it's a pleasure to see you again so soon.'

'I need that address,' I told him. 'My cousin is in imminent danger.'

'And what makes you so sure of that?'

I told him of Mahalia Ghosh. 'We believe whoever is after Dolly now knows her location.'

He pondered for a moment. 'Yes I can see the urgency, and I am of course willing to share that information with you. But as we discussed, the flow of information is a two-way street. Am I to take it that you therefore agree to our bargain?'

I closed my mind to the shouts of dissent. 'Yes.'

'Good, good.' He reached for the briefcase, opened it with a click and extracted a few sheets of paper and passed them to me. 'All that remains is to make it official.'

'Official?' I said.

'Paperwork, dear boy. We can't pay you a stipend without attending to the administrative side.'

It was a trap of course. The minute I signed those papers, I would be on record as working for him. The money might as well have been thirty pieces of silver.

'I do not wish a stipend.'

He waved away my comment as though it were smoke from a cigarette.

'Be that as it may, we still need to file the forms. After your years in the Imperial Police, I'd have thought you must know that His Majesty's Indian Government doesn't do anything without the requisite paperwork, filled out in triplicate, duly signed.'

I picked up the top copy. Two pages of tightly typed legal wording. Clauses and subclauses. There was no time to parse it, and anyway what was I supposed to do, debate the finer points of it while a killer stalked Dolly? No, these pages were the means by which Dawson would shackle me. My signature upon them just as solid as the iron manacles in which he held his prisoners in Alipore Jail.

He passed me a lacquered fountain pen and I signed the second page.

'Please date it,' he said, 'and initial the front page too.'

I did as he commanded, then did the same with the other two copies and returned to him his pen.

'Good, good,' he said. 'I'll keep these two, and this one is for your records.'

I took the paper from him, folded it and stuffed it into my pocket.

Dawson nodded. 'Well then, I see no reason to withhold the information of your relative's whereabouts.' He reached into his jacket and extracted a small slip of paper. 'You should find her here.'

An address in Howrah. Across the river. Round Tank Lane. House 18, Flat 6.

It looked familiar. I had seen it somewhere before, and then it hit me. Ronen Ghatak had lived in Round Tank Lane, in a *mess bari* at number 22. There were several entries in his ledger relating to payments made for renting a flat in the street. I had assumed that those payments were for Ghatak's abode, but what if it were for another flat? One rented by Mullick for other purposes? My heart sank.

'She is in danger,' I said. 'Do you have someone watching her?'

Dawson laughed. 'Alas I don't have the resources to watch everyone all of the time and she's hardly a matter of national security. But I can tell you that as of last night, she was still at that location.'

'Very well,' I said. 'Thank you, Colonel.'

I do not know why I uttered those words, and I instantly regretted saying them. It was like a mouse saying thank you to a cat for toying with him instead of killing him instantly. Dawson was not doing me any favours. He was playing with me for his sport.

He smiled like a priest offering benefaction. 'Oh, dear boy, don't mention it.'

I reached for the door handle.

'One last thing,' he said, calling out before I had a chance to turn it. 'I understand you went to see the mayor this morning.'

It made me wonder, if he had spies in place who could tell him that, then why the devil did he need me?

'What did you think of him?'

'A good man,' I said.

'Oh, absolutely. Jolly fine chap. But I hear you didn't ask him for a position.'

'That is correct,' I said.

He took a breath. 'I thought that was what we'd agreed?'

'I felt it would not be conducive to the future direction of my career.'

His features hardened. 'I think you should reconsider that decision.'

With the address of Dolly's hideaway now in my possession, some of my backbone began to return.

'I will not do anything I deem detrimental to the cause of independence,' I told him.

'Oh, of course not,' he said. 'Perish the thought. You'd be more of a conduit between the mayor and the administration. It's often useful to have a backchannel, so that both sides can know what the other is thinking; so that they can be aware of any red lines. If anything, you shall be assisting Anglo-Indian relations.'

I did not bother to reply, simply opened the door and stepped out. Sam, a cigarette between his fingers, was walking towards me, returning from the church.

'Well?'

'Howrah,' I said. 'She's in a flat in Round Tank Lane.'

'Right.'

Behind us, Dawson's car fired to life and shot off in a cloud of gravel and dust.

'You okay?' Sam asked.

'I do not know.'

'We can worry about it later. For now, let's go and find your cousin.'

I headed for the road. 'We need a taxi.'

Sam didn't move. 'I don't think so. This time of day, we'll get mired in traffic.'

'So what then?' I asked.

He headed off in the direction of the church and I followed. Rounding the corner, he stopped in front of an open lean-to. Within stood a motorcycle.

'That, my friend, is a Royal Enfield four-stroke 350cc. It belongs to the verger and he's agreed for us to borrow it, subject to the receipt of a twenty-rupee deposit, which I have paid. One would expect a man of the cloth to be more trusting and less materialistic, but there you have it. We live in tempestuous times, and needs must when the Devil drives, or rather when I do.'

He climbed on and suddenly the engine roared into life.

'Well, don't just stand there,' he said. 'Get on.'

Hesitantly I did as requested.

'Couldn't you have telephoned Lal Bazar and ordered them to send us a car and driver?'

'Where would be the fun in that?' he said, accelerating out of the courtyard and onto the road.

FORTY-ONE

Sam Wyndham

It wasn't far, not as the crow flies at any rate, but Howrah was on the other side of the river and crossing that was a mission in itself. I gunned the engine. With Suren behind me, holding tight to the frame of the Royal Enfield, we sped out of the churchyard and made for the pontoon bridge across the river.

The Strand Road was relatively quiet and we made rapid, if dangerous progress, at least until we reached the environs of the bridge. There things slowed to a quagmire with carts, lorries, rickshaws, bicycles, pedestrians, bullocks, horses and all manner of other creatures and contraptions fighting for access and grinding along in both directions in a fashion that seemed more attritional than sensible. Amid it all stood a policeman, marooned on his little traffic island like a shipwreck victim, arms flailing like an unfastened sail in the forlorn hope of instilling some order into the chaos around him and being roundly ignored for his troubles.

The air hung heavy with the stench of petroleum and sulphur and something unholy seeping up from the river. I put my foot down, barely avoiding collision with a fully laden number 8 bus coming the other way. We raced on to a symphony of horns, weaving between pack animals and vehicles at reckless speed, the distance to the far side closing inexorably. Ahead, rising up on the far bank like a Roman fort, stood the station, the city's navel, the source point for the umbilical cord that connected us to the rest of India.

As we approached it, Suren yelled in my ear. 'We're looking for Round Tank Lane. Do you know where it is?'

I gestured to the left, past the station, towards a large metal structure on stilts. 'I'm guessing that's the round tank. The lane can't be far off.'

We reached dry land and I turned left, hurtling along the Foreshore Road past the station, setting the water tank as our lodestar, past the walls of the wharves and warehouses that pockmarked Howrah like a rash.

I slowed down and pulled up next to an old man.

'Oh, *dada*, Round Tank Lane?' Suren shouted to him.

The man's reply was lost to me over the noise of the engine, but Suren caught it.

'Keep going. Second road on the left.'

I accelerated, all but throwing Suren off the back. He grabbed at my shirt, and at the last minute, pulled himself upright.

'You all right?' I said.

'Yes, though please try not to kill us both.'

Soon we were turning into the lane, a thoroughfare with two- and three-storey buildings on both sides rising to block out the sun. Once more I slowed.

'Which building?'

'Number 18.'

It wasn't much further, another hundred yards or so up the street. I stopped outside a dilapidated three-storey building and killed the engine. The house opened onto the lane, its doors and shutters painted dark green and with a rusting balcony running the length of the first floor. Weeds sprouted from cracks in the cement work. By Howrah standards, the building was almost pristine. Across the road stood a shoddy-looking tea stall of loose brick and bamboo and a sagging tiled roof that you wouldn't want to be standing under when the wind got up.

Suren jumped off the motorcycle and made for the door to number 18 and I followed him. It was a communal building which meant the main door was open, one wall of the hall beyond lined with wooden postboxes with names painted in white upon them. The one for Flat 6 had been painted over. Suren was already at the stairs, climbing them at a pace. I was about to follow when something, or rather someone, caught my eye. Outside, across the road, a figure was exiting the tea stall. It was only a second, but something about him struck me. The shirt. It was the same shade of blue as the one worn by the man who'd killed Mahalia. I shouted up to Suren.

'You carry on, I'll be with you in a minute.'

I stepped back out into the blinding light of the street. It took a moment for my eyes to acclimatise to the glare, but then I saw him, the man in the shirt, his back to me, walking up the street. I headed after him. His shirtsleeves were rolled up. On his left arm a crude bandage. He did not look round, simply walked on, head fixed, eyes straight ahead. I felt my entrails turn to ice. Were we too late? Had he accomplished what he'd set out to do? In my head swirled visions of Suren finding Dolly's lifeless body, just as I had found her friend's. But that could not be correct. A man doesn't murder someone then hang around the scene for a cup of tea. I continued to follow at a distance.

Suddenly he picked up his pace, making a beeline for something. Just then it hit me that I had no idea what Dolly looked like. Suren hadn't shown me any photographs of her. The bitter irony in that. I looked over my shoulder, hoping Suren might have come back out into the street, but there was no sign of him.

The man in the blue shirt was about fifty yards away now. He seemed to stop. It looked like he was talking to someone, but they were hidden from sight by his frame and passing traffic.

In an instant, everything changed. There came a scream as the man leapt to life, making for the entrance to a *gullee*, his left arm at his side, his right arm pulling a sari-clad woman in his wake. I reached for my Webley and ran, fighting past a gaggle of women already alerted by the noise. The man and his captive disappeared into the alley.

I kept going, fighting for breath, reaching the corner. There, twenty yards ahead, the man had the woman pinned against a wall. Suddenly he released his grip and reached into his clothing. Metal glinted. The woman screamed.

The rest happened fast. A knife raised. My Webley too. I shouted a warning. Too late. His hand at her throat. I fired and both he and the woman fell to the ground.

For an instant I just stood there, the Webley still in my hand, still pointed at the scene. Then, slowly, I came to my senses, then rushed forward. The man in the blue shirt lay slumped over the woman, blood oozing onto the dirt around them. There was movement, then a scream. The woman. She was alive.

I knelt down beside them. The man lay motionless. A bright red hole in the side of his head. I couldn't help feeling I'd seen him somewhere before, and not just at the house where he'd killed Mahalia. But where? I pushed him to one side and helped the woman up so that she sat with her back against the wall. By now she was sobbing, her face streaked with tears. She looked at me in fear.

'It's all right,' I said. 'I'm the police. Are you hurt?'

She didn't reply, just sat there, hugging her knees to her chest.

I put an arm around her. 'Are you Dolly?'

She looked up at me once more. 'Y-yes.'

'I'm a friend of Suren Banerjee. He's been looking for you.'

I helped her to her feet. Around us, a small crowd was gathering, drawn by the sound of the gunshot and the sight of a dead man.

I scanned them. Youths and loafers mainly. Not the type to be trusted. Then, at the back, a middle-aged man who looked more respectable. A shopkeeper, maybe.

'You,' I said, pulling out my warrant card. 'Where's the nearest thana?'

'Shibpur,' he said. 'One mile from here. Or Howrah, same distance.'

Another gentleman, older, dressed only in a checked lungi and vest, piped up. 'Police commissioner's bungalow, much closer, sahib. On Foreshore Road only.'

'Please go there and tell the guard on duty that there's been an incident. Tell them that a man is dead and to come immediately and to let Howrah thana know.'

I reached into my pocket and pulled out a grubby rupee note.

'Here. Take a bicycle rickshaw.'

I turned back to the first gentleman. 'Keep watch over the body until I return.' I put an arm around Dolly's shoulder and began to direct her out of the alley.

Before we had taken two steps, Suren burst through the crowd, relief blossoming on his face as he saw us.

'You found her! Thank the gods.'

'And in the nick of time,' I said. 'Our friend from Burra Bazar paid her a visit.'

He looked over at the body. 'Is that the ... ?'

'Yes,' I said. 'That's the man who killed Mahalia.'

He bent down, took a closer look and turned to me. 'He was on the train back from Bishnupore, the night Ronen Ghatak was killed.'

He was right, damn him. I had seen the man, fleetingly, disembarking, pushing through the crowd at Howrah. He'd been wearing the same blue shirt that night too. It stood to reason he was the one who'd murdered the secretary, which begged the question, why hadn't Madhu identified him? But that was a matter for later. Right now I had a dead body to deal with and a woman to question.

I took him to one side.

'Take Dolly back up to the flat and wait for me,' I said. 'I need to sort out our erstwhile assassin there.'

He headed back to the girl and took her hand. 'Come,' he said. 'You are safe now.'

'No, Suren-da! You must let me go! I need to –'

'You are going nowhere, Dolly. You are going to explain to us exactly what is going on and then, if the captain agrees, I am taking you home.'

She tried to pull away from him. 'I will do no such thing. Who told you where to find me? Was it Mahalia?'

His face darkened. 'Mahalia is dead, Dolly. You would be too, if my friend and I had not found you. Now you will come with me and tell me what I wish to know, or I shall ask Captain Wyndham to arrest you and question you at the thana.'

His words seemed to knock the fight out of the girl and I watched as he led her back towards number 18. I returned my attention to the alley to where my recently appointed deputy was doing a fine job of keeping back the onlookers.

It wasn't long before the cavalry arrived. Twenty minutes at most. I explained the circumstances to an officer from Howrah police station, a fresh-faced chap by the name of Kent. As his men took charge of the scene, I led him back to Round Tank Road and up to number 18, Flat 6. With a man dead on their patch, Howrah police would need to interview all witnesses. I just asked that Kent give me a chance to speak to her first.

Suren opened the door, his face grave. He didn't seem surprised to see Kent at my shoulder.

We followed him through a small hallway.

'How is she?'

'Unhurt,' he said, a certain irritation in his voice.

'She told you anything? Such as what the hell this is all about?'

'No,' he said curtly.

We entered a room that looked onto a wall. Like most native abodes, it was sparsely furnished: a bed, on which Dolly was now seated, a chair and paint peeling from the walls.

She looked up at us, then down again to the bare floor. I pulled up the chair and sat down opposite her.

'Dolly, are you all right?'

Her nod was all but imperceptible.

'Suren's told me a lot about you. He's been worried about you. Not only him, your family too. Now I'm going to ask you some questions, and I need you to tell me everything you can. Whatever you've got mixed up in has already cost the lives of several people. We need to know who's responsible.'

Dolly shook her head. 'I don't know. I don't know anything. I don't know who that man was.'

'Maybe,' Suren said, 'we should start from the beginning.'

'Why did you leave home?' I asked.

'That is not your business.'

'Does it have anything to do with J. P. Mullick?' I asked. 'We know he paid you a large sum of money. And this flat is rented in his name. Or maybe this has something to do with his secretary, Ronen Ghatak? He lived on this street.'

At the mention of the secretary there was a flicker of something in her eyes.

'Did you know Ronen?

'I told you,' she said, 'I do not know what you are talking about.'

I hardened my tone. 'Do I need to remind you that your friend Mahalia is dead? She was murdered this morning. By the very same man now lying in the gutter across the way. The man who came to kill you. Now you will tell me the truth, or so help me, I shall arrest you.'

She looked once more to the floor. Suren let out a sigh. I could see his anger rising.

'She was an innocent girl,' he said. 'She looked up to you. And she died protecting you. Now you will tell us what we need to know or I will personally ruin what little reputation you have left.'

Her face crumpled. 'What happened to Ronen?'

'Dead,' Suren said. 'Murdered two nights ago on the train from Bishnupore. You were at the station that night, weren't you? You were waiting for him.'

The woman began to sob.

'He told me ...'

'Dolly,' he said, 'too many people have died on account of you. Even I have made sacrifices to find you. You owe it to them, to *me*, to tell us what is going on.'

'Photographs,' she said.

'What photographs?'

'I ... I never thought it would lead to ...'

'Start from the beginning,' I said, 'and tell us everything.'

'I run a photography studio.'

'I'm aware,' I said. 'For women only.'

She nodded slowly. 'It was not doing well.' She turned to Suren. '*You* know what our people are like, Suren-da, always people criticising, whispering behind your back. People spreading all sorts of rumours, that the studio was a front for licentiousness, that I served the women alcohol. It is all nonsense, but so what? People believe it, business disappears and bills begin to mount.

'And then came Ronen. He just walked into the studio one day and said his employer was involved in the film business and he needed a photographer to take pictures of some of the actresses. It was a godsend. Suddenly I had a regular client providing regular business. And when I found out Ronen's employer was Jogendra Mullick, it seemed my problems were finished. All of those people who were saying things about me and the studio, they would be forced to change their tune. But though the business was good, it was not an answer to all my problems. I was forbidden from mentioning Mullick-da's name. Ronen said that if there was any hint that Mullick-da was my patron, then he would take his business elsewhere. And the type of girls I had to photograph – actresses, young girls – well, they only made people talk more.'

'Did Mullick ever come in himself?' I asked.

'No. The girls were brought in by Ronen. That is how I got to know him. It was he who told me the truth about Mullick, what sort of a man he really was. The photographs, like the films, they were all part of a scheme. Mullick wanted the pictures and he wanted the girls. He provided them everything, then took away their most valuable possession . . . I don't want to talk about it.'

'But you kept going?' I asked. 'You kept working for him even after you found out the truth?'

'I tried to stop, I swear it. I told Ronen I was not prepared to take pictures for Mullick any more. But he told me I had to go on. He said if I stopped, Mullick would just find another photographer and the money he paid, the money I relied on, would simply go elsewhere.'

'Why did you not go to the police?' Suren asked.

She shot him a withering look. 'And say what? That J. P. Mullick had asked me to take photographs of girls. There was nothing illegal in that. Of the other things, I had no proof, and who would believe me? It would be my word against the great Jogendra Prasad Mullick's, Ronen said, and he would ruin me.'

Once more she wiped her eyes with the hem of her sari. Suren seemed nonplussed.

'What are these, Dolly? Crocodile tears? You continued in the exploitation of these girls, and all for money?'

'No!' she protested. 'I did it for Ronen! You must believe me, Suren-da, he was a good man. He too hated what Mullick was doing, what Mullick made *him* do. We began spending time together. He would confide in me. He said he wanted to marry me, but that was a dream, nothing more, not until he was financially sufficient. His salary from Mullick was hardly enough to provide a roof over his head, and with the difference in caste, it would be impossible.'

'What has any of this got to do with their deaths?' he asked.

'It has *everything* to do with their deaths,' she said. 'It is all because of some accursed photographs I took eight years ago. It was Ronen who first noticed them. He was at the studio, looking through some books of my old photographs when he saw them . . .'

'Saw what?'

'You will need to see to understand.'

Slowly she rose from the bed and made her way to the door. I followed her as she entered a tiled room that acted as water closet, an Indian-style toilet at one end, a floor slick with water and a sink with a small dripping tap turned green with age. She reached for a mirror above the sink, taking it from the nail upon which it hung and placing it gently on the floor. Standing once more, she carefully pulled out one of the bricks which sat behind where the mirror had been. From the hollow behind it, she extracted a large envelope, bent in two to fit the space.

She passed it to me and replaced first the brick, then the mirror.

'Open it, please.'

I unfolded the envelope and extracted the contents.

'Photographs.'

I stared down at them, uncomprehending. They were photographs of Estelle Morgan. A younger Estelle, but recognisable. She was just as beautiful then, but with a radiance and an innocence that life would strip away. They were, I guessed, almost a decade old.

'How did you come by these?'

'I took them.'

For a moment the world spun. That was impossible. Estelle left India as a babe and had only just returned. As for Dolly, I very much doubted she had ever set foot outside it.

'How?' I asked. 'How could you have photographed Estelle Morgan?'

The woman bit her bottom lip. 'I didn't,' she said. 'I photographed a girl called Esha Murugan. She was from somewhere in the south. Orissa, according to her mother, but Murugan, that's a Tamil name.'

Pieces began to fall into place.

'Estelle Morgan is Indian?'

'Anglo-Indian,' Dolly corrected. 'A half-caste, though she was very light-skinned, even for an Anglo. She came to Calcutta to audition for a part in a play at the Regal. I had just started the business. She wanted some photographs taken and came to me. I took them and naturally kept the negatives. I developed a few extra copies. She was quite striking; so different from most of the women whom I photographed that I thought I might use her pictures for advertising. That was years ago. I had forgotten all about her.

'It was Ronen who made the connection. He saw the photos and realised who she was.'

So half-caste Esha had become pure English Estelle from Tasmania.

'Ronen said those photographs would be our ticket to happiness. He would show them to Mullick and put the idea in his head that he might bribe her. If the world were to know that Estelle Morgan had Indian blood, well, it would finish her career in America before it had even begun. He said Americans were much more hostile to the mixing of blood than even the English.

'And that is what Mullick did. He paid a thousand rupees for a set of those photographs, and he promised Ronen twice as much and an increase in his salary. Mullick then contacted Miss Morgan and threatened her. Either she come to India, star in his picture and no doubt be taken advantage of, or he would reveal to the world who she really was.

'I thought that was an end of it. I would be able to clear the bulk of my debts, Ronen would have his new position and salary and he would be able to approach my father and ask to marry me. But then he lost contact with Mullick. He telephoned me from Bishnupore and told me he'd no idea what had happened. Poor Ronen. I could tell he was scared, but he told me not to worry. He told me I needed to get all copies and the negatives out of the studio and to a safe place. I did as he asked, went to the studio and retrieved the negatives and all remaining copies. He gave me the address of this place, told me to come and wait here until he returned from Bishnupore.

'The next day, we found out that Mullick was dead and that my studio had been attacked. I didn't know what to do. In an instant we had lost everything. Not only was the studio gone, but his new position and the salary too. He would be fortunate to keep the job he had. There was no way he could approach my father and ask for my hand in marriage. It felt like a catastrophe. All those dreams of a life together, gone. Dead, alongside Mullick.

'I broke down, but Ronen said he could fix things. He could make it so that all our money worries would be over and he would still marry me. He would speak to Estelle's agent and sell him the photographs. I was to meet him at Howrah station, but he never arrived. Instead I saw you, getting off the train with Estelle Morgan.

I thought the police had arrested Ronen. I panicked and ran. I was too scared to go home. Instead I came back here. The only person I told was Mahalia. I asked her to check on the studio, just in case Ronen had gone there, but she told me the studio had been destroyed.'

She put a hand to her mouth.

'Mahalia,' she said, and then the tears started once more.

Suren made no effort to comfort her. As for me, my head was still reeling. Estelle was Indian. Anglo-Indian at least, but in matters of blood, the Anglo was irrelevant; it was the Indian that tainted her. She must have thought she'd escaped all of this when she had left India for England and taken on a new identity. Then, just as Hollywood and the world beckoned, her past had come calling. J. P. Mullick threatening to divulge her secret. But would Estelle sanction murder? To kill Mullick, and Ronen and Mahalia too? I could not believe that. I'd spent my life catching killers and she didn't fit the bill. She was just too ... too *innocent*. Not in the sense that she was as pure as the driven snow of course, but there was something about her character that suggested she couldn't countenance the taking of a life. She was about to become a star in America. She wanted *me* to be there with her.

Hell.

It was an act. Of course it was. She was an actress; I, the gullible audience. Deep down I suppose I'd always known the truth, but the previous night I'd dared to believe that her words might, just might, be true. That had been stupid of me. Her lies were little different from the countless others I'd heard over the years, they were just delivered better. I had to hand it to her. She'd played the part to perfection; the best damn actress I'd ever met.

Yet part of me rebelled against that conclusion. She had seemed genuinely shocked when we'd found Ronen Ghatak murdered on the train. She might be an actress, but a dead body is a dead body.

You couldn't mask your reaction to that, couldn't hide your shock; and she'd been genuinely horrified.

So that meant it had to be someone else. And there was only one other person who stood to gain. Her agent, Sal Copeland. He would also suffer if Estelle's secret came out. Who knows how much he'd invested in her? It might even ruin him. Copeland had come back on the train with Mullick. He would have known his whereabouts that night. And according to Dolly, it was Copeland whom Ronen went to in an attempt to cut a deal. Copeland would have known that any deal was dangerous. Ronen obviously suspected him of Mullick's murder. In his attempts to protect his prize asset, Copeland had laid himself open to bribery. Now, even if he got the photographs and the negatives, there would still be Ronen Ghatak out there with the knowledge of Mullick's murder. How long before Ronen used that information to extort more money? Where would it stop? No, Ronen Ghatak had signed his own death warrant the moment he'd contacted Copeland with the offer to sell him those photos. Of course Copeland wouldn't have carried out any of the murders himself. He would have hired a man, the one I'd seen on the station platform in Bishnupore, the one now lying dead in the *gullee* out there. Just another expendable Indian.

I turned to find Suren, his expression grave.

'I'm sorry,' he said. 'I know you were fond of Miss Morgan.'

'I'm still fond of her,' I said.

He stared at me as though I'd taken leave of my senses.

'This isn't her doing,' I told him. 'This is Copeland's work.'

'But she must have known about it.'

'We don't know that.'

'Three people are dead, Sam,' he said. 'Four including our assassin outside. One of them was a friend of mine. Or do Indian lives not matter to you?'

'Maybe you should ask that question of your cousin, Dolly,' I said. 'But I don't believe Estelle Morgan is behind these deaths.

'*Esha Murugan*,' he corrected. 'Her name is Esha Murugan and she has you beguiled. You need to do your job and arrest both her and her agent, before they leave this city and are gone forever.'

FORTY-TWO

Sam Wyndham

Suren was right. Until I could prove otherwise, Estelle was just as guilty as Sal Copeland. I would need to arrest them both, then sort the wheat from the chaff. There was no time to lose.

I made for the door.

'Sam.' Suren's voice. I stopped and looked at him. 'Should I come with you?'

I gave him a rueful glance. 'Stay here. Look after Miss Chatterjee. Decide what we should do with her. I'll deal with this myself.'

He made to remonstrate but then stopped. 'You are an honourable man, Sam. I have always known you to do the right thing.'

I couldn't help but smile. 'We both know that isn't true.'

'It is,' he said. 'Now go, and may the gods be with you.'

I ran down the stairs, out of the building and jumped back on the motorcycle. Within seconds I was gunning back along Round Tank Lane towards the bridge, dodging potholes and pedestrians while my head swirled with a torrent of thoughts. Estelle Morgan could not be a murderess. I could not, *would not*, believe it. But then a moment later, the opposite seemed just as likely. She was an actress, a damn good one, with the world at her feet. I was a washed-out Calcutta policeman. What was more likely – that she cared for me, or that she was using me? When put in those terms it was clear as day. It was an act and I was an idiot.

That I made it to the Great Eastern without killing myself or anyone else was down to the whim of the gods. Leaving the bike with the doorman, I ran in and made for the stairs, reaching the second floor and Estelle's suite. My breath ragged, I pounded my fist on the door, calling out for Madhu to open it. From behind it came nothing but silence. A chambermaid, alarmed by my manic presence came over. I turned to her, told her I was the police and asked for to unlock the room with her master key.

'But room is empty, sahib,' she said. 'Miss Morgan has left one hour ago only.'

Still, I persisted, and she did as ordered, unlocking the door and presenting an empty suite. I ran for the stairs once more, back down to the lobby, the front desk and the concierge.

'Miss Morgan and Mr Copeland,' I said, 'where were they going after checking out?'

He considered what to tell me, then seemingly remembered I was a police officer.

'I cannot be certain, but Mr Copeland enquired about trains to Bombay this morning. He asked for berths to be reserved for them on the 6 p.m. service.'

'How many berths?' I asked.

He looked perplexed. 'Pardon?'

'How many berths?'

'Four.'

Four berths on the 6 p.m. train. I wondered who that final berth was for. Maybe the man who'd killed Mahalia? The one I'd shot earlier. I checked my watch. Almost five. If there was an upside, it was that I still had time.

Once more I ran, out into the street, onto the bike and back in the direction of Howrah.

Dusk was falling, the red disc of the sun losing itself in the mists upon the western horizon. Soon, the station loomed large, its approaches jammed with vehicles, and in the gaps, an ocean of people, men and women swarming like ants in and out of the great building.

I weaved the motorbike between them, making it to within a dozen yards of the entrance. Close by stood a traffic constable, watching me with a certain disdain. I rode up to him, killed the engine and pulled out my warrant card.

On seeing it, he stood a little taller and saluted.

'What's your name, Constable?' I asked.

'Basu, sir.'

'Look after this bike, Basu,' I said.

'Yes, sir,' he said.

I left the bike and ran for the great portico at the entrance, joining the throng fighting to go through: soldiers and travellers and farmers and salarymen jostling to get home from the city.

The board said the Bombay train was leaving from platform 3. I made a dash for it, through the cauldron of the concourse, at points falling in with the flow of feet, at others, having to push and shove and fight against the tide till I reached the guard at the mouth of the platform. As fate should have it, the man was Anglo-Indian. I pulled out my warrant card again and held it up for him to see.

'I'm looking for a couple of first-class passengers, a man and a woman, surnames Copeland and Morgan. Travelling with an Indian maid. Have they boarded yet?'

The man thought for a moment, then consulted a list on his clipboard. 'I don't believe so, sir. They're not ticked off on the manifest. You're welcome to take a look.'

I ran on, checking the windows of the third- and second-class carriages, then climbing aboard upon reaching the first-class ones and going door to door, checking the individual compartments. A few heads turned as I entered. Englishmen mostly, well dressed and moustachioed, with the odd Indian among them. Of Estelle and Copeland though, there was no sign. I moved quickly through the carriage, reaching the far end and then pushing through into the next one, and then the buffet car, without any luck.

I checked my watch. Twenty to six. They were cutting it fine ... that is if they were coming at all. Copeland had been in a hurry to leave for days now, ever since Mullick's and Ghatak's deaths. They'd left the Great Eastern over an hour ago. They should have been here in plenty of time. Where had they gone and why leave it to the last minute to make the train?

I stepped off, back onto the platform and ran back to where the guard was still checking the credentials of would-be travellers, marking their names off his list. He looked up as I approached.

'Any luck, sir?'

'No, but if they do turn up, don't let them board. Get the railway guards to bring them to the stationmaster's office.'

'Yes, sir,' he said with a nod. 'Is that where you'll be?'

'At least until that train leaves.'

I left him and made for the stationmaster's office, once more fighting my way across the concourse, past the ladies' waiting room and the third-class waiting hall and booking office, till I reached the correct door.

Inside was a room manned by half a dozen men, secretaries and subalterns probably. I approached the nearest one, a pale man in a paler shirt seated behind a desk with piles of papers held safe from the sirocco of the overhead fan by an array of paperweights. Once more I brought out my warrant card.

'Police business,' I said. 'I need to use your telephone.'

He passed it across, I picked up the receiver and asked the operator to put me through to the reception desk of the Great Eastern Hotel. The plummy voice of the concierge answered.

'This is Captain Wyndham of the Imperial Police, again.'

'Yes, sir,' said the concierge. 'I hope you managed to locate the individuals you were seeking.'

The Burning Grounds

'No,' I said. 'I haven't. Did they order a taxi?'

'Yes, sir, and the doorman hailed one for them.'

'Go and speak to the doorman,' I said. 'Find out if they truly were heading to the station, and if not where they were actually going.'

I waited, agonising seconds that ran on longer than I had imagined possible. How long did it take to ask a simple question of a man not twenty yards away?

Finally the concierge returned.

'Hello?'

'Yes?' I said.

'The doorman says they ordered the taxi to Kidderpore Docks.'

The docks. I cursed myself. I should have checked with the doorman myself. After all, he'd looked after the bloody motorcycle for me. I hung up. A ship from Kidderpore would get them out of the country, *out of our jurisdiction*, far quicker than a train to Bombay.

The correct thing to do would be to notify Lal Bazar and the police at the port. Tell them to stop any vessel leaving and to detain Copeland and Estelle. And yet I did none of that. Instead I walked out of the office and through the crowds, out through the arches of the entrance, back to the policeman and the motorcycle.

Why had I not telephoned Lal Bazar or the police at the dockside? I told myself it was because I still had nothing but a theory, no hard evidence at all against either Copeland or, God forbid, Estelle. Yet that was just a sop to my conscience. The truth was, the minute I informed my superiors or anyone else of Dolly's confession, the whole situation would spiral out of my control, and I didn't want that, not yet anyway. Not until I'd had a chance to confront Estelle ... and if their ship set sail before I got there ... well, that, as Suren might say, would be fate.

Once more I headed towards the bridge, crossing it under the light of the full moon. I reached the Strand Road and set off south, skirting the river as the heart of the city flew past: the temples to commerce; the High Court and the Maidan; Fort William and the Prinsep Ghat. The docks were the other side of the canal they called Tolly's Nullah. I could see the lights of the ships twinkling up ahead. I could still stop and turn back. I could report that I had arrived too late, or that I had only gone to Howrah station and not found them there. No one ever needed to know that I had traced them to the docks. But then Suren's words rang in my head: *'You are an honourable man, Sam . . .'*

The gates to the docks were manned by a few uniformed durwans who preferred to wave me through rather than ask any questions. I stopped anyway and asked for directions to the harbourmaster's office.

'*Oi tho*,' said one of them. 'Straight on. Second building.'

Lights burned in its windows. That at least was something. I jumped from the motorcycle, leaving it in the dirt, and pushed open the door, into an office that smelled of mildew and stale urine, the walls lined with racks of superannuated files and rolls of paper that were presumably charts and logs, all tied together and quietly rotting in the humidity.

At a desk, under a large map of the river, charting its course south to the Bay of Bengal, sat a bald, dark-skinned native, a ledger open in front of him. My entrance seemed to startle him. He looked up at me, eyes wide as though I might be some malevolent spirit come to torment him.

He rose from his chair. A bespectacled little Napoleon in a half-sleeve shirt and a row of pens at his breast pocket like medals. 'This is restricted area. Port staff only.'

'I'm the police,' I told him. 'And I need your help. Do you keep a copy of the passenger manifest from each vessel?'

He looked at me as though I were mad.

'Of course not. Why would we keep such a thing?'

'In that case,' I said, 'I need a list of vessels that are due to sail tonight or which have left in the last few hours.'

'Two left since this afternoon,' he said. 'Three more tonight.'

'The ones yet to leave, where are they heading?'

He sat back down, turned a page in his ledger and ran a finger down its lines.

'SS *Themistocles*, bound for Bombay, then Mombassa, final destination Cape Town. SS *Bangalore*, bound for Madras; and SS *Coromandel*, bound for Singapore and Hong Kong.'

Singapore and Hong Kong. Out of India, into international waters and heading east. Probably the fastest way to California.

'The *Coromandel*,' I said. 'Does it take passengers?'

He looked up. 'Passengers and refrigerated cargo.'

'When does it sail?'

He checked his watch. 'In the next half an hour. Final preparations will be under way.'

'Take me to it,' I said. 'Now.'

He bustled out from behind his desk, grabbing a thin coat from a peg by the door. It was still sixty degrees outside and balmy, but anything below seventy and Bengalis will act as though conditions are arctic. I followed him out of the door and into the night, along the dockside and past a couple of rusting hulks.

'How far?' I asked.

'Close,' he said. 'Five minutes.'

'Maybe we could get a move on,' I said.

The man broke into a jog which required me simply to lengthen my stride to keep up, but then he reached his limit after thirty seconds and slowed once more.

'There.' He pointed to a vessel up ahead, its silhouette studded with a constellation of lights.

I left his side and ran on, the hull soon towering before me, the scene coming into focus: the outline of bodies on deck moving in synchronicity, men going through the motions of making ready to sail as the thrum of engines beat out a rhythm. From the funnels the first smoke, rising and fading into the night; and there, on the quayside, gangways thronged with coolies, their slender frames weighed down by the loads they carried upon their turbaned heads. Beyond them another, final gangway, less travelled. For passengers, I assumed, knots of men and women at its base, bidding their adieus, others waiting in line to have their details checked by the purser. I pushed past them, once more pulling out my warrant card and this time shoving it under the purser's nose.

'I need to see the passenger manifest.'

He passed it over without complaint and I scanned it, running through a list of around twenty names, not once but twice. There was no mention of Estelle or Copeland.

'Is this everyone?'

'Yes,' he said. 'Wait, no. There were a few late additions. They're overleaf.'

I turned the page and my stomach churned.

There, handwritten in black ink, alongside a couple of long Indian names I could not make out clearly, were two that stood out: Copeland, S. Mr, and Morgan, E. Miss.

I pointed to the names.

'Have these passengers boarded?' As I asked the question, I looked up to the top of the gangway. There, by the railings, stood Estelle's maid, Madhu, looking down at me. 'Never mind,' I said, 'I have my answer.'

The chap from the harbourmaster's office finally arrived, panting. I turned to him.

'This vessel is not to leave until I say so. Understood?'

I didn't wait for a response, simply left him and strode up the gangway, the maid watching me every step of the way.

'Where are they?' I asked her. 'Where are Estelle and Copeland?'

Madhu stared at me, unblinking, for a moment not seeming even to register my questions.

'Your mistress,' I said. 'Where is she?'

'She is in her cabin,' the woman said finally. 'She does not wish to be disturbed.'

'This isn't a social call,' I said. 'Take me to her *now*.'

She seemed to weigh my words before finally acceding to them. 'This way.'

I followed her across the deck, up a set of iron steps, through a hatch and along a corridor lined on either side by cabin doors. She stopped outside one and knocked.

'Miss Estelle.'

The door opened. Estelle saw me and took a breath.

'Sam? What are you doing here?'

'May I come in?' I asked.

'Of course,' she said, opening the door wide.

The cabin was sparsely furnished; just a bed, a desk, a chair and a wardrobe. Quite a comedown after the Great Eastern.

'I went to the Great Eastern. They told me you were leaving by train for Bombay,' I said.

'Last-minute change of plans,' she said, as naturally as though it were a change in the weather. 'Sal had a cable from Hollywood. He says we need to be there as soon as possible.'

'Sal,' I said. 'So this was Mr Copeland's idea?'

She looked confused. 'Of course. What's this about, Sam? Are you upset with me? Did you go to the station to wave me off? If so, I'm sorry. I just didn't think you'd be coming. I thought last night . . .' Her voice trailed off.

'It's not about the station,' I said. 'It's about Mullick. I know he was blackmailing you, and I know why.'

The colour seemed to drain from her face.

'I-I don't know what you're talking about, Sam.'

For once the act was transparent.

'I know who you are, Estelle, but that's not important to me. I'm only concerned with Mullick and Ronen Ghatak.'

She took a step back. 'Sam, you're confusing me.'

'I know your real name,' I said. 'I know about the photographs. You need to tell me everything you know about Mullick's and Ghatak's murders. It's the only way I can protect you. Was it Copeland? Is he behind this?'

She all but collapsed onto the bed.

'You have to believe me, Sam, I-I had nothing to do with their deaths. I didn't even know –'

'At the very least,' I said, 'you suspected, didn't you? You suspected Copeland was behind it. Your agent, going above and beyond the call of duty. Why though? Why would he murder for you? Is he in love with you? Is that what's going on?'

I willed her to say *yes*.

She shook her head. 'It's not like that at all, Sam.'

'Then why? Why did he do it?'

'You don't know that he did! He wasn't even on the train when Ronen was murdered.'

She was correct in that I had no proof, not yet anyway, but he was guilty. Of that I was sure. Other than Estelle, there was no one else who stood to gain. I didn't care if he was an American. I would arrest him and eventually he would crack.

'Where is he?' I asked.

A voice came from behind me.

'Right here.'

I turned to find Copeland standing in the doorway.

'Madhu called me. What's going on, Wyndham?'

'Mullick,' I said, 'then Ghatak, and now an innocent young woman. All dead. Murdered on your orders.'

'What? Are you insane? I haven't ordered anyone's death. How the hell would I even do that? And why?'

'Because Mullick knew Estelle's secret,' I said. 'Because first he then Ronen Ghatak tried to blackmail her and, by extension, you. If it ever got out that Estelle wasn't some belle of British stock from Tasmania, but actually an Anglo-Indian, it would finish her, wouldn't it? You told her as much. And how much money did you stand to lose? How much were the lives of those three worth?'

Copeland put his palms up. 'Whoa, slow down there a minute, pal. Yeah, Mullick was blackmailing Estelle, but I only found out once we were already here. Yeah, we had an argument on the train that night when the three of us came back from Bishnupore. I didn't mention it to Estelle, but he was insisting she spend the next week in the villa he'd rented. Just him and her. Said she'd be much more comfortable there. I told him to go jump.'

'And then you had him killed.'

'No! I never killed him or that secretary of his. I wouldn't know where to start.'

'You hired a killer, didn't you? God knows it's not hard in Calcutta. Well, the man you sent to do your dirty work is dead now, a nice bullet through his head, but we'll find the link between you and him. Till then, none of you are leaving the city.'

Copeland made to bluster something but suddenly he was drowned out by an almost inhuman wailing: piercing, distraught, like a wounded animal. The American turned in shock. It was coming from Madhu, the maidservant. Before I knew what was happening, Estelle had rushed to her side.

'What is it, *Ma*?'

The woman cried out again. Both Copeland and I stood in stunned silence as Estelle led the woman to the bed, sat her down and crouched beside her, the woman's hands between her own.

'*Ma*, what's happened?'

The woman wiped tears from her face. She looked at me with a hatred I hadn't seen before.

And then, finally, the truth hit me like a howitzer shell.

I cursed under my breath. I should have realised. The world spun around me.

I recalled the night on the train, when Ronen Ghatak had been murdered. It was no coincidence that she had been the one to find his body.

Ma. Not short for Madhu at all, but a word in itself, a word common to so many languages.

Ma.

'*You?*' I said. 'You're not just the maidservant, are you?'

Madhu looked to Estelle and then to me.

'Please,' she said. 'You need to understand. Estelle had nothing to do with this. I was only trying to protect her.'

I looked at her, that little Indian woman in front of me, bent over, tears running down her cheeks, and realised that I had never seen her properly until now. There it was, the resemblance to Estelle, ravaged by age and the vicissitudes of life, but distinct and definite nonetheless. And yet it had been invisible to me. Hiding in plain sight.

'You need to tell me everything, Madhu.'

She took a moment to compose herself.

'Is Gopal really dead?' she asked.

'If you mean the man who killed Mullick and the others, then yes.'

She gave a nod.

'Madhu,' I said, 'did you send that man to kill Mullick?'

She said nothing.

'And Ghatak, and Mahalia Ghosh, too?'

'I knew nothing of this girl,' she said. 'Believe me, I never asked Gopal to kill anyone, I just wanted him to get those photos from Mullick. I wasn't going to let him or anyone else hurt my girl. Not again.'

I turned to Estelle. Tears glistened in her eyes.

'Someone else did to you what Mullick had done to others?'

She looked away. 'There are more of his type than you would imagine,' she said. 'Certainly more than there are like you.'

I tried to steel myself against her words. Told myself I couldn't trust them. I turned back to Madhu.

'You say you never meant for anyone to be killed, but this man, this Gopal, he killed three people.'

'For the girl, I feel remorse. As for the others, Mullick deserved to die,' she said. 'His secretary too. Brutes who hide their wickedness with money. I knew a man like that myself, many years ago. A man who cloaked his barbarity in the whiteness of his skin and the coat of a doctor. I was his assistant. One night he forced himself upon me. I told him no, but he would not listen. The attack cost me my life, my future. But it gave me my daughter, Esha. We had to leave my village and move to Madras. It was hard, for many years, but Esha was fortunate because of her fair skin. A Catholic missionary school took her. The nuns taught her English, and as she grew, she looked almost like one of them. She could pass for European. So I told her, why not? Why not free yourself from this life? Become one of them.'

Estelle gave her mother's hand a squeeze.

'It's true, Captain Wyndham. Make of it what you wish. I gave up my name and became Estelle Morgan, from Tasmania, daughter of a retired English colonel. My career took off and I moved to London.'

Madhu took over once more.

'And when Esha met Mr Copeland and got the chance to go to America, it was like a dream. She would take me as her lady's maid and we could start again. When Mullick contacted Esha with those photographs that threatened to destroy her life, what choice did I have but to stop them? Gopal was a man I had known for some years. I told him I needed to obtain those photographs. I paid him to get them and promised him much more once he had done so. I even told him we would take him to America as Estelle's manservant. But I never expected him to kill anyone. When he murdered Mullick, I knew it was wrong, but I hoped that would be an end to the whole thing, I thought we might be safe.' She wiped a tear from her eye. 'But then his secretary, Ghatak immediately took over, looking for money rather than to take advantage of her, and I knew then that as long as those photographs were out there, Estelle was vulnerable. I had no choice but to get them back. Yet I was horrified by what Gopal did. I never wanted anyone to be hurt.'

I was not sure I believed a word of it. Maybe the mother possessed the same talent for acting as her daughter. Maybe they were all in it together. At the very least, Estelle must have suspected her mother's involvement, if not immediately, then certainly when Ghatak was murdered and Madhu just happened to find his body. Yet her shock, like her mother's pain and bitterness, seemed genuine.

'Please,' Madhu implored me, 'you can do what you want with me, I will confess to whatever you like, but on the condition that you let Estelle go and that you keep the secret of her background. You can say that I am insane, that I did it for money, whatever you wish.'

Estelle broke down. 'You can't do that, *Ma!*'

'It is all I can do, *makal*. And it is what I will do, if that is what is required to save your life.'

Estelle turned to me. 'Sam, please. Don't do this. You can let her go. You can say that Gopal was a madman. That he killed Mullick and the others without any need to involve her. Please. I'm beseeching you. Let her go.'

I closed my eyes and let her words sink in. I could do as she asked. I could turn a blind eye. If her story was true, and I feared it was, then I could only imagine what Madhu had gone through, first raped by a white man, then ostracised by her kith and kin, banished and left to bring up a half-caste daughter on the streets of Madras. To build a life from there, to build a future for herself and her child, to both suffer and to keep going, was an act worthy of respect. And then, to see all that at risk of destruction from a man like Mullick, a man who had everything but wanted more, I couldn't blame her for having him killed. But then there were the others. Ronen Ghatak – yes, he was blackmailing Estelle, and he was complicit in the actions of his employer, but to have him murdered? And then there was Mahalia. What crime had she committed other than that of protecting a friend?

I opened my eyes and looked to Estelle.

'I can't.'

FORTY-THREE

Surendranath Banerjee

I had not seen Sam for almost a week. That was not for want of trying on my part. He simply did not wish to see me nor anyone else. I did not blame him. Estelle Morgan, I could tell, had in those few brief days provided him with a glimpse of happiness, certainly more than he had known for a long time, and then it had come crashing down. He had taken her at her word: that she had not been party to any of it, and now she was en route to America with her agent while her mother languished in a Calcutta jail cell. Had any of it been real? Had she truly cared for Sam, or was it all simply an act? A ploy to keep him off balance and blind him to the facts? I did not know the answer, and to be frank, I did not know which of the two was worse. Whatever the truth, it would, I feared, only push him further into his misery.

Not that my situation was much better. The woman I cared for was on the other side of the world, and who knew how long before any love that she still harboured for me was extinguished? And all because of my own cowardice. Worse, I was now in hock to Colonel Dawson, in his pocket to be used at his whim, spying upon good people such as the mayor, Jatin Sengupta, and his wife. Even Dolly's safe return, for which I had traded my conscience to the Devil, though initially met with tears of joy and relief by her parents, provided me with little succour. I cursed myself for not saving the real victim, the only one who was truly innocent in all this: Mahalia Ghosh. In any case, Dolly's reputation was ruined. People were already whispering: her disappearance, just at the time her friend was killed; her links to the unsuitable types; her photographs of prostitutes and actresses; the incineration of her studio; it was all too scandalous for her family. Dolly was now on a train bound for Daaca to the house of an uncle, chaperoned by her mother, and I doubted she would show her face in Calcutta again for many a year. Such was our society. Shame was heaped upon the living to such an extent that it made one almost envy the dead.

My own future hung in the balance. I had started to work for the mayor, was provided with an office and a secretary and told to familiarise myself with a tome of arcane texts dating back to the 1700s, pertaining to the workings of the Calcutta Corporation. Suffice it to say the task provided much opportunity to pause and to think, and regret: about the way I had treated Elise, about Dawson and the trap in which I had ensnared myself, and about Jatin and Nellie Sengupta and my actions.

By the fifth day, I had reached a conclusion. I had picked up a telephone and asked for the number that I had been given by Dawson.

He had met me that night, on the riverside, close to the Prinsep Ghat, with the lights of Howrah on the far bank. I tried to make out the silhouette of the round water tank on the other side but it was impossible. Dawson arrived ten minutes after I had, emerging out of the darkness like an apparition.

'So, young Banerjee,' he said. 'Pray tell, what's on your mind?'

And so I told him.

I thanked him once more for providing the address of the building where Dolly had been hiding. It had probably saved her life. I told him I appreciated that I was in his debt, but suggested a reworking of the terms.

He stared at me over his pipe, in that gruff, superior manner that Englishmen have.

'What sort of reworking?'

'It seems to me that one good deed deserves another. An equally important deed, that would pay back in full your assistance with Dolly.'

He shook his head. 'It doesn't work that way, Mr Banerjee. And anyway, I truly doubt you have information of such merit.'

'Please humour me,' I said. 'If, hypothetically speaking, I had such information, something vital to the security of British interests in India, would that be worth a renegotiation of the terms?'

'It could,' he agreed. 'Hypothetically speaking.'

And so I told him what I knew in the hope that it would be enough to clear my debt. Indeed, upon hearing what I had to say, Dawson pondered and agreed that it was, if true, a matter vital to British interests. 'The slate,' he said, 'would be wiped clean.'

But the problem with slate is that, even when the chalk has been rubbed out, the ghost of a trace always remains. I was taking the Englishman at his word, and while that was supposedly his bond, the act of relying upon it had not always ended well for Indians.

And so I found myself once more in Premchand Boral Street, climbing the stairs to the flat I had shared with Sam for four years. It felt strange knocking on this door to which for so long I'd had a key, that rueful sense of familiarity with a place that was no longer one's own.

Some things, however, remain constant, and as usual it took Sandesh an inordinate amount of time to rouse himself and open his master's door. When he did, he seemed less than thrilled to see me.

'Suren-*babu*. Captain sahib *kāra'ō saṅgé dakhā kōrché-nā*.'

'Well, he will jolly well see me,' I said, and barged past him into the hall and then through to the living room. Sam was sitting on one of the cane chairs out on the balcony, his back to me, a large whisky in his hand no doubt.

'Sam,' I said, 'we need to speak.'

For a moment there was silence.

'Sandesh,' he called out, 'I thought I said no visitors.'

'I'm hardly a visitor,' I said, walking out to the balcony and taking the seat beside him.

'No?' he said. 'I suppose we must have just kept missing each other in the hallway for the last few years. What is it you want? Has another of your relatives disappeared?'

He took a sip of whisky.

'May I have one?' I asked.

'Help yourself,' he said. 'Sandesh! Whisky for Suren. And bring the bottle.'

I settled into the chair beside him as Sandesh brought the whisky and glass, poured a rather full measure. Sam swallowed the last of his own and reached for a refill.

'So what brings you here?'

I steeled myself and took a sip of whisky. The liquor tasted like a forest fire. I had never understood what Sam had seen in this drink, and despite my best efforts, found myself coughing, which at least brought a glimmer of a smile to his lips.

'Lagavulin not quite to your tastes?'

'It is strong,' I said, composing myself. 'I came to see how you were.'

He raised his glass and gestured to the world around him.

'I'm fine, as you can see. I'm even back in Lord Taggart's good books what with the conclusion of the Mullick case. He might even deign to let me get back to investigating more murders, which is nice. You know where you are with the dead.'

I let his comment hang in the air.

'So you see,' he continued, 'there's no need for you to worry. I am, as they say, *tickety-boo*. And you? How's your cousin Dolly?'

'Banished,' I said.

'To the ends of the earth?'

'Daaca.'

'Close enough.' He took a sip of whisky. 'So what now for you? How are you faring working for our esteemed mayor?'

'Let us say it is a little less exciting than a career as a detective.'

'I'll bet. Why don't you just go the whole hog and retrain as an accountant?'

'The work though will benefit others.'

He arched an eyebrow. 'And would that include Colonel Dawson?'

I sighed. 'I think maybe the colonel and I have reached an understanding.'

'And you think you can trust him?'

'We shall see.'

I wished to ask him of Estelle Morgan, of whether he truly believed in her story of innocence, but there was no point. It was better to let him brood than to rake over those coals once more. I took another sip. This time the whisky went down with fewer fireworks.

'I also came because I thought you might like to go for a walk.'

He looked at me. 'And why would I want to do that?'

'Three reasons,' I said. 'Firstly, I thought it might be nice for Sandesh to have some respite from you. Secondly, because I need your advice on something.'

That seemed to get his attention.

'Really?' he said. 'I'm not sure what advice I could possibly give Suren Banerjee, pride of the Calcutta Corporation. And the third reason?'

'Well, I think this particular walk might put a smile on your face.'

He gave a snort. 'Good luck to you. And how, pray tell, do you intend to achieve that?'

'You will just have to come along and find out,' I said.

Sam finished his whisky and I attempted several more brave swallows, gallantly reducing my own measure by half and hoping that evaporation might take care of the rest.

'Come,' I said, 'before it gets dark.'

We stepped out into the street, into the warm embrace of early evening. Somewhere, where exactly only the gods knew, birds were singing, their melody cutting through the infernal hum of man and machine. Even Premchand Boral Street, that most insalubrious of addresses, was bathed in that particularly sepia-toned light that I have experienced only occasionally and only in this city, that transformed it from a motley collection of structures into something almost halcyon, or at least as halcyon as a street full of brothels can be.

We set off southward, zigzagging our way towards Canning Street and then down towards the Maidan.

On such an evening, when the breeze is blowing off the river and the scent of wood-apple hangs in the air, there are few places in the world I would rather be than right here, in the city of my birth. For all its myriad sins and tragedies, it is, in its way, a symbol of what is noble in mankind, of what can be accomplished in spite of the odds. We and our oppressors had built this place, not from high-minded aspirations but simply for the expedient of commerce. And yet, despite its base beginnings, it had evolved to become so much more. The wellspring for art and science and literature and theatre, and the home of an entire culture, a hybrid one to be sure, part British, yet also wholly Bengali. In the entire world, this was the one place where I belonged; where the voices in my head made sense and my soul found peace. Thus it was with a sense of irony that I spoke next.

'I said I needed your advice.'

Sam nodded like a swami. 'Mmm, I was beginning to wonder.'

'I am thinking of going away again.'

'Really?' he said. 'For another three years?'

'It would be for less than three months, if all goes well.'

He looked at me and smiled. 'Let me guess. You've decided to go to France and marry that girl and hang the consequences.'

For a moment I was lost for words. What with his tendencies towards drink, self-flagellation and self-pity, it was easy to forget sometimes that he was a rather formidable detective; a reader of men.

'That is correct,' I said. 'How did you know?'

'Because you've been a miserable sod ever since you got back. Not to mention terribly and achingly earnest. In fact you've been a real bore. I'm only surprised it's taken you this long to realise that's what you need to do.'

'So, do you think it is the correct decision?'

He shrugged. 'It'll upset your father, no doubt, so *yes*, I do think it's the correct decision. A man's not a man until he has disappointed his father. And if it's any consolation, you people are so sentimental that it'll only be a matter of time before he forgives you.'

'Do you believe so?'

'Suren, it's time you stopped worrying about others and thought of yourself. You deserve happiness. And yes, I do believe he'll forgive you. An Englishman can hold the most trivial of grudges against his son for years, a Punjabi for decades, but a Bengali? Where his son is concerned, he'd be lucky to make it through to lunchtime without a change of heart. And if, by chance, he is still not speaking to you in a year, just give him a grandson. Now this girl . . .'

'Elise.'

'Yes, Elise. I need to know more about her.'

'Such as?'

'Such as everything.'

'Everything?'

'Well, yes. If I'm to come to France with you as your batman, I really do feel I should know a bit about the girl, don't you?'

I was not sure if I had heard him correctly.

'You want to come to France with me?'

'I don't *want* to go, but I don't really have much of a choice, do I? Someone needs to vouch for you to her parents, state that you are a gentleman of good character, and who better than me? How else do you intend to convince them to let their daughter swan off to the other side of the world with you? Or are you planning on not telling them and simply eloping? Running off to Gretna and getting some dour Scotch minister to marry you both?'

It was a good question.

'In truth I had not given the issue much thought yet.'

He sighed. 'Trust me, Suren. You do not want to elope. Your life together will be challenging enough without having to start it together in Scotland.'

'Very well,' I said. 'I accept your gracious offer.'

'Good,' he said, 'because you're paying for my ticket.'

For a while we walked in silence, down Chowringhee, past the Indian Museum and approached the entrance to Park Street.

'We should turn back,' he said. 'It'll be getting dark soon.'

I checked my watch. If Colonel Dawson held to his word, we had another fifteen minutes to reach our destination before the fireworks started.

'A little further,' I said, picking up the pace.

As we made our way down Park Street, it did not take Sam long to suspect that I may have brought him out under false pretences.

'Suren,' he said.

'Yes?'

'We seem to be heading in the direction of Miss Grant's place.'

'Really?'

'You know we are.'

'I see your powers of deduction are as sharp as ever,' I said. 'No wonder they call you one of the finest detectives east of Suez.'

He seemed surprised. 'They say that?'

'Oh yes,' I said. 'East of Howrah anyway.'

'Is there a reason why you're dragging me down here?'

'Let us call it a surprise.'

'If you think you can engineer some meeting between Miss Grant and me, then I'll beg you to stop right now. That ship has sailed.'

'Has it? I think you really do care for her. Maybe it is time *you* thought of your own happiness. Maybe loosen the bonds of the past.'

Ten minutes more and we were there, standing at the corner of Rawdon Street as the sun began to set. As fortune would have it, a chai-wallah with a bicycle and cart was passing and I flagged him down and ordered two *bhars*.

I passed a cup to Sam just as the first car roared into the street and screeched to a halt outside Miss Grant's building, closely followed by a second. A number of large men, Indian as well as British, wearing suits that bulged in all the wrong places, jumped out and made for the entrance.

Sam turned to me. 'Those look like Section H goons.'

'They do,' I agreed.

He stared at me as though the answers to his questions might be written on my face.

'Don't tell me you arranged to get Annie arrested? I know you're trying to cheer me up, Suren, but don't you think that's going a tad far?'

'Just watch,' I said. 'I have passed some information to Colonel Dawson. Enough, hopefully, to buy myself out of his debt.'

I finished my tea and threw the little clay *bhar* into the gutter, its terracotta shell splintering on impact into a thousand tea-stained shards. Reaching into my pocket, I brought out a packet of Charminars.

'Cigarette?'

Sam took one and I lit for us both from a book of matches. It did not take long before the men were back, a group of four of them with a fifth now held firmly between them. He looked stick-thin and shell-shocked.

'That's Ostrakhov,' Sam said.

'Yes,' I said, 'and no. I don't think that is his real name. At least that wasn't what he was calling himself a couple of years ago in Berlin. I saw him in a meeting hall, addressing Indian dissidents. I think he was going by the name Litvin. He would not remember me of course. I was just a face at the back of the room, but I remember him. I daresay he is not some penniless émigré but a Russian agent.'

'So you informed Dawson?'

'I searched my conscience, and yes, in the end I decided to. If the last few years have taught me anything, it is that in international politics, there are no such things as friends. The Germans, the French, the Russians, the British – you are all alike, playing your Great Game. If India is to be free, it will need to win that freedom through its own actions, not through the machinations of others. Besides, I do not think he was a suitable match for Miss Grant. Speaking of whom, I would imagine she might be rather distressed right now. She may benefit from the support of a friend at this most difficult juncture.'

He seemed incredulous, then smiled and shook his head.

'Suren Banerjee, you devious bastard.'

Acknowledgements

Returning to Sam and Suren after a gap of several years felt like a homecoming and there are so many people I need to thank for making it such an enjoyable experience for me.

Thanks to my agent, Sam Copeland (can't believe it's been a decade already) and the team at Rogers, Coleridge and White for making him look good.

A special thank you too, to all the booksellers and librarians across the UK, France, North America and further afield. You've introduced Wyndham and Banerjee to so many readers over the years. I owe you all a debt of gratitude.

Finally, thank you to my two boys for making life *interesting*, and most importantly to my long-suffering, darling wife, Sonal for putting up with me for two decades now. If that doesn't deserve a medal, I don't know what does.

Author's Note

This book had its genesis in a walk along College Street in Kolkata some years ago. College Street, or *Boi Para (the neighbourhood of books)* as it's sometimes called, sits not far from Sam and Suren's lodgings in Premchand Boral Street, and is a book-lover's dream. It's home to myriad bookshops and bookstalls selling everything from textbooks and bestsellers, to old tomes that might have been out of print for a hundred years. One of life's joys is wandering into its shops, browsing and discovering a gem or two that you wouldn't find possibly anywhere else in the world.

And that is what happened to me. I found a book on the life of the early twentieth-century Hollywood actress, Merle Oberon. I don't know why I picked it up. It wasn't my usual fare. Maybe it was the faded picture of this beautiful actress looking out from the cover, but I picked it up and flipped through it and within minutes knew I had to buy it, because Merle Oberon, one of the most glamorous stars of early Hollywood, had a secret past deeply entwined with India – a past she carefully concealed throughout her life due to the racial prejudices of the time.

Merle Oberon was born Estelle Merle O'Brien Thompson, in 1911 (or thereabouts), the daughter of a British railway engineer and a Sinhalese mother (though her actual lineage remains the subject of some debate). She grew up in Bombay and Calcutta, before moving to London, England in her teens to pursue her love of acting. There, she worked her way up from bit parts, eventually catching the attention of producer Alexander Korda, who helped craft her screen image and later became her husband and who facilitated her move to Hollywood.

However Hollywood's racial codes at the time prohibited mixed-race actors from playing romantic leads, especially opposite white stars. So Merle reinvented herself, hiding her Indian ancestry. She claimed to have been born in Tasmania, Australia, the daughter of an English officer. All mention of her upbringing was erased. Indeed, Merle never publicly acknowledged her Indian roots, even late in life. That erasure of her past could not have been easy.

She was the inspiration for Estelle Morgan.

Other characters in the book are grounded in real history. Jatin and Nellie Sengupta did exist; he was mayor of Calcutta; and the story of their love is real. What is more fascinating is that after Jatin's death, Nellie, an Englishwoman (born Edith Ellen Gray) remained devoted to the cause of Indian Independence and was elected president of the Indian National Congress at the Calcutta session in 1933. She stood in elections, represented Chittagong, and remained active in Bengal politics, especially during the 1940s. During the communal riots of Partition, she worked for peace and relief, refusing to leave Chittagong even when many others fled.

After India's independence in 1947, she chose to stay in East Pakistan (now Bangladesh), supporting local Hindu communities and working with relief organisations. She died in Calcutta in 1973.

Their story fascinates me.

About the Author

Abir Mukherjee is the bestselling author of the award-winning Wyndham & Banerjee series of crime novels set in 1920s India and the British Book Awards Crime Thriller of the Year 2025 *Hunted*. His books have been translated into sixteen languages and won various awards including the CWA Dagger for best Historical Novel, the Prix du Polar Européen, and the Wilbur Smith Award for Adventure Writing. He also co-hosts the popular Red Hot Chilli Writers podcast which takes a wry look at the world of books, writing, and the creative arts, tackling everything from bestsellers to pop culture. Abir grew up in Scotland and now lives in Surrey with his wife and two sons.